15

StoryEarth Chronicles

The Sting Baby

StoryEarth Chronicles

The Sting Baby

TINA LEAR

This is a work of fiction. All of the characters, names, incidents, organizations, and dialogue in this novel are either the products of the author's imagination or are used fictitiously.

Archway Publishing books may be ordered through booksellers or by contacting:

Archway Publishing
1663 Liberty Drive
Bloomington, IN 47403
www.archwaypublishing.com
844-669-3957

ISBN: 978-1-6657-4026-5 (sc)
ISBN: 978-1-6657-4024-1 (hc)
ISBN: 978-1-6657-4025-8 (e)

Library of Congress Control Number: 2023904555

Print information available on the last page.

Archway Publishing rev. date: 6/21/2023

FOR WILLIAM JAMES MCAULEY IV

The roads are many.
All begin and end in Oneness.
May every route bring you home to yourself.

Contents

THE NOTHING

HERE

Part One

The Netherjunctures of Ddrym

The Sting Baby

They argued until they were raw. It was Sting season, and Linn wanted another child. Bette did not. They'd been going at it for days.

Linn kept shifting how far the forks were from the plates, moving the cups. She blew her nose.

"Time isn't fallin' out our pockets, Linn! Remember, it was two whole years we gave so Wrem could come." She swiveled to face Linn standing in the kitchen. "Two years of service—for the elders, then for the children. And all the offerings we made of breath and blood, and the oaths we gave. And, Linn, even so, only one in every hundred Welcoming ceremonies bear the fruit of a newborn. That was the only time I ever wished we were a Primal couple. They sneeze and *Oops! Look! A baby.*" Bette went on, "But all those offerings weren't for naught. Wrem's here, and he's more than enough."

Finally, she said, "Linn, give me your eyes."

Her wife turned to face her.

Bette whispered, "A Ceremonial baby like Wrem doesn't come twice in a lifetime."

Linn stopped moving, looked down, and took a breath. Then she stumbled through the whole truth as a last resort. "It's...it's the Gathering...and...I thought maybe..."

Bette blanched. "What?!"

"No one would know. I mean, who's to say I *didn't* feel the pull—" Linn flinched as Bette flicked salt at her and hissed a protection spell.

"Take it back right now, woman," Bette said, slamming her hands on the table. "You're not smarter than the forest, Linn. The Sting baby pulls *you*. You Precinct idiots, you think the laws are just 'nice ideas.' This is Sting season we're talking about—"

"Yes, but—"

"These laws hold our world together. They are real, energetic forces. *No one would know?* If no one knew you jumped off a cliff, do you think gravity wouldn't smash you to the ground anyway?"

"Oh, Words, Bette. Why can't you just—I just want this. I want Wremmy to have a little sister or brother. For me it's just as real as gravity, and..." Linn's shoulders shook as she wept into her hands.

Bette turned away from her and looked out the window at their garden. "It's too bad your heart is sore," she said. "But I can't do this."

During Sting season, random beings were drawn into the forest by an unseen, unknown force where they coupled in twos and threes in all kinds of configurations. Normally, faithfulness between couples was held sacred. But for the eleven days of Sting season, it was a time to honor pleasure for its own sake, and anyone could join with anyone. There were no repercussions, jealousies, or hurt feelings because the same force that drew them into the forest was the one that erased all memory of what happened there once the season was over.

Another distinctive element of Sting season was its fruit. During the deepest dark of the eleventh night, a small number of Sting babies would come into being, usually at the base of older trees. A Sting baby was a newborn just like any other in StoryEarth, but they were only ever born on that one night each year. To this day, no one knows how, why, or to whom.

The next morning, Linn got up to wake Wrem. "Hey, sleepyhead." She stroked his hair as he burrowed further down into the covers.

"Come on, sweetlight. Mama Bette is putting out the offerings for the faeries. When she gets back, we'll be ready for breakfast. Let's go. Up." She drew his limp, little frame into her lap for a hug.

"Okay," he mumbled.

She whispered into his hair, "I'll make us some story time tea, OK? And some gigglecakes. Would you like that?"

"Yeah," he said, yawning. "But I getta go first."

"All right, you can go first."

But Bette didn't come back for breakfast—or lunch. As the morning stretched itself into late afternoon, Linn lost patience. *You made your point, Bette. Come on home now.*

Dusk came on. Linn took Wrem next door, where he ran into the house like it was his own.

"Scamp!" Celeste playfully flicked her kitchen towel at him as he sped by, then she turned to Linn. "What's up?"

"Bette left this morning. We fought, and she's still not back. And I...I—"

Celeste hugged her. "Go. I've got him."

Linn trotted down the lane, throwing Bette's name into the air. She'd stop every now and then to listen hard. In her panic, she'd forgotten the simplest idea. She found a soft place in the earth and took her stance, stood still, and tried to calm herself, remembering when Bette had taught her how to do this just after she'd left her Precinct life—so many years ago. She aligned her spinal energies with her clear message to everyone. *I'm looking for Bette. She's been gone all day. Please send her home if you see her.* The message went down her spine, through her feet, and into the earth—where anyone connected to her would receive it into their own knowing.

She had almost reached Blimmer's house. If Bette had gone anywhere to vent, it would be to her best friend. But just before she touched Blimmer's garden gate, something flickered in the corner of her eye. It was too far away to tell for sure. A person? A spirit? It glowed with a greeting light, so she knew it was safe. She walked toward it, then stopped abruptly. She closed her eyes and opened them again, to be sure. She felt faint.

It was Bette, weeping with joy. She held a tiny newborn Sting baby, lit from within. The two women swam in each other's eyes for a moment.

"How?" Linn whispered as she approached what was almost holy ground.

"I left angry this morning. I walked and walked. And then I started feeling off, something like a whole mess of bees stinging me from the inside out. They say that's the pull. The closer to the trees I got, the better I felt, just like they say. And then I seen her, so beautiful, just waitin' for me with those big eyes. And look at her light," she said, cooing to the baby, "Look at that wee happylight. And the faerie cloth, feel this, feel it—how soft." She was completely besotted.

"Bette! You!" They both laughed. "Of all people in the world, *you*."

"Ah, don't thank me. I didn't want nothin' to do with it. You can thank this little Sting baby scamp. She took me hostage. Weren't nothin' I could do."

Chapter 1

The Trouble
with Millie

Thirteen Years Later

Millie trudged into the kitchen, still in her jammies and yesterday's brown braids, sulking and half asleep. On her way to the dinner table, she dutifully dipped her fingers in the bowl and sprinkled the gratitude blessing over the altar for the faeries.

"Good morning, hon. Go sit. I made giggles for breakfast."

Millie rolled her eyes. "I'm not a little kid, you know," she said, slumping into a chair.

A plate of gigglecakes frosted with the leaves from their laughter bush sat on the table. The dark green leaves (frosting made from blended laughter leaves and compliments) trembled a little in anticipation. Millie started to take one, and it hopped away, just out of reach. She sat still for a long moment; then with predatory speed and precision, she nabbed the little green giggle. Her grip activated its properties, and peals of laughter cascaded out of the confection. Millie was in no mood for this. She ate the thing without cracking a smile.

She watched her Mama Linn work a pile of dough, folding soft edges into the center over and over, sprinkling in the Whisperflour, folding some more. It was the secrets cake for some special event at the StoryEarth Preservation Precinct.

Millie's grumpy mother, Mama Bette, was taller and stocky, with fair skin; sharp, blue eyes; and hair as short as you could have it and still have hair. She sat at her desk nearby, fretting over the schedule.

"Can we do five hundred hooray!cakes for next Thursday?" she asked Mama Linn. "Precinct wants to honor Myrtle Somebody, the outgoing Old Woman in a Shoe."

Linn went over to her calendar. "No. We've got the Bluebeard party and a Precinct event. Milliebug, I can warm you up some Cackle tea if you want. Would you like that?"

Millie had her head down on her outstretched arm, teasing the last giggle. "Do they have Cackle tea in the Precinct?"

"Yes, hon. They have all the same stuff to eat. But it tastes better here, don't you think?"

"I wouldn't know," she said, aiming her comment like an arrow. "I haven't been to the Precinct since Grandma Set's funeral, when I was only four."

Wrem clumped toward the kitchen in his forest boots. "Hallo, Mamas. Hi, bug." He put his coat on.

"G'morning, love." Linn wafted a plate of fresh, hot rolls under Wrem's nose and onto the table. "Buttered aspirations. And there's tea here. Help yourself."

"Sorry, Mama, no time. I'll take a couple aspirations with me though. Thanks. I've got Tree Care kids coming for class this morning. I'm late."

He tried to pull one of Millie's braids, but she batted him away. With a nod to Mama Bette, he popped the aspirations into a bag and went out the door. Millie sulked into a moody silence. "Mama?"

"Hm?"

"Why can't I ever go with you on a delivery?"

"We've been over this, hon. You're too old to go through as a baby—I carried you in my energy field then, but I can't anymore—and you're too young to go through as yourself. You need training. You're not ready."

"But—"

"Finish your breakfast and go see Drauml. I'm sure you two can keep yourselves busy today."

"Why can't you just train me now? You trained Wrem, and he gets to go with you all the time."

Mama Linn wiped the counter as she answered, reining in her exasperation. "Wrem was much older than you when I trained him. He was almost done with his second nine."

"Well, I'm almost that. I was nine four years ago."

"Not anywhere near how old he was. Talk to me in another four years."

"It's because he was a Ceremonial baby, isn't it?"

"Oh, Millie. All Things Told, not this again."

"It is. He always gets treated special."

Mama Linn ignored her, opened the cupboard, and hoisted out a couple of bags of definitions and explanations to peel and chop up for the order she was working on.

"I'm just the stupid Sting baby Mama Bette found in the forest. I'm never gonna get to do deliveries."

"Listen. Alphabet Delights is our livelihood. We're always going to do deliveries. It keeps our family alive, and gives the Ddrymmian region of Droaze something to brag about. When you're a full being, I'll have long trained you by then, and you can do all the deliveries then. On your own." Linn organized her ingredients.

Bette showed up at the kitchen table and scooped up the last giggle. "What's going on here?"

Millie buttoned herself into a scowl.

"Nothing, Mama Bette," Linn said. "Millie's just informing us that we love Wrem more than we love her because he's Ceremonial and she's Sting, and because of that, she'll never ever, in her life, get to deliver with us to the Precinct."

"You're not ready, girl," Bette said, her mouth full of giggle.

"I told her." Linn nodded.

"What do I have to be ready *for*?" Millie said, slamming her hands down on the table.

Mama Bette took over. "Millie, the border is no joke. You

need years of training to manage the energies. And anyway, what's on the other side of it that you want so bad? Ddrym not good enough for you?"

Millie got up and poured herself some more tea.

"There's nothin' to see," Mama Bette barreled on. "It's just like here, only ugly. They got trees and homes just like us but not as nice. Everything's all straight lines and hard angles. Only a fool would actually *want* to go there." She pointed that last part at Millie.

Linn shot Bette a look.

"*Plus,* you gotta make your way around confusing, big, sad, gray buildings to get there, and then there are them noisy, damned fast—"

"Cars!" Bette and Millie said it at the same time, one spitting, one swooning.

Linn stifled a laugh at the timing of it and pleaded at Bette with her eyes. *Don't go off on the cars again.*

But Bette was in the river of it now, and there was no stopping her. "I don't know what's so fancy about cars."

Millie concentrated on her breakfast.

"They're just for people too ignorant to go the way of nature. I'm talkin' about your own feet or Paulie's feet. Ain't nowhere we ever want to go that old Paulie can't get us there in fine time. Best horse in the world."

Millie mouthed those last words at the same time as Mama Bette, out of her line of sight. She picked up her plate and took it over to the sink, muttering through her teeth, "Cars can save you time." She scrubbed the plate harder than it was dirty.

"Time. Ha! You sprouts don't know anything."

"I'm not a sprout! I'm almost grown. I'm thirteen, Mama Bette."

"Well, since you're almost grown, then you already know that time is not for saving. You don't have little pieces of time that you save up in a box for later."

"Want some tea, Bette?" Linn moved around in the kitchen, trying to draw her wife's attention away from this conversation. But Bette's focus burned on Millie.

"It's not for rushing around so you can have more of it. You don't ever have any more of it than you have in your hand right now."

Millie scrubbed the giggles cupcake pan in the sink. "Never mind, Mama Bette. I just think it would be fun to go fast. You wouldn't understand."

"Ha! You want fast?" she said and slurped her tea. "Try being my age. You'll see how fast you went already. Linn, don't leave those Precinct trash publications lyin' around. It's makin' her wanna be one of them."

"Careful there, sport," Linn's tone cooling. "Remember, *I'm* one of them."

"Ah, but that's an entirely different patch o' grass, my love. You *left* them to come live here with me."

"I know, but—"

"The problem with this one here," Bette said with a thumb toward Millie, "is that she's never happy, always wantin' to go somewhere far from where she is and wantin' to get there faster in her shiny cars."

"It's not just about the cars," Millie shot back. "The Precinct is where all the Players live. I'd give anything to see a High Home or maybe even a Player! I think it would be amazing to *be* a Player."

The room got very still around Millie's busy hands in the sink.

Like sheet lightning, Mama Bette's voice came from far away but lit up the whole room with cold. "Don't ever say that again."

"What?"

"I said don't ever say that again."

"Why?"

Mama Bette stood up so fast, her chair almost fell over. "You want to be a Player? You want to live all high up above everyone, all la-di-da—"

"That's not what I meant—"

"Bette." Linn tried to make eye contact, but her wife was already on the move.

"Looking down your High Home nose on the rest of us poor saps here below? That's what you want?"

"Bette, stop!" Linn stepped toward them.

"Is it?" Bette was at the sink now and yanked Millie around by the shoulders so they were face-to-face.

Millie lashed out at her Mama Bette. "That's not what they're like. Players are in High Homes because they do important work!"

Bette's hand flew across Millie's face—and it shocked them both.

"Bette!" Linn rushed over to embrace Millie, but Millie wrenched away and ran to her room, yelling, "I hate you both!" She slammed the door behind her.

Silence roared in the kitchen. Bette looked down at her hand. She opened her mouth to say something, but when she looked up, Linn had turned and left the room.

Later, Millie heard only snatches of words like static through the walls, hissing whispers from mother to mother through clenched teeth. "Bette, it's been thirty years..."

"... ice-cold shell of a mother...the rotten end of a half-turned witch..."

Millie wasn't remotely curious. Mama Bette's mother probably looked at her funny thirty years ago. She went to sleep making plans, the kind that people make when they're very young.

Chapter 2

Paulie's Distress

After a muted breakfast animated only by the automatic gestures that develop over a long marriage, Bette sat down at her desk, and Linn went to prepare the delivery cart. Wrem came to help. "Where's Millie?" he asked.

Mama Linn responded while carrying a box of frosted compliments to the cart. "I heard her leaving early this morning. She's probably with Drauml, getting into some mischief."

He got Paulie from the barn and hitched him up to the cart. He went inside and asked his Mama Linn, "Where's the—" and then he remembered, lowering his voice to a stage whisper, "quietbox?"

"Very funny," Bette said. "Are ya ever gonna let it go?"

"No, Mama Bette. It's too much fun to remind you. To think there was a time you thought that a box lighter than air, that could carry an entire party, table, chairs and all, was somehow cursed—"

"I never said it was cursed."

"Ok," Wrem said, but he knew there was something else going on. "So Mama Linn? Where do you want the quietbox?"

"Just put it with all the other boxes in the back on the left," she answered. "It's a small party. Leave the stuff on the right. I'll unload all that when I get back."

"Sure thing," he said, going in again for the rest of the supplies. "You sure you don't want me to come along and help?"

"No thanks, honey. It's a very small party."

He gave Paulie an affectionate nuzzle on his way out. Paulie nipped at Wrem's sleeve. "Oy! Watch it." The three-year-old sorrel had been in the family since he was born, so Wrem and Millie often thought of him as their animal brother. He had a steady temperament, but he wasn't above the occasional roguery.

Linn came out to check the buckles of Paulie's harness, and he sidestepped a little. "Stop it," she said, jerking him back into place. He snorted, threw his head up, and pawed the ground.

"Paulie, what's gotten into you?" She went into the cart, checked everything off her list, latched the doors shut, hopped up into the carriage seat, and gave him the go-ahead. He didn't move.

"Paulie, let's go." She shook the reins firmly. Nothing. She waited a while before deciding to ask for help. "Bette?"

After a momentary silence, Bette replied, "Yeah?"

"Something's up with Paulie. Can you come check it out?"

Bette opened the front door, paused for a moment, and approached the horse, murmuring low with one hand under his muzzle, the other on his cheek. "Hey, troublemaker, what's going on?" She looked into his eyes. He threw his head up a couple of times and snorted again.

"His spirit's probably scraping on our troubles from last night." Bette was always more tuned to animals than people. She put her arms around his neck and whispered into his mane. She moved around him, staying very close to his body, touching him all over with a tenderness that Linn hadn't seen in ages. Whatever she said with her hands must have sung his energies back into place, because he settled right away.

"He's all right. Come back in one piece, will ya?"

"I will." Linn looked at her wife for just a moment without rancor. "Thank you."

Bette nodded and went back in.

Linn shook the reins and Paulie started walking. He was compliant enough. She passed friends and acquaintances, and greeting lights were exchanged. Ink and Paper, the dogs who'd adopted their neighbors the Rogger family, greeted Paulie like old friends, wagged their tails, and walked by his side down the path.

As the forest grew denser, the dogs peeled off, and Paulie forged ahead. Ddrymmians had forged a path for generations through the undergrowth, which now consisted of smokytalk trees and leggy, leafy history plants. The sunbaked scent of pine needles reached Linn's nose, and she began the shielding.

The border was a powerful force around the entire Preservation Precinct. As a line of demarcation between the Precinct and Ddrym, it had been put in place eons ago to keep both regions contained and protected. Energetically, Linn checked Paulie's bones as he plodded, spirit-wrapping them from skull to tail, soundproofing them from withers to hoof. Then she sent the sense shield all the way around his body. When she'd finished, she prepared herself in the same way. When she felt the tender force field of the border's outermost edge, she heard its warning wobble.

Paulie sidestepped a little, clearly losing whatever calm Bette had helped him find. Linn clucked her tongue and shook the reins. He sidestepped in the other direction. Paulie had never refused a command. She tried to calm him again as best as she could, but eventually lost patience and said, "We have a delivery to make. Now go!" She swung the reins sharply onto his rump.

Paulie reared up and turned left. Linn set her jaw and whispered, "Fine, have it your way." She pulled him even farther left till they came full circle and whooshed right through the border. As soon as he heard the wobble again and felt the pressure of its resistance, he broke into a hard, manic gallop.

Even when well prepared, it was hard to walk through the border, harder still to run through it. It was twenty yards deep and twenty yards high, but Paulie tore through it faster than Linn had ever seen him go. And as his legs seemed to fly them forward, a terrible scream pierced the air from behind. The horse—covered in sweat, eyes wild—continued his desperate run till they breached the Precinct side. Linn almost fell off, then remembered to release the snap shackles. Startled by the clicks that triggered his new freedom, Paulie jumped and then trotted away, the shafts bouncing and scraping the ground behind him.

The buggy and cart hit a rock in the road and went airborne—sending Linn flying into a ditch—then crashed onto its side, wheels spinning in the air. Paulie came to a halt in the distance. The screaming stopped.

Linn lay on the ground for a moment, breathing hard. Her right shoulder paralyzed her. Her right hip, almost as bad. She gritted her teeth and cried out in pain as she hobbled over to the cart. The doors were jammed shut.

"Millie?"

No response.

"*Millie!*" Linn banged on the door with her good hand.

A faint whimper came through. "Mama."

"Millie, listen to me. Open the doors."

"Mama, I'm burning!"

"Honey, you have to get out of there. I took a fall. I can barely stand. Can you move at all?"

A moment passed while Millie tested her range of movement. "A little. I can move a little."

"OK. Mill, we're both hurt, but maybe together, we can do it. Are you ready to try?"

"OK."

"All right. With all your might, now. One...two...three, *push*."

It didn't work right away, but they pushed and pulled and grunted, stopping to recover from pain, then trying again until the doors finally flew open, one coming clear off, clattering to the ground. Linn tried to help Millie climb out of the cart. The searing heat of Millie's legs added to Linn's pain.

"Mama, don't! It hurts!"

"It hurts me too!" Linn stood close by as Millie tried to get out on her own. But as soon as the young girl's feet touched the ground, her knees buckled and she crumpled into a heap.

Linn bent over her child, helpless. Millie was still breathing.

Linn put out the call for help. She felt for the energy lines in the land with her feet, but could only put her full weight on one of them, hoping it would still work. She found a strong spot, and sent the call in treespeak, reserved for real emergencies. *Sting child with bordercheat fever! Mother with shoulder and hip injuries. Broken cart and buggy. Help! Precinct side of the border, near Emmering/Droaze line.* She was in shock, and could not move her body to invoke the healing protocols for Millie, and so she prayed to the sacred ground underneath them and the air and the trees around them to breathe their healing somehow up into her daughter's burning body.

In less than nine breaths, she heard the familiar deep wobble of the border being breached. Lohm, a well-known healer and a longtime friend of Linn's who lived in Near Emmering, rode toward them from the Ddrymmian side with several of his friends, all on horseback. Linn waved at them from beside the cart as they surveyed the damage and looked at Millie on the ground.

"Had a stowaway." Linn nodded over to her daughter.

He blanched. "And she's still alive?"

Chapter 3

Bordercheat Fever

Lohm directed the group to see to the cart, then went straight to Millie. She was trying to move, first to lie on her back, then to fold over her knees. Nothing was bearable. As Lohm tried to move her into a sitting position, her skin almost blistered his hands. Finally, she lay back, her eyes closed, and she breathed in fits and starts. She seemed to be fading fast. "Millie, can you hear me?"

She barely nodded.

"Is there water coming up in your throat?"

"Not anymore. I—" Her voice was thin and shaky.

"Not anymore. That's good. Any buzzing or clicking in your spine?"

"I'm on fire. Please make it stop."

"Millie, just answer me. Is there any buzzing or clicking in your spine?"

She was quiet for a moment. "No. Please make it stop, the burning."

"Ah, Millie, listen to me. You've got the bordercheat fever. The few who've survived an untrained passage, they suffer with intense heat—can't nothing be done about it. It's gonna be terrible bad for a while, and the only thing you've got for it is your mind and your grit. I can give you something for the fear. For that, you use your mind. Should help some. But for the pain, you'll just have to be tougher than a girl your size. You're gonna be tougher than *it,* you hear me?"

He held his hands as close as he could to her head and sent an ice-blue light through his arms, into her brain, and down her spine, all throughout her nervous system. Linn watched as a faint, pale blue light radiated from within her daughter's body.

"When you need it," Lohm said, "close your eyes and go underneath your skin with your mind. Open your arms, palms out, and then listen to your body-knowing till you feel the cooling layer. Try it now...arms out. Palms up...that's it...keep listening. Yes. Do you feel it?"

She relaxed, then said, "Wow, yeah."

"Good. Rest now. I'll give you some water in a bit, but you need to stay still for a while, right where you are, before you'll be able to drink it. Don't move. Let me tend to your mother." Then he turned to a woman in the group, a healer training with him, and said, "Sarah, can you please watch over her. Make sure she doesn't move."

Millie shifted uneasily on the ground, asleep as Lohm helped Linn walk to the nearby stream. "Is she gonna make it?" Linn asked under her breath as they made their way through the grasses.

"I think so...but...Linn...it's the bordercheat, and...I just don't—"

"I know. I know. Just tell me what to do to give her the best chance."

"I gave her an ice layer for the fear. But she'll be in black pain anyway. Movement in the cart will make it worse, but there's nothing for it except grit. And watch for the singsong. If she starts talkin' all singsongy, it's a sign that the Door to Elsewhere is near. Stop right away and get her hands, any way you can, directly into Ddrymmian soil. Remind her where she's from, where she is."

"I will."

"So what about *you* now? Lemme look you over...well, it's clear you put your shoulder out."

"Yes."

"Okay, let me...let's get you over here. Do you think you can sit down? Let's try." With great effort, he helped her over to a boulder by the stream. Then he said, in a calm, soothing voice, "Linn, look at me. Breathe. Relax. Breathe again, and—" quick as a cat, he'd popped her shoulder back in its socket. She yelped, then chuckled as she tested its range of motion, as he opened his backpack and took out a blanket, a cup, and a great skybrill bird feather.

"All right. Now I'll do whatever I can for your hip, but I can only help you get back home. See Grelle or someone once you get there." He helped her to the edge of the water, and spread out the blanket. This water, known as the Little Seed Stream, was revered by all for its healing waters. He eased Linn down onto the blanket. Then he filled the cup, and she drank. Afterward, he had one of his friends refill the cup and bring it to Millie.

Linn said, "Paulie tried to save us."

"What do you mean?"

"Paulie, our horse. He...he tried to...he must've known she was in the back."

"Yeah?" Lohm kept her talking while he rummaged through his bag, looking for the right powders.

"He wasn't himself. He fought me at the border. He tried so hard to save her." She started to cry as Lohm began to call inwardly on his healing allies.

Linn kept her eyes on Millie, who had to put the cup down because the water boiled at the touch of her lips. But Linn could tell that even just the drop she got from the Little Seed Stream was delicious. She hoped it cooled her daughter's throat somewhat at least.

The friends worked on righting the cart, hammering the doors back into place, and realigning the wheels. Millie watched Lohm kneel at her mother's side. When all the water was in Linn's system, he made some gestures with the skybrill feather that invited the soul of the Little Seed Stream to flow through her shoulder and down through her hip. Her mother's body jolted a little, then relaxed. He dipped his hands into the stream, flicked the water onto her body at the pain points, then filled those joints with white light and sealed it there.

When he helped her back up, her hip was still a little sore, but the sharp pain was gone. And her shoulder—she moved it in every direction, smiling.

"Lohm, you are a great tree in our forest. Thank you."

"Remember, that's only gonna last till you get home. Please see Grelle or somebody to finish the work I started. And, Millie?" He turned to make sure she heard him. "When you lose heart, remember, hold your arms out with your palms open, facing front. Breathe in and activate the ice-blue layer of light just under your skin. It'll calm you for a bit."

Millie nodded.

Lohm's friends had re-hitched Paulie, and Lohm went over everything one last time. They were good to go. As they prepared to leave, Lohm caught the hint of a gesture from Millie and yelled at her, *"Wait! Don't!"* She jumped. "The light will double you over with pain, dear. No greeting lights from you, Millie, for *anyone,* until you feel better."

"Thank you, Lohm," Millie said, grateful he'd caught her in time.

"May you be showered with blessings," Linn called out.

"Blessings are everywhere," they answered.

Once their friends had passed back through the border into Ddrym, Mama Linn did her best to settle Millie in the back of the cart on extra blankets and tablecloths she always kept there. "Is the ice blue layer working?" she asked her daughter.

Millie winced with every movement. "I guess. A little."

"All right. We'll talk about all this later. Let me check the quietbox to see if there's anything left to deliver." And with that, she opened it and almost wept with relief. It must've hovered during the crash, because every single hooray!cake was intact. Everything was in its place. This was why quietboxes were worth the great expense.

Linn got out and locked the cart doors. She made her way

up into the buggy and shook the reins. They rolled and thudded along, as gently as possible.

Millie, riding the pain of her fever, lay down and listened to the sounds with her whole body. Her discomfort eclipsed the fun she would have had otherwise, but still, she noticed what she could. Strange, loud trumpets would erupt from behind the cart. They were irregular, with no discernible pattern. Then there would be the whooshing sound of something bigger breezing by. *A car!* Against the background of Paulie's rhythmic steps clip-clopping, there were whistles and low, grinding mechanical sounds. There was a steady beeping that stopped after a while. Even through her scorching skin, Millie vibrated with curiosity.

The road became smoother, and Millie was able to rest. In and out of sleep, she heard conversations, but she couldn't make out the words. Some greeted her mother like they knew her well. Millie bathed her mind in the strange sounds of this magical realm—the Preservation Precinct—the sacred organization that preserved the spirit, structure, and accuracy of all the stories in all of StoryEarth.

The cart finally rumbled to a stop. Mama Linn secured the reins and came around to open the doors. "Don't move, Millie, and rest. Oh, I'm so late!" She held out her hands for the quiet-box, and it floated right into them. She took it, closed the doors, and walked away briskly, carrying the whole party in her hands.

But she'd forgotten to lock the latch. Millie pushed gently against it with her foot. It moved! She hoisted her fevered body up to peek out, and as she did so, a girl stomped out of the back door of the house.

"I don't care!" the girl yelled over her shoulder. "I'm not doing it. Not ever!" It was both an oath and a curse as she ran away, passing right by the cart. Millie opened the door a tiny bit more. Through the crack, Millie watched in wonder. The one yelling was a blond Precinct girl about her age, running from a magnificent house, wearing an immaculate, light blue dress, pressed and fragrant. Her shoes shone like a second skin, only bright blue with a sparkle that seemed to have been rubbed on with clear white magic. They must surely be at someone's High Home.

Trying to get a better look, Millie pushed on the door ever so slowly. The squeak of it made the girl turn around. Their eyes met, and their hearts stopped.

The girl had a look of alarm on her face as she stared at Millie, whose chest had grown bright with an automatic greeting, unbidden. As predicted, this doubled her over in agony, and the searing pain, with a voice of its own, twisted up through her throat into a helpless wail as she brought her light back into her bones. This sapped the last of her strength, and she collapsed onto the cart floor. The High Home girl scrambled backward toward the hedge. She stood there, panting. Silence.

After several minutes, the girl approached the cart warily, terrified, and said, "Uh...h-hello?"

No sound.

For a few moments, the girl stared at the cart. *It's too quiet in there,* she thought. She took a deep breath, went to the door, and opened it. She poked her head in and saw a girl her own age, sheet-white and covered in sweat, lying on some blankets, her eyes sunken in, her body jerking every so often.

"Hey," she whispered. "You OK?" The High Home girl tried to shake her awake, but as soon as she touched the sick girl's body, scorching heat seared her hands. She flew back out of the cart, and flapped her hands furiously, trying to cool them off.

"I'm going to get help!" she yelled, and she ran hard into the back door of her house. In no time, Mama Linn flew out the same door, heading for the cart.

She squatted next to her daughter. "*No!* Millie, stay with me. Millie!" She tried to quiet herself. *What does she need? Ice-white. Ice-white.* She summoned the healing color and it flowed through her hands, accumulating till she could spread it out over and around Millie. When the covering was complete, she moved back a little and bowed her head, crossing her hands over her heart, whispering, "Keepers of all the elements, Invisible Friends of Wisdom on the Other Side, please bar the door. Please don't let her in. I'll take care of her. I'll take better care of her, I promise." Tears ran down her face as the protection layer sank slowly into Millie's body.

Mama Linn watched her daughter's frown disappear, watched her shoulders soften, her legs slowly release to the relief as the feet fell away from one another, toes out. She had fully received the layer of ice-white. After some time, Millie opened her eyes. Her mother mimed hugging her, and they held each other's eyes.

"I'm getting us home as fast as I can. Please stay with the ice-blue that Lohm gave you. I added some ice-white that should shield you a little more from the movement of the cart."

She walked over to Paulie and whispered into his ear, "Go gentle, but go *fast*." As soon as she was up on the buggy with the reins in her hands, off he went. He moved almost catlike, choosing his steps carefully and moving quickly down the pathway toward the border.

Before reaching the clearing near the border, she prepped Paulie as she'd done on the way in. Off in the distance, she heard the sound of a galloping horse. And just as they approached the edge of the field, she saw her friend, Lohm, coming at her at lightning speed.

He drew his horse to a trot, and turned around so he was riding by her side. "The Larksheners made a tunnel," he said, pointing to it.

She looked toward the border, and saw a subtle passage through it—like a giant sleeve of quiet: a Larkshener silktunnel. She'd only heard of it as folklore. She never dreamed it was real.

Larkshen was one of the four regions surrounding the Preservation Precinct. It had been there the longest, their people the oldest in StoryEarth—ironic, since they had no vocal chords. They used their whole bodies to 'speak.' They were said to be StoryEarth's original race, a hotly contested issue in the Preservation Precinct, but accepted in most other parts. Larksheners were a green-skinned folk, mysterious, intuitive, and profoundly connected to the land itself.

And here they were, standing in two lines, each with their backs against the "walls" of the invisible silktunnel. Their feet were wide apart and their arms stretched out, fingertip to fingertip.

"I realized you can't prep Millie if she's got the fever, so I called them," Lohm said.

"But how does it—"

"No time to explain. Everyone will be safe in the tunnel. Just follow me." Lohm took off, and Linn shook the reins, but Paulie wouldn't follow. The horse sidestepped a little, skittish and snorting.

Lohm saw the problem and rode over to the elder Larkshener, signing with his arms and hands in Larksheni. The elder, Stofe, was their leader—a short, stocky man with graying hair and the darkening green skin typical of a Larkshener with many nines behind him. He nodded and walked up to Paulie, bowing before the animal. Paulie brought his head down so they could touch foreheads, while Stofe rested his wrinkled hands on the horse's cheeks. They remained there for a few breaths. When the moment was complete, Stofe returned to his spot at the mouth of the tunnel and nodded to Linn.

Lohm led the way again, and Paulie followed without hesitation. When they were inside the silktunnel, a silence deeper than the middle of the night came over them. Linn offered her greeting light to each Larkshener as she passed; they nodded in return. When they'd reached the Ddrymmian side, she turned around for one last look, and it had all vanished—no tunnel, no Larksheners, just trees and the last low wobble of the border's voice.

"I'm going with you. There's no way you're doing this alone," Lohm said.

"Lohm, it's a long way. Are you sure?"

But he was already on the path, moving fast enough for Linn and slow enough for Millie.

Chapter 4

The Long Solitary

Lohm led the way home with Linn close behind. Trying to braid hypervigilance, haste, and calm. They had only just crossed over into Droaze when Linn heard something and said, "Aww." Her tender tone struck Lohm as odd. He looked at her as she listened. She cocked her ear toward the childlike tenderness, a song coming from inside the cart. She smiled at Lohm—and as soon as she saw his face, her scalp tightened, and her mouth went dry.

"We have to get her on the ground," Lohm said, "right now." They dismounted and threw open the doors of the cart. Millie's eyes were glazed over. Linn yelled, "Millie!" She answered, singing,

> Look over there, the leaves in her hair,
> The leaves in her leaving, the door to her lair.
> The moon lights the way as it closes the day
> And opens the Door to Elsewhere.

"Spirits help us," Lohm said.

Mama Linn was already in the cart, gathering blankets, tablecloths, anything she could put between their hands and Millie's fiery skin. She gave some of it to Lohm and together, they padded themselves and moved Millie out of the cart and onto the ground.

Holding Millie's hands to the forest floor with a couple of pot holders, Mama Linn said, "Millie, feel this. This is your home; this dirt is where you were born. This is what we brushed off your faerie cloth blanket when Mama Bette found you." She pressed down on her hands through the pot holders.

A shadow passed through Millie's eyes but only for a moment before she lay down. *The leaves in her leaving, the door to—*

"I'm going for help." Lohm got on his horse and rode like a madman toward his home in Near Emmering.

The forest listened as Millie sang her little chant in a whisper. Mama Linn tried a different song, the one Millie used to love when she was a tiny sprout, singing louder. *"Seven little puppies all in a pile. Puppy one and puppy two take a nap for a while—"*

"Linn."

Linn jumped up, so startled that she nearly knocked the poor woman over.

"Balimaya! How did...? Lohm only just left—*just* now!"

"I know. I left a footcall for him to return home. I will tend to Millie so you can make the journey just fine."

Linn, nervous and trusting at the same time, asked the old woman, "But how did you know...?"

"My dear. The forest has many voices. And I've known for several hours that Millie was in trouble. The hyphen between me and anyone connected to Bette alerts me when there is a disturbance." The ample, dark brown woman was a Long Solitary. She'd given herself to life among the elements many nines ago, barely a woman when she first took her first vows. Long Solitaries live in silence for years, during which the elements speak through them, teaching them, guiding them until they become conduits for healing in the world.

Balimaya was a particularly powerful one. Her white hair was shorn, and contrasted with her dark brown skin. A living blade of marsh grass from near the Little Seed Stream encircled her left wrist, and her generous body wore the deep blue robes of a Long Solitary with grace.

"It's the bordercheat fever," Linn cried out. "Millie snuck into the cart, and I— It was...it was a delivery, and I didn't know. *I didn't know.*" Linn was now hysterical and weeping. "And we went through. And Paulie—"

"Linn, calm yourself. You are doing her no good in this state. Let me see to the child."

"Just don't touch her. She'll burn your hands off."

The old Solitary scoffed, and Linn gasped as she knelt down and took the girl's face in her weathered hands without flinching. Millie lay on the ground with a limp smile on her face. Eyes open but unseeing, she sang in a dreamy whisper. Balimaya rooted around with her thumb in the little pouch hanging between her voluminous breasts. She then pressed that thumb onto Millie's forehead and kept it there for a moment, holding the back of her skull. She seemed to be syncing her breath to Millie's.

Now Balimaya joined Millie's melodic chant with her deep voice, but she sang different words.

Look over here, a life that's so dear.
It walks through my story; it tells me its tears.
The sun lights the way, the body, the mind,
And ushers me back to right here.

She sang in harmony with the girl, her voice penetrating Millie's bones. After a few rounds, Millie faltered, confused. Then she "remembered" the words, the new ones, and along with Balimaya, sang her way free of the trance. They sang together like this three or four times, till the old Solitary was sure the girl was safely on this side.

Tears ran down Millie's face. She looked away. "Why did you do that?" she asked the old woman. "All the pain had gone. They were waiting for me. I wanted to go."

"Millie Fireflower, you have important work to do, and you can't do it from Elsewhere. Give me your eyes, girl."

Millie turned slowly toward the old Solitary.

"You have to stay here so you can accomplish it."

"Nobody needs me here."

Balimaya could feel where the hooks were in Millie and how to pull on them. "Oh yes, they do. You don't know it yet, but you'll be famous. You'll be known all over StoryEarth for what happens because of you." Millie's energy shifted, and the old Solitary went to work. "Get up," she commanded.

Mama Linn rushed to help her daughter. Balimaya prevented her. "Do you or do you not want this girl to make it home alive?" Then she addressed Millie, saying, "I am Balimaya. I trained your Mama Bette when she was younger than you. I am going to give you some tools. They will serve you well. But you must stop trying to be bigger—or *smaller*—than you are. Now get up!"

With some trouble, Millie did get on her feet. And for the next hour, she received direct training from the most revered Long Solitary in all of Ddrym.

"Every living form lives to express itself. Every blade of grass. Every squirrel, every tree, every person. That means you, too, Millie."

The woman stood across from her, making very subtle hand gestures as she spoke to the fevered girl. "It's important you stay on your feet as I teach you. You must stay briskly awake. So. Repeat after me," she said, "I am a blade of grass like any other."

"I am a blade of grass like any other," Millie said, wanting only to lie down, and making herself stand erect.

Balimaya went on, "I root in the soil and reach up for the sun. I drink the rain. And I dry off in the wind." Millie repeated it, thinking it a little childlike.

"Like every blade of grass, I regulate myself according to soil, sun, rain and wind."

And in between each phrase, Balimaya showed her how to respect the molecules of her heating mechanisms, to understand what they were trying to protect her from. She showed her how to converse with her innate ability to allow cooling streams of energy to flow, to direct them where they would do the most good. It was only the beginning, but the few techniques she taught her would at least keep her safe till she was home.

In that one session, Millie learned spoken instructions, chants, prayers of praise to the elements and breathing exercises to calm and soothe her own nervous system. Millie learned so quickly, showing such proficiency that Balimaya offered to continue training her in the years that followed, as she had Bette. The connection lived on.

As Balimaya prepared to leave, she said to Mama Linn, "Keep her up in the buggy with you. Fresh air will help. The burning is down by half, but remind her no greeting lights till all the heat is gone. It might take some days. Feed her now but only a little bit. And of course, fill your flask with water from the stream, for both of you. She must be home by dusk."

Mama Linn knelt before the big woman and kissed the grass bracelet on her wrist. "May every action I take from here on bring blessings to you."

The old woman placed her hand on Linn's head. "And may those blessings enrich all of StoryEarth in turn. See that she gets home soon."

After Balimaya's departure, mother and daughter faced each other. Awkward and exhausted at once, Mama Linn asked her, "How are you now?"

"I'm tired. It hurts a lot, but I feel like I can make it home."

"OK. Let's load up." Both of them at half strength, they did their best at putting blankets back in the cart, and climbing into the buggy, making sure Paulie got a good drink before proceeding. They rode in silence for long enough to begin processing all that had happened. Linn looked over at her daughter from time to time.

"Are you up for a little conversation?" Mama Linn asked her.

"Sure," Millie said, a little tentatively.

"Okay. The border works like this: There's a force field on its outer edge to protect the unshielded from accidentally going through. Its job is to repel. When you get near it, it makes you feel like moving away from it. Once you're trained, you'll know how to shield yourself and move through it anyway." Mama Linn stopped speaking and tried to stay calm. Paulie's steady steps helped. "But you were locked inside the cart, weren't you? Right? Millie, look at me!"

Millie jumped and looked at her mother.

"So you couldn't respond to the repelling." And then the words tumbled out louder and louder, her anger growing with each syllable. "What happens then is your lungs are flooded with blood, and your nervous system bursts into a million tiny fires just under the skin. Yes? Answer me!" Her eyes blazed at her daughter, then looked straight ahead again.

Millie nodded, flushed with shame.

"I don't know how you lived through it, but as furious as I am with you, I thank All Things Told that you're still with me right now."

Millie's eyes filled with tears, and she gave her mother the mimed hug, not knowing if she was still too hot to be touched. "I'm so sorry, Mama."

Mama Linn sighed and shook her head. "I just...almost *lost* you, Millie. I can't lose you."

They rode on for a little. Then she pulled Paulie to a stop, and rummaged around in a bag she'd been carrying on her good shoulder. "I have some sandwiches here. You should eat a little."

She pulled out a small second draft sandwich, gave half to Millie, and took half for herself. Millie nibbled hers down, leaving the crust like she always did. Linn looked at her daughter. "Why are you so fixated on the Precinct?"

Millie finished the bite she was working on, looked down, and fiddled with her shirt sleeve. Paulie nibbled on some grasses nearby.

"Listen, I have an idea," Mama Linn said. "Stay still."

Mama Linn got down from the buggy, and drew her own light up through her body and into her hands overhead. It was much brighter than a traditional greeting light. Her presence intensified until she shone like a brilliant body of light-carrying light. Mama Linn walked a wide circle around Millie like this, with her hands overhead, leaving a wall of barely perceptible blur in her wake.

Millie had never seen her Precinct-born mother work this kind of light, and she sat with her mouth open, watching. When the circle was complete, the wall had become a privacy bubble. This transparent sphere within the forest held them safe from anyone's hearing. But Mama Linn added a layer of protection. Moving fast, she shielded the bubble from sight as well, sealing the process by drawing up a phosphorescent dark blue light from within her and covering the bubble with it. Then, she climbed back into the buggy.

"This is a heartspeak, Millie. No one can hear us, or see us. And here's what's important. The members of the heartspeak are oath bound not to judge or retaliate in any way, not ever, no matter what is revealed inside it. This applies especially to the initiator of the heartspeak."

"Really?"

"Really. So answer me. Why are you so fixated on the Precinct?"

"OK then. How come you're *not* fixated on it? You're Precinct-born. It's your home. And you never talk about it."

"It's complicated," she said. "Has to do with Mama Bette, but that's not my story to tell. She had a terrible experience in the Precinct, and I don't feel like putting salt in that wound, even without her here. The story itself is a wound."

Mama Linn passed her the flask of water. As Millie drank, Mama Linn said, "I had good times there, to be sure. But I left because of differences I had with how they do things."

"What differences?"

"Oh, Mill, I don't know. It feels...tight...there, lots of pressure. It's in the air. And I just felt better, a thousand times better, here in Ddrym, especially Droaze, where your Mama Bette lived...lives. It just 'fit' me better."

"Do you hate the Precinct like Mama Bette does?"

"No, I don't. Living there as long as I did, I know its value, its dedication to Story. But I also know its danger, how it goes too far in its 'preservation' of consistency. I much prefer Ddrym. Sometimes I wish I'd been born here. You were born here, and *Sting* at that, so you have gifts I could never hope to have. It's—"

"Mama, please." Millie rolled her eyes. "What gifts do I have that you could never hope to have?"

"Well, for one, your energy work. It took me years to get to where you were by the time you were seven. You have a knack for it. And then there's your backsight."

Millie's eyes went wide. "I've never told anyone," she said, "not even Wrem. How did you know?"

Mama Linn laughed. "My sweetlight, I've known since Bette found you in the forest. We watched your movements as a baby. There was never any way to sneak up on you, even just to observe. You always knew we were there. And how many times did you whip around like a sprite and scare Wrem to his willies with a 'boo!' right before he was about to do it to you? We all know about your backsight. It's a Sting gift. Not every Sting, mind you, but a few have it, and you're one of them."

Millie decided to trust the heartspeak. She said, "Tell me something good from when you lived there. I never get to hear anything good about it."

Her mother sighed and looked at her daughter's hungry face. She shifted her weight, favoring her injured hip. "I tell you what, call on your healing elements now, the way Balimaya showed you. Let's have one more drink from the stream, stretch our legs, and we'll talk the rest of the way home."

"What about the heartspeak?" Millie asked.

"It comes with us till I release it." And with that, both of them a little better for the food and the rest, they climbed, grunting, into the buggy, and the heartspeak repositioned itself to travel with them, covering them all—Paulie, Linn, and Millie, the buggy and the cart.

As Paulie pulled them through the Dimbling Forest in Near Emmering, Mama Linn told Millie about her favorite Precinct event: the annual StoryEarth Good Will Ball, the one event each year where Players and common folk rubbed shoulders as equals. Millie knew all about it. *Players Magazine* devoted an entire issue to it once a year, and the event was one of Alphabet Delights' biggest accounts. She listened, entranced, as Mama Linn relived it through the eyes of her twelve-year-old self, watching the pageantry, meeting the stars. As Millie listened, she began to grow pale.

"Millie, you OK? Should we stop?"

"Yeah, I think I need...I feel..."

They pulled off the trail again and stopped. Mama Linn held Millie's hair back while she vomited. Afterward, Millie sat and concentrated on the breathing techniques she'd just learned.

"I am a blade of grass like any other..." One by one, she realigned her energies. She regained her color, and they started up again.

Mama Linn knew that, as unpleasant as it might be, it was important to give Millie a broader picture of the Precinct. "I was only four when I watched, from our window, a woman being led to the Nothing. She was sobbing in handcuffs, and they shoved her down the street, these two uniformed Precinct agents. She begged them for a quick darkening instead, anything but the Nothing. Because at least she'd be ended, and through the Door to Elsewhere—whereas in the Nothing, she might live forever in a place where nothing can save you, nothing can see you, nothing works and nothing happens.

"Your Grandma Set tried to pull me away from the window. I asked her, 'Why are they being so mean to that lady?' She told me the woman had said a wrong word in the story she was embodying, so she had to go to the Nothing. That's the law."

"I've heard that a million times," Millie said. "It seems so arbitrary: 'That's the law.' But why is it the law? It makes no sense."

Mama Linn thought about it, as Paulie plodded forward. "In Precinct school, we learned that before the Precinct was formed, eons ago, there was chaos. There were half-truths and lies and crazy histories and upside-down fallacies that paraded as Story. It was a mess. No one knew how a story went because anyone could change it. Because the ending kept changing, no one ever knew what happened. And no one could tell it. There were too many versions. No one knew which one was the real one.

"Then everyone got fed up with not knowing. There was a

revolution. It was headed by a powerful orator, Andrew Flort. His followers insisted on consistency, predictability. The creatives rebelled. Wars were waged over and over, one side winning, then the other, back and forth, for centuries—until finally, the two sides agreed on occupying different territories with a border to separate them. Everyone who agreed that a story, once told, should never change at all—they were the richest, the strongest, and they claimed the center territory of StoryEarth. They named it the Preservation Precinct.

"And the people more interested in creativity and flexibility would live on the fringes of the Preservation Precinct. They called it the NetherJunctures of Ddrym, and it was made up of—"

"Droaze (our region), Near Emmering, Far Emmering, and Larkshen," Millie interrupted.

"Yes, but the Larksheners have always lived in Larkshen," Mama Linn continued. "They were there long before any of the rest of us, and eons before the wars."

At that moment, because they were hidden by the heartspeak, a forest sprite flew right into Paulie's neck. The sprite let out a scream that sounded something like a very distant ringing in the ears, and flew awkwardly away with lots of up and down movement. Paulie tripped a little, but quickly regained his composure. Mama Linn and Millie looked at each other from inside the heartspeak and stifled their laughter, even though they couldn't be seen or heard. Bad form to laugh at a sprite.

"Well, I always loved our visits to Grandma and Grandpa Set." Millie relished the opportunity to speak about the Precinct. "My favorite part was learning all the stories exactly in sequence."

Mama Linn smiled. "I remember. You were quite a skilled memorizer."

"I remember Grandma Set teaching me to say, 'Language is our primary form of nourishment,' before I even knew what that meant. And the best day ever was when Grandma Set said I would make a great Player." As she said this, her mother saw Millie smile from way inside her young bones.

Something invisible came over Mama Linn's face, but she

made herself keep listening. Millie shared her dream of serving Story, something much bigger than herself—to serve it directly and perfectly with her whole heart, to be part of the ancient lineage and practice of being a Player. Millie never dreamed she'd ever be able to speak this freely with her mother.

Mama Linn steadied herself, remembering the precepts of the heartspeak. When she opened her mouth again, she said, "Millie, my darling, our kitchen feeds *all* the StoryEarth beings—from Players all the way down to the administrators of the Precinct—so in a way, we serve every part of Story on the deepest levels."

Millie thought this over.

"Just think!" Mama Linn went on. "When you take over the family business, you'll be serving much more than *a* story. You'll be serving Story itself in all its possible manifestations."

Millie blushed with pride at the implication.

"Wrem might be Ceremonial, honey," Mama Linn said with heartspeak frankness, "but his spirit chafes against the Precinct. He gets in his own way a bit. Hasn't found his Oneness with them yet, so he could never represent us there. You, my beloved daughter, you are our best hope.

"One of your most important gifts as a Sting, which I should have mentioned first when you asked, is your profound ability to befriend, no matter the origin of a person. Maybe it's because Sting babies have no way of knowing who their mother or father is, so they're kind to all because anyone might be their relative.

"We were so lucky to have found you. Don't you see? You'll be the perfect face for Alphabet Delights, delivering all our goods to the Precinct, able to move easily between both worlds. Seeing them as One through your Ddrymmian eyes and befriending all with your Sting nature, you're already on the road to the heroic service of Story. In fact..." But she stopped abruptly.

"What?" Millie pressed.

"No, never mind... I just— Never mind."

After a long moment, Millie asked her mother, "When can I train for the border crossing?"

Mama Linn answered, "No, Millie. Don't even think about it for now. You just put us all in mortal danger. There are serious repercussions to your actions. Your mother and I will have to talk it over with the circle of elders. I don't know what the consequences will be, but I do know that you probably pushed your border training back by many seasons."

Millie bent her head and wept. She was thirteen. She wanted what she wanted. And everything stood in her way.

Once they reached the clearing and saw Ink and Paper running toward them, Mama Linn withdrew the heartspeak. She and Millie waved to the Roggers, and Paulie quickened his steps, feeling home nearby. As they drew up to the front door, Mama Linn whispered, "We'll have to have a family meeting tonight. Shield up and go straight to your room. I'll call you when we're ready."

Millie got out and tapped her heels down on the ground twice, the way she'd been taught as a child. She drew up power from the soil to create a psychic bulwark against any onslaught, a procedure that was meant to be employed during high stress.

Once inside, she ran to her room and hoped for the least awful of any number of awful outcomes. She heard loud voices. She heard Wrem coming home from his Tree work. And then she heard the knock at her door—family meeting.

Chapter 5:

Shadow Woman

Millie kept all Balimaya's teachings fresh. She could be heard speaking, "I am a blade of grass like any other, I root in the soil and reach up for the sun. I drink the rain. And I dry off in the wind." After many breathing exercises and prayers to the elements, Millie's skin finally gave up its heat. But now she had new problems to deal with.

All of Ddrym knew about Millie's brush with the Door to Elsewhere. The elders rebuked; the sprouts pestered—youngsters who were just as curious but not as brave as she'd been. All were a little spooked by the fact that she'd survived it. She couldn't go anywhere without having to answer for herself in some way. As the weeks wore on, she became sullen and defensive.

The Circle elders offered guidance about the nature and scope of the infraction. Elder Shekwey, who was head elder for the entire region of Droaze, counseled her mothers to use the whole process not as punishment but as mulch for Millie's development. Bette had a hard time distinguishing between the two. Linn fought to mitigate some of the severity and won on only one front: Millie would get a day off from working dawn to dusk, every nine days. Bette made sure that there wasn't a minute of inaction on Millie's part during those eight days.

First, she had to lay out the faerie offerings for the entire property. This was much more work than just tending to her own windowsill. Now she was responsible for the other bed-rooms, the warmroom, and the thresholds at both the front and back doors. This meant getting up long before everyone else.

Next, she had to do the circlewalk around the garden, leav-ing offerings at each station for the elemental spirits—these offerings were complex and specific, and they changed with the seasons. She also had to keep the enormous garden fed, weeded, and watered. Again—before teachings, afterward, and during everyone else's resting days.

Third, she would clean out Paulie's stall every day and keep it stocked with fresh feed, water, and hay. She had to brush him out as well.

Finally, and most importantly, when she was not doing these other chores, she was on kitchen duty. This served two purposes: 1) It kept her busy, and 2) It provided her with a rich education that would serve her well in the future. She was being given the keys to the kingdom day by day—Mama Linn's recipes.

There was no time for rest, except nighttime and mealtimes. Millie was constantly exhausted, but she had a couple of tricks up her sleeve. Sometimes she would lie down for a brief nap in Paulie's stall. He always moved or whinnied to wake her if he saw someone coming. And she learned to eat slowly to maximize her sitting-down minutes.

Whenever Millie could get Mama Linn alone, she would say, "Mama, can you please just let me rest for a few minutes?"

But Mama Linn was a stone. "Nope. You can rest at night and every ninth day."

Millie submitted to her mothers' disciplinary measures. But underneath, her link with the Precinct only grew stronger. She turned her frustration into a campaign of compliance. She per-formed her tasks with angry precision. *I will do everything fully and beyond reproach.* As she weeded the simile and metaphor patch, clearing the row of clunky phrases and dangling partici-ples, she thought, *I will wait as long as I have to.* She pulled up cuss weeds. *Eventually, I will reach the fullness of my two nines, and then I will go.* She sprayed everything down with water. *I will leave this backward, boring place and go to the Precinct, where I belong. I will drive a car and party with Players, and—*

A presence tingled in her consciousness. She stood up and looked around. No one there. Returning to her gardening, she opened her backsight for a better view of the world directly behind her. Kneeling over her work, she pulled up some misspelled words and then felt it again. Her scalp now tingled with an image. She saw an old woman, an ancient, anemic face with long, thin, blanched braids. The woman seemed to be wearing cloudcloth and ash. Her colorless hands were wrinkled, and dark blue veins snaked up her forearms.

Millie stood as tall as she could, given her trembling feet. The woman made no attempt to hide herself this time, but her form was unsteady and translucent. For the first time, Millie thought, *This is a shadow woman! They're real!*

Her greeting light came up automatically, traveling from within her breast through her arm and into her hand, and the shadow woman returned the gesture. When the woman's lavender light swam into Millie's, the young girl became utterly still. She wanted to run away, but her feet seemed to grow roots into the ground. She suddenly knew what it was to be a tree. They held each other's gaze. Millie's breathing slowed, but her heart quickened, and her mind seemed to have gone into some kind of unholy hibernation. Silence. Stillness.

The back door slammed, and with a loud clap, the shadow woman was gone, as though she had never been there. Millie shook her head and blinked her eyes.

"The garden isn't gonna spit the weeds out on its own, Millie! Get to work!" Mama Bette was carrying laundry to hang on the line.

Shaken and confused, Millie bent down over the plants and pretended to weed while her mind scrambled, trying to piece together what had just happened. She longed to tell Mama Linn about it, but didn't trust her anymore. She returned to her task, feeling Mama Bette's eyes on her as she sent her questions into her work. *Who was that? What did she want? Why me?*

Chapter 6

A Year of Penance

For months, that moment in the garden hovered in the fading margins of Millie's days. She would awaken with a pounding heart, troubled and impatient, wishing she could see the shadow woman again, then hoping she wouldn't. She learned in Circle Teachings that shadow people always showed up for a reason, but the reasons were never the same from one person to another. The elders admitted that all their knowledge about the shadows was useless because their very nature was shifting, ephemeral, and imprecise. The best advice in the event of a visitation was to shield up and invoke Oneness.

But Millie wanted to know more. Mama Bette had always been a reliable source of Ddrymmian wisdom and lore, so once, during lunch, as casually as possible, Millie asked her where shadow people came from. Bette asked her, alarmed, "Why are you asking about this?"

"No reason, just wondering."

"Well, don't talk about...them—ever. It's dangerous."

"OK, but—"

"*Shht!*" Bette held up her hand as a gesture for her to stop, and Millie went silent. And then she noticed a force field between herself and ever speaking about it to Mama Bette again. It was almost physical. She found she couldn't even apologize about bringing it up.

Did Mama Bette do that?

Bette's head was bowed as she murmured something, moving her fingers together in specific ways. Millie watched her carefully, then looked over at Mama Linn, who seemed out of her depth. The subject never came up again.

Feeling very much on her own, Millie refined her plan of deceiving her mothers into trusting her again. When the moment was ripe, she would escape. But as time went by, things shifted. Bette and Linn watched her carefully, noticing changes that they weren't ready to give credence to yet. Millie was punctual and thorough. She did as she was told and sometimes threw in extra touches. For a while, her diligence had a sarcastic edge to it. But that eventually dissolved as she began to genuinely appreciate her native Ddrymmian traditions.

One late afternoon, she was scrubbing pots in the kitchen when Wrem ambled through the door with his friends Bluke and Riss. They hung their work coats on hooks by the door and brought the scent of cedarwood and soil into the kitchen with them. "Hallo, the house!" Wrem called out.

"Hallo, the boys," Bette muttered absentmindedly without looking up from her desk. She nodded to Millie. "Take care of them, please."

Millie left the pots in the sink and began setting out the crispy jokes and salted anecdotes that Linn had prepared for them before leaving. She gave them each a tall glass of iced song. Wrem asked Millie, "Where's Mama Linn?"

"She's doing a Listening with the Rogger family."

"What's their problem with her?"

"I'm not sure, but I think she committed the 'atrocity' of teaching a little Precinct game to one of their children during a break in the Reaching ceremony last week. And they thought she was polluting their daughter with Precinct ways."

As the boys found their seats at the table, Bluke said quietly, "Can you blame them?"

"Wait a minute, Bluke," Millie said, passing out the forks. "What about 'seeing Other as pollution is the first act of war'?"

At her desk, Bette put down her pencil and cocked her ear.

Millie went on, "So much talk about Oneness in our world without the walk. For the Roggers, Precinct is Other. Where's the Oneness in that? But we're no better, if we're mad at the Roggers, even for being mad at us for no reason. Then the Roggers are Other to *us*. That's why Mama Linn went over to listen. She's at least trying to find Oneness."

Mama Bette couldn't hold back any longer. "Right you are, Millie," she said, coming in for a frosted anecdote. "And as you know"—she took a big bite and kept talking—"Oneness being Oneness, no one is wrong."

The boys and Millie nodded respectfully. Then Bette swallowed her bite and muttered, "We just have to find a way to sit around the same fire without knocking their blocks off." They all had a good laugh.

Millie returned to her work at the sink while Wrem updated Mama Bette on their progress. "We cleared the circle for the Turning ceremony—right near that bendy crook in the Little Seed Stream—the place had a welcoming spirit."

Riss jumped in. "We placed mad good offerings last night at the trunks of the main trees there, and—"

"And today," Bluke broke in, "the trees gave their permission! All of them!"

Bette arched her eyebrows. "That was fast."

Riss said, "Trees *and* stones. It were amazing and all because of our treefriend here." Wrem's relationship with the forest and its inhabitants bordered on legendary, even though he had only two nines to stand on.

The boys had come in for a bite before setting out again to finish. As they were shoving the last of the food into their mouths, Pim Pfahler showed up at the door. Millie dusted herself off and went to open it. "Hallo, Pim," she said.

Their neighbor stood at the door wearing a silk turquoise porkpie hat, an iridescent-green bird feather in the hatband, fixing her in his gaze with his all-business black eyes. Pim never said an unnecessary word. He was thought to be a TwoBody

Peacock, but no one could prove it. There was controversy, even in Ddrym, over whether TwoBodies existed at all. The myth was that TwoBodies changed from their human form into their animal form and back in absolute privacy. So because no one had ever seen it, there was no way to prove it.

But Pim was a sure clue that they must exist because, on one too many occasions, a gorgeous peacock had been spotted walking around, usually with its feathers down, pecking at the ground just moments after someone had seen or met with Pim in that very place. Some had even seen its feathers up and fanned out in a breathtaking display of superiority. Of course, no one could be sure it was Pim, but still...

He seemed in a hurry. He removed his hat and said, "Linn here?"

"I'm sorry, no. Would you like to come in? We've got plenty to eat."

"No," he said. "Bette?"

"Yes, let me get her. Mama Bette?"

"What?" Bette said from her desk in the other room.

"Master Pim is here, would like to have a word with you."

"OK, here I come." Bette went to the front door and stepped outside, shutting the door behind her.

He was a strange man. No one had ever gotten close to him. Nobody disliked him really, but he was hard to like. In the Ddrymmian community, however, he was revered for his grasp of the theatrical. His fondness for fabrics and colors and his deep relationship with shapes and textures found their expression in magnificent robes, headdresses, and ceremonial decorations. His sensibilities were extraordinarily fine-tuned, making it sometimes difficult to live next door to him.

When Bette came back in, they all looked at her. "What?" she asked.

"Oh, come on, don't play dumb with us. What did he want?"

She looked at them for a long moment, trying to decide whether to tell them. "The laughter over here threw off his color sense. He's asked us to keep it down for an hour while he recalibrates."

They all stifled themselves as best as they could, choking down snorts hanging on to their mouths. Wrem finally said, "OK, let's get back to work." In their clumsy, grown-boys way, they all brought their plates to the sink, thanked Millie, and headed out.

Millie developed a rhythm with the days, and she eventually became an authentic sister in the community. Over time, her angry diligence softened and dissolved. Her childhood friends Drauml and Bari were growing into themselves as well. Technically, she had more in common with Bari, who was also Sting. Plus, they always celebrated the same finding day.

But her connection with Drauml was always a little deeper. Drauml was Primal, and her mother was Mama Linn's best friend. Drauml's parents had always been Uncle Rollo and Auntie Celeste to Millie and her brother.

Millie's time of atonement had ripened her in ways that no one foresaw. By the time she was in her fourteenth year, this Ddrymmian Sting had shown a rare understanding of the Oneness principle and a knack for garden management. (Mama Bette had been an excellent teacher, if a rough one.) She also became quite adept at tree-singing, energy healing, and baking.

She learned the difference between honoring faeries and appeasing them, and in the process, she developed a strong connection with their house faerie, Flurjahm. He seemed to travel with her everywhere—sometimes visible, sometimes not. He appreciated that Millie never called attention to his kind, and she never bargained with him. She was what they called in their language "a sweet wind."

Flurjahm had been Bette's and Linn's house faerie since long before Millie was born. During her year of penance, she learned all his idiosyncrasies. Through trial and error, she discovered how much he loved cream, butter, tiny bells, anything shiny, holly berries, and bright coins. He appreciated his elderberry wine served in a half walnut shell. On the flip side, she also learned how much he hated iron, disorder, Saint-John's-wort, stinginess, and being watched. Furthermore, neither he nor his friends would come around if there was discord or anger in the house (unless they'd created it themselves with a prank).

Because she took such good care of him, he would send her a few extra minutes every now and then, elongating her nap in the horse stall. Sometimes he would express his joy to her by emitting the scent of licorice and riding on her shoulder throughout the day.

One cold, blustery afternoon during Turning season, the Circle students took refuge inside for their midday meal. The sanctuary was low and cozy, with a fire burning in the fireplace. They ate at tables in their established groups. Millie's Sting friend Bari had gravitated to some more dogmatic Ddrymmian kids who held that Oneness was the superior way and that all things Precinct were inferior, not seeing the inherent twoness of that thought. One of Bari's friends, Shayla, called out, "Hey, Millie! Come sit with us."

Millie paused for a moment. Shayla was in a clique of girls who had shunned Millie after her bordercheat escapade, but recently, they'd softened a little. "OK," she said, setting her bowl and cup down on the table. They ate in silence for a while.

Shayla finally said, "Did you hear about the Player for Horton?"

"Horton?" Millie replied.

"From *Horton Hears a Who!*"

"Oh, no. What happened?"

"He blew it. He said 'I heard it' instead of 'I hear it.' And just like that, he's off to the Nothing. I mean, *we* know the Nothing is not really a place. But wherever they *do* take them must be pretty bad, because no one ever comes back."

Florence piped up, "Bari thinks it's possible Precinct people might change...someday. But I think they're idiots, and they'll never learn."

Millie sighed. "You do remember," she said, "that my Mama Linn is Precinct."

Florence faltered for a second but quickly recovered. "I do.

And that's exactly the point. She's *here,* right? She left that place and came here!"

"Not because everyone in the Precinct is an idiot though." Millie looked around for any excuse to get out of this conversation.

"Well," Florence felt the need to add, "I think if they punish their Players so harshly for messing up one tiny word, then they're criminals."

In Millie's backsight, she could see Drauml way behind her, looking around. Millie turned and called out to her. Drauml nodded to a table nearby. Millie got up, turned to Shayla, and said, "I'm gonna go hang with Drauml. But thanks to Oneness," she tried to say without rancor, "no matter what our differences are, there's—"

They cut her off with "Room for us all." They rolled their eyes and giggled.

Millie sat down with Drauml. Digging into her meal, Drauml asked Millie, "What was that all about?"

"It's just them being them...I'm sick of how nobody sees the two of it."

"The two of what?" Drauml asked, savoring her steamed sequitur—a slightly bitter, green, salty vegetable with crunchy stems and sweet buds at the top.

"The two of favoring Ddrym over Precinct or the other way around," she said, seasoning her dictionary stew with ground clarity. "Don't they see they're turning their backs on Oneness? Aren't we taught that it's *all* one world?"

When lessons ended, Millie hurried home with her jacket collar pulled up against the wind and her hands deep in her pockets. The day had gone badly. She'd overheard Florence imitating her and everyone laughing. As she made her way down the path, she thought she caught a whiff of licorice in the air. She smiled at the small comfort, but it all disappeared when a strong gust of wind nearly blew her over.

She detoured through the forest where there was a little more protection from the wind. There was a stooped elder ahead of her. Her robes were blowing a little as she held onto a tree for balance. Millie trotted up to help, then noticed the translucent gray arms, the dark blue veins, and the fact that there wasn't enough substance inside the robes to hold them up. The shadow woman turned to Millie and offered her greeting light, this time an indigo globe, pulsating.

Feeling again the desire to run and the inability to do so, Millie panicked. But eventually, she had nowhere to go, and so offered the woman her own greeting light. She tried to shield up before their hands met, but wasn't fast enough. The lights mingled, and Millie's feet rooted down into the soil. In the profound silence that followed, their eyes met, and it was as though Millie had fallen headlong into the shadow woman's world.

She felt herself reaching, stretching toward something with her essence, never arriving, never being able to grasp. There was a frantic nature to it. Searching, she always felt it was maybe behind her or maybe over there where she'd seen something out of the corner of her eye. It was a deeply unsettling, unsatisfied sense of almost—but never quite—obtaining something precious.

By now, Balimaya had trained her in dealing with sprites, spirits, and elves, but she was new at it and trying desperately to remember what to do. She made a stab at it. "One...Oneness flows through us all," she stammered. "You are not different from me. You are part of me as I am part of you. We have no power over each other. We are One in the Oneness of everything."

Millie felt one last piercing lurch for something just out of reach, and then she was alone again, no shadow woman anywhere. She immediately shielded up and ran home. After closing the front door behind her, she hung her coat on the hook and began unwinding her scarf.

"Millie," Mama Bette said, and Millie's stomach wrenched into a knot the way it always did around Mama Bette. Her mother's voice had an unfamiliar tone to it, though, as she came to greet her. Millie noticed tears in Mama Bette's eyes just before she was suddenly gathered up in her mother's arms.

Then Mama Bette held Millie at arm's length and said, "I just got a message from Elder Shekwey, and as you know, he is the elder for the entire Droazian region of Ddrym. They want you to assist with the sprouts class, the three-year-olds! This is the surest sign that you have reached them with your heart. I'm so proud of you."

At these words, Millie herself burst into tears and hugged her rougher mother tight, sobbing with very old grief and new openings. Their greeting lights shimmered in and out of view, which can happen in times of strong affection.

The year of penance was lifted, and Millie was free to return to her normal schedule. With the sprouts class as almost a bonus. A good many months went by in this way, and Millie continued to grow in the community.

Then came her Finding Day, which always included a surprise of some kind. Once, Wrem had hoisted her up onto Paulie, and they went on a picnic way into the forest. He introduced her to his favorite tree. He taught her to sing with it. Once, when she was little, her mothers and their friends had arranged a pajama party. On this particular Finding Day, though, Mama Linn said, "Why don't you skip your circle teachings and take a walk with me."

"I can't skip circle teachings. They—"

"I already spoke to the circle elders. They gave it their blessing. Let's go."

They walked around the house to the back gate, and onto a pathway that was well worn, but not by Millie. They walked for almost an hour, in a direction Millie had somehow never explored.

Then, Mama Linn said, "See that?" pointing to an open field. "That's where we're going. You lead the way."

Millie walked ahead of her mother. And after a few minutes, she heard the warning wobble, and felt an almost nauseating revulsion. She spun around, stumbling away from it, remembering the intense pain and heat. She started to shake. She went numb. Her mother took Millie in her arms to calm her trembling.

"Memory is big. But you are bigger, Millie," said a familiar voice, not very far away. "You, and the moment at hand, the one right under your feet and inside your eyes—you are much bigger than any memory, any fear. Remember that."

Millie looked up.

"Balimaya!" The expression in Millie's face brought the sun, the moon, and the stars out to shine all at once. Mama Linn stepped out of the way, and motioned for Millie to greet her teacher.

She and Balimaya exchanged greeting lights, then Millie knelt and kissed the marsh leaf on the Long Solitary's wrist. The woman pulled Millie up and said, "Are you ready, girl?"

"I don't know," Millie said, still shaken from the memory.

"Well, let's ease our way in, but first," the solitary said with a twinkle in her eye, "let's agree on one thing. I don't have all day, so let's save some time and you just call me Miss B, like your Mama Bette used to, all right?"

Millie smiled and said, "Okay," looking over at her mother, full of gratitude.

It was an intense day with Miss B. First the old woman took care to discuss Millie's original experience with the border.

"You lived, Millie," she said. "You must let the suffering through it live too. Be kind to it. Give it a soft place to sit in your heart, and it won't bother you so much. Eventually, it will turn into strength and become your ally. For now, just don't push it away."

They stood up and faced the border, looking through its invisible power—toward the Precinct. Miss B took her pouch out of its hiding place in the middle of her breasts, powdered her thumb, then pressed it into the fleshy part at the base of Millie's thumb.

"This will help with some of your fear and nausea," she said. "Now, stand up straight." Millie did, feeling the effects of the powder, and Miss B's belief in her.

"First, you must ground yourself in Oneness, the Oneness of

everything—Ddrym, the Precinct, elders, full beings, children, babies, easy people, difficult people. Everything is one.

"Second, you must have a specific purpose for breaching the border. Fix your mind on that purpose. While we're training, your purpose will be to learn how to get to the other side without harming yourself or anything else. Envision it in detail. Nobody breaches this border in either direction without a specific, peaceful purpose.

"And third, you must offer your greeting light to the other side to signal that you mean no harm. These are all things you must master before I can even teach you the shielding skills. Let's give it a go."

They began there. Millie worked diligently every day at getting the border to trust her greeting light. Once she'd accomplished that, Miss B knew she would be safe to continue on her own with her mother. Millie begged her to stay, but Miss B said, "Dear one, you have a destiny to live into, and so do I. Mine is as a Long Solitary, and," she said, chuckling, "I've had enough of humans for a while. But I'll be coming every three or four seasons, so keep working on what I've taught you. The roads are many…"

"All begin and end in Oneness," Linn and Millie responded.

Mama Linn spent hours teaching her concentration exercises. She showed her how to wrap her own bones with soundproofing energies and how to create a sense shield around herself and eventually around another being. They practiced after Circle Teachings almost every day. Mama Linn also trained her with Paulie and the cart, showed her the spot on the path to the Precinct where the pine-scented needles signaled that it was time to begin Paulie's shielding, when delivering with the cart.

Millie proved herself capable almost right away, with a notable knack for establishing Oneness and finding the thread of kinship with the other side. That was no surprise. But Millie's aptitude for the rest of it—creating the soundproofing and the sense shields and managing the more subtle energies necessary upon exiting the border—was astonishing. She would be the perfect successor to the family business.

Millie was looking forward to representing Alphabet Delights to the larger world. Especially to the Preservation Precinct. Her own heart hid itself from how much she looked forward to that.

Chapter 7

A Secret in the House

Walking home from their Circle Teachings, Millie and Drauml carried baskets full of herbs. Their homework was to make several healing expressions: 1) three tinctures, one for nausea, one for anxiety, and one for sloth; 2) a powder to improve poor memory; and 3) three teas—one for calming, one for clarity, and one for dignity. Drauml gave Millie a curious look as they walked.

"What?" Millie asked.

"Nothing."

"Oh, Drauml, when you get that look, it's never nothing. Come on. What?"

"I just— You know Lims?"

"Words, I do. I wish he would leave me alone."

Drauml thought that one over.

Millie pushed. "Well, what then? What about him?"

"He's dreamy, Millie! He's kind and good with birds, and... and...he likes you."

"I know," Millie said quietly. "But he doesn't understand."

"What's there to understand?"

"Drauml, I'm Sting."

"So? I mean, it's not really true what they say, right?"

"Depends on what you've heard. But if it's what I think, of course it's true."

Drauml stopped and stared at Millie. "You don't join? Like, ever? I thought it was...just..."

"Never. Ask Bari. We don't feel things the way Primals do."

"But then you'll never have a sweetfriend? Or a lover? Or... Ever?"

"No. Haven't your parents had this 'talk' with you yet?"

"Yeah, but they skimmed over a lot of it." Drauml faltered as they walked quietly for a while. "Can I just ask you this?" There was some tenderness in her voice.

"Sure."

"Is it that...you don't join...with boys? I mean, are girls more..."

Millie laughed hard at this, and it broke the tension. "No, silly, it's not like that, not at all. I don't know. I just don't feel like sharing my body with anyone. No Sting does. We have other connecting lines to the people we love." She took a moment to return her friend's questioning eyes. "Stings receive and show love with deep friendship and affection. Do you like Lims?"

Drauml's face flushed. She looked down at her shoes and said, quieter than a fallen leaf, "Yes."

"Then you should let him know." Millie smiled.

"No! What if he doesn't like me?"

"Ha ha. What if he already knows all about me, and he's just using me to get closer to you?"

Drauml grinned and pushed her friend in the shoulder.

"OK, Drauml, I'll see if there's a way to find out. But if he does like you, you have to tell him how you feel."

They giggled about the many ways this could be accomplished and were still laughing when they came through the front door of Millie's house. They overheard an intense discussion between Linn and Bette. "But hear me out," Linn said.

"No, this is nonsense. It's elf scat."

"Bette, listen to me. Just listen for a minute."

"Linn, I will not stand here and—"

"Fair hearing!" Linn's voice shot out, sharp and clear.

The minute the girls heard the words "fair hearing," they blanched and backed out of the house, closing the door as quietly as possible. When they were a safe distance away, Millie said, "I want to go back and listen so bad."

They walked through the woods to their favorite talking spot: an old oak with branches that all but reached down to help the girls up. One branch had two perfect indentations close to the trunk for them to sit together. They'd spent the best part of their young years in that tree.

"Don't even say that," Drauml said.

"What could they be fighting about that would make Mama Linn invoke *fair hearing*?"

Drauml was thoughtful for a while. "The last time I heard those words," she said, "my mom and dad were about to disjoin. She had to invoke it just to get him to listen to her through a whole sentence."

"I never knew your parents had fought like that."

Drauml laughed, then gave her friend a reassuring smile. "Looking back on it now, it was really funny watching my dad try to not say anything till noon meal the next day. Scary at the time, but now...it turned out OK. They're really good. She had to learn to speak in a way that went in easier for him. And he just had to stop yelling long enough to hear her, to really listen."

Millie gave a lifeless smirk. "Mama Bette's never been a great listener. I wish I knew..." They looked at each other for a moment.

"No, Millie," Drauml pleaded. "We can't. Fair hearings are completely private. You know that. You know what happens if we get caught."

Millie grinned. "Yeah, but that's only if we get caught."

"How can you even think about it at a time like this? You're respected now. You're helping teach the sprouts!"

But Drauml hadn't even finished the sentence before Millie was already stealing back toward the house, through the brush, and down the path. Drauml did not follow. Millie was foiled though. One of her mothers must've heard her coming and invoked a heartspeak, because the angry voices disappeared into a sudden smack of silence.

Chapter 8

The New Idea

A few days later, Millie began her morning like she always did: She set out her offerings, made her bed, dressed for another teaching day at the lake with the elders, and clomped down the hall in her gardening boots for breakfast. When she came into the kitchen, everyone stopped talking. Mama Bette's face had hardened, and Mama Linn's was inscrutable. Wrem stood behind Mama Bette's chair as if in solidarity.

"What's going on?" Millie asked. No one spoke for a long moment.

Mama Bette, always ready to spit out what's what, told her, "Your mother here thinks that because you're so brilliant at managing the border, you should go to school on the other side of it."

Millie laughed. Nobody else laughed. She jerked her head back, asking, "Why?"

Mama Bette pounced. "That's my girl. Good question! Why would you want to do such a thing? You see, Linn, her roots are here. She's asking why. She's assisting the elders, she works with the little sprouts, she's growing a great garden, and she is conversant with Oneness. Especially Oneness—so why would she need to go over there and get all mangled up in the world of Twos?"

Mama Linn let Bette finish, then answered her daughter

evenly, "We aren't getting any younger, your mother and I. Wrem is deep into his work with the trees, and while he'll always be able to help with loading and unloading, he's not comfortable dealing with the Preservation Precinct, and you are.

"So because you'll be succeeding me as the face of Alphabet Delights to the whole of StoryEarth, you need to be easily conversant with Precinct ways, as well as the Ddrymmian ways that are in your blood. My thought is that if you go to the Precinct high school, you'll have those years not only to learn all their ways but maybe to forge some friendships that could anchor your presence in their minds as a Ddrymmian they can trust. It's an investment in the future of our business. Do you understand?"

"I think I need to sit down," Millie said, suddenly unsure of all she thought she knew. She'd dreamed of this chance all her life. She had tried in a hundred ways, unsuccessfully, to make it happen. But now, standing on the ledge of its coming to fruition, she felt a torrent of conflicting emotions. She wanted desperately to go to school in the Precinct, but that would mean being tied forever to Alphabet Delights.

I guess some contact is better than none at all, Millie thought. *But...* Her mind was racing.

Mama Bette shook her head and sighed. They were all quiet for a while.

"Is it even...allowed?" Millie asked.

Linn sat down next to her as she answered, clearly having done some research. Evidently, deep in the archives at the Preservation Precinct, there was a law governing the transportation of students between the Preservation high school and all the regions of Ddrym. This law predated the Big Split.

But in the chaos that followed that negotiation, this quiet little law detailing what route children should take to the school got overlooked, and it was never changed. Mama Linn planned to use that law to assert Millie's right to enroll in the school. They talked at that kitchen table for as long as they could before Millie had to leave for her Circle Teachings and Wrem was called away by the trees. The subject paced around in everyone's minds all day.

At dinner, Mama Linn announced that Millie would be accompanying her and Wrem on the next delivery. Linn wanted to start acclimating her daughter to Precinct practices as soon as possible. Bette had fought hard but eventually acquiesced.

Millie could barely breathe. "Who is it? Which Player?"

"Lonner Mastin for *Rumpelstiltskin*. His little daughter just got a prize for something, so they're throwing a big party for her and her friends."

"When do we leave?" Millie asked.

"Tomorrow." That was the good news.

The bad news was Mama Bette was coming too. She hadn't been to the Precinct in decades, but she wasn't about to be left out of this moment. Once everyone had eaten their fill and the kitchen was clean, they all went to bed, and nobody but Wrem slept that night.

The following morning, Wrem went out to get the wagon. They had upgraded. It was of respectable size—not as large as the Framms' in Near Emmering but not small either, just right for Alphabet Delights' needs. There was, of course, a buggy seat for the driver, the wagon itself, which held three people comfortably, and a large trunk in back for all the supplies. Wrem had built cupboards and drawers with his own hands, having first asked the trees respectfully for the wood. His reverence was no doubt why packing was always stress-free. Massive amounts of food and supplies went in, but because of Wrem's genius—and not a little faerie involvement—everything was easily accessible. What didn't fit (as well as foods that were meant to be surprises) went into quietboxes.

He harnessed Paulie, who was patiently swishing off flies with his tail. Paulie was strong and steady, never spooked by the cars, and preternaturally attuned to Wrem's guidance from the driver's seat. An occasional whinny let them know he was ready to go.

"Whoa there, Paulie. We're gettin' there," Wrem said.

Linn went through the checklist with him. "Thirty hooray!cakes?"

"Check."

"Laughing balloons?"

"Check."

"Tablecloths for two large tables?"

"Check."

"Twenty napkins, dessert plates, forks, spoons?"

"Check."

Bette chimed in, "Invoice!"

Wrem and Mama Linn smiled at each other. "Check."

Linn continued, "Magic BabySquirrel party favors."

Millie said, "Oh, they're so lucky—"

"Check. Mama Linn, I got it. It's all here."

"All right, then. Millie, up you go."

Millie got into the back seat, followed by Mama Linn on one side and then Mama Bette on the other. Wrem sat up front, took the reins, and said, "OK, Paulie, go." The horse perked his ears up and heaved forward, moving into a nice pace. Millie fidgeted with joy.

They'd been traveling for the better part of an hour, with Bette watching Millie carefully. She said under her breath to Linn, "I hope this goes the way you think it's gonna go."

Linn poked her head out the window and called up to Wrem. "Are we to the pull-off point yet?"

"It's coming. Five long breaths, and we're there."

They'd agreed to stop at a nook in the road just before the border, where they could review all the reminders for Millie before crossing into the Precinct. Much rode on her behavior and affect. They stopped by the stream off from the roadway, protected by an outcropping of brush, where Paulie could munch on some of his favorite grasses. Everyone got out to stretch their legs.

"OK, Millie," Mama Linn said. "Let's go over it one more time. Wrem over there is going to be Mr. Mastin, and I'll be his maid." She nodded to Wrem.

"I want coffee! Now!" Wrem had no respect for Players or the Precinct in general, so he was having his fun with it.

Mama Linn played along. Bowing, she whispered, "Yes, my lord, coming right away." She scurried off into the bushes.

Bette motioned for Millie to ring the bell. Millie did so, making a ridiculously large, low sound. "Diiing-doooooong." They all had to laugh, even Mama Bette.

Mama Linn, recovering, said, "Look, we don't have much time. This is serious." She looked away to recompose her face. "So the bell has rung. What's next? I come to answer it." She mimed answering the door with a withering gaze, looking down on Millie. Millie's greeting light began to shine in her chest.

Bette and Wrem both jumped on this. "No, no, no, no, no!"

Millie shrank back, paralyzed. Linn gave them both a look, then put her arm around her. "It's OK, Millie. Just remember, Precinct folk are afraid of the greeting light."

"I know! I forgot. I just forgot."

"Well, at least this way, you made your mistake here instead of there," Mama Linn offered cheerily. "You got it out of the way where it was safe. Let's start over, from my opening the door. What would you do differently?" Linn mimed opening the door and looked down on Millie.

Millie kept her voice low and said, "Delivery from Alphabet Delights for the Mastin High Home."

Linn arched her eyebrows for effect. "You're rather young to be a delivery girl."

Millie gave a curtsy, just as Linn had taught her, and said, "My name is Millie. I am the daughter of the founders of Alphabet Delights. They let me come along to learn the business."

Then Linn gave her the standard response. "Very well, then. The service entrance is around the back."

"Thank you, ma'am." Another curtsy, and she'd passed. A sigh of relief went through everyone, Millie included.

They loaded up again and traveled the rest of the way in silence, with Millie willing her greeting light deep into her bones so it wouldn't escape again unbidden. When they got to the border, even Mama Bette could scarcely conceal her pride watching Millie execute the first steps of the border prep. Mama Linn was right. She'd probably be ready to do it on her own before they knew it.

Wrem and Linn switched places. Linn being Precinct born, she had instinctive habits that kicked in automatically. On deliveries, she was the face they saw most often, and they knew her, so Precinct customers were less dubious of her Ddrymmian catering service.

When Wrem climbed back to join his mother and sister, Millie asked him, "When are you going to be joined, Wremmy?"

He gave her a look. "Where's that coming from?"

"Nowhere. It's just, Bari's brother got joined during Water season, and she asked me when you were getting joined, and I said I didn't know anything about it."

He laughed. "Well, Docken is a good friend, and he found himself a right, good woman. I'm happy for him. Me, I'm sworn to the trees."

"Really? You'll never be joined?"

"No, that's not it. It's just that my life right now is made happy by being with the trees, hearing their songs, mending them when they need it, tending to their life. Not really lookin' to be joined. But it might happen someday."

Millie looked out the window, memorizing every single detail about the Precinct landscape—the square junctures where others had to stop to let you by, or you had to stop for them; the buildings built up so tall into the sky; the diamond-shaped windows; and, oh, the *cars*. All the different colors, different shapes, different sounds.

Lonner Mastin's High Home was through the center of the Precinct and well into the northwest hills, a cave deep in the rocky side of Mount Gorbelain. Players get to have any kind of High Home they want, so there are many different kinds in the Precinct. Mastin's entrance was the farthest he could get from any neighbor in the Precinct. They had to travel up a steep, narrow rocky road, and Paulie's sure-footedness served them well.

Suddenly, Linn sniffed something in the air and pulled Paulie to a halt. She was the only one who knew they had arrived.

Everyone got out of the wagon and followed Linn's gifted sense of smell all the way to a place that looked like nothing in particular—grasses, rocks, weeds. She pointed out a tiny green circle of moss against the mountainside and told Millie to push it gently. They heard nothing. They waited. Eventually, the rocks faded into an opening roughly the size of a door. Millie's jaw dropped. A short, stout being larger than a dwarf but smaller than a man scowled at them. *"What?"* he yelled, and they all jumped.

Millie did her best. "D-delivery f-f-from Alphabet Delights for the Mastin High Home."

"Humph. Over around back, by the trees."

Before the door disappeared, Lonner Mastin himself caught sight of the little group from down the hallway. "Easy, Mac. They're friends." He gave Linn a warm handshake. "Linniblitt Fireflower! As I live and breathe. I knew the cakes were coming, but didn't know you'd be delivering them yourself."

"Oh yeah, I always do. How long have you been Rumpelstiltskin?"

"Only about two weeks. Took over from old Pat. He faded to white recently, and I got the job. It's been at least ten years and you don't look a day older. Who's this?" He gestured to Millie.

"Lonner, this is our daughter, Millie. She's going to take over someday, so we've begun her training."

"How do you do, sir." Millie curtsied.

Linn went on, "And this is my wife, Bette, and our son, Wremming."

They exchanged nods.

"Well done. Maggie's at school still. All excited about the party. Mac said where to go?"

"Oh yes," Linn said.

"Good. If you'll set up, Mac'll help you out and take care of payment. Safe home, Linni. We should catch up the next time you're on this side."

"Absolutely," she replied.

They walked around to the back, with Wrem counting the big boulders to find the second hidden door. After the fifth boulder, there was a grouping of young pines, and just as Millie was looking for a tiny moss bell to ring, one of the boulders vanished, and they were face-to-face with Mac again.

"Everything goes in there," he said, pointing to a room beyond the mudroom and through the kitchen. It was a room so magical that it might have been plucked from one of Millie's faerie fantasies. Everything was in creamy yellows and pinks; sparkles were in the air, mingling with the faint scent of honeysuckle. Two tables were ready for setting.

Mama Linn jolted Millie out of her amazement. "Come on, you. There's work to do."

While Mama Bette unfurled and placed the tablecloths, Mama Linn gave Millie directions. "Take these and place them like I showed you. Ten settings to a table—one at each end, four on each side. Set the same way for both tables."

Wrem carried in all the heaviest boxes. He also brought in the quietbox with the Magic BabySquirrel party favors. Mama Bette tied all the laughing balloons to their respective chairs. A harmonious rhythm carried through all their actions. Mama Linn finished by setting the hooray!cakes on platters at each table. They fussed with all the settings until it was just right.

Mama Linn stepped back to see the effect. "What do you think, Millie?"

No answer. Millie was gone! Mortified, they went in search of her, hissing her name. She had wandered into the den, eyes wide, fingers curious. She picked up a book and opened it. It was filled with strange characters she'd never seen. She put it down, then stroked the blanket on the back of the couch.

Mama Bette found her in a reverie, pressing the blanket against her cheek. She took Millie's hand in a hard grip and dragged her back through the party room and the kitchen and out the mudroom door. Mama Linn was close behind her, whispering, "Bette, calm yourself, please."

Wrem had the presence of mind to touch Bette gently on her shoulder, making eye contact. He said quietly and with an authority that only another full Ddrymmian would feel, "She goes in the wagon. Stays there till we're done."

Mama Bette released her grip. A sober-faced Wrem nodded toward the wagon at Millie, and Millie ran for it, shutting the door quietly behind her.

Mac came in to check their work, his scowling visage in stark contrast to the pink-and-yellow paradise he had to sign off on. You wouldn't think him the type to know, but he said in a low growl, "Any napkins with ponies on 'em? She got a thing for ponies lately."

Wrem went into the wagon and dug up some they had left over from a previous run. He and Linn replaced the existing napkins while Bette cooled her heels at the door. She hadn't trusted Linn to pay close enough attention to the dangers of bringing Millie to the Precinct. Now she fumed with how right she was.

Mac looked things over. Linn handed him the invoice and said, "We'll take payment when we come back to collect everything." He signaled his approval with a grunt.

As soon as they were back in the wagon, Mama Linn jumped in front of the conflict. "Millie, what in stupefying syntax were you doing in Mr. Mastin's living room? What made you think it was allowed?"

"I don't know. I was just—"

Bette jumped in. "You were just, you were just what?! You were handling things, picking them up! You opened a *book*!"

"I just wanted to see it, Mama. It was strange. There was no way to read it."

Bette immediately turned on her wife. "There it is, Linn. This is why the whole idea should just rot in the compost heap. I go in and catch her fingering a book that she herself says 'there's no way to read.' It's an Other book."

"Bette, there's nothing wrong with Other books," Linn said, looking out the window.

"Oh! Nothing wrong. The very word 'Other' says all that's wrong with it, proof that in the Preservation Precinct, Oneness means nothing—other languages, other customs, other everything, High Homes, low homes."

"There are no low homes, Bette."

"Everything that isn't a High Home is a low home. Poor dimwits just don't know it."

"Bette, stop it. Practice the Oneness you say you value. Millie can learn to read Other books. There's room in Oneness for that. Leave room. *You* leave room for other ways of being in the world."

"Well, I'll tell you what I'm not leaving room for. A Ddrymmian daughter learning all kinda elf scat about other worlds and...and—"

"Bette, stop. *Stop.*" They made eye contact. Linn held her palm up, facing Bette, and said, "We are too angry right now. Until we have cooled, let us not speak further of this."

Bette barely touched Linn's palm and settled herself into a furious quiet, looking out the window, while Millie sank out of view between the two women.

Chapter 9

The Fight

When they arrived home, Bette and Linn went to their separate corners—Bette to her desk and her papers and Linn to the kitchen, where she immediately began chopping insults and slicing complaints for the grumble she was making for the family that night. It was a perfect way to discharge the energy from her argument with Bette. She decided last-minute to throw in some minced mirth, a touch that only she would think of, which was what made Alphabet Delights so successful.

But what had begun in the wagon only worsened with time. Weeks passed. Bette paid bills, wrote letters, opened and pawed through her various drawers to look for a particular pen that was never there, moved papers around on the desk, and so on. She'd open her mouth to say something and then shut it and hunker down over her work. Linn did her requisite cooking but spent every spare moment out in the garden or with her friend Celeste next door. Or she'd decide that now was the time to do a thorough cleaning of the windows.

For his part, Wrem always sought refuge in the trees. But he'd never felt his mothers so divided and he could sense that Millie was caught in the middle. He went to her room and sat on her bed while she played Clap! with Flurjahm.

There was a myth in Ddrym that if you had a faerie in your hand and you clapped at just the right time, they would momentarily dissolve into a sparkling grass-green explosion of light and then reassemble into themselves. Of course, this never happened. Faeries were just too fast. But they loved the fact that people thought it possible, so they made themselves visible on rare occasions just to tease them into trying, over and over. Flurjahm was having a ball.

"Hey, Milliebug, whatcha doin'?" Wrem asked.

"Nothing." She didn't look up. Concentrating on Flurjahm, she watched him smile up at her from her palm, letting her see him full on. She tried clapping him green again for the hundredth time. The carbonated birdsong of faerie laughter tingled her ears.

"Hey, Millie."

"What?"

Wrem took her hands gently, and Flurjahm vanished. "Look at me."

She looked up at him, tears brimming now. "I want to go to school over there so bad. But...I've never seen them like this."

He put his arm around her. She melted into him. "Ah, Millie. You know them. They're always at different points on the Circle. It's what makes Oneness interesting. They'll be OK. Anyway, come on with me. I need help with Paulie. Wanna help me brush him?"

"OK." They left through the back door and walked over to the barn, where Paulie lived. Wrem started to give her the currycomb he'd fashioned for her when she was little, when she still needed the stool to brush him out—then he realized she was grown now. He gave her the big one instead. She went to work. She brushed Paulie's grateful flanks while Wrem cleaned out the stall, replenishing it with fresh hay and water as they spoke.

"Mama Bette is very tough, I know. But she's tough because she don't want nothin' to happen to you."

"Well, nothin's ever *gonna* happen to me if they don't let me go anywhere. And why do you always take her side?"

"Millie." He had to think about how to say this. "In the Precinct, people think crazy things about Ddrym. They don't know us. They believe that we're some kinda weird monsters or something."

"But they can just look at us and see that we're not."

Paulie swished his tail and shifted his weight to the other foot. Millie walked around the other side of him, keeping her hands on him, staying close, whispering low, "OK, Paulie, I'll do the other side."

Wrem tried to explain it. "See, a few of them, long ago, saw us giving the greeting light, which—well, they never seen it before. It hit them fearful. And also, very long ago, someone witnessed a TwoBody right in the middle of a change. Ever since then, they been makin' up all kinda elf scat about what else might be true. People that were scared got the stories bigger and scarier all the time. So now Precinct is mad scared o' Ddrymmians. And fear sometimes makes people wanna blot the fearful thing out."

"You think Mr. Mastin was afraid of me?"

"Well, not him exactly because he's a friend of Mama Linn's, and Mama Linn is Precinct. But you saw him walk a wide circle around Mama Bette, dincha? Didn't really know what to make of her—or me."

"I didn't notice."

"Littletree, you gotta learn. Precinct folk aren't all bad. They just scared o' what they don't know. So just steer clear, and it'll be fine."

"But did you see his warmroom?"

"They call it a livin' room."

"Did you see it? It was so beautiful. And there was a book there written all the way through with words I've never seen."

"Yeah, well, you got no need for those. Circle teachers are best. We need to listen to plants and trees and wind and water and light. Faeries got to have their due and spirits too, all the elements." And then his voice changed a little. "We got enough to learn without all that Precinct nonsense."

As time passed, Millie noticed that Mama Linn and Mama Bette almost never talked to each other. They were polite, and it made her sad. She'd seen Mama Bette stew in silence, but this lacked the heat of stewing. She'd seen Mama Linn grow expressionless and concentrated, but she'd never seen her so blank. They exchanged brief, accurate conversations and clipped greetings and goodbyes. And worst of all, everything in the kitchen was spotless.

At dinner, Wrem and Millie sometimes glanced at each other, their faces full of questions neither could ask. One night, Millie tried for some levity. She had a good one all loaded up. She spoke. "What's the difference between an elf and a preservation agent?"

"Not now, Millie," Bette said.

Wrem tried to help her out. "I dunno, Millie. What is—"

"I said not now!" Bette's voice shot out, smacking sharp like the thwap of a flyswatter.

There was an icy moment, then Mama Linn slapped her napkin down on the table and left the room. In the queasy silence that followed, Millie's shoulders—rock ledges at the top of her torso—did their best to keep the feelings from spilling over, but to no avail. Millie's tears tumbled down her cheeks, quiet as the room, and she said in an impossibly small voice, "Mama Bette?"

"What?" Bette shoveled more journalism hash into her mouth, still chewing the bite before it.

"We can't keep on like this."

Bette finished chewing, swallowed, and looked down.

Millie felt the strength of her own truth. "I miss you smashing your papers down on the desk and complaining about the Precinct. I miss Mama Linn makin' a mess in the kitchen. I miss how it was. I miss noise and people talking, not all polite like it is now but, you know, back-and-forth talking. Everything's so complicated now. I wanna go to school over there, but I love it here too. And then I went on the delivery and broke our family!"

Mama Bette got up from her chair and put her arms around Millie tenderly. The girl wept in her softening mother's arms. Wrem cleared the dishes. No one had noticed Mama Linn standing back in the hallway, her own tears falling silently.

"Hey, squirt," Bette said, "nothing can break this family. Nobody can. It's just sometimes..."

She looked up and caught Linn's eyes and didn't look away as she said to Millie, "Tell you what, maybe it's time for a Listening."

Linn looked at her hard. This was what they'd been fighting about for weeks. Now maybe there was a sliver of hope.

"But you don't like Listenings," Millie said, remembering the many diatribes she'd overheard about it.

"I don't. I never seen the point of them. But maybe it's the only way to get the rocks out of the dirt in your garden."

The call went out the next day. Linn stood at her front door and sang out her longing through her feet into the ground. Soon Celeste felt her own feet open. She lived right next door and had known and loved Linn since the first day she'd met her twenty years ago. She stopped scrubbing the grass stains out of her son's pantleg, closed her eyes, and let the call all the way in. When she learned it was from Linn and Bette, she sighed with relief and foreboding. "Finally," she whispered to herself. "This has been a long time coming."

Lohm felt it as he was doing inventory at the market. Pim Pfahler felt it at the gazebo where he was having supper. The Roggers felt it at their farm in Droaze, and even the Framms felt it while harvesting cheerfruit from their orchard in Near Emmering. Everyone did. Three of the Larksheners who'd been part of the silktunnel that saved Millie so long ago felt it. Even some of the Ddrymmian carpenters and janitors who worked in the Precinct felt it.

Some made their plans to attend the following day. Some declined. No judgment. It was commonly held that whoever showed up made the circle whole, and no one who wasn't there belonged there.

Chapter 10

Ddrym Weighs In

Elder Shekwey, Pim Pfahler, and even Balimaya came to hold the Circle energies. Bette had always spoken so highly of Miss B and with such affection that Millie and Wrem had always thought of her as their invisible, mysterious grandmother. But after the bordercheat fever incident, as well as the border training, Millie had her own direct line to the old Solitary. They sat on either side of her.

People wandered in here and there in comfortable clothing, carrying their sitting pieces, setting them down. After a longish time, the Circle finally settled and felt complete. Elder Shekwey opened the Listening with the Ddrymmian blessing. *The roads are many. All begin and end in Oneness.* Pim had placed a stunning round quilt in the center of the Circle for Bette and Linn to sit on. It was thick, soft, and tightly woven with the image of an earth-toned star on a dark blue background.

Linn and Bette sat and faced each other. Bette spoke first. She spoke of her commitment to giving Millie a true Ddrymmian education—without interference from the outside—until Millie had truly brought the spirit of it all the way into her bones and was fully grown. Then she could do whatever she wanted.

Linn spoke about the fact that they weren't getting any younger, and she emphasized the importance of laying the groundwork now for the business to continue when they could no longer handle it. She spoke about the need to encourage Millie's fluency with Preservation Precinct culture and build trust with Precinct folk so that when Millie took over the business, the foundation was already set.

Bette had a chance to rebut with all the dangers that could befall the girl stemming from Precinct superstitions, and Linn used those very superstitions as the symptom of how deep the need was for trust building so the prejudices could slowly dissolve. Linn said, "This is why we need Millie to be exposed early. I know it will be hard, but Millie is extraordinary, and I know she can do it. Children adapt much faster than adults, and that goes for Precinct children too."

When they had each spoken their peace and responded to each other's concerns, those who made up the larger circle began sharing their hearts on the matter. Jamie Strok, a young treesinger, said, "I think it's great that one of us gets to go to school in the Precinct. Could be the beginning of more talk between the two places, more listening."

"Ah, Jamie, you're a dreamer," his father said from across the circle. "Talk to your uncle Stimp. Three nines he worked over there in one of them cursed High Homes. Only had his stomach troubles to show fer it." Several of the older members mumbled in solidarity.

"But that was long ago. Things have changed, Elder Strok," said one of Jamie's friends.

"You don't know that," Soralla Mitchers said with the conviction of one with almost no true information. She barreled on, "Nothing has changed over there. They're all rules and regulations and punishments. I say we don't lower our standards. Millie stays here."

A surprising number nodded.

Celeste spoke up. "We all profess to honor Oneness. How is it that the Precinct is suddenly outside that Oneness? Since when? We were taught since we were sprouts that the roads are many. All—all—lead to Oneness." A few nodded in agreement.

"Not the roads to the Precinct! They're idiots." Blick Rogger raised his voice in opposition to *any* encroachment of Precinct on Ddrymmian ways. His wife, Seala, remained silent.

Wrem got agitated, responding with great effort toward respect, but Blick had no such concerns. He called Mama Linn spineless, and when Wrem stood up in response, Blick stood up too. Elder Shekwey lifted his hands. "Silence!"

The circle quieted, except for Blick, whose animated muttering continued. Someone nearby shushed him. Then Balimaya, in a very rare show of position, spoke up. "This Circle is large enough for all our views," she said, the deep voice of the wisdom she'd gathered from the trees resonating throughout the circle. "Respect for one another, however, for *all* others, must be kept." The old sage paused, her spirit as large as her body harvesting her next words. "In fact, that's what we're doing here. Linniblitt and Bette have called us so we can help them sit with a challenge, not so we can decide who's right or who wins.

"Let us close this Listening with light so they can make space for their discomfort, knowing that there are no easy answers. Let us send them home more sure-footed in their differences, willing to walk side by side. And let us all," she said, holding Blick with her stern but compassionate gaze, "remember that the roads are many, and *all* begin and end in Oneness."

With that, everyone summoned their light, everyone but Blick, who'd stepped out of the circle. Seala seemed caught, hesitated, then eventually stayed. The circle overflowed with light, everyone sending it with their hands toward the center, where it pooled, accumulated, filled, and surrounded Bette and Linn, who maintained eye contact with each other until the radiance consummated itself and faded.

Bette held out her hands to Linn, who took them. Tears flowed from both women. There was no good answer to this, but their hearts were more open, and each was a little more willing to make space for the other's views. When they were complete, they leaned toward each other, touching foreheads. At that point, everyone bowed their heads. Bette and Linn stood to address the circle, spoke their thanks, and everyone went home.

On the way back from the Listening, Millie walked with Wrem behind their mothers. Millie said, "Hey, Mama Bette."

"What?"

"When we get home, will you please bang some papers around on your desk?"

They burst out laughing, all of them.

"OK, squirt. OK."

It was a while before Millie accompanied them on another trip. But she was deep in her Circle Teachings, so every day there were sessions of Treespeak, Healing with Herbs, Letting Be Practices, and StoryEarth History. She palled around with her friends. Wrem sang to his trees. And all was right with the world. But not for everyone.

One resting day, Bette brought a basket of her favorite salted paragraphs over to her friend Blimmer's, and they shared cups of hot telling, discussing each other's lives. Wrem was out, training some new forest tenders. While Millie read in her room, Linn made a new batch of sounding boards—massive loaves of bread that were a big favorite in Far Emmering because of her special ingredient, sarcasticum. It was a perfect day for baking, not sunny but not raining either. She'd just put another batch of loaves in the oven when there was a soft knock at the door.

"Coming!" she said, brushing herself off, washing her hands. When she got to the door, Seala Rogger was there with her little girl, Blaisey, on her hip. She was sweating and out of breath.

"Oh! Come in, Seala. What's wrong? Here, let me take Blaisey." And the little girl went easily to Mama Linn as Seala hung up her coat.

"How are you, my little giggle? Come and have some gossips. They're on the plate right there. Have a seat, both of you. Blaiseygirl, let me get that coat off you. We'll put it right here on the chair."

"Kank you," Blaisey said in an adorable little voice while her mother helped her up onto the chair.

"How old is she now?"

"She'll be two this coming Sorting season." Seala wrung her hands at the table, her eyes darting here and there.

"She's got a lovely spirit, Seala. Well done. Listen, why don't we— Hang on a minute." Then she called down the hall, "Millie?"

Millie answered from her room, "Yes, Mama?"

"Can you come here for a moment? We have visitors."

Millie came down the hall, and her face lit up when she saw the little girl. "Hey there, monkey! Oh, Mrs. Rogger, so good to see you." Greeting lights were exchanged all around. Because of her youth, Blaisey's baby light was continually pulsating on and off.

"How are you, Millie?" Seala said.

"I'm fine, thank you. Especially now that Blaisey's here." Millie held her arms out for her little 'monkey,' and Blaisey climbed into them right away.

Little Blaisey had been abruptly taken out of Millie's sprouts class, so it was surprising to see them there. Millie had missed her little charge. Blaisey had a really sharp mind, and Millie loved watching it work. "Mama, could we take a couple gossips with us and go play in the forest?"

Grateful for her timing with this request, Linn said, "Of course. But stay close by. And put your coats on. It's chilly out there," handing her the coat she'd just taken off the child.

Millie took Blaisey through the front door, their hands full of napkin-wrapped gossips. Linn sat next to Seala and poured her some tea.

The young woman jumped at the sound of the door slamming as their daughters left. She fidgeted and cupped her hands around the hot tea. Linn waited and filled her own cup. They sipped amid the pool of calm that Linn always managed to create around her. "What's in your heart, my friend?"

Seala started to say something and then closed her mouth and sipped her tea. She nibbled on a gossip. Finally, she said, "I don't know what to do."

Linn waited some more, then answered, "Does something need doing?"

"Well, now it does. Blick is...I don't...we don't agree with—"

"Our plan for Millie? I thought we'd already—"

"No, Linn. Please let me get this out."

"I'm so sorry."

"We don't agree with...each other...about Millie." Seala raised her eyes to meet Linn's, then went on. "I was moved by your Listening session, both with all of us in the Circle and how you spoke to each other when it was just you and Bette, and I—"

Just then, there was violent banging at the door. "Open up!" It was Blick.

Seala's cup went crashing to the floor. She sat frozen in her chair, shaking, sheet white. Linn grabbed a towel for the mess. They stifled their words into quarter whispers.

"What do you want to do?"

"I don't know. I don't know."

"OK, go into Millie's room," Linn said, frantically pointing the way. "Down the hall, on the left." Seala took off her shoes and ran on muted feet to the room. Linn walked to the front door.

Blick yelled through the door, "I know she's in there! I've checked everywhere else. Open this door!"

Linn's stomach tightened into a knot. With eyes closed and both of her hands in the calling shape (with the tips of thumb and ring finger together), Linn pressed her feet into the ground and sent a treespeak through her feet to Wrem for his return. Then she opened the door.

"Hello, Blick," she said. "I see that you're angry. Please come in, and let's talk."

"I will not. This is no place for any self-respecting Ddrymmian." He tried to look past Linn to see into the house. "Seala! Come out right now."

Linn prayed for once that the children had disobeyed her and were far enough away that they couldn't hear this. She summoned her calmest tone. "Come in. Let me hear what you have to say. I have some hot water on the stove."

"Talk, talking, listening, talking, listening. Rotted flesh covered in maggots for all the good it's done. And besides, your listenin' ain't worth nothing. You're a traitor." His rage crested on his voice and crashed into the kitchen. "Seala! Now!"

Seala, shaking, spoke from behind Millie's door. "Blick, I will come with you after you've calmed yourself."

"Curses, woman! Get your sorry ass out here or—"

Suddenly, the squawk of the neighborhood peacock pierced the air, and he strutted aggressively toward Blick from next door, feathers up. When Blick turned around at the noise, he backed up from the bird, then fell into a dark silence. Beings who had heard the commotion had come out of their homes, approaching quietly, maintaining a wise distance. Ten or twelve neighbors had come to calm the confrontation. The peacock got about three paces away from Blick and stood his ground, feathers fanned, quivering with focus.

Just then, Wrem came trotting in from the forest. The girls were running after him, thinking it play. He threw his hands out to the sides, signaling that the girls should stay back, and Millie ran into him from behind. She giggled. "Ha! I got you!" And then she noticed the crowd and the quiet. Little Blaisey saw her father and stopped breathing.

For a moment, no one said anything. Then Blick turned to Linn and said, "I hope your whole family rots in the Nothing." For a second, the world became hyper focused, and the gravity of that utterance fell on everyone present.

Linn felt her own hard grip still on the door handle and smelled the peacock feathers; she could even smell the pine scent that had traveled back in Wrem's hair. Then she remembered herself. "May we all make space with that great emptiness, in which there is room for all ways of being." She was careful not to use the word "Nothing" while still showing respect for its presence, wherever it might be. Everyone took it as an invitation to offer a calming greeting light. Linn offered hers first. Wrem wrestled with his anger and then offered his. Others followed suit. It was worth a try.

"Take your cursed light back!" Blick shouted as he walked away. "Stick it where your grandmothers won't go lookin' for it! Poison it is! Traitorous poison, you hear me?"

The peacock charged Blick, running him off at full speed.

Blaisey hid behind Wrem's leg.

Everyone's light was still alive; it traveled as a stream into the house to find Seala. There, she let it fill her and returned hers outward as she appeared in the doorway, trembling, relieved, and moved to tears by their gentleness. Millie scooped Blaisey up and ran to the house, where they hugged their mothers. Lorkan, a neighbor from two houses down, said to Seala, "You and little Blaisey are welcome in our home. We have room."

And that set off a tender cascade from others present, all declaring, "*We* have room!"

Seala addressed them all. "Th-thank you, everyone. If...if it's OK with Linn and Bette, I'll stay, um, here...until...I guess until I know what to do next." And with that, Linn put her arm around her, and they turned to go back inside.

As the gathering dispersed, Wrem cast a watchful eye outside their home before going in and closing the door.

Chapter 11

Preparing for School

Seala and her daughter stayed with Millie's family for a few days, then they left for Seala's mother's house in Far Emmering.

Together, Mama Bette, Mama Linn, and Wrem doubled down on Millie's future as their key to Alphabet Delights' longevity. They committed as a family to slowly integrating her into Precinct life by getting her into a Precinct school. They sealed it with their light, passing from left hand to left hand, into the heart and back. Millie couldn't sleep.

The first step was to obtain an application at the school for Millie to fill out. A wedding was coming up between Nancy Tix and Evan Stimble, the Players who embodied Superwoman and Robin Hood respectively. It was all the rage. Alphabet Delights had been contracted to do the reception. Linn and Wrem called on well-trained friends to help them out. On their way to the reception, they made a brief stop at PPHS, and Linn ran in to pick up a blank application. They protected it as though it were a diamond, and gave it to Millie the next day. Linn helped her fill it out, and their bond grew ever stronger.

Soon, though, the enormity of the challenge became all too clear. It had been so long since a Ddrymmian student had been inside a Precinct school that the very idea of it hardly had room to exist. Eight thousand years. Naturally, the resistance was fierce. But an idea had to start somewhere, and Linn had sent her proposal via holograms to all the Precinct School Board members before attending the council meeting. No one thought much of it, as it was sure to fail. But procedure was procedure, and she'd followed all the proper steps.

After all, she was a Precinct-born, former citizen, and her parents, before they passed through the Door to Elsewhere, had been influential and generous to the Preservation Precinct Administration. So Linn knew they had to at least give her proposal a chance to be considered.

When it was her turn to speak, she began with "The roads are many. All begin and end in Oneness."

Murmurs of assent.

"And what relevant words to ground us in discussing the subject of the many *actual* roads that might join my daughter's home in the Droaze region of Ddrym and the Preservation Precinct High School in the Stapes region of the Precinct." An uncomfortable silence followed.

"The Preservation Precinct and Ddrym are fundamentally One in the world of StoryEarth." A few people coughed.

When she got to the part about integrating Millie into their educational system, the head of the Precinct educational council cleared his throat and interrupted her closing words, saying, "Thank you. We'll take the matter under consideration." Linn saw the council people look down at their HCbs[1] and heard the telltale *whoosh* of several deleted holograms.

Weeks passed. Linn continued to remind the council of the law, stopping by the council house when making deliveries, leaving messages in their message boxes. Her only hope was that their devotion to the written word might bring a resolution to this impasse. She turned her campaign into an art form. She and Wrem delivered curiously well-timed delicacies to important members of the school board, education lawyers, teachers, influential parents, and sympathetic judges, all with their breath held and fingers crossed.

The council tried but simply could not circumvent the clear

---

[1] Holographic Communications boxes.

language of the ancient law stipulating exactly by which roads Millie was to get from her home in Droaze to the school in the Precinct. So they agreed to Linn's proposal and began laying the groundwork on the Precinct side.

There was such parental uproar over it at the school that the school board was forced to compromise. They placated Bette and Linn by allowing Millie to attend, and they placated fearful Precinct parents by allowing *only* Millie to attend. This would give everyone time to acclimate to the idea. And Millie could be a test run for whether it would work at all.

To this end, Millie's mothers laid groundwork of their own. They invoked the Oneness principle on the Ddrymmian side to cultivate support at home for the idea. Also, they made it their business to understand more about the current Precinct culture so that Millie could assimilate more easily. For instance, Linn had begun to notice the recent change in fashions. These days, they wore tight little scarves around their necks with tiny bells attached to the ends. During a delivery to the Precinct, she bought one for Millie from a friend's store, and put it away as a first-day-of-school gift.

As Mama Linn intensified her teachings about all things Precinct, Millie sometimes visited the boundary alone, practicing going through and coming back. During one of these practice sessions, a familiar figure shimmered into view. Millie had just completed the opening rites: remembering Oneness, stating her clear intention, and calling up her greeting light. Just as she moved on to the next step, her left cheek tingled, and the shadow woman came dripping out of the oak leaves of a nearby tree.

Millie shielded up hard and fast. The old shadow cocked her head appreciatively as her greeting light came up from within her, this time a small, blood red, strong-lit globe materializing into her colorless palm. The first time, it had been lavender. The second time, indigo. She held it out to Millie. Millie did not reciprocate. "What do you want from me?" she asked. "Why do you keep coming?"

"You keep calling," she said, stepping closer and thrusting the light toward Millie again.

"I do not," Millie said, backing away. She thought about sending a message to Wrem or Mama Linn.

"Oh, I wouldn't do that if I were you," the shadow said, reading her thoughts, moving around the girl, shimmering in and out of visibility with more malice this time than ever before. "If they think..."

Millie jumped as the shadow hissed right into her ear from behind, her breath a mix of rot and mold.

"If they think you're calling shadows, what will they think you've been doing all this time at the border?"

"But I'm *not* calling you. Go away."

The shadow woman laughed, like a cat toying with its prey, her voice menacing and sarcastic. She said, "What happened to 'We are One in the Oneness of everything'?" One of her white braids reached out by itself and tickled the end of Millie's nose.

Millie threw caution to the wind now and treespoke her call for help. *Wrem! Now! Droaze/Near Emmering line, at the Precinct border.*

The shadow woman shook her head and said, "All right, have´ it your way. But in the time it takes him to get here, I will give you the gift you won't admit you want."

"I don't want anything from you!" Millie meant it, and turned to leave.

In a flash, the shadow's face was inches from Millie's. "Yes, you do!"

Millie's shielding had been pierced. She felt the shadow's cold palm on her cheek and began to sink into her spell. Her senses dulled, and she rooted into the ground, deeply still and silent like before. Once she was in it, she never wanted it to end. The forest had disappeared, and she was on a story set at the Preservation Precinct. She walked through it, trying to understand which story it was for, but then she was backstage. She saw a golden sign on one of the dressing room doors and gasped. It said, PLAYER MILLICENT FIREFLOWER.

Her very skin vibrated with need, with the reaching, the outstretched spirit, the almost getting there. She only wanted to open that door and be that Player, but distant running footsteps broke the vision, and the shadow woman vanished down the tendrils of a nearby fiddlehead fern.

Wrem was breathing hard. "I came quick as I could, Millie. What's wrong?"

She looked at her brother and stammered, "I...I, uh, I don't know. I was practicing the opening rite for the boundary, and... and I suddenly felt full of fear. Then I felt...real strange."

"Ah, Millie, maybe you got the words in the wrong order. That can happen sometimes. You'll be all right. Let me help you now. Come with me." He offered her his arm, and they walked slowly home together. She was dizzy and so confused; she was relieved to see him yet sorry he'd interrupted. They conversed about everything and nothing, and she had the strangest sensation of missing him from somewhere far into the future. She hugged his arm closer.

The vision had lit a fire in every cell of her body. The possibility of becoming a Player was real. She threw herself into her boundary training as never before.

Every night just before sleeping, she'd go over what she'd learned from Mama Linn—how to greet people in a Precinct way (waving or grasping right hands or nodding *without light*) and how to make promises (again, without light, just saying, "I promise," and then grasping right hands). She also tried to think of things she might have in common with them, watching for Oneness everywhere. *We're all people. We all want to be happy.*

Her favorite part of the training was going in with Mama Linn and Wrem to make deliveries. She got so good at restraining her light that it wasn't restraint anymore—it was just the gear she shifted into for the Precinct. As the time drew near for her to enter Preservation Precinct High School, her confidence grew, and her mothers were at peace with their decision.

Millie had always had a deep, nuanced understanding of Oneness. Mama Linn cautioned her about assuming that everyone had that same understanding. For that reason, she gave her the most important survival techniques she would need. First, lay low for a few months. Just pay close attention to how everyone interacts, what works, what fails. And second, once she truly knew the differences between Ddrym and the Precinct (as silly and artificial as they might be), she was to tone down the expression of all things Ddrym (her backsight, the lightworkings, etc.).

The week before school started, Bette and Linn noticed Millie frequently swatting away the faeries. Like most Ddrymmians under stress, her ears were twitching. Gangs of faeries made sport of catching and hanging on to the edges, the bravest of them actually anchoring their feet just under the helix and whispering insults into the ear in a language known only to them. She could not go to school in this condition.

Bette gave her a smooth, dark centering stone, training her to send her energies down through her arms and into it instead of letting them creep up into her ears. Millie caught on very quickly, and as Mama Bette had promised, when she mastered this skill, the faeries lost interest and left.

"Keep it in your quietpocket," Mama Bette said.

"Okay," Millie said, smiling.

"No, ya don't get it. Your *quiet*pocket."

Millie cocked her head, perplexed.

"See, your ol' Mama Bette can learn new tricks after all, can't she? Ol' Paulie and I went to Far Emmering to talk to the people from where we got the quietbox for Alphabet Delights. Asked 'em if they got anything smaller, like if ya didn't wanna lose somethin' little. They showed me this." She pulled out of her own pocket a little translucent bag only slightly bigger than the stone. Its color was somewhere between flesh and dirt, when it was visible enough to have color.

"Ya keep it wherever no one'll likely go lookin' fer it. And because it's a quietpocket, all you gotta do is press it to you," Mama Bette said as she mimed pressing it between her own breasts, "and it stays. It remembers its home. Go ahead." Millie was a little shy, but she took the magical quietpocket with the centering stone in it, and opened the buttons of her shirt so she could press it to her chest.

"Thank you, Mama Bette. Really." She looked at her mother, and felt a rare moment of care and connection. "I love you."

"Ah, pshht," Mama Bette said, waving her off. "You're my little Sting. My little pain in the backside squirt. I gotta love ya. No choosin' about it." Which made Millie smile.

Chapter 12

The Ddrymmian Student

The Pirate's Parrot was the most popular watering hole of all the gathering places in the Preservation Precinct. Of course, each group had their 'home' bars. Players tended to hang out at the Plot Pivot. Precinct agents often lied to their spouses while loosening their ties at Rules & Regulations. Admin people went to the cheaper places like Thimbles or the Hammer & Nail. But the Pirate's Parrot welcomed everyone. Beings from many otherwise disparate groups were welcome, and many backroom deals were made there as a result.

The screens above the bar broadcast all the important events. Information was shared about what new stories were coming into play and who had been cast for what roles. There were also audition schedules, understudy placements, and so on. Every half hour, they would list the coming Continuing Education workshops with titles like Wand Handling, Bloodcurdling Screams, Leaving the Evil Stepmother at Work, Daily Preservation Disciplines, and Knowing Your Player Benefits. If it was happening in the Precinct, you found out about it on the screens at your local bar.

At a certain point, everyone hushed to hear about the new Ddrymmian student coming into PPHS. "Hello, Elizabeth Maggish here coming to you from StoryEarth Broadcasting

Company. It's a big day for StoryEarth. After much controversy, for the first time since the Big Split over eight thousand years ago, a Ddrymmian student will be enrolled at Preservation Precinct High School. Here to tell you more is our correspondent Fairlin Brape. Fairlin?"

They cut to an underling at the school who basically spouted out the same noninformation everyone was used to by now from the press. But you could have heard a faerie fart as they listened anyway.

"Ddrymm*scat!*" someone shouted from the back.

Someone shushed him.

When the newscast went on to the next issue, heated discussions boiled in the bar. The few progressives in the place were quietly thrilled.

As Millie and her family approached the wrought-iron gates of PPHS, they saw the SBC van and a reporter with cameras and a microphone at the ready. Fortunately, Bette had stayed home. Millie's ears were already tingling. She fingered her centering stone in her pocket, and it helped. The anxieties that had bubbled up somersaulted in her rib cage and immediately swam in the opposite direction, down through her arms and into the stone.

Wrem noticed and said, "Good move, Milliebug. You can do this."

They stopped before reaching the front gates. Linn gave Millie a big hug, saying, "Remember, sprout, Oneness everywhere. Don't you worry about the TV people. Let me handle them. Watch my right hand. As soon as I give you the sign, just walk right around me through the gates."

Mama Linn strode ahead of them, approached the reporter, and spoke quietly to her, and after a few minutes, with a flick of her right hand down by her hip, she signaled to Millie that it was time. Millie looked up at Wrem. "Go!" he said as he pressed a blessing into her shoulder blades during his embrace. And off she went, gripping her stone hard. She was thrilled, terrified, and determined. She walked through the gates, up the four steps, and into the building, suddenly aware that everyone was staring at her.

Because of Bette's strict house rules forbidding Precinct "news," Millie had no way of knowing that her own image (which had been included with her application) had been broadcast all over the screens for the past few weeks. Everyone at that school, everyone in the whole Precinct, knew her face. Fortunately, she was saved by a short, graying but precisely coiffed woman holding her hand out.

"Hello, Millie. I'm Ms. Shoze. I work in the office, and I'm here to help you find your classroom."

Millie shook her hand, nervous about keeping her greeting light in check. "Thank you, Ms. Shoze."

The woman said, "Let's go then." And she began walking quickly enough that Millie had to trot to keep up. Everyone gawked as they went by.

Millie gripped her stone so hard that her arm was sore by the time they arrived at her classroom. She was struck by how square everything was, hard corners everywhere. And all the classes were held inside, not out in the trees, where she was used to taking lessons.

The students were finding their seats, putting supplies in their desks. A blond girl walked in, and when she saw Millie, she stopped so suddenly that a bottleneck of teenagers bumbled behind her at the door. As she found her seat, she smiled at Millie, and Millie smiled back, reminding herself, *No light, no light.* All the students came from several different junior high schools in the Stapes region, so most didn't know one another. But some were already longtime friends and ignored the startlingly loud bell. They went on talking, laughing, finishing up stories.

Mrs. Taprus was a tall, bony woman who had probably come out of the womb with her hair pulled back in a rigid fist at the base of her skull. She was sick of teaching, sick of this group of snot-nosed elf spawn. Her retirement loomed like a mirage in the desert. But in spite of this, she was still an excellent teacher.

The talking grew more rambunctious. Mrs. Taprus took off her glasses and looked into the class, her eyes roving from one student to the next. She waited. The room finally grew silent.

"So!" she said, her tone so brisk that they all jumped. "Welcome to your first year of high school. I trust you all have your books and are ready to go. I know some of you already know one another, but there are many newcomers here, so we'll play a little game to begin. Let's go around the room, say your name, what neighborhood you're from, and what your favorite food is. I'll begin. My name is Mrs. Taprus. I'm from Near Hills. And my favorite food is thoughtful observations on a crisp slice of premise. Next? Let's start on this side of the room."

Millie panicked. She had forgotten to pay attention. As the others gave their answers, she frantically tried to remember her training. Mama Bette had told her, "If they ask where you're from, don't try to say 'Ddrym.' You won't be able to do it, and it'll call attention. Just say, 'I'm from the NetherJunctures.' And do it like it's the most natural thing ever." And they had practiced for months.

"Millie?" Mrs. Taprus said as Millie suddenly felt everyone's eyes on her.

"Um, y-yeah—I mean, yes. M-my name is Millie Fireflower, and I'm from..." She forgot everything, and Ddrym filled her mind. An unusual, almost spiritual silence overcame everyone in the room for a moment. She recovered her senses and said quickly, "I'm from the NetherJunctures."

But it was too late. Some of them were squirming in the moment of deep sweetness they'd felt. And then they were giggling. They'd heard about it from their parents, but it seemed so strange. Ddrymmians really couldn't say the word "Ddrym." They really did call it "the NetherJunctures." Heat rose into Millie's face. All that work for nothing.

Mrs. Taprus chided herself. She had forgotten about this particular Ddrymmian idiosyncrasy when suggesting the exercise. Already tired of her work, she saw double the work ahead. She knew she'd have to be vigilant about shaping acceptance and respect in this class full of Precinct brats with parents who'd taught them their original distrust. She wished, for the girl's sake, that she'd learned to better manage her energy. But there you had it.

Mrs. Taprus slid her dismay behind her inscrutable face and said without missing a beat, "Lovely. And welcome, Millie. It's our very good fortune to have our first student from Ddrym in generations. We look forward to learning more about the NetherJunctures. And your favorite food?"

Nobody heard what it was. They were already coalescing into exclusive groups among themselves as the minutes went by. By the time the bell rang, Millie wouldn't belong with any of them. They would make sure of that.

At lunch break, Millie had no idea what to do. The configurations of girl friendships seemed impossible to penetrate. Millie watched from inside herself, shy and baffled, as everyone either went outside or to the cafeteria. In Ddrym, they would have exchanged greeting lights, and everyone would feel more or less safe to approach. But with no light to tell the person's heart by, how did you know who wanted to be approached and who didn't? She decided to go outside.

A few boys ambushed her as soon as she came through the door. "Hey, Millie! Are you a TwoBody? We heard there are TwoBodies in Ddrym...and monsters."

She fingered her centering stone. *Watch for Oneness everywhere. They're beings. I'm a being. Oneness there. They're just scared of what they don't know. Don't react. Don't react.*

"Yeah, do you know any monsters? Do they eat their own babies? I heard they eat their own babies."

A skinny boy named Frank came up to the group and mumbled, "Come on, guys. Stop it."

"Whatsamatter, Frankie?" a boy named Grommle said. "She your girlfriend, huh? You guys going steady?" His friend Lum and the others howled, holding their sides, laughing hard at the thought.

Horrified, Frank yelled, "No! It's just…"

Millie had turned to walk away as she heard him say, "It's just…it's not right. It's against the rules! To bully people!" He tried to hold them back, but they were already hot on her heels like a pack of wolves stalking a deer.

"Do you have any sisters?" Lum took over. "What kinds of monsters are they? Can you change into your other TwoBody self? What is it? A…a…a—"

"Is it a rat?" With this, Danny, the runt of the litter, struck gold. They mimed a rat's face eating cheese as Frank hung back from the group.

Millie tried getting away, but Lum got in front of her, with the others encircling her. "Go ahead. Show us what you've got. Let's see you do it."

Grommle elbowed Lum. "Wait a minute. Watch this," he said. "Hey, Millie. Where are you from? Huh?"

She was ready this time. She yelled, "I'm from the NetherJunctures!"

Grommle, all wide-eyed and innocent, asked, "Yeah, but what are they called?"

Millie closed her eyes and stood straight and tall like her mothers had taught her to. Breathing deep, she pressed her feet into the ground and pushed her fingers into the centering stone. But it was no good. She started to cry, squeezing the stone with all her might. The only Oneness she felt now was the Oneness of being singled out for ridicule, the Oneness of being the only one, excommunicated from a group she never even got to be a part of in the first place.

Suddenly, she felt someone take her firmly by the arm. "These are half-wits, elfin rejects." It was the girl who'd smiled at her. She led her away, but when the boys followed, she spun around and yelled, "Stop it, you guys! I mean it. Go eat bird scat, all of you." They dispersed. Then she said something to Millie under her breath, and in the giggles that turned to raucous laughter shining through the young Ddrymmian's tears, she rooted herself forever in Millie's heart as her dearest friend.

"I think we might have met, sort of. When I saw you in class, I wondered if it was you. Your mom is Alphabet Delights, right?"

"How do you know that?"

"Well, she delivered to our house. I think I was around twelve and...I...I saw you. No, you saw me first, and you fell down in the cart. You were really sick. I ran and got your mom. I'm Agnes. Pleased to meet you." Agnes held her hand out. Millie shook it, no light.

"I'm Millie. But I guess you already know that. What High Home was Mama delivering to that day?"

"Oh, Eleanor Grath, Player for Cinderella, the sixth in as many generations of Cinderella Players."

Millie did her best not to hyperventilate. Agnes was used to it.

At lunch, the girls at Agnes's table twittered with anticipation. Millie had been on TV—or at least her picture had—and they all wanted to be seen with her. Agnes noticed Millie standing in line to get her food. She walked up to her and said, "Why don't you come sit with us." She motioned to her table. "My friends are a little rowdy, but they won't bite."

"Thanks," she said, and made her way to the table.

One of the girls found an extra chair, and they all scooted over to make room. The one named Sarah blurted out, "Millie, could you please try to say 'Ddrym' again? That felt so dreamy!"

"Sarah!" Agnes snapped, noticing Millie's cheeks warming.

"What? I mean it. I never felt so good. Millie, I'm so sorry. I didn't mean to make you feel bad. It's just I'd never felt that before, and it was so grea—"

"Sarah, stop. Please. It's her first day. Give her a break. Let's just eat our—*ew*, what is this?" Agnes said, looking down at her bowl. It was a delicious-smelling stew in a golden liquid thick with meaning. Inside the liquid were little orange, green, and yellow bits of prefixes and suffixes and chunks of whole words here and there.

"It's dictionary stew," Flibbey said and then added very softly, "I like it."

"It's gross," Grace offered, watching Agnes.

"I don't know how you can gag it down," Agnes said to Flibbey while eating it with a fair amount of abandon just to confuse Grace.

Millie put her toe into the conversation. "I think it's pretty good." The table went quiet for her, listening. "I mean, my mom is a really good chef, and she makes a dictionary stew that would silence this one. But that's not a fair comparison. This is actually not bad. I like it too."

Flibbey shot Millie a shy glance. Millie winked at her.

Agnes knew they'd successfully navigated around some social rocks and said, "Anybody want mine? I'll trade you for some extra sides." Trades were negotiated around the table, and everyone began chattering about their favorite stories, Players, and costumes; their dreams; their romances; and what they would specialize in once they graduated. Millie listened, watched them move, and tried to memorize all she could about them.

Chapter 13

Frank's Friends

The first year set Millie's Precinct bones and established her as a viable member of her class. Some students would never stop mirroring their parents' disdain for an integrated school—Grommle and Lum, for instance. But they became the minority, and Millie's Sting nature helped solidify authentic friendships with the larger whole.

It didn't hurt that Agnes was her best friend. Agnes was the clear heiress to the Player role of Cinderella, given that she was next in line after six Cinderella generations in her family. Her mother was the current one, famous throughout StoryEarth, and everyone wanted to be near Agnes because of it.

Destined to step into the role once she was old enough—possibly right after graduating—Agnes confided in Millie that it was the last thing she wanted. What she wanted most was a choice. She wanted to have to audition for a role and earn it. But at least she had made one choice of her own: Millie as her best friend. And that definitely increased Millie's standing in everyone's eyes.

Agnes loved all things Ddrym. She'd read everything she could about it even before she met Millie. Most of the adults in her life chalked that up to teenage rebellion. And Millie loved all things Precinct. Agnes showed Millie how to drive the sporty little Fissbin her parents had given her, and Millie taught Agnes how to manifest her greeting light.

On Millie's sixteenth birthday, she invited Agnes to her home. Millie knew by now how to shield other beings through the boundary. Agnes redeemed herself to the Fireflower family by offering her greeting light. (A Precinct girl! From a Player family!) She also brought with her a gift, a bouquet of herbs and flowers with specific meanings conveying her best wishes to Bette and Linn.

When Millie visited Agnes's High Home, she received a slightly cooler reception, but it was cordial enough, and she managed to get through it without incident. Millie's experience of visiting there only fueled her fire for Precinct life. The Grath High Home was built in the grand mansion style: long driveways, marble fountains, manicured lawns on the outside, and chandeliers and ballrooms on the inside. Eleanor Grath even maintained a horse and carriage as a hat tip to her Player status as the sixth Cinderella in as many generations.

The day Millie got home from that visit, she looked at their cramped kitchen, walked down the narrow hallway to her tiny room, and slumped onto her bed. She started making drawings of what her High Home would look like if she ever became a Player.

Millie also befriended the skinny boy Frank, who had tried to defend her during that terrible first day. He was an odd boy—a creature of habit and a slave to particular sequences of activity, which opened him to ridicule from his friends. But they were careful never to go too far, treating him like a kind of mascot. They kept him in their circle for proximity to his father, an esteemed Preservation Precinct agent, Agent Nine Eight Nine. Who knew when you'd need a friend in high places?

It was Pecking at the Ground season, and so the air was neutral—neither hot nor cold. Frank was born during this season, which gave him his keen persistence. He'd loaded his tray at lunch and made his way over to the table his friends always shared. But the boys were sitting in a different configuration. Grommle was in what had always been Frank's chair. Fred and the rest of the guys had formed a *U* around the table, each in a different seat. The empty chair for Frank was across the table from where he was used to sitting.

He stopped. There was an awkward moment while he tried to act casual and sit in the empty chair. He got behind it, put his tray on the table, pulled the chair away, then abruptly shoved it back in. He tried again but couldn't follow through. On his third try, one of them broke and started laughing, which sent them all into spasms of hilarity. He was mortified.

"Sorry, man," Grommle said, getting up out of his chair and offering it back to Frank. "We just wanted to see what would happen."

Frank didn't know what to say. He was furious, but if he left, it would bring him even more of the attention he'd never wanted in the first place. He had to sit down.

They were merciless, imitating him trying to sit in a different chair. They were turning their plates a quarter before taking a bite. It was awful. Frank got up to leave when the principal—a tightly wound, well-dressed man named Mr. Flarribon—came in and walked directly to their table. He addressed Frank directly. "Mr. Grambling, please come with me." His friends looked almost impressed, thinking maybe (*no, unthinkable!*) he was in trouble.

No one saw him after that. All day Millie heard bits and pieces.

"He's in so much trouble it's a Precinct secret."

"No, I heard his dad was arrested."

"His mother committed suicide."

She looked for him after school. She'd been everywhere. Finally, at the end of the hallway leading to the sanitation area, she saw him sitting on the floor near the wall, his arms around his knees, rocking back and forth. His head banged softly over and over on the wall. His eyes were open and vacant.

Millie rushed over to him. "Frank! What's happened?"

No response.

"Frank."

Nothing but the thumping of his head on the wall. She tried

sitting directly in front of him to make eye contact, but there was no one in there to reach. The only thing he could do was rock and let his head bring him back to his body over and over.

Millie decided to break one of her family's precepts and let herself use her Ddrymmian skills just this once. She sat beside him, dropped into a deep silence, and listened for his energy. After a few breaths, it came. It was a combination of panic, heartbreak, and disbelief. Something truly terrible must have happened, and it wasn't physical. She continued listening.

The way showed itself. She would need to create a strong link with him to bring him out of this state, but how? She sent her psychic tendrils out for his etheric frequencies, and when she felt them, she would concentrate on matching them without succumbing to the attached emotions. It was advanced work that she shouldn't have tried, but she couldn't just leave him there like that.

The link connected her to him, and she felt twice her size and nauseated by the swirling emotions. *What was it again? Something both directions? That's it. I am one with him, and he is one with me. If I can feel his frequencies, he can feel mine.*

As soon as she remembered that simple Oneness equation, he began to settle. She breathed slowly and deeply, as Balimaya had done for her at the border many times. Because she and Frank were linked now, he also breathed slowly and deeply. His head stopped bumping against the wall. She felt the panic subside. But the heartache was deep, and she had nothing for that.

Frank moved back into his own eyes. He looked over at her, a solid, comely girl with hazel eyes and brown hair tied back in a simple ponytail. She wore simple clothes, all earth tones. Comfort, a being made of comfort—she was looking back at him.

"Tell me how you feel, Frank. What happened?"

"My...my...my f-f-f—" He shook his head. She noticed his energy slipping into treacherous territory again, so she called him back. She kept the link alive between them and tried to keep her emotional balance while talking to him.

"OK, OK. Is it all right if I walk with you to your house?"

He nodded. They got up and hoisted their book bags onto their shoulders. She went all the way to his house with him in silence. She let him be in his world completely while keeping the link alive. He had never felt companionship of any kind, not even from his parents, so he was unsettled by this new feeling with no name. He also didn't want her to leave once they got to his address.

"Thank you, Ms. Fireflower," he said, holding out his hand to shake hers.

She smiled uncertainly, frowning too a little, but decided to shake his hand and match his tone. "You're welcome, Mr. Grambling. Please take care of yourself. Whatever it is, maybe take the day off tomorrow?"

"It's against the rules not to come to school on a school day," he said with no expression.

She thought about this for a moment. "It's also against the rules of physics to push the body's heart past its limits. We learned that in our second year. Which rules are more important?"

Mrs. Grambling opened the door and peered at the two teenagers through a veil of alcohol, grief, and shock.

"Hello, Mrs. Grambling. I'm Millie Firefl—"

"I *know* who *you* are," she snapped.

An awkward moment passed between them, and then she saw Frank and cried out, "Oh, Frank!" She threw her arms around his stiff, unyielding frame.

Millie backed away quietly and headed home, hoping she would learn what had happened. When she got through her front door, she rushed to her room and turned on her new HCb. She watched a hologram of the SBC breaking news:

"In a stunning development, we've just been notified that senior continuity agent for the Preservation Precinct, Agent Nine Eight Nine, Mr. William Grambling, has been stripped of his designation this morning and will be banished to the Nothing tomorrow at dusk. The charges are Long-Term Distortion of Story Intent and Manglement of Meaning."

Millie sat on her bed with her hands to her mouth in horror. This was Frank's father.

"This unprecedented breach involves the evil witch in the story of *Snow White and the Seven Dwarfs*. Over the course of the past seven years, the witch, embodied by Player Miriam Boldwell, has begun to seem more sympathetic. This was noticed when public sentiment began gradually turning against Snow White. Lately, the indicators in the monitor rooms showed a marked decrease in White's popularity and an unprecedented growing appreciation for the witch, which gave rise to the inquiry. Analysts have said this could not have gone on for so long without widespread corruption at the Continuity Department. An investigation has been set in motion today.

"We were not able to reach Oscar Woundliss, president of the Preservation Precinct, for comment. A former employee in the Continuity Department, however, speaking on condition of anonymity, alleged that Mr. Grambling had been a secret member of the illegal group of malcontents called Another Way, which evidently has been trying to subvert Story preservation for decades. We will keep you updated as this story unfolds."

Instantly, the holograms went into everyone's kitchens— even in the NetherJunctures. PRESERVATION AGENT NINE EIGHT NINE INDICTED WITH STORY CORRUPTION.

For a few days, Frank was absent from class. Millie rang his doorbell every day, but no one answered. Eventually, he showed up at school to discover that his friends had dropped him like a misspelled word. They no longer even acknowledged him, not even to ridicule.

At lunch, he sat at a table alone. Millie approached with her tray. "Is it OK if I sit with you?"

"I don't recommend it," he said dryly. "Think of your reputation."

She smiled. "You let me decide what I do about my reputation. I repeat"—she decided to up the ante, matching his formal tone—"Mr. Grambling, would it be permissible for me to sit with you?"

He sighed, trying to hide his gratitude. "Yes, Ms. Fireflower. It is permitted."

Agnes showed up minutes later. It cost them some of their friends, but after that, Agnes and Millie almost always sat with Frank during lunch, carrying on with their lives in a way that made room for his idiosyncrasies without calling attention to them. The two girls never made fun of him for the way he rotated his plate a quarter turn before taking a bite or how he always ate the same things on the same days of the week. And they never asked him to be other than himself, even though he continued being painfully formal with them and rarely altered his facial expression. He'd never experienced a friendship that didn't involve his being the butt of a joke, so this took a little getting used to. He was never what you'd call jovial, but he became pleasant enough.

One day, Millie was the last one at the lunch table, putting her tray down and getting settled. The kids across from their table whispered something while looking at her, then broke into peals of laughter. Agnes said, a tad louder than necessary, "Watch out for the cow droppings next door."

"Don't bother, Agnes," Millie said, her mouth full of sautéed text. "I'm used to it."

Everyone chewing at the same time created a momentary silence. Then Frank said, "I feel sorry for them. A Ddrymmian girl, the heiress to a Player's dream role, and the misfit son of a Precinct traitor all at the same table. Their brains are probably exploding, unable to compute."

Millie snorted the water she was drinking out her nose, and Agnes's silverware bounced around from the force of her banging on the table in silent hilarity. Frank looked confused. Millie said, "Frank, that was choice. Very, very good. I didn't know you were so funny."

"I'm not," he said straight-faced, which made them laugh even harder.

In the end, all three did very well in their chosen fields of study.

Frank nailed all his exams, and never veered from his

desire to clear his family name and become a Precinct employee. His endurance of ridicule in high school eventually wore the bullies down. His attention to detail, consistency and integrity in his school work singled him out with the Precinct elite who recruited potential agents for which the school was known. He graduated with honors, and mixed feelings. Would his father have been proud? Or would he have been disappointed, given the fact that he'd thrown in with the hoodlums at Another Way? No one comes back from the Nothing, so he would never know.

Millie's family had shown him kindness and acceptance during his years at school. And today was no different. Mama Bette and Wrem stayed pretty much to themselves, but they greeted Frank with a certain begrudging warmth. His behavior had always been impeccable on the rare occasions that he'd visited Millie's home. He, Agnes and Millie were a tight threesome during those years, and he developed an ease in Ddrym that he'd never expected. Linn engaged him in polite conversation, respected his discomfort with affection, and told him how she looked forward to the great contributions he would no doubt be making to the Preservation Precinct.

Agnes dreaded her place in the family legacy of fame as Player for Cinderella, but she consoled herself during her school years by learning more and more about Ddrymmian ways. She visited Millie as often as her parents would permit. And when she did visit her, she would glean from Mama Bette everything she could about Oneness, about how Listenings were done, about the garden and its guardians, both visible and invisible. And she had helped Mama Linn in the kitchen, washing dishes and telling her all her boy troubles, soaking up her wisdom and comfort, laughing at Precinct puns that only she and Mama Linn would understand.

Millie and Agnes had grown very close—as close as is possible between a Sting and another being. On graduation day, amid the happy chaos of all the students reveling in the fact that their schooling was over, and going off with their families to celebrate,

Millie pulled Agnes away for a private moment, before their own families swooped in.

She led Agnes by the hand to the spot where Agnes had comforted her, when the boys had been so merciless on that first day of school. They stood on that spot. Millie put her hands on Agnes's head, just behind her ears. She said, "There's something I want to give you that only a Sting can give you." Agnes met her eyes, shy for sure, but respectful of Millie's serious tone. "Please close your eyes."

Agnes closed her eyes. *Oh no! Is she going to kiss me?*

Millie felt her anxiety, and said, smiling, "Calm down, Agnes. It's me. I'm just giving you the only truly meaningful thing I can give you."

Agnes felt the heat of Millie's hands on her skull, then the gentleness of Millie's forehead against her own. Suddenly, all was quiet.

The blessing hallowed her body before it reached her ears.

"May you feel the light in your bones. May it shine out from you in the dark. May our bond live strong beyond our limits. And may you know your Oneness with all beings."

Warmth, like a substance woven together with joy and silence, paused at her forehead, waiting for permission. Whatever training Agnes had received from her Ddrymmian 'family' helped her appreciate this innate courtesy that some energies have. She inwardly gave her permission, and a shining tear left a small trail of thanks down her cheek. She felt her body fill with Millie's love and friendship as Millie spoke the last words of the blessing. Agnes opened her eyes and looked at Millie, who smiled. They bowed their heads.

"Now you're my deepfriend," Millie whispered, before looking around them to read the energy of the crowd. It was time to return to the chaos. "We better go back."

Agnes's mother, irritated as always, said, "Agnes, All Things Told! Let's go."

Agnes turned around and said to Millie, "I'll see you when I see you."

And just then, for the first time of many to come, Millie gave her the sign of a Sting deepfriend bond. With her index and third fingers together, she touched her forehead, and pointed them at Agnes. Agnes returned the gesture.

Chapter 14

Millie Takes Over

After graduation, Millie began working in earnest at Alphabet Delights. Linn's hands were beginning to cramp while kneading the bread, and Bette's right hip would complain during Water season. The healer Grelle had taken care of the family ever since Millie was born. But her salves and spells only went so far in relieving these ills. So Mama Bette and Mama Linn were thrilled to have Millie back in the home all day.

Millie had always thought she had a big head start just by virtue of knowing where everything was and how the garden worked. But now that the weight was shifting more authentically onto her own shoulders, she realized how much she didn't know. "How long do you marinate the complaints before putting them into the grumble?" she asked Mama Linn.

"No, no, honey! The complaints have to dry overnight. It's the insults you marinate. And make sure to use a tiny spoonful of sarcasticum. Once it goes into the grumble, that's what brings out all the flavor."

Linn passed on her recipes (some of them so secret she would only tell Millie inside a heartspeak). Wrem and Bette showed Millie how to work with garden energies, how to time the planting, the many ways to water a plant, what to sing for different outcomes, and which faeries were best trusted with which unseen element.

Most overwhelming, though, was the practical side of things. Everyone fawned over Linn's creations, but they had no idea how much Bette did in the background to make them possible, things no one ever saw. Bette knew what supplies to order, how much, when, which brands, and from whom. She knew who owed money, with whom to never do business, and the difference between "negotiating" with Precinct customers and "coming to Oneness" with Ddrymmian customers. Without Bette, they all would have starved into darkness long ago—she could do this stuff in her sleep.

Millie wondered if she'd ever be able to do it at all. There were two of them but only one of her, so when the business actually did transfer to her (sometime in the very distant future, she hoped), she would absolutely have to hire someone to help.

But for now, she thanked All Things Told that her mothers were in relatively good shape. She worked at their sides, bringing her youthful energy and often her good ideas to the table. She relished the fact that she could move freely between Ddrym and the Precinct and crossed the border at every chance she got. Bette and Linn, for the first time since they started their little enterprise so many years ago, could envision some true rest at the end of a lifetime of effort.

Millie was working on a new project in the garden. She'd broken up the soil for a row of discussion beans they'd started in the greenhouse. When Wrem noticed the frequencies had gone soft and sour at the northwestern corner, they worked with those energies all afternoon. The sun had cooked them both, so they sat down to rest under the maple tree near the shed.

"I'm done for," she said, offering him some cool musings from her cup.

"Thank you," he said, sipping from it and leaning his head back against the fence. "It's a hot one today. Hope the flattery buds hold up."

"I think they will. They were covered during the worst of it."

"Good."

A long silence passed between them. She leaned away to brush something off her pants, using the opportunity to watch him with her backsight. "What?" he asked, fiddling with a blade of grass.

"Nothing."

"No, you were looking with your back. From you, that's never nothing."

They laughed.

"I don't know. You just seem...different...in a sort of lovely way."

In the past three or four seasons, Wrem had fulfilled his forest duties admirably, but he hadn't lingered as long before coming home or left as early in the morning for his work. He was spending more time with the family and with their friends, Drauml in particular. She wondered about this, whether there was something developing between them.

In Ddrymmian fashion, there was no rush to start this conversation. They sat in the shade together in a companionable quiet. They shared the cup of musings, passing it back and forth. But her unasked question hung in the air, polite and patient, and he could pluck it and peel it or not. He plucked.

"I've been feeling a bit—how'd you say it?—*different* lately."

"Yes?"

"Yep. Always thought I'd be a forest friend the whole of my life. Never felt pulled like my buddies into joining with women. The trees give me their songs when I work with 'em all day, and I'd come away with my depth filled to full up. It were a good trade, I always felt. And it's still a good trade. But I been...I don't know. Lately..." He blushed and looked away like he was checking out a far part of the garden.

"Say her name, Wremmy. I know already. Say it," she said, smiling.

He laughed out loud with relief. "Ah, it's no use. I'm addled. Drauml has tangled up my head. I can't sleep. Can't get to the end of a thought in her presence. The words just go tumblin' around in my face, and I feel like an idiot."

Millie laughed hard and beamed at her brother. The fatigue she'd felt before disappeared. "Wremmy, that's just wonderful!"

"Is it?"

"Of course it is! How could it not be? You've given some good, strong years of your life to the forest. Forest friending isn't for life, you know that. You are in the middle of a change. So it's just—this is your time to be joined. And to my very best friend!"

"Well, here's what I been gonna ask you, if I ever got the courage," he said. "Will you—I mean, can we just talk it through a bit? Not sure what to do. I haven't been able to think straight for a while now."

"Of course," she said as they got up and gathered the tools to put them back in the shed. "Let's have a walk in the forest."

Later that week, Millie orchestrated a midday dinner for several of their friends. It was a reunion of sorts—so many of them had begun separating into their respective pathways. Drauml showed up more beautiful than ever, with her long brown braid graceful down the middle of her back and wearing a dress she'd been saving for a special occasion—it had living flowers in the fabric. She'd spared no expense. She had even used her mother's cedarwood essence behind her ears.

Wrem saw her come through the door, and his heart sent a sunbright greeting light that she met with her own. Their palms touched, and with a sober face and a love that went all the way down to his feet, he saw the rest of his life in her eyes.

That Saving season, Wrem and Drauml were joined and began building their cottage nestled in the trees nearby.

As the next few years unfolded, Millie's activities brought more trips to the Precinct, more friends, and more complications. At twenty-two, Millie came up with progressive ideas that were regularly met with resistance. It was Turning season, the season for changes, so these ideas weren't completely unexpected.

The haggling started, however, when Millie wanted to bring in another, younger horse to give Paulie a break. Bette had a fit. "You might as well take the money and throw it all to the faeries after dark! Paulie's perfectly fine. He's only twelve. He's in his prime!"

"I know, Mama Bette, but I want him to live a *very* long time, and if he keeps having to do all the pulling—especially now that we have more business—we'll be shortening his life."

"Nonsense."

"Here's how I see it," Millie continued. She could go toe-to-toe with Mama Bette better than anyone. "We have Paulie pulling every two days for a while, then let him rest for a bit. The young horse can take the greater share of the work. And down the road, it protects us for when Paulie has to go Elsewhere. We'll still have a fairly strong horse to carry forward. It's an investment in our future success."

Bette shook her head. "You sound just like one o' them now, 'success' and 'investment.'" She made a face. "Didja forget what we're about? We keep the faeries happy to bring a smile to our home, and we tend and sing to the land so *it* will be happy. It gives us its rich harvest out of its own happiness!"

"I know, Mama. But you were the one who taught me that if we don't pay attention to the practical details, we'll go under." Millie made a note to watch her Precinct language with Bette.

"Well, I didn't mean—"

"All I'm saying is, let's bring some extra kindness to our friend Paulie. He's been so good to us. Let's bring him a friend and nourish our livelihood in the process."

Bette knew she was being manipulated, but eventually conceded to the logic. She knew the Framm family in Near Emmering. They raised horses to supplement their cheerfruit income. She told Millie she'd go visit them and sniff things out. But Millie, keen to get this piece in place, beat her mother to it. She asked around till she heard about the Framms' three-year-old paint horse. She couldn't stop pestering her mothers about it.

Mama Bette snapped at her, "I was getting to it."

"I know, Mama, but you're on Ddrymmian time, and I have Precinct concerns."

Bette cocked her head and frowned. There was an awkward beat.

Millie jumped into it. "I'm sorry, Mama Bette. I lost my balance for a minute, thinking too much about the business and not enough about our life together. I was just so impatient, so I started asking around, that's all. Forgive me?"

Bette softened and said, "Aw, hon, I remember what it's like to want what you want. Believe me."

Mama Linn walked in just then, and they had to recount the whole thing.

"He's ready now, Mama Linn," Millie said about the horse. "He's beautiful. I've seen him. Someone will snap him up for sure. They're asking thirty suns, which is pretty fair."

Mama Linn did the math. "When will you have time to give them thirty suns?"

"Maybe they'll let us pay it a bit at a time? Because it's us?"

One week later, after some clever negotiating, Millie rode him home, her new, handsome horse, Cliffer. She would pay her suns one at a time every season. At thirteen seasons per cycle, she'd be done in a little over two cycles. She was ecstatic, appreciating his lively step and his quick responses, admiring his alertness—his ears turned in every direction as they went home, gathering information. Paulie trailed behind good-naturedly, and Millie was careful to give him extra snuggles once they got home so he'd know he wasn't being replaced.

The next hurdle was a disagreement about deliveries. Sitting at the table over dinner, Millie broached the idea of making the Precinct deliveries alone.

"Why in the Sea of Non Sequiturs would you want to do that? Something could happen, any kind o' problem, and you wouldn't have your brother there to help you," said Bette.

"Well, that's exactly what I wanted to talk to you about," she said. "I think Wrem is being pulled in too many directions right now. He's finishing his new home, he's tending the trees, and they've got him teaching treecraft to youngsters as well, but the thing I really wanted to tell you is"—she looked behind her for dramatic effect before whispering—"he and Drauml may be trying for a baby!" One little white lie wouldn't hurt.

It was impossible for the mothers not to smile over this—a grandchild. They were all quiet for a moment. And both Bette and Linn felt a tenderness for their daughter, so typical of a Sting, trying to balance things out for everyone—first Paulie and now Wrem.

When the three women approached Wrem during their fortnightly family dinner, he was actually quite relieved. So was Drauml. They ironed out some of the obstacles (what to do about heavy equipment or a wagon breakdown or if one of the horses had a problem), and Mama Linn gave Millie a list of Ddrymmians who work in the Precinct who'd be willing to help out in an emergency. By the beginning of Sorting season, only a few weeks away, Millie had the deliveries all to herself.

Two weeks after that dinner, Mama Linn went to the forest to forage for mushrooms, where she smelled an unusual scent— something she'd rarely come across. It had a hint of rage and heartbreak in it. Following it, she came upon Wrem treating a tree for birch blight. She waited till his song ended and said quietly, "Sweetheart, remember, tomorrow night, you and Drauml are coming to dinner."

He looked at her for the longest time.

Her heart grew tight. "What?"

"Ah, Mama," he said with a sigh, putting his arms around her in a real hug. "Nothing. I was just...thinkin' about something else."

She left with a heavy heart. *It's joining trouble*, she thought. *Everyone goes through it. But they'll find their way. Both of them are such good people.* She made an intention to provide a delicious distraction tomorrow night and to shower them with familial love. All would be well.

The next day, Millie came home from a delivery and tripped over the threshold. She dropped her bag, and all its contents went flying. She rushed furiously to put everything back. "Hi,

Mama," she said with a thin laugh as she put her coat up on the hook, missed, and tried again with too much force.

"Go outside, Mill. Your energies are banging around the whole place. See to them first," Linn suggested.

"You're right. You're right. Yep. Be right back." She walked out into the garden and stood still, pressing her thumb into her well-worn centering stone. It took a few minutes, but once she was calmer, she came back in.

Linn still picked up a whiff of something acidic, just a trace of something raw and sickening that she couldn't place. "What's going on?"

Millie tried to think of how to answer. In Ddrym, lying wasn't just frowned upon, it was virtually impossible, because it would indicate the presence of Two (the truth and the lie). She chose her words carefully. "Dearest Mama," she said, looking at her with something that strangely echoed Wrem, "it's something I have to solve on my own. I'd rather keep it to myself till I've sorted it out."

"OK," Mama Linn said. "You know you can talk to me if you need."

"I know."

Later that evening, Drauml and Wrem arrived arm in arm. Mama Linn had gone all out. There were decorations at each place setting. She'd sculpted different birds out of sugar-spun story line and placed them at the settings—a hawk for Bette, a black-capped chickadee for herself, male and female cardinals for Wrem and Drauml, and a hummingbird for Millie. Warm hugs went all around, except between Wrem and Millie, who barely looked at each other.

Mama Linn noticed it and shifted into full-force joy to blot it out. She got everyone to the table, donning her cooling gloves to pull every kind of sensual deliciousness out of the oven, taking plates that had been prepared in advance and placing them in the center. There was a bottle of elderberry wine. Drauml poured it around.

Mama Linn began the meal. "We honor the presence of our

sprites and faeries, especially Flurjahm. We thank the garden and all the elements for providing our sustenance. And we open our hearts with gratitude to the language we're about to consume. We bow our heads to the Oneness that feeds and holds us all."

They dug in. Drauml said, "I've found the most wonderful little spot in the dirt at our place where we can grow heads of composition and rows of yellow shouts. *And* there are fiddlehead limericks just jumping up out of the soil on their own. Nobody planted them."

Millie said, "That sounds wonderful, Drauml."

"Does it?" Wrem spat out, staring at Millie.

"Wrem," Drauml said softly, shocked.

"Yes, it does, Wrem. I think it's a great idea," Millie replied, meaning something entirely different and returning his glare.

The whole table went cold. Mama Bette finally blurted out, "What in black stars has gotten into you two?"

Wrem returned to his meal as Mama Linn offered, "If need be, we can have a Listening right here, right after dinner."

"No!" Millie and Wrem said at the same time.

"Well, at least you agree on that." Mama Linn heard weak laughter from Drauml and Bette.

"All right, then," Linn continued, "let your troubles rest for a moment while we eat in peace."

Turning to Drauml, she went on, "By the way, Drauml, did you ever talk to Pim about your fabric? For the curtains? He's such an odd man, but I think he's the best when it comes to warming your home."

Millie did her best. "There's a great place in the Precinct called Fantasy Fabrics. If you want—"

"No, she *doesn't* want," said Wrem. He said it with a baseball bat in his voice.

"Wrem! Gather up your heart. Where are you?" Drauml chided him. He had never answered for her before, and she wasn't about to let him start.

"I'm out of sorts, OK?" he shouted. Then he looked at Millie.

"Maybe I drank something that didn't agree with me." He pushed his chair back and got up.

On his way outside, he mumbled, "I've always liked trees better than people anyways."

Wrem did succeed in calming himself and returning to the dinner for his mothers' and his wife's sake, but the rest of the evening was an exhausting exercise in doublespeak, with no one saying what they meant, everyone dying to know what the trouble was, and Millie and Wrem oscillating between insult and apology.

In the weeks after that fateful dinner, he started complaining openly about her Precinct snobbery. She bristled at his Ddrymmian provincialism. They built their walls, each waiting for the other to practice Oneness and acceptance. They reluctantly tried a modified Listening (with no one else in attendance), but it ended with them further from each other than before—which is why Listenings are never done without a third friend present.

They eventually settled into a rhythm of avoidance. Wrem spent most of his time working with and teaching about the trees. Millie and Cliffer delivered all the Precinct orders, which were growing every week. Wrem and Paulie were called on every so often to deliver a couple of Ddrymmian orders during the busiest times. Drauml helped out in the kitchen, hoping to make herself a bridge between them.

Mama Linn kept herself busy. She tried to calm her wife's unease by being indefatigably upbeat. She left her little notes of encouragement. Bette would find them on her desk or sitting near her faerie offerings in their bedroom. She even found one in the bathroom tucked into the spray of lavender flowers. It said, "Whatever is troubling our children, we must remember the one breath breathing us in and out each day."

Chapter 15

The Decision

One resting day, Millie had come back from dining with the friends she'd met in Near Emmering on one of her delivery runs. It was late afternoon in the Reaching season—all the leaves, plants, and flowers reached for the sky, and everyone keenly connected to their goals and ambitions. Drauml was at the Circle meadow with Bari, helping prepare for the seasonal ceremony a week away.

"Mama Linn?" Millie asked.

Linn was deep in thought, kneading the ruminations dough. "Yeah, hon?"

"Is Mama Bette around?"

"I think so. She was just looking for her glasses. She's around here somewhere."

"OK. Can I talk to you both?"

Linn felt something in her legs go weak. She said in her even voice, "You bet." She pressed her feet into the ground, lengthened her spine, and softened her neck. And then she snapped right back into the ball of tension she'd been for the past many weeks.

"Mama Bette?" Millie's voice echoed down the hall. She searched through the house until she found her other mother outside, pulling towels and sheets off the clothesline. "Here, let me help you with that," Millie said as she took the bundle from

Bette. "Can you come inside for a moment? I need to talk with you both."

"Yap," she said, and they walked inside with their arms full of clean laundry, while Bette summoned the kind of courage you'd need for a march toward the Door to Elsewhere.

Everyone sat at the table. "Is Wrem part of this? Is he coming?" Linn wanted to know.

"He didn't want to be here." But as Millie spoke, the back door opened, and there he was, out of breath, his eyes asking Millie something. She just kept her eyes steady on his as her answer. He stomped over to the table and sat.

Linn, startled but relieved to have everyone at the table, got up to make some conversation tea. "This is good," she said, hoping she meant it. It was good to have everyone there, even on the lip of whatever this was. At least the tension would break. Maybe.

"So," she said as the kettle warmed over the fire, "Millie, you said you had something to talk to us about?"

"Yes," Millie said, suddenly sick to her stomach. "So, um, Mama Linn," she looked at her mother and tried to invoke a thread going back a decade or so, "remember a conversation we had so long ago? I think it was on the way home from the silktunnel..." Mama Linn nodded. "Well, I said, then...I told you how much I, uh, wanted to..." Then Millie realized that the longer this took, the more painful it would be. She already had the center stone in her hand. "I've been hired by the Preservation Precinct."

No one said anything for quite a while. "Hired" was the first stumbling block. When would she have time to do anyone else's work with all the work they had at Alphabet Delights? "Preservation Precinct" was the next hurdle. What could possibly be in the Precinct that was more important than shouldering her increasing load at home? Linn's stomach began to ache, ears twitching.

Bette, in her typical fashion, said, "All right, let's have it between the eyes. Who hired you? And how in black-and-blue stars are you gonna manage your time here? You can barely keep up as it is."

Millie had rehearsed for this moment for so long, trying it on in front of a mirror, trying it with the trees, trying it with Agnes play-acting the part of her angry mothers. And nothing, none of that, prepared her for the actual, live-action breakage of heart coming now. "I've been hired for a story...to replace Barbara Cratcher."

After a beat, Mama Bette said, "But that's not possible. Barbara Cratcher is a...a Player."

"Yes. She retired, and I'm going to be the new Player for Mama Bear in *Goldilocks and the Three Bears*."

There was a moment of blank nonresponse while the news connected to all the belief points in everyone's mind.

Bette wheeled on Wrem. "You knew!" Wrem flinched. She went on, "Every fortnight at this table! Conversation tea and elf dribbles! When were you gonna tell us?"

Wrem tried to hold his head up. "I was sworn to One Knowing. I tried everyth—"

"You couldn't break the precious One Knowing for the sake of this family?"

"No, Mama Bette. *No*. It's a vow. It's not for breakin' whenever you want."

"You young saps, you got no sight. You think everything's all grand and clear, the lines clean and straight. It's your *family,* Wrem. It's the only thing ya got." She shot a glance at Millie.

"No, Mama Bette," he said softly. "I got my word, and if I don't keep my word, then who am I?"

"Your word! I got a word for ya—"

Linn lunged for the bell at the center of the table and rang it for silence. With effort, Wrem and Bette stopped talking. Millie knew that Bette's fury at Wrem was only a rehearsal for what was coming at her. Linn felt nauseated, her heart banging in her throat as her mouth went dry. Everyone's ears twitched. The faeries were beginning to notice. She paused before speaking; having been the one to call for silence, by custom, Linn was the only one allowed to break it.

She said to the table, to no one, to everyone, "I'm curious about how long Wrem knew, of course, and how he found out, but I also know that if Millie's mind is made up, it doesn't really matter how long he knew. We don't interfere in the affairs of full beings. And Millie is a full being now." Linn's skin prickled. "Have you signed the contract?"

"Yes."

Linn, being Precinct born, knew better than anyone at that table what it meant. It was the end of everything. Now, if they were lucky, they would see her in person only a few days every cycle, that's every thirteen seasons. Now, if she made any mistakes, even the smallest one, they would never see her again. She would be sent to the Nothing.

She turned to Millie. Over and over, her mouth opened and then shut before anything could come out. She did not want to believe the dogs of grief and betrayal baying inside her belly. "This is our family business! Your family," Linn said. "*Your* business, essentially. Did you think of that?"

"Mama, it's all I've thought about for years! But you never asked me. You never asked if I wanted to do this."

"Yes, we did!" Linn replied.

"When, Mama? When?" The tears were now rushing down Millie's cheeks. "When did you ask me? Was it when I had barely one and a half nines behind me? When you *told* me how lucky the family was that I was going to take over? That's all you ever said. You never *asked*."

Bette jumped in, enraged, "You were completely enthralled with it. You loved preparing and making deliveries with us—" She blew her nose.

"Because it took me to the *Precinct*."

Wrem said, "Oh, right. Twist the knife a little deeper, wont-cha! I don't think we felt it enough."

She shot back, "Don't make me the villain here. I just want my life." She looked around at her family. "Where is your precious Oneness when it comes to that? The Preservation Precinct is not *Other*. What I want is not *Other*. It's just other than what *you* want! And besides, Mama Linn, you followed your dream to come here. You left your home. Why shouldn't I?"

"Because no one else was depending on me, Millie. I just left disappointed parents. No one cared enough to tell me why I shouldn't. But you leaving us here, you're leaving an entire... an entire..." And she bowed her head into the unspoken finish.

A thick silence fell on them all. For Bette, it was a blow to the bones. She closed her eyes and got up from the table and sat down at her desk. She put her head in her hands and sighed. Then she picked up her pen and started writing.

Millie asked her, "What are you doing?"

She paused, looked at Millie for what would be the last time, and said, "That's none of your business anymore, is it?"

Linn ran out of the room, down the hallway, through the back door, and into the garden. She fell to her knees, weeping in the middle of the exposition heads ready for harvest. Millie followed her out. She approached her, uncertain whether she should leave her be but knowing she had to try. "Mama."

"Don't. Just...don't."

"Mama, listen to me. I know you don't want to, but hear me out."

Linn stayed put, digging her hands into the soil over and over as her daughter spoke.

"As a Player, I'll get paid very well, more than I need."

Linn made a sound of disgust.

Millie went on, "But the 'more than I need' will go to our family business. It could be great for us all in the long run."

Linn spat out, "I will not have Alphabet Delights benefiting from the fruits of injustice."

"But, Mama—"

"There is no 'but' to that."

"The benefits are all-encompassing. If anything happened to any of us, we would have access to the best healers anywhere in StoryEarth. They're very open-minded about it. Could be a Precinct doctor or any kind of healer anywhere in the NetherJunctures. It's great security."

Linn was inconsolable. She buried her face in her apron and wailed. When the wave had passed, she wiped her face with her apron and said, "You don't see it, Millie."

"What don't I see? Tell me."

"I raised you. I taught you everything I knew so we could grow this business and be part of the larger circle here in Ddrym. And now...you've thrown it all away. Who will take over now? Who will do it?"

Millie knelt next to her mother, listening.

Her mother seemed to calm herself into a kind of anger. She went on, "Everything I fought for to get you to school in the Precinct"—her tears climbed up and shot out again as she shook them away—"the fight with Blick and his friends...and some of my friends...and even your Mama Bette. Mama Bette..."

Linn paused to remember it. "By the grace of Oneness, that woman heroically got over her resistance, and she and I wheedled, bribed, researched, gave our very souls to winning over the Precinct government—thinking we were sending our roots farther down into our own family soil. And instead, all that—*all* that—was for nothing, all of it. And now you're leaving us for a...a..." She whispered her shame into the ground. "A High Home."

Never had Millie felt so low. She had been ready for a fight, but when the time came, her stance went up in smoke. In the past year, she had methodically worked her way into the trainings, the auditions, and eventually the coveted role of Player. She had done it covertly, always using only Cliffer for those trips, because she was afraid Paulie would somehow give her away. She had told herself that she was ultimately doing it for her family, that her new Player status would help the whole family, that they'd easily be able to hire someone—maybe even Drauml—to take her place.

Frank Grambling had helped, since he was now Agent Four Seven, but she had basically accomplished this on her own, and it was a phenomenal feat. She was the only Ddrymmian to achieve Player status in...well, ever. She knew she should have told her family earlier. She should have said something about her desire for this while she was still in high school.

She remembered with a pang the day her mother had told her that working for Alphabet Delights would be serving Story in the most comprehensive way, that it would bring her into plenty of contact with the Preservation Precinct. What she hadn't realized then was how deep a hold the Precinct had on her. Every mention of it in conversation, every visit for deliveries, and certainly almost every day of her Precinct schooling sealed her love of it.

Millie tried to find her stance again. She remembered her resentments, her justifications. They'd planned her whole life for her without once consulting her. And then she remembered something else. "Mama, one of the most important things I learned in Circle was 'Let your own yes grow within you. To use anyone else's is theft.'"

After a moment, Linn responded, "There is another Circle teaching you managed to forget. 'Never hide your true heart from your loved ones.'"

Millie had no answer for that. She left her mother to grieve in the garden.

She had only a few weeks to get settled. Her High Home, the construction of which she'd been covertly overseeing for eight weeks, was ready, empty, and waiting for her things. She had to decide what to bring and what to leave behind. Also, she needed to prepare for the traditional leave-taking ceremonies: the Telling (for your friends and the larger community, where you state your intentions about a major transition in your life), the Deeper Telling (for intimate time with your family, for recommitments to the heart of wholeness), and the Going (a ceremony just between you and the elements, enacted when passing through the boundary between now and what you are going toward). It would be a tumultuous and awkward week. She would need every bit of her training to steady herself.

Shock reverberated throughout the NetherJunctures. Family

dinner tables as far as Far Emmering bristled with conflict, conjecture, and condolences. Despite the Ddrymmian distaste for excess, the younger set was fascinated. A Ddrymmian becoming a Player—how had she done it while maintaining her duties with Alphabet Delights? How had she done it at all?

Many knew of Millie, of course, from when she lived through the breaching of the boundary unshielded in her mother's delivery cart. But many also loved her. She had been their friend, she had helped them in times of need, she was a good listener, and she could mend hard feelings between troubled beings. That she would actually leave Ddrym for the Precinct was nonsensical, though. And that she would go there to become a Player was by turns baffling and appalling.

Millie's biggest challenge was not anyone's contempt but rather their scripted civility—sometimes lifted word for word right out of the Circle Teachings. They said these things with genuine effort, trying to find their way to her without showing their reactive thoughts. "May you prosper in all that fulfills your growth." "The roads are many. All begin and end in Oneness."

She was exiled from her family's relaxed interactions, bound to the careful words of strangers. Wrem hardened with each passing day, answering forest calls from Larkshen and Far Emmering, which kept him away from Drauml, starting early in the morning and extending into the deep dark.

Toward Millie, Bette had gone profoundly silent—with words, body language, eye contact. There was no reaching her at all. She devoted herself completely to the office, the numbers, and finding someone to replace Millie. (There had also been talk of just letting the business go once they could no longer manage.) The faeries disappeared into the forest. Offerings were left untouched for days at a time.

Linn suffered in her particular way: She cleaned. She moved appliances to clean the floors better, dragged furniture out of corners so she could mop and sweep, and took curtains off the rods, washed them, and hung them out to dry. She worked hard to maintain her fury at Millie. It felt better than the agonizing grief of watching her daughter disappear into the Precinct machine.

Millie loves the solid structures and clear directives of the Preservation Precinct, Linn thought. *They're so much easier to live with than the ambiguity of Circle Teachings and how they never tell you which way to go. She has no idea what's coming. She thinks that Precinct agent, Frank, is her friend. Ha. She has no idea. No idea.*

But Linn had work to do. *There is another load of wash waiting...and bread to make and announcement salads for the...for the Telling.*

Drauml came to Millie's house and rapped on the door. Bette was in the garden; Linn was pulling something heavy out of the oven. "Millie! Door!"

But Millie was already there. She opened it, and before there was even time for greeting lights, Drauml took her into her arms, hugging her hard, anger and love fighting for prominence. She whispered into her shoulder, "How could you do this?" She cried for herself, her friend, everyone. "Bari is too upset right now. But she said to let you know she'd be at the Telling."

"Thank you," Millie said, never meaning it more than at this moment. "Will you please, *please* come in for some tea?"

Drauml held Millie's eyes in her own, filling with tears. "I'm sorry, Millie. I can't."

"I understand."

"May you prosper in all that fulfills your growth," she said, meaning every word.

And Millie responded with equal sincerity, "The roads are many. All begin and end in Oneness." They exchanged greeting lights, and Drauml turned to leave for home.

Chapter 16

Leaving Ddrym

The Telling

Millie was grateful that there was a ritual for this. Usually, she bristled at the long, drawn-out, timeless nature of Ddrymmian ceremonies. But now she was comforted by the fact that there was a ritual where everyone knew what was expected of them—even as they faced a wholly unexpected situation. The drumming, the humming, the gentle stamping of one foot and then the other in place: all of it helped each being find their place in the Circle again, their place in life—well, almost everyone.

As the gathering grew, Millie remembered part of why she preferred the Precinct—a place where if you said it would be over by four, it was over by four. If you said you'd be there at eight thirty, you were fully expected to be there at eight thirty. Here, getting people together at the same time was always like herding a mischief of faeries. Everything took five times longer than necessary.

They formed a circle that grew with every being who joined. Pim had been sensitive to the difficult nature of this ceremony and had chosen muted earth tones and elegant restraint in his design. It was well-attended enough. Whoever wanted to show support for the family would be there, even though it might be misinterpreted as support for Millie's choice. She knew not to hope for much.

Wrem made it clear privately that he would be there as head drummer for his mothers and his mothers only. By contrast, Drauml and Bari stood as close as they could to Millie in honor of their friendship. Elder Shekwey was there, as always, to lead.

The drumming went on for longer than usual. It seemed they were waiting for something. And then one of the little ones pointed over to the pathway and said in his baby voice, "Bamaya!" Balimaya, or Miss B. as Millie had come to know her, approached from the northern path. Despite her spine being stooped a little now, she seemed somehow even more commanding than ever in her deep blue robes. She had lost some weight, and her gait was slow, but she carried herself with elegance and grace. She steadied herself with a cane.

Millie burst into tears when she saw her. Balimaya had been a Long Solitary all of Millie's life and rarely came out for public ceremonies. The last time she'd seen her was at Mama Bette and Mama Linn's Listening, almost eight years before. Millie ran to her and offered her greeting light, which the old woman warmly accepted and returned. Millie took her arm and guided her to the elder's place in the circle, mute and flooded with gratitude.

This one interaction shifted the entire circle's energy. It was not as if they were all suddenly in favor of Millie's decision to leave, but their vision of it had expanded. Balimaya's presence had cast this move in the light of Oneness and helped them rise out of narrow opinion and into a larger space—for those who could go there.

The ceremony started with a long drumming session, followed by chanting and invocations. The traditional stations of a community home-leaving ritual unfolded one by one. It took hours. Finally, when Water and Earth, Air and Fire, Space and Story had answered Elder Shekwey's call-and-response chant, Millie spoke the news that everyone already knew. She spoke it cleanly, and lights were exchanged. The first great hurdle of Millie's official exit was behind her.

Afterward, she walked Balimaya as far home as the woman would allow. When they got to the ancient sequoia at the crossroads between Larkshen and Droaze, Miss B turned to Millie and said, "I must go the rest of the way on my own, child."

"Of course." But Millie stood still, not wanting the woman to leave.

Miss B then signaled for Millie to kneel. The old woman then put her hands on Millie's head. As white light flowed from the Long Solitary's hands into Millie's body, the old woman gave her this blessing: "The Nothing is not what anyone thinks it is. May you never have to face it directly. May you prosper in all that fulfills your growth. The roads are many."

Matching her formal tone, Millie responded, "All begin and end in Oneness. May all your inhales bring nourishment, and may all your exhales bring peace." She kissed marsh leaf on Miss B's wrist. They exchanged light one last time, and Millie was filled with it the whole way home.

The Telling ceremony had had a somewhat mollifying effect on the family. Tensions had softened, and they were able to at least converse as long as the subjects were of absolutely no consequence. Flurjahm made a couple of furtive appearances.

Their most difficult moment lay ahead of them, the Deeper Telling. It was to come the following day, before Millie took her leave of Ddrym. They had collectively decided, without knowing it, to pretend that nothing at all was happening. Dinner went smoothly. Night came and went.

Millie realized it would be her last faerie offering at this particular bedroom window. She hoped Flurjahm would come with her, but didn't know whether the atmosphere at her High Home would appeal to him. She'd grown up in this room. Some things remained from her childhood: a tiny rocking chair Wrem had made for her, the chest of drawers given to their family for her room when she was found, and a basket of baby toys they kept for visiting parents with small children.

But most of her childhood lived in this room, in the deep, worn, glowing comfort of well-loved objects: the candlestick that lit her musings when she wrote her thoughts as a girl (which she decided last-minute to bring with her to her High Home), the bedside table where her Precinct books would pile up, the closet that held all her clothes—now only the ceremonial robes remained. Everything else was in the quietbox she'd received roughly from Bette, who had tossed it into Millie's bedroom, mumbling, "We were gonna chuck this anyway."

Millie did not sleep. She rehearsed a million scenarios for what she might say to her family at the Deeper Telling. In the end, she woke with a start, having drifted off in the middle of the night.

The Deeper Telling

It traditionally came at the last minute before the goer turned to go. The Deeper Telling was a chance for everyone in the family to recommit to Oneness despite the impending distance between them. There was a protocol for this, but it was rarely followed. Moving away from Ddrym (so often the cause for a Deeper Telling) was controversial, so it was almost always fraught with emotion. Those who opposed the impending separation most strongly either didn't show up or used the ceremony to voice their opposition one more time.

Millie, filled with anxiety, couldn't wait to get to the other side and start her new life. But suddenly, she was dawdling. Her legs wobbled a little. She checked and rechecked her shoulder bag and the quietbox, her face reflected in the window. Ddrym did not have mirrors, but she often sneaked a peek in a window. How a being "looked" in Ddrym was known to be subjective. It depended on who was looking and how each being felt inside. So the Precinct obsession with mirrors was always a source of amusement to Ddrymmians. *Mirror, mirror on the wall, who's the fairest of them all?* Proof that mirrors were good only for evil. She checked herself in the window and saw her own face— blank, nervous, drawn, defiant. Better she had not looked.

Linn's movements in the kitchen, the little clinks and taps and swish-swish swishes, made a musical collection of sounds that Millie committed to memory. She could smell the buttery sweetness of her mother's famous patois puffs rising in the oven. There was a big party coming up on the set for The Elves and the Shoemaker, and they'd ordered five hundred of them. As she entered the kitchen, Millie's eyes were alive with extra precision, noticing the worn indentations in the butter dish, dust on a window ledge, droplets of water from where Linn had rinsed then shaken-out heads of translation just before chopping them into a salad. These were things she would probably never see again.

Bette sat at the table, stone-faced. Linn busied herself with finishing the cleanup, wiping down counters, getting the cooling racks ready for the batch in the oven. Millie wasn't exactly sure what to do next. Usually, the family accompanied the Ddrymmian being to the boundary, in whichever direction they were going. That was unlikely in this situation. She decided to be direct.

"Will you be coming with me to the border, or would you prefer to do the Deeper Telling here?" she said, her eyes fixed on what used to be her chair at the table as her thumb pressed into the centering stone in her pocket.

Linn replied, "How about we accompany you to the edge of our yard, and you can take it from there."

"OK."

"Are you— Is it happening now?" Linn's voice faltered a little.

"Um, I guess. Yes."

Linn stopped what she was doing for a moment. She looked at the oven. "I need to wait until this batch is done. It'll only take a few minutes. Want some steamed soliloquy? Fresh this morning."

"Sure. Thanks, Mama."

Millie got her bowl and utensils out, spooned out a serving of the porridge, sprinkled in a dusting of comfort, and ate in silence. Bette left the table to go do something at her desk. Everyone had calcified into their own corners. It was a perfect time to go.

Once the patois puffs came out of the oven, Millie rose to put her coat on. She'd already staged her quietbox outside the front door. As she shouldered the bag that held her Precinct papers, her new ID badge, and the rest of her credentials, Bette and Linn looked at each other and moved toward the front door. Millie opened it and went out first per protocol. She picked up her quietbox. They followed her to the border of their yard. Millie put down the quietbox, turned around, and faced them.

The family started first. Linn looked at her daughter for a long time as she waited for her own words to come up. Finally, she took a deep breath and, defeated, spoke slowly, mindful of every word. "Millie, I am in so much pain. Perhaps someday I will come to terms with this path you are taking. I can only hope that you will remember your deepest teachings and that you will not, wittingly or unwittingly, betray your Ddrymmian roots." She put her hands on her daughter's shoulders and fixed her eyes on her.

"I do not understand you. I do not trust you. I am angry, and I suffer. But I—" And here she faltered, forcing the words through her broken heart. "I also do...love you...very much." A moment passed, and she seemed like she was about to add something. But she looked down at the ground instead. Then, Linn took hold of Millie's shoulders and looked directly into her eyes. From her deepest Precinct-born self, she whispered a wish, a warning and a watchword, all in one prayer: "May you say all your lines correctly." Then she bowed her head to signal that she was finished.

When it was Bette's turn, several times she looked as though she might say something, only to shut her mouth abruptly. Here she was, face-to-face with her own daughter, the little bundle of light that had called her into the forest, that had drawn out of her the very love she hadn't known existed. Here was her daughter, who had shown so much promise and who had become an enemy, turned away, turned her back on an entire family and heritage. Bette closed her eyes, pressing her feet into the ground, looking for deeper words to say. But her heart had gone into such hiding that language had accompanied it, and there didn't seem to be any point in summoning it back. All she could do was give Millie her eyes briefly, then bow her head.

Millie waited one more instant to listen for Wrem. Finally, she took her turn.

"I love and honor you both. I always have, and I always will. I'm grateful you found me in the forest, Mama Bette, grateful you chose to bring me into this family. You may not understand my decision, but please stay open to the possibility that it may result in many positive consequences for us all. I hope someday you'll forgive me for not telling you sooner." They all shifted on their feet. "I was thinking maybe Wrem would show up, but I guess not." She looked into the forest around them, in every direction one last time, just in case. "Please tell him how much I love him and that I will hold him in my heart always."

Then she said, "May the Oneness that pervades the whole of everything breathe through us all."

Linn and Bette repeated it, tears coming to Linn. They exchanged their lights one last time. Then Millie turned around, picked up her quietbox, and left. Linn and Bette went back into the house, shut the door, and looked at each other for a minute. Bette wrapped Linn in her arms.

The Going

When she reached the border, Millie turned toward the trees of Ddrym and performed the Going ceremony. "In the name of Oneness, I call on the six elements—Water and Earth, Air and Fire, Space and Story. I call on the spirits and the whole faerie family to hear me." She waited in the fullness of her greeting light. Little by little, she felt presences arriving, though she could not see them.

When the gathering felt complete, she went on with the words Miss B had taught her to say if she ever left Ddrym for another land. "Thank you for keeping me safe after my Sting birth until Mama Bette could find me. Thank you for all the times, known and unknown, when you kept me from harm and guided my feet back home. I am blessed with growth and going. The road I walk takes me away from Ddrym for now, but this road is one of many. And all begin and end in Oneness. The Oneness that breathes in my heart, I promise to bring to all things. May all beings inhale nourishment. May all beings exhale peace."

And just as she turned to go through the border, someone whispered in her ear, "Enjoy." Millie's blood froze as she whipped around just in time to see the shadow woman blowing her a kiss goodbye with a wink.

Her skills at border prep had become second nature. Every step she took from Ddrym brought her closer to the Preservation Precinct. Once she breached the Precinct edge of the border, she was consumed with exhaustion. Agnes was waiting by the side of the road in a brand-new yellow Fissbin. They greeted each other with their special deepfriend sign. Millie got into the car and sat still for the longest time.

Agnes finally said, "Where to?"

Millie said, "I am so tired."

Agnes turned the key. "I bet. Put the seat back and rest. We'll go to my place. My driver will get you to your High Home tomorrow in plenty of time to meet your staff."

Millie fell sound asleep before she could even thank her.

Part Two

The Preservation
Precinct

OFFICIAL SCRIPT, PLAYER MILLICENT FIREFLOWER

GOLDILOCKS AND THE THREE BEARS, Act 1, Scene 2
STORYEARTH: OFFICIAL PRESERVATION PRECINCT CAST

GOLDILOCKS   - Tiffany Staevla
PAPA BEAR   - Seth McLeod
MAMA BEAR   - Millie Fireflower
BABY BEAR   - Sam Canffer

> *The family of three bears enters from stage left, having been out to pick berries. One by one, they hang their jackets up on hooks just the right height for each. They move to the dinner table.*

PAPA BEAR

Why, look. It seems someone has eaten some of my porridge!

MAMA BEAR

Oh my! Looks like someone has eaten some of my porridge too!

BABY BEAR

Papa! Mama! Look! Someone ate *all* my porridge! There's nothing left for me.

> *The family gets up from the table to investigate, moving into the living room.*

PAPA BEAR

Look. Someone has sat in my chair.

MAMA BEAR

Look! Someone has sat in my chair too.

BABY BEAR

Oh no! Someone sat in my chair and broke it to pieces!

> *The family moves to the bedroom door. PAPA BEAR opens it.*

PAPA BEAR

What is going on here? Looks like someone has slept in my bed!

MAMA BEAR

Mine too! Look at the covers. They're still wrinkled.

BABY BEAR

Look! There's a girl in my bed!

> *BABY BEAR has spoken so loudly that GOLDILOCKS awakens, screams, and runs out of the house, never to return.*

THE END

Chapter 17

Millie's High Home

The day after she left Ddrym, Millie woke up disoriented in Agnes's High Home. Had the whole thing been a dream? Was she back home? It looked like she was in her bedroom back home, only it was more expansive somehow. She sat up and rubbed her eyes. She held her breath. Any minute now, Mama Bette would bellow at her from her desk down the hall. A soft knock at the door made Millie jump.

"Silly girl. It's me," Agnes said, bringing in a breakfast tray for Millie. "I'll be right back. Gonna go get mine." Within moments, she came through the door with her own tray. They sat on the bed together, trying to be careful not to spill or knock anything over.

"Agnes, why does this feel like I'm back home in this room? It's spooky in here."

"Oh." She laughed. "That's because I designed my High Home based on Ddrymmian principles—and I learned everything I know about that from you and your family. I so loved the way my spirit felt over there. You can imagine how thrilled my family was about this," she said. They chuckled.

Millie let this sink in as she began eating her breakfast. Agnes had brought a pot of hot, steaming coherence for them both, spiked with sweet haiku; compliment biscuits frosted with sincere regards; and a bowl of fresh intentions, little marble-sized berries, red and round and sweet, as they were at their ripest now. "Agnes, this is so lovely." And for a moment, the light Millie had given her at graduation radiated from her, and Millie smiled, taking it in.

"You know, sweets, not all people know how to keep their Stinglight, once received. I had a feeling you'd be one of the ones who could."

"I had no idea what to do with it. Still don't. I just think of you, and suddenly, I'm warm and full and free."

"That's it. That's what to 'do.' Nothing to it. It's too simple for most."

"Well, here we are, me, the seventh Cinderella Player, and you, the new Mama Bear, on your first day in the Preservation Precinct as a full-time Player! It is a day to celebrate! You ready to meet your new staff?"

"No. I'm so nervous. What am I going to say to them?"

"Just remember, it's *your* High Home. Think of what's important to you. What are your favorite meals, and when do you like to eat? That's what you tell your chef. What do you want your butler to do? What specifically do you want him *not* to do that butlers usually do—"

"I don't know anything about butlers! I mean, except telling delivery people to go around to the service entrance, I don't know what anyone does on a High Home staff."

"OK, so first of all, calm down. Your ears are acting up. Where's your centering stone?"

Millie laughed and got out her stone, working her fingers into it.

Agnes went on, "You're not going to get it perfect on the first day. Everyone has to get used to one another. Just don't be shy about speaking up when things don't go your way. They can't read your mind."

"OK."

"Anyway, you already know the chef is the person who cooks, and the washerwoman you asked for will wash everything washable. The butler is the person who kind of holds the house together. He'll coordinate all the workers who come in for any reason. He'll organize and facilitate all your parties and events. And he'll keep watch over the other employees to keep the quality of service up to snuff."

"Thanks."

"Also! I heard your groundskeeper is a Ddrymmian, so there's one person you won't need to worry about."

Millie brightened. "Really? That's wonderful."

Agnes had to leave for work, so just before going out the door, she said, "I've asked my housekeeper, Emily, to draw you a good bubble bath scented with cedarwood and lavender. And my driver, his name is Liffmer, will drive you to your new Home when it's time. I have to go now. Good luck! And, Millie, you'll do fine." Agnes stopped and smiled at her friend. "Millie." Millie had been looking out the window, far away. She tried again. "Millie."

"Yeah!" she said, pulling herself back into the room from the window.

"You'll be fine. These first few weeks are bound to be bumpy. I know it was hard for you to leave your family. Just try to stay focused on what's in front of you, all right?"

"You're right. Hey, Agnes? Thank you for everything you've done for me."

"Nonsense."

After her bath, Millie took a brief centering walk. Then it was time. Liffmer carried her quietbox out to the car and opened the back door of the long, shining limousine. She was in her best clothes—a Feorge Laker suit with live lilies of the valley at the sleeve edges and down the lapel. She wore her nicest shoes. Her quietbox and the rest of her bags were loaded into the trunk. With her heart still shaking from the enormity of what she was about to do, Millie watched the Precinct city center disappear as they got closer and closer to her High Home.

The paved road turned into a dirt road that turned into two tire tracks in the grass, and then it was just a field. Meanwhile, the trees had gotten more present and prominent. "Ms. Fireflower, I'm afraid this is as far as my directions go. I'm confused."

"Oh, I'm so sorry, Liffmer. I forgot all about the security feature. Please wait here."

She got out of the car and stepped carefully on the grasses as she searched for the tree with the hummingbird carved into the notch where two branches met near the trunk. When she found it, keeping the carving on her left, she walked five paces and made some subtle gestures with her hands. She whispered, "The roads are many. All begin and end in Oneness." Slowly, the thousand-year-old oak shimmered into view. It was a stunning tree in and of itself, but even more magnificent with a Ddrymmian-built High Home nestled into its branches—conceived and constructed with incredible attention to the spirit of the Player who would live there.

She turned around to speak to Liffmer. "There it is."

"I thought I'd seen everything," he said, breathless. "But this is truly the most beautiful sight I've ever laid eyes on."

"Isn't it? Let's go."

He jumped out of the driver's seat, fetched the bags, and helped her down the path and up the stairs to the doorway, where Millie drew up her greeting light. Her soft butter-yellow radiance lit up Liffmer's face behind her, and the door vanished.

She entered, drinking in all the warm touches—small bouquets everywhere, even a lovely offering for the faeries in the living room, which was equipped with a couch and two armchairs upholstered in the wool from the happy sheep on her property. The wooden table was polished and shining. The open shelves of the kitchen held all her simple dinnerware, cups, saucers, and the like.

Special Weather Windows looked out onto the forest in every direction. These were custom-built windows that collected and radiated the heat of the sun in the cold seasons, and in the hot seasons, thousands of invisible perforations opened and cooled the breeze on its way through.

When the driver had brought in all her belongings, he

wished her well and went on his way. She shook Liffmer's hand warmly before he left. Then Millie went over to the windowsill where the faerie offerings were placed. There was an envelope next to it. The letter inside was in Frank's inimitable voice and handwriting.

> *Dear Ms. Fireflower,*
>
> *Welcome to the family of StoryEarth Players, and congratulations on your assignment. I trust you will find your High Home satisfactory. The Precinct's familiarity with Ddrymmian culture is not what it could be, so I enlisted Ms. Grath to help with some of the decisions about the smaller touches. Please feel free to adjust anything not to your liking.*
>
> *Looking forward to your continued embodiments as Mama Bear.*
>
> *Sincerely, and may you say all your lines correctly,*
>
> *Agent Four Seven*

She folded the letter with a smile and put it in a drawer. Then she paced around, waiting, calming her nerves, hoping Flurjahm would like the offerings.

At the appointed hour, Millie walked out to the main entrance of her Home, marked by what she came to call the "hummingbird tree." At exactly eleven, the Transport bus came rumbling in. She waved at the driver, who answered her with a glare. A loud, hissing noise accompanied the opening doors, and her staff disembarked, looking much the worse for wear.

First off was a bear of a man, named Breller, who looked like he hadn't bathed in weeks. Then, a meticulously clean Both-er named Blaze with a picked-the-short-straw look on his face. This was one of the staffers' favorite hires for Millie, as Blaze belonged to a group of beings that was most disdained in Precinct culture. They were too feminine to be seen as men, and too masculine to pass as women. Blaze was extremely defensive, and scanned for conflict everywhere he went. After a momentary lag, two figures came toddling off together—Shank, a Larkshener man, his dark green skin marking him as an elder of his race, helping Lydia, a woman probably older than he, down the stairs. She had white hair and a very chatty, uncertain way about her.

Once they were all off the bus, Millie nodded to the driver, who stepped on the gas, raising as much dust as possible as he peeled off. Her heart sank. Here she was, a Preservation Precinct Player with her brand-new staff, and no one looked happy about it.

"Well," she said, more cheerily than she felt, "I know it was a long drive. You must all be tired. And that bus driver didn't do us any favors, did he?" Silence. She soldiered on. "My name is Millie Fireflower. Welcome."

They each said their name in response, except for the elderly man, who made a sign with his hands that Millie seemed to understand. She hesitated and then signed something back, hoping it was right.

"So why don't I show you to your quarters, and you can change into other clothes if you wish? Then let's meet in the warmroom—uh, the living room—in a half hour." She turned around, bent her fingers into their secret shapes as she spoke the words, and her High Home appeared to them. Despite themselves, they realized this was not a typical High Home.

They traipsed behind Millie in awkward silence, except for Lydia. "My, oh my. Why, this is lovely, isn't it? Who could guess it was even here? I wonder how long it might have taken to build. I remember once, a long time ago, when my son..." They'd all stopped listening.

Millie showed them the grounds, the house in all its glory, and finished with their very nice, modest quarters on the ground floor. Their rooms encircled the trunk of the great tree. The massive tree trunk was energetically fitted with steps all around it that could lift you to the next level. Only Millie and the staff could access that lift. It would take some training to teach them how, but that had been factored into the breaking-in period.

Millie's living space was above theirs, with a second very private area near the top branches, where she could sit and feel the wind, observe the animals, listen for birds, converse with the elements and spirits, and watch for faeries. Throughout her years there, she would come to scan the pathways below, hoping to see someone—Mama Linn, maybe? Perhaps someday Wrem? Drauml?—from her family coming to visit.

Unbeknownst to Millie, her staff had been assigned to her as an insult. Millie had certainly earned the role of Mama Bear on her own merits, but Frank, now Agent Four Seven, had helped too. He'd told her about the upcoming audition and had even been there on the very day when Wrem discovered her in line to try out. Agent Four Seven had almost had to step in during that confrontation. He'd also made some subtle maneuvers during the casting decision. He had deftly managed all the predictable resistance to the *D* word so that Millie never even knew about it.

But the resistance had been there. It was most notable in the lower levels of the Precinct. The agents in charge of staffing her High Home were legally bound to follow through with hiring every kind of employee she requested. But because most of the agents were vehemently opposed to a Ddrymmian holding such an important role, they did what all bureaucrats do in such cases: They followed the letter of the law with cruel precision.

She'd asked for only four helpers: a butler, a chef, a washer-woman, and a groundskeeper. Snickering into their sleeves, they hired the most difficult qualified beings available. Her butler was a Both-er with an infamous chip on their shoulder who, despite being professionally trained and certified, couldn't manage to keep a job longer than two or three months.

Her chef was a mediocre misanthrope who'd only cooked for the Precinct Correctional Facility, which was reserved for lowlifes whose crimes were of a less serious nature than encroaching on the integrity of Story—crimes like theft, or fraud, or assault. Naturally, the PCF wasn't fussy about food quality for their prisoners, but he did have fifteen years of experience.

Her washerwoman turned out to be an elderly, almost infirm woman just barely able to do the job. She was from the farthest eastern edge of the Precinct, the poorest of neighborhoods, but she came with letters of recommendation from the many families she'd worked for in the past.

And her groundskeeper was a Larkshener, and Larksheners were famous for their groundskeeping skills. The only problem was that Larksheners were nonverbal, speaking only with their hands. All were qualified, but all were problematic in their own way.

High Home staff members were usually supremely happy to serve Players in such an important way. But Millie's staff were in it for the money and nothing else. They did their duty without bringing anything extra to the table. The Precinct Agents who had staffed Millie's High Home relished their revenge on this Ddrymmian interloper.

Unfortunately for them, it was her Ddrymmian nature that foiled their plan. Her employees had been bumping into one another every day, trying to get their jobs done. Blaze once told Lydia to "shut up" in a fit of exasperation. And the last straw was when Breller threw a ladle at Blaze for making a derisive comment about his food. Millie called a meeting.

Once they were assembled in her dining room, she lit a candle and said a brief prayer to the spirit of Oneness, then introduced them all to the concept of a Listening. She laid out the rules, made sure they all understood, then opened up the Circle.

Blaze wanted to go first. "Breller, seriously, you need to bathe. Brush your teeth. Something!"

Breller jumped up, hands already fisted.

Blaze threw Millie a look, shaking his head, waving his hand in front of his nose, and saying, "Ms. Fireflower, you don't even know. Whew."

Millie cut in just as Breller was winding himself up, saying, "Why, you little—"

"Stop!" she said. And to her surprise, there was utter silence. "Both of you! Blaze, don't say another word. Breller, you sit back down. Now listen, all of you. This High Home is a Fireflower home, and you are my people, and we are going to sit in this circle until something opens up, and I don't care how long it takes. And that *is* a *threat,* by the way, because I'm Ddrymmian, and I've attended ceremonies that were four and five hours long. So if you want to go to bed at a reasonable hour tonight, you will participate respectfully, starting now. So...Blaze...try again. Find something closer to home. Speak only about yourself and your concerns."

"OK." Blaze had another go at it. "Well...the other thing is, I didn't know that I'd be dealing with a Larkshener here. I don't speak Larksheni. How am I supposed to oversee his work if we can't even communicate?"

"I know, I've been thinking about that. I only know a few phrases in Larksheni myself. Let's come back to this at the end. Thank you. Anything else?"

"Actually, yes. My papers list me as a Both-er, but all the pronouns in the document are 'he,' 'him,' and so on. Anyone with eyes can see the 'she' in me. But I'm not only 'she' either. I would much prefer 'they,' 'their,' and 'them.'"

"OK," Millie said thoughtfully, "let's put that on the list of things to hold in the group. Is that all, or do you have more to say?"

"No, I'm done," Blaze said, strangely calmer.

Millie signaled that it was Breller's turn. He sat in thought for a good minute, clearly reliving the many slights he'd already received in the past few days. Finally, he spoke. "I only ever cooked for prisoners. It never mattered," Breller admitted, "whether it were good or no. In fact, bosses liked it better when it weren't. Then I was cook for the Precinct office cafeteria for a while, samwiches an' such. An' I didn't come lookin' for this job." He said it a little louder than necessary. "They come and give it to me!" He thumped his chest with his thumb. "I were fine at the cafeteria. Don't need no highfalutin work where everybody lookin' down on me, too good fer ma food."

They waited. He added, "That's all. Just dunno why I even got this job, is all."

Millie said, "Thank you, Breller. More to think about. I didn't know you didn't ask for the job. It helps to know that. We'll revisit this in a little while. Lydia?" Millie had been shushing Lydia during everybody else's turn. But when it was Lydia's turn, she just sat there. "Lydia?" Millie prodded.

"I...I...never really been, or had, the whole space to meself to talk in. Dunno what to say."

Millie helped, "Do you have problems here that you haven't had a chance to bring up? As long as it's respectful, you can bring up anything here, and we will listen."

"Well, I...I know I'm on in years. But I done outlived all my folk. My man faded to black years back, buildin' somebody's High Home on the side of a mountain. My son went black from the drink. Damn that Hammer & Nail Bar. Hammered the nails right into his coffin, it did. I'm grateful fer th' work. But my hands hurt, and my back hurts, and I got a heart fulla tears. Ain't nothin' nobody can do about it."

There was a silence in which Lydia's suffering resonated with everyone else's.

"Thank you, Lydia. So sorry for your terrible losses. The body has a way of carrying those losses, but perhaps there is something we can do to help you find some relief. I will sit with it. And now, Shank, do you have anything for us?"

Everyone looked at him, and no one knew what to do next. There was a candlestick in the center of the table. Shank reached out and brought it closer to himself, and no one knew what to expect. There were uncomfortable chuckles.

Millie said to the rest of the group, "Let's just wait and see what happens."

They waited.

Then Shank pointed to the candle, and put his forearms together, pointing upward, and gently wiggled his fingers: *candle*. They all did their version, smiling a little. Shank's face lit up.

Then he got up from his chair and stood by Breller, put his

left hand on Breller's right shoulder, and then brought his own right fist to his own heart. He repeated the gesture with Blaze, then did the same for Lydia. *Workers.*

When he stood by Millie, though, he crossed his arms and put both fists to his chest. *Our boss.* They weren't sure what that meant, but they got close enough. He sat down then and respectfully put the candle back into the center of the table.

Millie said, "Thank you, Shank. Oh, how do we say 'thank you' in Larksheni?"

Shank stretched out his hand and wiggled the fingers, then snapped them shut softly. So they all tried it in his direction, with varying degrees of commitment. His eyes grew shiny, and he looked down.

Millie said, "For my part, I am in unknown territory. I know there are those who are against Ddrymmians, so I must be careful. Some of you may have been hired for this job expressly to punish you or me or both. But we are not going to let that define us. Tomorrow, let's discuss ways of bridging our gaps.

"But I can tell you these things right now. They're in no particular order.

"One, I want to learn more Larksheni from Shank, and perhaps we can do this together. Two, I would love to spend more time in the kitchen and work with Breller to create a great menu we can all be proud of. Three, the new guideline is that we will all refer to Blaze with the 'they' pronoun from now on. We'll probably need reminding, so please feel free, Blaze, OK? And four, Lydia, I know a healer in town. She worked for Agnes's mother. I will make an appointment for you to see her. She is excellent at translating arthritic pains, hearing underneath them, and giving them solace. As to heartache, I, too, carry heartache. I think everyone in this circle knows their own version of it. We should all try to remember this and be more compassionate toward one another. Let us stand up together...

"And please repeat the following words: The roads are many." They repeated. "All begin and end in Oneness." They repeated. Only Breller added, "Whatever that means."

The staff and the Player who had awakened that morning were not the same staff and Player who went to sleep that night.

In the beginning, Blaze oscillated between brooding shame and pugnacious defensiveness of their status as a Both-er. But they soon saw themselves anew through Millie's eyes. They learned to relish their Both-ness, their ability to bring forward a commanding presence to anyone posing a threat while shifting into a stunning graciousness and beauty when Millie entertained.

They excelled as a social secretary. They made sure there was candlelight and fresh flowers at the table for all Millie's meals. They learned the art of timely orders for all the foods, seeds, and supplies for the kitchen, the garden, the grounds, and the faeries. They had to be trained in faeriedom for the placing of offerings, but were a quick learner and soon attained mastery over whatever task they undertook.

Breller, the chef, was sullen, fastidious, and unimaginative, and he hated Both-ers. But he began to soften the more time Millie spent with him in the kitchen. She taught him some of her mother's recipes by finding the way into his sense of humor. His favorite was grumble stew, and he grew especially deft at this delicious dish. She also got Shank to start an herb and vegetable garden just outside the kitchen door, so Breller would have easy access to all the best options. His offerings began to improve. He was very insecure and covered it up with threats and bluster, especially around Blaze. Of her four staff members, Breller was the slowest to come around, but come around he did. He even agreed to a regular bathing schedule.

Lydia's drawback was the incessant talk. Millie was clear about her need for quiet, but also showed her some kindness by ordering her to see the Precinct healer for the pain in her back and her hands. Millie even worked on her energy lines for a while, helping bring a smoother function to her capabilities. Eventually, Lydia was able to find her own silence and do a much better job.

And Shank—well, Shank was a Larkshener, and Larkshen

was part of Ddrym, so for Millie, he was the easiest to understand. But that understanding was more theoretical than practical. While he was adept at landscaping, gardening, and keeping the High Home under cover, the whole property (including Millie) had to learn the Larksheni signs to communicate with him. Millie was too enthralled by the privilege of being a Player to even feel this as an inconvenience. She learned along with the rest of them how to communicate in Larksheni signs. Once everything was in place, Millie was well pleased with her High Home and the cohesive crew she had managed to create.

As to the story she'd been given, she had worn herself deep into the cozy nature of it, settling right in. She'd internalized the script well before her first day, which came one week after she and her staff moved into her High Home.

A few months in, she'd witnessed Jillian Snip, the Player for Wendy in *Peter Pan,* being led away from the Precinct and away to the Nothing after making a tiny mistake in speaking. Millie could not shake Jillian's beseeching eyes as she went by in handcuffs. It seemed so wretchedly unfair, but it was what they'd been trained to expect from the beginning. No one had ever returned from the Nothing. Millie renewed her mastery of every single move, gesture, word, and inflection for her role.

Chapter 18

Making Precinct Friends

Years went by. Millie was twenty-four, then twenty-five, then twenty-six. The story in which she was embedded began to fray at the edges. Her own tiny hints of boredom terrified her. It was like finding a bottle of cyanide among the spices. She did everything she could to banish it. She attended Player Refresh! workshops, even frightened herself with books from the library about the Players who'd been sent to the Nothing, and their varying desperate attempts to die at their own hands before they had to meet that particular fate.

But she was well ensconced in Precinct ways and had developed great friendships—mostly with Players, per protocol. At least once every season (except for Empty season, as it was customary to cease all types of celebrations during Empty season), the cast members of her story would take turns hosting a dinner, and she'd always bring a little something Ddrymmian for Sam, the young Player for Baby Bear, because he pestered her endlessly about her life across the border. Once, it was a game of Stimfott! and she taught everyone, even Lacy, Sam's mother, to play. Tiffany didn't want to play the game, so she was designated scorekeeper, and she was merciless at it.

Sam loved it when it was Millie's turn to throw the party. On his first visit there, he and his mother experienced the vision of arriving, and he said, "Mommy! Can I go climb it?"

Lacy looked at Millie.

"Of course, you can, Sam," Millie said. "Just be careful. The back side of the tree likes to sleep and sometimes gets grumpy if it's awakened from a nap. Make sure to pay your respects calmly and quietly before you go up."

The grown-ups smiled and entered the magical High Home. Seth had brought a lovely bouquet of flowers. He seemed to trip all over himself that evening. Millie was eventually able to put him at ease.

She also tried to cultivate connections outside her story. She loved palling around with Players like Guy Flacksom (Captain Hook), Sherry Nicks (a crowd member in *The Princess Bride*), and Stick (Tigger).

Of all the Players she knew, Stick was the biggest surprise. He was a dour, lethargic pain in the ass, but he had such a dry sense of humor that his was always the loudest table wherever he showed up to eat. He would sit in his deep slouch, chain-smoking and muttering one-liners into conversations, which resulted in roars of laughter, drawing more people to the table. This caustic, morose alcoholic embodied one of the most cheerful, confident, energetic roles in all StoryEarth. Preservation had a knack for casting, and Stick as Tigger was the best proof of all. He would fade to black before that role went to anyone else.

As for her friend Frank, she saw him once on her way to work and waved. "Frank! Hi!"

He bent his head and walked briskly by without speaking to her. She caught up to him, saying, "Hey! Have I violated a rule? I thought this was allowed. Frank, we know each other from before my appointment as Player, so it's OK, right?"

"Yes, but...the lines are too murky. I'm not sure what the regulations are with respect to Ddrymmian Players. Please refrain from addressing me in the future unless it's for business. And please use Agent Four Seven when you do."

She remembered his dogged resolve to restore his family

name and figured this was the main engine in his life, so she respected his wish. But it felt strange to remember they'd once been so close that, for a crucial time in their youth, she and Agnes had been his only friends. Except for the first Mama Bear audition, two subsequent callbacks, and the exchange just described, she hadn't seen him since high school.

Ever since Millie had given Agnes the Stinglight, their bond as deepfriends had only grown. Agnes had learned from Wrem all about tree energies and from Mama Bette about gardening and herbs. She had gotten to know the Fireflower kitchen much better than her own in the Precinct. And Millie had even taught her how to put out the morning and evening faerie offerings. She was the perfect bridge between Millie's two worlds. That was, until Millie chose the one over the other.

Mama Linn had sent one hologram telling her all was well and that Wrem and Drauml were expecting a baby during Flicker season. But that had been two years ago. There was nothing since then, except for Drauml's footcall announcing to the general community that she'd borne a boy, and his name was Kite. Millie had tried to send holograms, but they always showed up as "unseen" in her HCb. She sent gifts to Wrem and Drauml's child, but she never knew if they'd arrived. At least they weren't returned.

She felt that she'd lost that part of her life forever. Several times, she used her feet. She sent out her message in treespeak to Mama Linn, Mama Bette, Wrem, and Drauml. "I love you all, and I think of you often." The only messages she got back were little tremors of acknowledgment from Mama Linn and Drauml.

> *The family of three bears enters from stage left, having been out to pick berries. One by one, they hang their jackets up on hooks just the right height for each. They move to the dinner table.*

PAPA BEAR

Why, look. It seems someone has eaten some of my porridge!

MAMA BEAR

Oh my! Looks like someone has eaten some of my porridge too!

(I've never gotten why we all left the house if the porridge was just put down on the table.)

(Blah, blah, blah...the rest of everyone's lines)

BABY BEAR

Oh no! Someone sat in my chair and broke it to pieces!

(OK, can we talk about the chair? If it was so "just right," then why did it break? So many problems with this story.)

(Blah, blah, blah...the rest of everyone's lines)

The End

Chapter 19

The Seed of
the Switch

More years passed. Two? Three? Millie had lost count. She was twenty-eight years old. The days went by in an endless succession of too hot, too cold, just right, too hard, too soft, just right. There were times when she thought heretical thoughts, when she was bored to starving, when she questioned why this was even a story worth telling in the first place, much less embodying. It was becoming a chore, a hard one—despite all the perks, which she rarely took advantage of anyway.

Of course, she didn't dare speak of this to anyone, not even Agnes. It was impossible to know whether Preservation was listening in, and the risk of losing everything and being sent to the Nothing was too great.

So she tried to make the best of it every day. And at the end of the day, she did love coming home to her beautiful tree house, even if she sometimes wished for more, for a different story, for anything to change, to be different, to happen in a surprising way.

It was the end of a particularly long day for Millie. Seth was trying to catch up with her as she ran out the stage door. "Hey, Mama Bear!" he yelled at her retreating figure.

She turned around and yelled back, "Seth, please. My name is Millie."

He stopped, holding a heart-shaped box of chocolates. "OK, sorry," he said softly. "These are for you." He offered her the box, walking slowly toward her.

"Oh, Seth. I mean...you really shouldn't do this."

"What do you mean? I thought you liked chocolate."

"I do, but...well..."

"They're just chocolates. Take them."

"OK," she said, resigned. "Thank you."

Then he asked her, "Mama Bear, are you OK?" Old habits die hard.

"Yeah, sure. Why?"

"I dunno. You just seemed a little off today."

"No, I'm just fine, Seth. See you tomorrow. And thanks for the chocolates. But don't bring me any more gifts. And call me Millie when we're off set, OK?"

"OK."

Even Sam had never called her anything but "Mama." She'd grown so impatient with the Goldilocks story that she didn't know what to do.

Her body made its way to the Plot Pivot, where she found a corner booth in the back and sat down, hoping Agnes might show up. She ordered a flaming argument, up, no chaser. A young woman shyly asked her for her autograph, which she gave almost without looking. Then she saw Agnes's ball cap with her signature mess of hair stuffed up inside it, and in that same moment, Agnes felt her Sting friend's presence. She joined her at the back, slumping over the table.

"I am so glad you're here," Agnes said, getting settled. "I can't take this one more day."

Millie looked up at the surveillance cameras with a question in her face. She knew the rules, and disparaging the Player work was an infraction that could get you into real trouble.

"Oh, Millie, relax. They've known from the beginning that I didn't want this role."

"Really? Are you sure it's safe to talk here? I just had somebody ask me for my autograph."

Agnes thought about it. "Yeah, you know, let's go to my house. Or...wait. Can we go to your place?"

"Of course!" Millie said, glad for the company. They downed their drinks, paid, and left for Millie's High Home.

Deep into the forest and almost to the Ddrymmian border, stood the hummingbird tree. When they reached it, Millie spoke the syllables, and lifted the veil that hid her magnificent High Home from the rest of the world. In an instant, the ancient oak, Millie's magical living quarters, appeared, welcoming them with its spirit. Agnes never tired of this moment.

Blaze greeted them at the bottom of the stairs and asked if they needed to set an extra place at the dinner table. Millie was desperate to be alone with Agnes, so she told Blaze to please ask everyone to go to their own homes and leave them to themselves for the night. Shank wanted to stay for protection, but Millie was adamant.

She signed to him, *The shield is protection enough. No one even knows we're here.*

Shank responded, gesticulating, *How can you be sure no one followed you here? You are too trusting, Lady Millie.*

Millie moved her hands and fingers nimbly, replying, *The veil goes down when you leave, and the energy shield will be up. We are invisible and safe. Go home.*

He was respectful but adamant. *I will station myself at the outermost point.*

She knew there was no arguing. And she trusted him. Master of illusion, he shifted himself into a sleeping squirrel and slept on the leaves at the edge of her High Home border.

Once they were alone, Millie made herself and Agnes a secrets cocktail with a twist of fate. Then they sipped in silence. After a good nine breaths, Agnes went first. "Millie, I know we've talked about this before. But if I have to stick my foot out for that wretched glass slipper one more time, I'm going to lose it. I'm going to scream."

Millie replied, "You've always said. But I can't imagine not wanting to embody Cinderella. I would die for that job. You wanna talk about 'can't do it anymore'? Step into my paws for a while. My big dramatic moments have me parroting Papa Bear. 'Someone has eaten my porridge too!' and 'Someone has sat in my chair as well!' I'm out of my mind with boredom. What I wouldn't give to be in your glass slippers."

"You don't know what you have, Millie. My mother and her mother and her mother all had this role. I didn't even get to try for anything else. I got railroaded right into the audition. It wasn't even me who applied for it! My mother announced it to me. And it's either wretched servitude or grand palaces and pretty dresses. I want...I want...what you have. Your story unfolds inside a cozy little home, and it's about a cozy, loving little family. The simplicity is something I've yearned for all my life."

"I know," Millie said. The drink loosened her tongue a bit. "Quit complaining, my unhappy friend. Let's just switch places." They laughed and started riffing.

"We'll stop time, and then—" Agnes said, giggling.

Millie picked up where she left off. "Um, wait, we'll stop time and then run like blazes, you to my story, me to yours." They got up and mimed running to change places.

Agnes had a go. "And...and...I know! Wait! We somehow have the costumes all ready, and we jump into them, and—poof!—time's up. It starts again, and you're Cinderella."

"And you're Mama Bear."

"And nobody notices!" They howled with laughter, squeezing their legs together to keep from peeing.

It took a moment for the laughter to become an uncomfortable silence with eye contact. Millie broke it. "Well, that's not going to happen."

"I know," Agnes said. "But I sure wish it could."

"But it's not."

"But, Millie, think of it—"

"Aggie, stop it. It's not. Don't even think about it."

"But that's the thing, Millie. I don't even get to think anymore. I used to think all the time. It was my favorite thing to do when we were kids...to think, to imagine."

"Well, I'm bored to black," Millie said. "And I'd love to change places, but I'm not fond of the idea of being sent to the Nothing and losing all my benefits. My choosing this pretty much destroyed my family as it was. All I need now is to fail at it and destroy them again."

"OK," Agnes surrendered.

They talked of other things. Millie made a delicious, simple grumble that she'd learned from her mama Linn, with justification salad. Agnes helped her with the dishes. They laughed at some in-jokes that no one but a Player would find funny.

It got late, and Agnes had her coat on, ready to leave. She had her hand on the door when she turned around and asked Millie, "If you knew it couldn't fail—I mean, really knew that we could switch places without anyone ever knowing—would you do it?"

"In a heartbeat."

Chapter 20

Agnes Approaches Mix

For months, the idea wouldn't leave Millie alone. The conversation had somehow germinated the possibility of a switch and now it was incubating somewhere in her world. Millie worried that the Precinct had gotten wind of her dissatisfaction or that their conversation at the Plot Pivot had been overheard or that they'd built listening devices in her own home that she didn't know about.

She reminded herself that Preservation cared only that each story was told in exactly the same way each time—same words, same body, same costumes, same message, same ending—without alteration, without fail, without end. And she went about her life, trying as best as she could to enrich it in the Precinct with the continuing education courses available to her.

On Saturday night, the bartenders at the Pirate's Parrot could barely keep up. Everyone was in rare form. When Mixko came through the door, he found his friends and sat down. They had worked together as Watchers for years, developing into a close-knit team. They were each assigned certain stories to watch all day, looking for infractions.

Fobbler, the more flamboyant member of the team, sat with them at the bar. Fob greeted his friend Mix with a good-natured threat. "Enjoy it while it lasts, you sorry excuse for a goblin-inker. Just know: I'm coming after you."

Everyone knew this must be the latest installment in their ongoing prank feud. These feuds were the source of much entertainment—and not only between the team members. Anyone who knew them relished in the details of whatever prank had last been visited upon Mix or Fob. Bink enjoyed these pranks the most, being the youngest Precinct Watcher, with all of two nines and a handful of years.

"Oh joy. What did he do this time, Fob?" Bink asked.

"Spit it out." Other friends gathered. They wanted blood.

"The bastard hid all my pants, all of them."

There was a low, appreciative "whooooaaah" that culminated in spasms of laughter.

"That's rich," Jayth said, an old friend of Mix's, also a Watcher.

"How?" was the biggest question here.

Hiding Fobbler's pants was no small endeavor. His defining characteristic was his pants. Of course, as a Precinct Agent, he never got to wear them (except within the walls of his own house) because it would "reflect poorly on the department." But he was famous for his collection, and any time he hosted a gathering, no one missed the party—if only just to see which pants he'd be wearing.

The more colorful or crazy the design, the better he liked them. He had pants shaped like a toaster (where your legs went in the slots). He had psychedelic paisley pants that created sensations in the body of the onlooker. He had pants made of singing wool: some that sang the blues, some that sang opera, some that sang folk songs. He had pants that did the walking for him. He had pants that clung to his skin and pants that flowed in the breeze. He even had pants that vibrated, but he couldn't wear those, even to his own parties. He had hundreds of pairs. Fobbler had built a special room onto his small home just to accommodate them.

That Mix could even find room to store them all after stealing them, much less the time to accomplish this feat, was a mark of his brilliance. He tackled the space issue by studying the molecular structure of each pair. Once armed with that information, he created a rough digital contraption that miniaturized them to about the size of one's hand. Not one for half measures, Mix then decided to hide all the pants in plain sight—adding a delicious degree of difficulty. Fobbler had to take a day of sick leave just to find them all, the first pair being the most difficult, as they were all hidden outside, and he had to go out in his underwear to begin.

Finally, she arrived in jeans and a T-shirt, ball cap on with her blond hair stuffed into it, no jewels. Mix felt his body relax for the first time since he'd seen her last. He loved her dressed-down look. Her family hated it. Tonight she looked even more low-key than usual, almost like she didn't want to be recognized. He bought a round for Fob and the rest of his coworkers, then bid them all adieu and joined his friend at one of the booths in the back.

"Hey, Agnes, what's up? Your message was a little weird."

She looked down and fiddled with her cocktail napkin. "I don't know, Mix, it's the same old crap. I'm just so...I don't know...tired of—you know what? Forget it. I'll figure it out. I mean, look at you," she said, admiring his face, fresh with recent laughter and pumped up with his friends' clear respect. "You're doing what you want to do, and you're having a blast at it."

"Hold on," he said. "You think that being a watcher looking for infractions all day is what I want to do with my life? Agnes, the fun I'm having has nothing to do with work. I'm so bored that I have to fill the time by pranking my friends. I got Fob so good the other day—"

"What did you want to do with your life?"

"What?"

"What did you want with your life? Before."

"Ah, come on, you gotta hear this. I hid...*all* his *pants.* Fobbler's pants!"

"Brilliant. So what did you want to do with your life?"

After a long pause, he said, "It doesn't matter," and the life drained out of his face.

The server brought their drinks. Agnes waited till she left. "Really? I don't believe you. But humor me—if you aren't doing what you want to do now, what would you rather be doing, like, long term?"

Because it was Agnes asking, he tried to answer her shyly, "I don't know." He fiddled with the cocktail napkin. He looked around, ran his hands through his hair. He drank some. Employing a Ddrymmian technique she'd learned from Millie, she waited.

Finally, he said, "I guess I wanted to get inside the heart of how things work. Machines, electronics and stuff. Make them do amazing things. I've always loved the insides of clocks, computers, cameras, mics. But you already know that."

"Yes, I do," she said pointedly. She caught his eyes and held on.

He looked away before he spoke. "So why'd you ask me the question?"

"Because"—she was starting to have dangerous fun with this—"I have an idea that is so perfect for you but so big I'm not sure I can even talk about it. The only one who could even help me imagine it would be you. We can't really talk here. We need to go to Millie's place."

"Millie? Why? What does she have to do with anything? And anyway, I can't go to Millie's place. You know the rules. I don't know her."

She put down her drink. "Are you actually going to say to me with a straight face, *Oh, I couldn't possibly. It's against the prior friendship regulation?*"

"Ag—"

Laying it on thick now, bringing the back of her hand to her brow, she said, "*We weren't acquainted before I got my permanency papers—*"

"Come on, Ag. I just don't want to push it." He looked around like he was worried about something. "I've been trying to lay low for a bit. Agent Four Seven is on my ass all the time."

He'd known for a long time that Millie was Agnes's best friend. What he hadn't known, because he didn't like to think about it, was how much it bothered him. Something about it, something about the way she almost literally lit up when she mentioned Millie.

"Right...right," she said. She paused to think for a moment. "Right. Well...would you mind taking a walk with me sometime, like, out in the forest? I'd rather talk out there anyway. That wouldn't be against the rules, would it?"

"Not any of the ones I care about," he answered, and they laughed, catching each other's eyes again for a little longer than usual. They got up to leave.

Once outside, he began to feel the loosening effects of his meanings mojitos. "When did you say we were meeting?"

"I didn't," she said, grinning at him. "Let's do it this Saturday. It's Flicker season. The air is crisp and cool, so wear a jacket, OK?"

"OK, *Mom.*"

"Yeah, well, wear a jacket. You don't always take the best care of yourself, you know." She hugged him. "So next Saturday." She turned him toward her and held him at arm's length. "Mix, look at me."

He did.

"Next Saturday at ten." She started to release him, but as he drew her back in, she resisted and said, "Say it back to me so I know you got it."

"Next Saturday...ten." Then he embraced her. "Hey...Agnes," he said into her neck.

"What?"

"You're the best friend I've got. Do you know that?"

"Mix, when are we meeting?"

"Um...tomorrow at eleven."

She playfully punched him, and he doubled over in mock pain, grinding out the words, "Next Saturday, ten o'clock." Then she got into her little car and drove away.

> *The family of three bears*
> *enters from stage left,*
> *having been out to pick*
> *berries. One by one, they*
> *hang their jackets up*
> *on hooks just the right*
> *height for each. They move*
> *to the dinner table.*

(You can do this, Millie. Come on, think of the beautiful High Home you live in.)

PAPA BEAR

Why, look. It seems someone has eaten some of my porridge!

MAMA BEAR

(Just do your lines and be done with it.)

Oh my! Looks like someone has eaten some of my porridge too!

(Blah, blah, blah...the rest of everyone's lines)

MAMA BEAR

(Focus. Put your heart into it. They'll know if you don't.)

Look! Someone has sat in my chair too.

(Blah, blah, blah...the rest of everyone's lines)

MAMA BEAR

(Oh, All Things Told, if I have to say this one more time—no, focus! Remember the benefits. The Precinct sets aside funds for

my family every season to help in case of need. I'm doing this for my family.)

Mine too! Look at the covers. They're still wrinkled.

(Blah, blah, blah...the rest of everyone's lines)

THE END

Chapter 21

The Secret Summit

By the time Agnes and Mix finally met up in the forest, he'd forgotten how much more beautiful she was when she got away from the city. It was like old times, when they'd been in permanency training together during the summer after high school at the StoryEarth Institute—him in the Precinct Watcher courses and her in the Player courses. As they walked together through the trees, he could smell her intoxicating perfume, and there was a freedom in her conversation that he didn't know he'd been missing. After the initial pleasantries, he pushed her for what was on her mind.

"I put on that ball gown, and I feel like I'm suffocating. All I want to do is be in my jammies and *read* a story instead of being it."

"I know, Aggie. You've been singing this song for a long time though. It will pass. Have you ever tried pranking someone in the cast? Takes the boredom out of things from time to time. I can help you."

"Yes, well, that's kind of what I want to talk to you about, only it would be a gigantic prank."

"Awesome!"

"But I need your help."

"I'm in."

They walked for a while in silence while the sun spied on

them through the leaves. Squirrels raced up and down the branches. The percussion of a woodpecker played underneath a diffused little orchestra of breezes and birds in branches. She began explaining, "I'm not alone."

His hand went into hers without thinking. She didn't pull away. It threw her off track for a moment. She smiled and looked at the ground as they went on walking.

"No, you're not," he said. "I'm here for you. We've gotten through darker times than th—"

"No. Well, yes, and I thank All the Words in the World for you. I do. But I meant I'm not alone in being unhappy with the role I've been assigned as a Player."

"So? Life is hard for everyone in *some* way."

"Yeah, but I, um—how do I say this?"

He stopped walking and faced her. "Spiked stars, Aggie, what are you talking about? Just spit it out."

"Mama Bear. Millie Fireflower for Mama Bear."

"What about her?"

"She is unhappy in *her* role."

"Oh, well, that changes everything." He let go of her hand and picked up speed, muttering, "After all the controversy it took to get her in a Player role, now it's not good enough for her? I usually don't side with the Precinct, but I gotta tell you, Aggie, I don't feel sorry for her. They did the best they could. She's probably living in some palace up in the mountains, so she should be grateful for whatever she's got."

Agnes was keeping pace with him but suddenly stopped. "Mix, I need you to trust me now...look at me."

"What are you doing? Ag?"

"Just trust me, Mix."

"I trust you, Aggie, but—"

"Settle down. I want you to look in that direction."

He was too confused to resist.

She made a shushing gesture, and put her hand on the hummingbird tree for a moment. Then she took a deep breath, and turned toward where Mix was looking. Nothing noteworthy there, really. Agnes made the hand gestures necessary, and exhaled into these words: "The roads are many. All begin and end in Oneness."

Mixko's eyes grew wide as the air around them shimmered. His hair lifted off his scalp, and he thought he heard a sound— something like a humming, only the sound wasn't aural; it was physical. The sound tingled the air and his eyes and his mind into ever greater clarity as the veil grew thinner and thinner, till Millie's High Home showed itself in all its cozy magnificence.

Shank appeared with it, though, directly in front of Mixko, and he brandished a shovel like a weapon, ready to level him to the ground should he signal any ill intent. Agnes stepped in front of her friend. She'd learned just enough Larksheni to make a beginner's sign of *safe man, friend* to Shank, so Shank stood down.

Mix remembered how they'd laughed in the monitor rooms when they'd heard how Millie's High Home had been staffed. They were all sure her staff would implode within weeks. But this loyal Larkshener had obviously been there for many years.

Shank led the two to the front door. Agnes rang the bell and knocked a secret rhythm. The door dissolved, and Blaze was there to welcome them in. While Agnes made the introductions, Millie came running down the stairs from the upper branches.

"Agnes! You made it. And you must be Mixko. I'm so glad to meet you. She has said such wonderful things about you."

Mix was disarmed by her immediate, easy warmth. She was well-spoken and gracious—nothing like the odd, uneasy Ddrymmians Mix had heard about. Millie led them into the living room, where there was a tray with stacks of discussion sandwiches, a plate of gossips and frosted tells, and a little bowl of tiny, savory ideas.

"Can I get you something to drink? We have some nice, hot conversation tea, or if you'd like something a little stronger, I can bring you a snifter of conclusions."

"No, tea is fine."

"Me too, Millie. Tea is great," Agnes said, so relieved to be over the first hump.

Once they were all settled with their teacups, Millie gave Blaze a long list of errands to do. They were more than happy to get out and about on a Saturday. "By the way, I've given Breller the day off, and he's gone to see his family. He'll be back by supper. But Shank will need to go with you to buy more seeds and supplies for the new greenhouse he's building. Oh! And I almost forgot. Lydia has gotten herself ready. You must take her to the healer. She has an appointment at ten forty-five this morning and will need to be picked up by noon. I told Shank to harness the horses up to the bigger wagon. It will be more comfortable for everyone."

As much as she had loved the idea of cars as a young girl, Millie found herself insisting on using the Ddrymmian modes of transportation at her High Home. The only exception was for official events, where she was obligated to arrive in a long, black limousine.

When they were all gone, Agnes started the meeting. "So, Mix, here's what we want to talk about—"

Millie cut her off abruptly. "Agnes, wait. Just for extra measure, I'd like us to use a heartspeak."

"What's that?" Mix was a risk junkie, but he usually wanted to know what he was risking.

"It's a NetherJunctures practice. We create an orb in which whatever is said cannot be seen or heard by any other living thing outside the orb."

"What? How do you know? The Precinct would have known about this if it were an actual, and actual—"

"This is a fairly common practice where I grew up. I understand how it seems superstitious to anyone with a honed sense of logic. But I can assure you, it's real. My mothers used to use it when they didn't want me to hear their conversations." She paused, remembering. "It's real."

She shifted her energy, made eye contact with him gently, and asked, "Are you okay with trying it? If you're not, I won't do it."

He looked at Agnes. She was utterly calm.

"No. Go ahead," he said. "Do I need to, um—"

Millie replied, "You don't need to do anything except to come close for a moment."

Mix and Agnes walked toward her and stood a little closer than was comfortable. Millie summoned her own bright light and let it grow within her until it transcended her skin and enveloped Agnes and Mix, whose eyes grew wide as the light emanated from her. (In the Precinct, they've heard that Ddrymmians work with light, but few have actually experienced it, so a lot of them don't even think it's true.) Then she summoned a deep blue light from within herself, spread her arms wide in a circle, and turned in every direction while the light found its purpose there. And finally, she stood still. During that pause, Mix and Agnes felt the third layer seal them off from everything else. Now the three of them were inside a sphere that protected them in four ways—from being seen, heard, misunderstood or betrayed.

Mix looked around. He'd watched it all happen, but nothing looked different.

Millie said, "You won't notice the protections of this heartspeak from within it. But they're there. Also, one more thing. It is a sacred law of the heartspeak: The members of the heartspeak—especially those who initiate them—are oath bound not to judge or retaliate in any way, not ever, no matter what is revealed inside it."

Mix was processing too much to even have his first questions about all this. He remained silent.

"Mix." Agnes snapped him back into the moment. She stated their case. "We want to switch places."

He stepped back to allow them the room to do that.

"No," she said, laughing. "I want to be Mama Bear, and Millie wants to be Cinderella."

Mix just looked at her.

"Mix, you're a genius. You can do anything. You can figure it out. We have all the time in the world."

He didn't know how to tell her. This could never happen, never in a million years.

"Listen," Agnes went on. "Here's the thing. What matters to the Precinct is the preservation of Story integrity, right? In other words, the exact words said in the exact order by the right character, who wears the exact same clothes every time. Done with heart and commitment. Every day."

"Yes." He was still trying to catch up.

"So what do they care if it's her or me embodying the story?"

"Well...they care because...because—well, they care! A Player switch has never been done. Look, if they let you guys do it, then everyone disenchanted with their role would...I mean, it would be chaos."

"I know, but they wouldn't be 'letting us do it.' They wouldn't even know it was being done. It's perfect."

"Well, it's not perfect unless you actually do it without them finding out."

"Yeah. That's where you come in."

Millie watched this conversation carefully, trying to gauge where Mix stood.

"Oh, Aggie, please. I don't want to put you in jeopardy like that. Plus, no offense, but I don't know Millie, and I don't know if she can do Cinderella really. I mean, you're taking an enormous risk here. Plus your mother. What are you gonna do about that?"

Agnes was unmoveable. "Forget about my mother. Mix, think about how embodiment works. It's not like we just switch costumes. It's *embodiment*. So when we do our work as Players, we actually become the characters we're playing. She'll bloom into Cinderella's actual face and body, just like I do. And like— oh, who plays Charlotte from Charlotte's Web?"

"Stephanie Pisque."

"Stephanie. Think about it, Mix. Stephanie's a big woman. And when she embodies, she morphs into this perfect little spider. No one can tell it's her any more than they'll be able to tell it's Millie as Cinderella or me as Mama Bear."

"Ag." He really looked at her. "If we get caught, it's the Nothing for all of us."

Silence as they took it in. Coming from the risk junkie among them, it carried a greater weight.

"But only you and Millie and I would know."

"And all your castmates."

"Yes, but they won't know till the moment of the switch, and after that, no one will want to be implicated as a co-conspirator. They would have to accompany us to the Nothing. So no one's going to say anything."

"And *how* is this supposed to happen?" he asked.

Millie stepped in now. "It's a very long shot. But maybe there's a way to disconnect all the timekeepers as well as the cameras for each set on all the sets of StoryEarth—"

Mix laughed. The preposterousness of it.

"Stay with me, Mix. Just hear us out. Maybe there's a way to disconnect them for long enough that we can run to each other's sets—we're lucky they're so close together—change costumes, and be in place when everything is connected again. I mean, it might take a year or two to research and set up.

"We would, of course, train and rehearse during that time. It seems right on the verge of being possible. And whenever you need to discuss the details with us, we can meet here or at Aggie's, always in a heartspeak."

"One problem," Mix said, holding his hand up. "All this is moot because I'm not supposed to have any interaction with you, Millie. I didn't know you from before my Preservation permanency commitment."

Millie thought about this for a moment. "OK, but maybe we could meet at a Preservation-sanctioned gathering or someone else's party. Then we'd—Wait! The annual StoryEarth Goodwill Ball! That's coming up next month. We would have met there anyway. So anytime after the ball, we can talk to each other without reproach."

He thought for a long time. You could see his formidable intelligence flirting with his respect for this mother of all pranks. You could see him fighting with his survival instincts. You could see him *wanting* to give this to Agnes. The women kept still.

Finally, he broke the silence. "I am not saying I will do this. I'm not even saying it can be done. I am only saying I will think about it. And we won't discuss it or have any contact whatsoever—including you, Aggie—until the ball. Is that understood?" Turning to Agnes, he said, "And I was never here."

"Understood," Millie and Agnes said at the same time.

"I need to go now."

Millie rose and offered her hand. "I know you were tricked into coming here and meeting with me. But I thank you from the bottom of my heart for just considering this idea, even if nothing ever comes of it. Thank you."

"You're welcome," he said. "And thank you for showing me your beautiful High Home. It's extraordinary."

As Agnes left with him, she threw a hopeful wink in Millie's direction.

Shank escorted them to the edge of the yard, still a little wary of Mixko. Once they were on their way, Mix turned around to get one more look at the High Home, and nothing of it remained, just the forest—leaves filtered by the sunlight flickering through them, a light breeze that made everyone pull their coats in a little, sparrows flitting here and there, the occasional scurrying chipmunk, and some ancient oaks. He realized, in that moment, he wouldn't have been able to identify where Millie's High Home was, even if his life depended on it.

Mix and Agnes held hands all the way back to their cars at the turn off where they'd met up.

Chapter 22

Agent Four Seven's Challenge

Over and over, Agnes and Millie stifled their delirium at even just the prospect of their switch. As so often happens when suffering is about to end, the suffering itself seems more bearable. Millie felt the old affection for her castmates. She embodied her role with renewed presence. All its original sweetness came back to her.

And for Agnes's part, every time she put on the dress, she was almost happy at the way it dug into her skin, imagining how much more comfortable she would be as Mama Bear. She brought an extra measure of grace to her role as Cinderella, feeling magnanimous toward everyone on set.

Agnes and Millie managed to behave as ordinary friends for the whole month leading up to the Goodwill Ball. They met only as often as they normally would—always at the Plot Pivot and often in groups of other friends. They sometimes shared meals together, talking about nothing and everything as though their whole lives weren't shifting right beneath their feet.

Neither of them had any contact with Mix, who was feeling his own version of that renewed commitment to his work. Despite his reputation as a maverick, he had real integrity and was always the first one in and the last one out. He liked his codes clean and all the connections to the cameras clear.

He did hours of thinking after work and got very little sleep, doodling on papers that he would then burn, lest they be decoded. Sitting back in his chair in the monitor room with his feet up on his desk and twiddling a pencil back and forth between his fingers, he ran a thousand scenarios. The idea of the heart-speak haunted him, and he wondered if he could ever learn to make one himself.

Everyone had left for the day, and Mix assumed he was alone. He jumped when the door to the monitor room opened. "Agent Four Seven, sir."

"Mr. Stenfar."

"What can I do for you?" Mix got up from his chair. "Is there something wrong?"

"Well, yes. It's an issue that begins innocuously enough, but it can lead to the disintegration of all that we're about here at Preservation."

"Sir."

Agent Four Seven hesitated.

"I know," Mix interjected, wanting to get ahead of this one, "the Pooh incident. I really think he meant 'to the room' when he said 'into the room.' He was probably exhausted."

"Well, there's no excuse for it. We provide the best working conditions in all StoryEarth. He had no cause to be exhausted. Anyway, he's been dealt with. But that's not what concerns me. The watchers caught that breach and tagged it. What concerns me are the breaches that were *not* caught, not even picked up by the cameras installed on the sets."

Mixko was perplexed. "How could that be? We just installed new ones last season. They were supposed to be even more powerful than the last ones. What did they miss?"

"I stationed some spot checkers on various sets. Been moving them around every couple of days. One of my guys on the *Secret Garden* set noticed that the Player for Master Colin Craven screamed only three times instead of four. When they realized that no consequences had been exacted on the Player, they asked me why."

"I see."

"Mr. Stenfar, I know we've had our differences. But you are the best watcher we have, even though your employment records are replete with internal complaints for disruptive behavior."

Mix took it for the backhanded compliment it was. "Sir."

"So I also know that you've designed systems before. It was in your school records that your design for the mapping system used by the bus drivers made a substantial difference in their efficacy, cut their drive time by a good twenty percent."

"It did. But I haven't worked on anything that complex in quite some time."

"Oh, I think you probably have," Agent Four Seven said, looking at him square in the face. He was no fool. The Fobbler's pants incident had no doubt made its rounds.

Mix said nothing and maintained a straight face. "What do you want me to do?"

"I want you to create an entirely new surveillance system."

"But—"

"I know. We've upgraded the current surveillance system many times, but they're just not cutting it. Given the recent undetected breaches, I think we need something a little outside the box. Top quality, but something no one has ever thought of before. This is why I came to you."

"Thank you, sir. I'm honored. But this will take some time."

"I want to announce the new system at the next Preservation Precinct Convention. See to it that the system is in place by the first day of that convention."

"Sir, to be honest, that only gives me six seasons, which isn't nearly enough time. It means a complete revamp of the entire system throughout the whole Precinct. I mean, even with my guys helping me—"

"Oh no, Mr. Stenfar. No one else can know about this. Your continued employment here depends on your keeping this endeavor, and my request for it, in the strictest confidence. I have complete faith you will come through with the desired result at the appointed time.

"It's the cameras. I think that's our weak point. Consider designing something where they not only pick up visuals, but maybe detect body heat, eye movements of the Players. I don't know. Anything that can help us truly be...the *Preservation Precinct*. That helps us preserve the integrity of each story."

Just before closing the door behind him, Agent Four Seven said, "I'm going to promote you to Head of Watcher Systems, which will mean an increase in pay but a reduction in your actual watcher hours. You'll still be coming in half days for watcher duty, but the rest of your time will be spent on this project."

"Of course, sir. Thank you, sir."

Four Seven left happy—ish. He hated Stenfar's cocky, entitled nature and had long wished to wipe the wry smile off his face. This was a win-win. If this cocky bastard was up to the task, the Precinct would have an unimpeachable system, the best imaginable, for which Four Seven would get the credit and, no doubt, a promotion. If he wasn't, Four Seven could sack him and never have to look at his smug face again.

Mixko Stenfar sat back in his chair, his brain on fire. He had two conflicting undercover requests. He had to deliver the one while secretly accomplishing the other. Each one posed almost insurmountable challenges. Each one was intended to thwart the other's success. Either one could end his career. Now he was happy.

Chapter 23

The Annual
StoryEarth
Goodwill Ball

Beings in the Precinct had a love/hate relationship with the StoryEarth Goodwill Ball. Yes, the Precinct provided 90 percent of all StoryEarth employment—for the Precinct Agents, the Security, the Watchers, and the administrative staff, as well as for Player positions and all their personal High Home staff members, all the way down to set design, makeup, costuming, script supervision, janitorial services, and the like.

But the strictures and harsh penalties for the slightest mistakes, the straitjacket environment, and the sense of always being watched definitely took its toll. So every year on the first full moon after Sorting season, the Precinct threw an extravagant bash to which every single being in the Precinct was invited. All the "previous friendship" regulations were suspended for twenty-four hours. And they spared no expense—only the best musicians, light shows, and entertainment.

With the Goodwill Ball only two days away, Millie found herself oscillating between excitement and dread. They would be meeting Mix there, and Agnes would "introduce" her to him. But would the new Precinct cameras see through it? Would they know she had met him before? What had Mix decided? Had he determined it was even possible? How would they talk about it? They'd waited so long without making a single false move; the tension was unbearable.

Millie had to choose a gown. She'd done this every year, and every year it was harder than the last. She flipped through all the hangers in her closet. The golden one. She loved the slight train at the back and the boatneck trimmed with pearls, but for some reason, it seemed like too much. She always wrestled with her Ddrymmian upbringing when dressing for these events. She chose a quieter one, pale blue with live Queen Anne's lace blossoms at the sleeve edges. Then she changed her mind back to the golden one. But what about the lovely off-white with the poofy skirt?

This went on until just hours before the ball, when Blaze couldn't stand it anymore and intervened. "Ms. Fireflower, may I? Here, wear this...with these shoes. And here's the jewelry." They put their hand on the exact right gown for the occasion—a stunning black sheath with a high neck and a very low back— open-toed high heels, a gorgeous necklace of golden sage leaves, matching earrings, and a small clasp purse for her lipstick and mascara. She looked ravishing.

"Thank you, Blaze. You always come through."

The day had finally arrived. Preservation sent a car and driver to each main Player, adding to the dramatic flair of the event. By previous agreement and to maintain her Ddrymmian privacy, Millie had arranged for the car and driver to arrive at the border of the forest. Shank had driven her to the pickup point, and when the black limousine pulled up, she stepped out of her modest vehicle and into the fancy one.

They drove to the StoryEarth Center Hall. Thousands of trumpeting lanterns lined the long driveway to the entrance where the press waited to take photographs of incoming celebrities. As a child, Millie had always thought she'd love this part, but the reality of it was nerve-racking.

"Hello, Preservation friends. Elizabeth Maggish, special

correspondent reporting for SBC, coming to you from the StoryEarth Center Hall, where the annual StoryEarth Goodwill Ball is held. And a stupendous event it is from the looks of it. Here comes Lonner Mastin, Player for *Rumpelstiltskin*, with his lovely daughter, Maggie, at his side…and pulling up just behind him, we have our one and only Ddrymmian Player, Millie Fireflower! Millie, could we have a word?"

Millie hated this part, but there was no way around it. "Of course. Hello, Elizabeth."

"You've come a long way from your first days at the Preservation Precinct High School."

"Yes, I have. So grateful to be here. As usual, it's an absolutely gorgeous event."

"Yes, it is. I'm sure it's a nice change from the costume you're in most of the time, yes?"

"Ah, yes," Millie said with the obligatory chuckle. "Well, it's a little less comfy, but it's always a great evening for Mama Bear to let her hair down." She struck an over-the-top diva pose, and the crowd behind the rope went wild.

"Yes, it is! Well, I'll let you go. I know you'll want to greet your family inside, as I understand Alphabet Delights is catering the event after a very long time away. How proud they must be!"

Millie's entrails shrank as she kept the practiced, blank smile on her face. She said her polite goodbye and sped away down the red carpet, hoping no one noticed her ears twitching.

She found the ladies' room and raced into the first open stall, then locked it behind her and stood inside, trying to manage her breath. Most of the ladies in there knew her, so she had to be careful what they heard, even in there, *especially* in there. But at least she had a moment to collect herself.

First, the ears. With a pang of guilt, she remembered Mama Bette giving her the centering stone, and telling her firmly: "Let your anxiety flow downward into the stone so it drains from the ears." She undid the top of her dress just enough to reach the quietpocket, and took the stone out. She let her anxiety flow from her head and her ears, through her arms and into the stone. After a moment, that seemed to do the trick.

Then she performed her usual quieting practice. She pressed her feet into the ground, softened the backs of her lungs, and lengthened the back of her neck. She tried to remember Oneness in all things. So many Ddrymmian teachings had become visible again in her mind, ever since she'd created the heartspeak for Agnes and Mix.

The StoryEarth Goodwill Ball had always been one of her family's biggest accounts at Alphabet Delights. She had accompanied Mama Linn on countless occasions to deliver their delicacies on this happy day, and for the last few years before her fateful announcement, she and Wrem had even done it on their own. Mercifully, when Millie was hired as Mama Bear, the event had been catered by other companies, Edible Heaven being the most prominent. Did her mothers boycott the event, or was the Precinct being sensitive to her situation? The former was way more likely.

What was Alphabet Delights suddenly doing here? The thought of approaching the buffet table in her finery and seeing Mama Linn and maybe even Mama Bette filled her with both dread and longing. She imagined the table loaded with yippee!puffs and spicy stuffed conference poppers—she couldn't bear it. What would they say to each other? What could she possibly say to them? But her centering had helped, and so, somewhat calmer, she exited the stall, washed her hands, and took a deep breath, looking into the mirror. *All roads begin and end in Oneness.*

She put the stone in its quietpocket, and pressed it into its home between her breasts, threaded her arm back into her dress, and went out to mingle the way she learned to during the Player permanency courses that summer so many years ago. When her family thought she was 'going to summer school.' Which wasn't technically a lie.

She found many of her friends—Mimi, of course, holding forth about the breadcrumbs and the children in the oven;

Sydney, her favorite props guy, who was deep in discussion with the set designers for *In the Night Kitchen;* and a couple of the background Players for *The Princess Bride* whom she'd befriended during one of their parties last year.

Her stomach was off, so she decided not to eat. It was safer that way. She was telling Stick something funny that had happened with Baby Bear when her legs wobbled underneath her. She'd caught sight of her Mama Linn behind the buffet table across the room. It was the first time in five years.

Linn was reloading the trays being brought around by young servers. Drauml had just hoisted something heavy out of the cooler and set it on the table. Linn looked it over, put her hands to her low back, and stretched for a moment. Coming out of that stretch, her eyes met Millie's through the crowd.

Both she and Drauml had seen Millie and froze for an instant. Immediately, Linn looked down, and Drauml busied herself with arranging the little peace treaties, small shish kebabs of skewered chunks of grudge, gravity and grace—freshly grilled. She replaced them on the empty trays coming back from the rounds.

Millie made her way to the table. Drauml had already left to circulate again in the crowd.

"Mama."

"Hello, Millie." Her name, now a motherless child in her mother's mouth.

Linn's face was tired, and a gray streak Millie had never seen swam from Linn's hairline to the back of her head. She loaded a new tray with sandwiches, moving them around, rearranging how many would fit.

"How are you?" Linn asked the grown woman across from her, now an elegant stranger in black.

"I'm doing well. How is Mama Bette? How are you?"

Something hardened on the way out of Mama Linn's mouth, and she could not answer. Everything Millie thought of to say into the silence felt wrong. The difficulty stretched out and yawned.

"It's good to see Drauml. Did Wrem come with you to help unload?"

"Yes, but he had stuff to do. He'll be back to help us break everything down."

"Hey," Agnes whispered just behind Millie's ear. Millie jumped, and they both laughed. Agnes had snuck up to her just after coming in from the entrance, where she'd managed to get through the press gauntlet. So intent on surprising Millie, she didn't notice the woman behind the table.

"Millie, I want you to meet somebo— Oh! Oh, my Word! Mama L—Ms. Linn!" Agnes felt such genuine warmth for Linn, the mother she still wished she'd had. "How are you? And how is Ms. Bette?"

Linn's throat tightened with tears, hearing the girl—the young woman—correct herself from the familiar to the formal salutation. Tears she could not cry for Millie rose up in her eyes for Agnes. Her presence lit up all the memories, the things she'd taken for granted, Millie's young girlhood, and how much they had all loved one another.

Linn had felt great affection for Agnes, had actually loved her. Even Bette had been impressed by her desire for simplicity and connection, given her upbringing. But Agnes had been instrumental in Millie's defection, so the tears were pulled back into bitterness before they could ever fall. "We've been well enough, and you?"

"Well enough," Agnes said. "I try to keep in mind something you told me long ago: *Sometimes the life you can't stand is merely a birth passage.*"

Linn remembered one of the teenage heartstorms, some boy problem she'd brought to their home for healing, and looked at Agnes as she tried to find her sense of Oneness. "Yes, that is still true."

Agnes said to Millie and her mother, "It's good to see you, Ms. Linn. I should leave you two."

"No, it's fine, Agnes," Millie said. "I have to mingle anyway. Excuse me, Mama."

"Of course."

And just like that, it was over. Millie trailed after Agnes, who led her into a crowd of rowdy young men enjoying the tail end of a very good joke. Agnes pointed to Mix and said, "Mix, this is my friend Millie Fireflower, Mama Bear from *Goldilocks*. But you guys already know that 'cause she's on your monitors every day, right? Anyway, Millie, this is my friend Mixko Stenfar."

"How do you do, Mr. Stenfar?" Laughter erupted from the group. There were hoots and hollers.

"Oh, there'll be no living with you now, eh, *Mr.* Stenfar?" They ribbed him, all of them bowing low.

"Shut up, guys. We are obviously in the presence of a lady. A little respect, please." And with that, he clicked his heels together, gave a gentlemanly bow, and kissed Millie's hand.

Just like Prince Charming might, Millie thought. *Is it a signal? Is he saying he will do it?*

She had a sense of humor, so she played along and gave a deep curtsy. The boys had fun with this charade, so each of his buddies got their turn. Fobbler, Bick, and Jayth. They all treated her well, laughed, and she was in. But her mind was racing. She knew they couldn't talk here. But he had said he'd give his verdict by this date. How would he do it?

Drauml came around with a tray of flaming limericks. It was all Millie could do to keep her light from issuing. As Agnes and the boys picked off the snacks, Millie said to Drauml, "It is really so good to see you, my friend. How are you?"

Drauml gave a sad smile and said, "I'm well enough."

And then her eyes lit with something mischievous Millie had never seen before when she went on to say, "Your brother has certainly been a thorn in my side."

"Really? Well...you could do worse as thorns go. And the children? I understand you have two now. Did you receive my gifts? I never heard, so I wondered if he'd rerouted them or something." Millie tried to make it easy for Drauml to tell her the truth.

"No, we received them," Drauml said. "But Wrem is very stubborn. We had many Listenings over it, and we compromised by donating them to the Larkshener children, who are in dire need of toys and lovely clothing that never soils."

Millie caught her tears at the corners of her eyes before they fell. "I'm glad they went to a good cause." She swooped her face in front of Drauml's face to make sure she saw her. "Please make sure to tell him I love him and that I think of him and honor him in any way I can every day."

"I will. Gotta go now. Tray's empty." And off she went into the crowd.

More food and drink were ingested. Millie did some circulating, touching base with her contacts, making new friends, occasionally glancing over at the food table to see how her mother was doing, and hoping to catch a glimpse of Wrem.

The entertainment was a famous troupe of color manipulators called Glory in Glaween. They accessed visual frequencies, turned them into sounds, and then moved with those sounds, all of which culminated in physical sensations for the audience. It was a thrilling experience, and it kept everyone rapt for a good hour and a half. For Millie, it looked like a gaudy imitation of what happened during the Ddrymmian seasonal ceremonies, without the subtleties or spirit.

Alphabet Delights was in the process of packing up for the long trip home. Millie caught sight of that and went over to say goodbye. Drauml put the china in a quietbox with the other heavy items and took it out to the wagon. "Mama, you look so tired." Linn was clearing the table of glasses.

She continued working without looking up and said, "I'm fine. You should go back to your friends."

Millie stood there, breathed in and out, waited, and watched her mother. When neither of them made a move to get any closer, Millie left quietly, saying, "Goodbye, Mama."

Linn turned around. Their eyes met one last time, and she said, "All roads...*all* roads, Millie." Her tears came now. "All roads begin and end in Oneness."

Millie came around the table in one move and hugged her mother, both of them holding on tight while actively suppressing their lights. "Please give my love to Mama Bette."

"I will." They wiped away each other's tears, shared one last look, then resumed their former positions.

The party eventually condensed itself into the afterparty. Beings had left in twos and threes, until only a smattering of them remained: agents, Players, and some higher-level administrative staff. Millie and Mix and Agnes were among them.

They all gathered in a cozier antechamber, one with smaller chandeliers and lit fireplaces, to sip their musings from expensive snifters and tell favorite tributes about one another. These were, of course, more roasts than tributes and were often dominated by tales of pranks perpetrated either by or *on* Mixko Stenfar, which left everyone wiping their eyes with laughter. Millie's feet ached, but she could not leave without the verdict.

At the tattered end of the night (the beginning of morning, really), the diehards played Favorite Story. When it was Mix's turn, he said, "Mine is *The Prince and the Pauper,* where the beggar and the prince realize they look so much alike they could switch places. It's just so much fun, and there's so much room for comedy."

Millie and Agnes did not dare make eye contact. It was on!

Chapter 24

Linn's Collapse

The ball was over, and the wagon was packed. Linn looked like she could barely make the trip home. Wrem sent Bette some requests through his feet before he got in the buggy. Drauml made Mama Linn comfortable and sat with her in the back, while Wrem trotted Cliffer home as fast as possible.

When they arrived, Bette was ready. She had a pot of hot prayers on the stove and had the poultices for her back made up in case they were needed. Drauml and Wrem helped Linn out of the cart. She was sweating and very short of breath. Bette's face blanched when she saw her. "I should never have let you go," she muttered under her breath.

The women helped Linn into her nightgown. Bette had warmed the sheets for her. They tried to get her to drink a little tea, but Linn was unable to do it. "So tired," she whispered. They let her sleep. Bette put out another call to Grelle.

Drauml's heart was pounding. Things had seemed to go all right at the ball. There hadn't been any words. She couldn't think what had happened. She and Bette sat at the kitchen table and drank some tea, mulling it over, trying to sort out what was going on here.

Soon enough, there was a knock, and Bette led Grelle to the bedroom. The healer placed her palm on Linn's forehead, asked her some questions, and took her temperature. She was very cold but not shivering. She should have been shivering.

"Bette, I know you warmed the bed already, but fill the bed warmer again with coals right away. Get it in there under the covers. Drauml, bring more blankets. That's it," Grelle said as they complied. "Good."

The healer gave Linn a few more sips of hot prayers tea with one of her tinctures in it; she held Linn's feet and sang the ailing woman's energies back into her meridians. After about an hour, Linn seemed better. She was sleeping peacefully, and her temperature had come back to normal.

Grelle said, "She's going to have to rest for a week or so. I know this will sound strange, but make it a gently active rest. She needs her people around her. Bring friends over. Have them come and sit with her and tell stories. Give her small things to do, not big things. She must be kept *just* active enough that it tricks her into resting." Bette knew what she meant but wasn't sure how she'd pull it off.

Drauml and Wrem reluctantly left for home. Bette got into her pajamas and climbed into bed. She looked at her wife. She had loved her so much for so long, this stubborn, wise, sweet, brilliant pain in the ass. She put her palm on Linn's cheek. She kissed her forehead.

Bette fell into a fitful sleep, waking with her heart pounding, having dreamed that the house shook, and the great Elsewhere came for Linnie, and no one could do anything but watch. And then it was Millie screaming for help from thousands of feet down in a chasm. She got up twice during the night to check the offerings she'd left for the faeries, hoping Flurjahm would be especially pleased with her gifts.

Chapter 25

The Big Switch

They trained for over five seasons, almost half a year. Mix set up a schedule and guidelines for how to rehearse the technology and movements without attracting unwanted attention. They would use the heartspeak and rehearse only during each new moon, when the Precinct performed its maintenance protocols for all StoryEarth sets.

Because of his special assignment from Agent Four Seven, Mix was expected to visit each location often so he could establish the digital, molecular, and energetic connections between all the Story sets and Precinct headquarters. So he pretty much had carte blanche. That was the good news.

The bad news was he himself was being watched. Four Seven valued him enough to give him the challenge, but didn't trust him. So it wasn't unusual for Four Seven to show up for spot checks without warning. These took place with unsettling irregularity.

Once, the only thing that saved them from being caught was Millie's backsight. She saw Four Seven approaching the outside door. They'd been inside a heartspeak on the *Cinderella* set when she felt him coming. It was too close a call. They decided to meet less frequently from then on, and they got together only at either Agnes's or Millie's High Home, never on set.

Agnes taught Millie everything about how a princess walks, talks, and behaves; how to curtsy; how to shape her hands to receive a gentlemanly kiss; how to fashion her face into the demure, graceful recipient of good fortune. Millie taught Agnes everything about a bear suit, about working with a child Player, about where the pitfalls might be in the role. She told her about her castmates, their idiosyncrasies, what made them happy. This would no doubt help during the transition. They each went over the other's script until they could recite the lines in their sleep. This was paramount. And then they just dreamed together, waiting for the day to come when Mix was ready with his magic.

Only once more did they risk an impromptu meeting. When Millie arrived at Agnes's High Home, the servants were sent home, the heartspeak was invoked, and they began to talk. Millie said, "When the power goes down, it's going down only on our two sets, right?"

"Right," Agnes replied.

"Well, what are we actually going to say...to our castmates? I feel so bad for Seth and Sam. They're going to be terrified. And I'm worried about Tiffany because she hates me and would probably jump at the chance to get me in trouble."

"I know," Agnes replied. "Same with Brad. Well, Brad *and* Pauline. But remember, they won't be able to do anything *during* the switch because Mix fixed it so that all communication on our sets goes down both ways for that whole time. And none of the cameras will even register that we're down."

"Right," Millie remembered.

"And when the red light goes back on," Agnes continued, "the cameras won't know it's a different Player because of how embodiment works. I mean, you're inside Cinderella's actual face and body. I'm inside Mama Bear's body."

"Right. But...but...but what about our castmates? What am I going to actually say when the power goes down?"

"Millie, we've been over this. You're going to tell them how much you value them as Players, but you just can't do it anymore, so you and I are going to switch. We've planned it for many, many seasons. When they freak out, and they will, you tell them that the power's going back up in twelve minutes, so please just, you know, 'do what I tell you.'

"And then you tell them that archival footage is running while we're down, and you describe exactly where the story is going to be starting up again at the twelve-minutes-later point. I'll come in to your set, we'll change, you'll run to my set, and we're done!"

Millie went over it in her mind until she was calm again.

And then sooner than they thought, sooner than they were ready for, the annual Preservation Convention began. Mix had given his signal: a copy of *The Prince and the Pauper* just showed up on each of their doorsteps. No one knew when or how. Millie and Agnes realized that before night fell, they'd be inside their new lives.

Normally, not that this happened a lot, the cast would wait patiently while Preservation fixed the problem. But today was different. Millie and Agnes knew they had only twelve minutes. Mix had set it up for exactly that amount of time, during which the watchers would be unwittingly seeing archival footage.

The instant Millie heard the silence of no power, she turned around and yelled, "Tiffany! Come out! Urgent cast meeting!"

Seth whispered, terrified, "Mama Bear!"

"Seth, it's OK."

"Don't you mean 'Papa Bear'?" he asked, nervously indicating the sensors in the corners of the room.

"Mama?" Sam trembled, looking from one to the other, trying to understand.

Tiffany arrived, mute and horrified, nodding toward the sensors with her eyes bugged out.

"Tiffany, all of you, the sensors are down. Plus, no one even knows they're down. Archival footage is playing as we speak. But we only have twelve minutes." Millie was talking so fast that she could see them not processing. She tried to slow down.

"Mama Bear, what—"

"Stop calling me that, Seth. Cinderella and I are switching places. She will be Mama Bear, and I'm going to be Cinderella."

They gasped.

Seth breathed out, "Oh help us, Beings All." He was shaking his head.

"People! The story sensors have been *disabled,* along with all the connectors, from here to Cinderella's palace, so Preservation *can't see us.*"

Seth looked at the door, expecting agents to come storming through at any moment. Millie took hold of his furry face and said, "*Hey!* Pay attention! I'm going to say this again. They can't see us. No one even knows we're down. Agnes and I have worked this whole thing out. So—"

"How did you—"

"Never mind. So—"

"When would—"

"Never *mind*! So—"

"Mama Bear, are you nuts?"

"Seth, *my name is Millie,* not Mama Bear." And as she walked through the set, quickly changing it to its twelve-minutes-later state, she went on, "I know this is a great shock, but I just can't do this anymore, and neither can Agnes. She wants to be here, and I want to be there. So we figured out how to do it, and now it's happening. Now remember, you're going to pick up twelve minutes from where we stopped off—"

Seth was baffled. "Why don't you want to be here?"

"Hon, it's the stupidest story in all StoryEarth. What happens? Goldie comes in—porridge, chairs, beds. Then we come in—porridge, chairs, beds. We see her, she screams, and she leaves. It shouldn't even be a story."

They all jumped at this, questioning the worth of a story, a capital offense on a set. They could lose their lives.

"You guys, the sensors are down."

They all stood motionless. What was the protocol? No one in the history of StoryEarth had ever even tried such a thing.

Tiffany finally used her voice. "All Things Told! We're going to be banished to the Nothing because of *you*."

Sam remembered the story and recited with her, "Where nothing can see you, nothing can save you, and nothing can dry your tears."

"Don't be ridiculous." Millie hissed, watching the clock. "That's what happens when you get *caught* changing a story. And we're not even doing that. Just take your places and get ready to pick up twelve minutes from here—Baby Bear will just have said his line about the broken chair. Please move yourselves into the story at that point—Sam, break the chair—so everyone can go on enjoying this brilliant little tale."

Tiffany took offense. "What, you don't like it?"

"Tiff, not now."

"You actually don't get that this is a cautionary tale about cultural trespass and the displacement of the young female in our culture's psyche..."

"Oh misspelled words, Tiff, *shut up*! Go take your place immediately, or you really will end up in the Nothing. You and everyone else!"

Tiffany returned to the bedroom, slamming the door on her way out.

Millie turned to Seth and Sam. "You guys, I really wish we had more time to talk, but we don't. Cinderella's going to show up in about"—she looked at the clock—"three minutes. She and I are going to trade costumes. That way, when the sensors go back on in"—she looked at the clock again—"six minutes and twenty-nine seconds, everything will go exactly as planned. You guys will all pick up right after Sam says his line about the broken chair, and I'm going to be 'locked up' on the other set, banging on the door, right before meeting the prince...and Preservation will have their precious 'fully intact story,' and we will have our new lives, and everyone will be happy!"

Sam whooped. "Yay! We getta go live in a palace!"

Millie faltered. She fussed with his costume, smoothing

down the fur on his head. "No, no, no, honey pie, not all of us, just...um—I'm...I'm the only one who's—I thought you loved it here."

"Well, yeah, well...I thought *you* loved it here." There was another silence, with everyone regrouping. Sam went on, "Don't you like us anymore?"

She crouched down so she was eye level with him. "Sam, listen. Do you remember trying out for the part? Remember memorizing Baby Bear's lines?" Sam nodded. "Yeah. Well, that's what they are. They're just lines, and you're embodying a part, and so am I. But I don't want to embody my part anymore. I want a different one. So I found you a better—"

Seth broke in. "Wait a minute. Did you—do you need more help around the house? Is that it? Sam"—Seth looked in the kitchen for something to help with—"help your mother fluff the cushions and go check on the beds. Sam, please. Help your mother."

"Seth, you're confusing him. I'm not his mother," Millie said. She called out to Sam, "I'm not your mother, Sam."

And turning to Seth, she said, "I'm not your *wife*. I'm not *your* mother! I just can't do this anymore."

"Millie, you can't just change everything around—"

"But don't you see? That's the beauty of it! I'm not changing anything. All the words will be in exactly the same order...just the way Preservation likes it."

Sam reentered, his head down, mumbling, "I wanna go to the palace."

Seth nodded toward Sam. "Really? You're 'not changing anything'?"

"Seth, why are you so— What's the problem?"

"Nothing. There's no problem."

"We all did the same training, right? We auditioned for StoryEarth parts, and we got them."

"I know."

"And this part is not a challenge. Anybody can do it. Trust me."

Seth twisted his paws together. "It's just...we've been doing this story together for so long. I'm used to you."

Sitting in his chair at the dinner table, waiting for his cue, Sam twiddled his spoon on its end, trying to spin it like a top. His other elbow on the table, paw holding up his head. He mumbled, "I wanna have a sword and ride horses and feed the alligators in the moat and—"

Millie took him tenderly by the paw and led him to the living room. "Sam, remember you need to be over here. Sit on the floor by the broken chair."

Just then, Agnes blasted in, breathless. "Am I late?" She left a trail of soot everywhere, her hair tied up haphazardly in a kerchief. Millie wiped her footprints clean so there'd be no evidence. Then she and Millie proceeded to quickly disrobe and trade outfits. Seth and Sam caught themselves just in time to look away.

"No. You're actually a little early," Millie reassured her.

Agnes looked around. "How's it going?"

"Let's just do this."

"I brought the pretty one too, just to make sure one last time that you know how to wear it. My place? They're freaking out a little—"

They laughed. Millie said softly, "I know. Here too. You go first. Try these." Then she handed her the bear legs, making sure the feet pointed the right way.

Agnes lifted her rag dress over her head and gave it to Millie. "And I'm just maybe freaking out a little too because I wasn't sure whether—" She hoisted her shoulders into the rest of the bear outfit. "I mean, what if, you know, the whole thing just— I can hardly...I don't know...I mean, nobody over there, like—you can't believe what they—jeez, it's weird being...myself...while I'm on a set." One of her zippers stuck. "Oh trolls!"

Millie told her to watch her language as she helped her gorgeous friend turn from a magical princess into an overweight, frumpy, middle-aged bear with arthritic paws. "Poof out your tummy a little more."

Agnes relaxed her belly and sighed with relief.

"Shoulders more forward. Remember, you're always picking up after your family, all day long. That has to show in the shoulders." Seth and Sam looked at each other.

"Let me see the back." Agnes bear-waddled around in a circle, looking over her shoulder at Millie, giggling a little.

"Perfect," Millie said.

Agnes felt free and weird and shy.

Then it was Millie's turn. Agnes had brought the palace dress. "Do this one first, and remember what I told you. Get the glamor going in your center before you step into it."

When Mille got it all the way on, buttons done, her heart sank. "It feels awful. Why does it feel awful? Oh, Agnes! It's not right. It doesn't want me." It puckered unattractively in front. She was still slumped forward from years of Mama Bear duty and the infuriating "me too" with the porridge and "me too" with the chair.

Agnes said, "Nonsense. Stand up straight! I told you to get your glamor going. Do it from the inside, remember?" The minute she did so, closing her eyes and lengthening her spine, something about the dress responded with a sudden, thrilling grip like a hug. There was presence in the bodice, and the skirt breathed itself into fullness around Millie's body.

An aura of glitter, barely visible, began to tingle into existence around her shoulders. The signal was weak, but it strengthened as Agnes reviewed with her some of Cinderella's signature moves—how to pick up the gown when stepping across a threshold, how to curtsy, how to hold her hand out for a kiss. It was clear they'd been over this before a million times, but now it was real, and they were nervous. Everything was a little harder to pull off.

Agnes looked her over. "You look gorgeous. OK, now put it in your bag, and let's get these rags on. Time's almost up." She handed her the dirty dress, the tattered scarf for her head, and the worn-out shoes. Millie quickly made the change, putting on the drab outfit, remembering the ashes for her face and arms and knees and feet. The palace dress jumped into the special gig bag marked "Cinderella" that Preservation had supplied Agnes with when she got the role.

Then she took Agnes over to Papa Bear, who had now turned back around, watching this baffling scene, holding Sam's little paw. "Agnes, here's Papa Bear. His Player name is Seth. Seth, Agnes." They nodded to each other.

"And this is Baby Bear. His Player name is Sam. Sam, this is Agnes, your new Mama Bear."

Agnes looked around, taking it all in, remembering why she wanted it so badly. They'd pulled it off. For so long, life had been a living dungeon for them both, and now they were each stepping into their own versions of paradise. She looked down at him tenderly. "Hello, Baby Bear."

Sam threw a minimal "hi" in her direction and stood closer to Millie. "Mama?"

Millie took Agnes by the hand and showed her around the set. "My name is Millie, Sam. This is your Mama Bear now."

"Mama, I wanna go with you. I don't want a new Mama Bear."

"Well, you may not think so now, but wait and see...you're gonna love her." She showed Agnes where they kept the towels and the sheets, and they walked through the efficient, compact little kitchen. Agnes was completely smitten.

Meanwhile, Seth had been steaming. "How dare you put us in jeopardy like th—"

Then something beeped in Millie's pocket, and everyone jumped. "Words! This is it." She and Agnes looked at each other. She looked one last time at Seth and Sam. "I'm sorry, you guys." She went over to hug them. Seth was frosty, but then he wouldn't let go.

Sam said, "Mama, I wanna go with you."

Her tears threatened the whole game, so she strangled them in her throat. "My name is Millie, Sam. My name is Millie. My name is Millie. And listen. Mama Bear here"—she pushed Agnes in front of her—"will take great care of you."

She looked at the clock. "You guys! Places!"

They scrambled to their places. Millie picked up her bag and flew out the door in her rags. Agnes stood, with Seth and Sam looking down at the broken chair.

Chapter 26

Monitor Room
Shenanigans

Hey, Fobbler, I think we've got an infraction here."
Everyone's eyes swiveled over to Bink's screen.

Fobbler bit. "I don't see anything."

"Me neither," Bink said. "I just thought it might liven things up to say it. This is such boring rat passing. Most boring job in StoryEarth."

"No, Bink," Mix said. "The most boring job is listening to you whine about it."

"Shut up, Mix."

Echoing their little boyhood scraps, Mix shot back, "No, you shut up."

"No *you*," Jayth jumped, never passing up an opportunity to razz his friend, Mix.

Bink had to laugh.

Mix offered him the bowl of jokes he'd been snacking on. Tiny, spicy, multicolored crisps, with mushy interiors. On the first chew, they laughed inside your mouth. "Here, have some. Make you feel better."

Bink popped a couple in his mouth. He crunched on them as he scanned his screen, looking for infractions. His hand went over to the bowl, feeling for more, which he munched on gratefully. Mix was right. He did feel a little better.

Bink couldn't resist though. He took one of the crispier jokes and aimed it at Fob's head. He squinted, calibrated, then flicked it with his thumb and middle finger off his other palm. Score. Bounced right off Fob's forehead. Fob rolled his eyes and sighed. He opened his drawer, looking for more ammo, and found it: a box of erasers. He returned fire. Eventually, all five watchers had become little boys, laughing, throwing too hard, and just barely avoiding damage to the screens on which their jobs depended, on which everyone's job depended.

On the *Cinderella* set, everyone was frozen in place, waiting for Millie. Stepmother stood behind the settee, Anastasia at her side. Hortensia was preparing to sit. Prince Charming was still kneeling with the slipper in his hand. The air was prickly with tension as Millie barreled in, trying to calm herself, muttering under her breath, "Okay, okay, okay, okay."

Claire (Stepmother) muttered, "Why do we get stuck with the Ddrymmian?"

"My name is Millie," she said over her shoulder as she ran by.

"Seven seconds, everybody!" Millie said from offstage, quietly counting down so they'd know exactly when to start. When she reached "action," everyone immediately snapped into character.

STEPMOTHER INGRID   - *Claire Steller*
ANASTASIA   - *Laura Faiblen*
HORTENSIA   - *Pauline Borb*
PRINCE CHARMING   - *Brad Wraimsich*
CINDERELLA   - *Agnes Grath*

STEPMOTHER INGRID

Step aside, Anastasia. It's Hortensia's turn. *(To the Prince)* Your Highness, my eldest daughter, Hortensia.

> *ANASTASIA steps aside as HORTENSIA takes her place on the settee, kicks off her shoe, and winds her foot seductively around in front of PRINCE CHARMING, waiting for the slipper. He tries to put it on her. It does not fit.*

HORTENSIA

No, no. Please. Try again. It's just a little bigger from all the dancing we did last night *(wink wink)*.

PRINCE CHARMING

(To Stepmother Ingrid) Begging your pardon, ma'am, but is there no one else in this house? No other daughter?

STEPMOTHER INGRID

No, no other daughter.

> *(Loud banging on a door offstage.)*

No one else, save a wretched, ungrateful little wench who is our maid. Or who pretends to be.

PRINCE CHARMING

May I see her?

ANASTASIA

What?

HORTENSIA

You jest!

STEPMOTHER INGRID
(stammering)
I'm...I'm—well, I'm afraid that's not possible.

PRINCE CHARMING

Why not?

STEPMOTHER INGRID

Well, b-because, well—

ANASTASIA

She's cleaning horse stalls, and oof, does she ever stink whenever—

STEPMOTHER INGRID

If I may be so bold, Your Highness, the maid is not fit to be presented to royalty. She has no training, no manners whatsoever, and—

> *Again, loud pounding from offstage. Nobody moves. More pounding.*

PRINCE CHARMING

Do you need to—

STEPMOTHER INGRID

No, certainly not. Hortensia, go see to that racket.

(HORTENSIA exits.)

Actually, Anastasia here is quite the little flamenco dancer. Show him, darling.

*(ANASTASIA freezes,
aghast.)*

My pet. Don't be modest. Show His Royal Highness the Prince how well you do that passionate flamenco dancing. You are so good at it. Remember? The one that goes like this?

> *She demonstrates, banging
> her feet loudly, almost
> obliterating the sounds
> offstage. Anastasia catches
> on and goes with it, but
> the knocking, CINDERELLA's
> pleas, and HORTENSIA's
> shushing get louder and
> louder, until just af-
> ter ANASTASIA finishes her
> dance with a flourish, we
> hear offstage...*

HORTENSIA

Stay out of this, you ugly little toad, or Mother said we can leave you in there to rot! You got that?

> *In the silence, HORTENSIA
> realizes that everyone has
> heard. Beat.*

PRINCE CHARMING

I think it's best you let me meet whoever is in there.

STEPMOTHER INGRID

(Reluctantly bowing low) As you wish. *(To Hortensia, who is still offstage)* Hortensia, sweetheart, would you please escort our kitchen wench to the living room?

ANASTASIA

What? But so, what did you think of the danc—

> *She is quickly shut down by STEPMOTHER INGRID. HORTENSIA drags CINDERELLA into the living room and roughly pushes her toward PRINCE CHARMING. CINDERELLA's and PRINCE CHARMING's eyes meet. She tries to leave, but HORTENSIA shoves her back toward him. CINDERELLA does a deep, refined curtsy.*

PRINCE CHARMING

Your name, miss?

CINDERELLA

My name is Millie.

Chapter 27

The Breach

There was a moment the size of a mustard seed where nothing happened.

Then the world split in two with the searing sound of a siren screaming up and down the scale, alerting the Preservation Precinct to a story breach. When this particular alarm sounded, everyone in any story simply froze in place while the situation was sorted out. It happened. But none of them had ever heard the louder, lower, two-tone, discordant *buzz-buzz-buzz* going through the entire compound, signifying something infinitely more serious.

In slow motion, her castmates gasped in horror. Some weren't even completely sure they heard what they heard. No Player in history had ever said their own name during an embodiment.

Chapter 28

Crisis in the Monitor Room

Mix couldn't move. His stomach dropped into his thighs, and his mouth was a desert. Meanwhile, his cohorts flipped out.

"Trolls! Trolls in ballgowns, what just happened?" Bink whispered.

"Look at her," they said, looking carefully at the *Cinderella* set in the monitor.

Fobbler said, "Mix, why would Agnes say such a thing?"

Mix was staring at the screen with his mouth open, sweat stains blooming down his chest, under his arms. The rest of the crew looked at him sideways as they scrambled. Mix had the most prominent stories on his roster because of his status as Head of Watcher Systems. *Cinderella* was one of his biggest responsibilities. It wasn't his fault that a Player messed up, but it was taking him forever to go into action about it. And that could look bad for him.

"*Mix,* the archival footage! Go!"

He flipped the switches numbly, immediately.

They were all watching his monitor, which still showed what was actually going on, trying to figure it out. Bink got it first. "The Ddrymmian's name is Millie, right? Millie Fireflower? The one they hired for Mama Bear."

Jayth muttered, "No way."

"I mean, there's no way it could be her. That's Agnes, right? But still...how—"

Then, as if they'd been jolted by electricity, they all realized their own stories might be at risk. They dived back into their own monitors, making sure their stories were on track.

Bink, glued to his screen, asked, "I've got the freak-out scene in *Rumpelstiltskin*. Fob, you got *Tinkerbell*?"

"Yeah, I'm good. Everything looks good. Jayth?"

"All good. Pooh is at the hive. Bees are getting riled up."

Agent Four Seven exploded through the door, and they all jumped. "What in black stars is going on? Stenfar, what are you waiting for? Shut the story down. *Shut it down!* What did she mean, 'Millie'? Are we talking about the Ddrymmian? And if she's in Cinderella's role, where in black stars is Agnes Grath?"

Trying to summon his professionalism through a shocked daze, Mix said, "We're only just seeing this, sir. Jayth, you do shutdown protocol while I track Agnes down."

"No, Stenfar, you don't move," Four Seven said. "You shut the story down. I've already got agents headed to the *Goldilocks* set. If she's not there, believe me, they'll track her down." Agent Four Seven disappeared as quickly as he'd arrived.

Mix went into action. He made the appropriate connections, muted all his other Story sets, jammed his foot on the emergency, grabbed the mic, and began speaking, "Attention, *Cinderella* Players." His voice shook a little. "The *Cinderella* story is temporarily shut down. We are running archival footage for the time being. All cast members except the Player for Cinderella, please retire to the green room until further notice. The understudy is on her way."

Fob looked at Mix and said, "What just happened?"

Years ago, Mix had been hired as a Watcher for the monitor rooms. He'd completed his Preservation permanency training with such high results that he became something of a legend. His parents, both prominent Preservation agents, were proud but guarded. On the positive side, his grasp of the legal structures that made up the Preservation Precinct, combined with his astonishing technical mind, vaulted him higher in the Precinct's esteem than anyone in the history of its training program had achieved.

On the negative side, he was creative. This was a problem, especially for someone so well versed in the inner workings of the Precinct. Some of his interpretations of the statutes made his professors squirm because of how hard it was to best him in a debate. This happened more often than anyone was comfortable with. When he was handed his certificate of completion at graduation, the students gave him a standing ovation. The bank of professors looked on with somber faces.

All his promise, all his potential, and his brilliant future had crashed and burned with the simple utterance: "My name is Millie."

Chapter 29

Agent Four Seven Makes an Arrest

Agent Four Seven got to the set faster than anyone thought possible. He practically kicked the door down. At the sight of Millie, he froze. All his procedural prowess, his righteous indignation, and his emotional momentum abandoned him. His body went cold. He was heartsick. It was, after all, Millie. This one being had been his one and only friend, Millicent Fireflower—a woman he'd only ever really known as a brilliant, kind, and fiercely loyal girl, as Millie.

He couldn't stop his tenderness toward her now, seeing her completely resigned to her fate, Millie herself, not Cinderella anymore, but Millie, in Cinderella's rags and worn-out shoes— making what he had to do next so much harder. He had to escort her directly to an unthinkably horrible fate, to do it publicly so everyone could see, to deliver her to the place beyond the outer edges, from which no one had ever returned, to the Nothing.

At the Pirate's Parrot, Bink ordered the drinks to be delivered to the back booth, where he and Jayth and Fobbler would hunker down and ask unanswerable questions into the air at one another until they were too drunk to care. Everyone watched the screens, where news of this unconscionable breach was already being announced and re-announced in a loop. "Breaking news from our studios at SBC in the Preservation Precinct. I'm Elizabeth Maggish, and it appears that the Player for Cinderella—thought to be Agnes Grath, the renowned heiress and seventh in seven generations of Cinderella Players—was actually our sole Ddrymmian Player, Millicent Fireflower. In an unprecedented Preservation breach, somehow she managed to take Ms. Grath's role.

"It is uncertain at the moment where Player Agnes Grath is. Foul play is suspected. Representatives at the Precinct head-quarters have confirmed a full investigation is underway, and we will be notified as soon as there is more information."

Maggish, along with her colleagues at the sister stations in Droaze, Near and Far Emmering, and Larkshen, broadcast a constant stream of old footage—pictures of Millie in high school eleven years earlier, clips of her as Mama Bear, old inter-views with her former teachers and classmates, and even Agent Four Seven's headshot. As to how it happened, that remained a tightly shrouded mystery, and Preservation threatened dire consequences if reporters started messing around before they could complete their investigation.

Mama Linn was up to her elbows in novella dough when a wave of dark nausea came over her. Drauml saw her doubled over and sinking to the floor. Bette came rushing in.

"Something terrible," Linn said. "Something terrible..." She said it over and over like it would lead her to the what of it. Bette put a wet rag on Linn's forehead, sat on the floor with her, and held her.

At that moment, her friend Celeste burst through the door, her own face ashen. She took one look at them and said, "You heard."

"No. What happened?" Bette's scalp tingled.

"It's Millie," she said, turning on their screen.

They watched in horror. No one knew more than this: Millie had somehow snuck into the Cinderella role and then said her own name. No one knew why or how, but one thing was sure: They would never see her again.

Wrem ran in, breathing hard and slamming the door. "You heard."

Mama Linn caught his eyes. "We'll never see her again."

"Good," he said under his breath.

"Wrem! How could you say that? She tried to find us for years, and we wouldn't let her. We just sat here, spouting on about Oneness while we fed a big, fat Two right here in this family, shutting her out, not returning even the treespeaks she sent. You and your Mama Bette and your precious Ddrymmian pride. It's a rotten tree with poisoned fruit. We don't, any of us, know the whole story. We don't know anything about her at all. And now we'll never see her again."

Before Agent Four Seven could say anything, Millie begged him in the name of all that had ever been said aloud to let her see her mothers one last time. But the pathway from the Precinct to the Nothing always went through Larkshen, which was much too far out of the way, so that was out of the question.

"Agent Four Seven, please! What about the Players Agreement? Isn't there something in there that stipulates—"

"Ms. Fireflower, the Players Agreement doesn't protect criminals. Your hands, please."

She held out her hands, and he clicked on the cuffs. He took her by the elbow as they exited the building and started on the path. A Player being escorted to the Nothing was always taken there through the Precinct Center, on foot for maximum visibility.

"But it was an accident! I didn't mean to change the story. It just...I don't know, I just—"

"Said your own name!"

"By accident!"

"Ms. Fireflower, you know that's not what this is about. Something happened just now that was not an accident. It must have taken an inordinate amount of planning, covert planning, which is inexcusable."

People lined the streets in shock as they walked by. Almost

208 của Tina Lear

everyone in the Precinct had gotten used to the idea of Millie as a Ddrymmian. She had become one of the most beloved Players in the Precinct.

"There might be a sliver of hope, however, if you're willing to tell us exactly how this whole thing happened. Who else was involved?"

She looked away for a moment, then answered feebly, "It was an accident."

"Ms. Fireflower, whoever got you into this certainly didn't care about your well-being. They gave not one whisper of a thought about what might happen to you. This is no time for some romantic idea of honor. Your very life is at stake. Save yourself."

She remembered that first night when Agnes and she were drunk and laughing about how this might go. It was all her fault for even bringing it up. None of it would be happening if she could have just shouldered her small burden of boredom and carried on. "No one else should suffer for my stupidity."

They kept walking while each waited for the other to blink. As they made their way toward Larkshen, the news traveled much faster than they did, and the traffic grew. People drove to various viewing points and set out their lawn chairs to ogle. Some brought their children to teach them a lesson. Millie thought of Mama Linn and how terrible it had been for her when she was little, and now—oh, she prayed that Mama Linn would not be watching. But how could she not? The Precinct's communications reached into all four regions of Ddrym, through their own HCb's and through word of mouth.

Agent Four Seven performed the protocol for getting through the Ddrymmian boundary. Once they were deep into the region, Larksheners appeared. They bowed their heads as Millie and Agent Four Seven passed, as was the custom, but Millie noticed their hands. Every one of them made the secret sign for "You are in our hearts," soft fists with thumb protruding between the index and third fingers. Shank had taught her this sign. She dared not make eye contact, even to thank them, lest they be swept

up in her punishment. They had always been the strongest op-
ponents of fundamentalist Preservation Precinct philosophy.

It took them the entire afternoon to reach the far edge of
Larkshen, where the landscape began to lose its color. The sun
turned gray; trees grew anemic, their faded leaves holding on
but barely. The path they'd been walking had been fringed with
deep green grass. As they progressed, the marrow of Millie's
bones registered a psychic chlorine poison in the grass as it
withered into two endless, graying frown lines bordering the
trail ahead of them.

Several times, the pain in her bones was so great that they
had to stop. Agent Four Seven did not seem affected at all. Was it
because he was not Ddrymmian? Or because he was uniquely who
he was? Eventually, the path was bare, no grass at all—just wide
swaths of dirt and the occasional ash-colored flower lying on the
ground. She remembered Wrem's magical touch with living things.

Agent Four Seven stopped at an unmarked place in the road.
Millie doubled over and sobbed. He let her have her grief for a
moment, but then, newly energized, he tried again—more force-
fully this time.

"Ms. Fireflower, listen to me. Look at me!" She'd never heard
such direct talk from him, so she complied. "You are a person
of worth. I know it because...I know it. You have made a fatal
error. I have no idea what the backstory is to this insane turn of
events, but this? What we're doing now?" He pointed toward the
invisible border to the Nothing, "This is unnecessary.

"All you have to do is tell me who talked you into this terrible
idea, tell me everything you know, and you can live a somewhat
normal life. You may still be in prison, but your family can visit
you. You'll see them again." He caught her eyes. "The Nothing is
a fate worse than darkening. There is *nothing*, nothing happens,
nothing can save you, nothing can hold you or let you go, and
you are kept alive but just barely, and only so you can continue
suffering. The Nothing never *ends*."

"So end me *now*!" she shouted, shaking. She finally seemed
to be understanding.

"I can't! You know that." But Agent Four Seven fumbled here, wondering which would be worse, wondering if he could. If he would.

Millie sat down on the ground, feeling her own end in front of her. "You can."

He hunkered down in front of her, and said, "Please, *please,* help me help you. Think clearly, Millie." His voice broke on her name, and she shot him a look that brought both their younger selves to the fore. He swallowed, and went on, his voice subdued, almost conspiratorial. "You did not do this alone. You have information that could save StoryEarth and keep you alive on this side of the Nothing."

She looked as though she might say something. Her eyes to the ground, her whole body seemed poised to speak.

"Millie? Millie! Ms. Fireflower."

But in the end, her stubborn silence won.

Agent Four Seven stood up and sighed. He began his difficult task. "By the powers entrusted to me, I, Preservation Agent Four Seven, Fairy Tales Division 719—"

"No, no! Not yet! Wait!" Suddenly, she was up on her feet.

It worked, he thought. *She's going to talk.*

"Who helped you?"

"Nobody. I just, please...don't do this."

Heartsick, he continued. "In deference to all remaining and unaffected blameless Players and with respect for the precious connection between StoryEarth and all stories everywhere and—"

"This isn't happening. Dirges, what have I done?"

"Especially keeping sacred the safety of the story life of all the children of Earth do hereby—"

"Frank!"

Hearing his childhood name stopped him for a moment. He opened his mouth, closed it, and went on, "Necessarily and in absolute accordance with—"

"Frank! When we were kids? Before Mama Bear? Before Agent Four Seven?"

"All the laws—"

"Frank, listen to me!" She got in front of him, turned, and faced him. "Listen. You don't have to do this—"

"Ordinances, mandates—"

Agent Four Seven, now in clear difficulty, stumbled. He paused. She jumped into the center of it. "Frank, you could—I don't know—do something different."

He took a deep breath, redoubled his effort, and went on, "Ordinances, mandates, statutes, and requirements in StoryEarth—"

Truly desolate now, Millie broke from all tradition. She grabbed him by the lapels, her cuffs clanking against his chest—unthinkable—and were it any other combination of agent and Player, she would have been darkened on the spot. But he was in so much pain now that he just stood there and let her do it.

"Frank, please...please...listen...listen to me. Look at me. Frank, it's me." Her eyes were wide, pupils dilated with terror, and her words scrambled out as she raced her fate, trying to get to something better first. "You and me, remember? I was your friend when nobody else would talk to you. I was your best friend. You don't have to do this. We could go somewhere. We could—"

"Do hereby permanently decommission you, Millicent Araklane Fireflower, from embodying any and all roles in StoryEarth, from now into the farthest reaches of the spoken word."

Her body went numb. There was a distant ringing in her ears. She tasted metal. She'd heard about the Nothing all her life, but she hadn't really believed it existed. Somewhere in the back of her mind, it had always been just an effective myth to keep everyone in line.

But here they were at the border between everything she knew and the actual Nothing. Everything she'd left behind dripped with greenery, lush, full, growing, and alive. Everything facing them was dry, dull, mute, gray, empty, hard, and flat. "What happens now?" she asked.

He looked her in the eyes for the last time, his own brimming with emotion. He unlocked the cuffs, and said, "Nothing." Then he pushed her as gently as possible but firmly through the boundary. He thought he could do it, but he almost failed. He performed the ritual that created the seal using his strongest voice, tears streaming down his face. Her form grew blurry, and he was glad. He hoped she wouldn't hear the tears in his muffled voice from the other side, as the seal closed. In one breath, he was cut off from her, and she was cut off from everything. Forever.

Outside, Agent Four Seven had to finish the grueling ritual, invoking Preservation Precinct Regulation 1593.278, *Breaches,* part 4, "Wrong Words," and part 19, "Systems Subterfuge." He intoned, "Forces that govern the spines of all stories, of all myths and magic—for her crimes against the covenants between Player and Story, decommissioned Player Millicent Araklane Fireflower is hereby consigned to the Nothing for all time. As a representative of the Preservation Precinct, I, Agent Four Seven, hereby sever the link between her and all stories to which she has ever been connected. I hereby seal off her access to StoryEarth."

Next, he took a deep breath as he raised his arms above his head, then exhaled with a massive verbalization of syllables known only to certain Precinct agents. His arms came down, creating a visible seal to shut off the space made when Millie had entered the Nothing. It was powerful, opaque and fluid. He had effectively closed the border to the Nothing. A faint, deep warbling sound lingered for a while.

Agent Four Seven walked heavily to the nearby Precinct rest house. It was erected for Precinct agents to sleep and restore their strength before returning to work the next day. He put his hand on the scanner at the door, entered, took his shoes off, and fell into a fitful sleep on the bed.

Chapter 30

Chaos in the Precinct

T he Big Switch," as it became known throughout not only the Precinct but all four NetherJunctures as well, strained friendships, split families, and upended life as everyone knew it.

Agent Four Seven had always been cool and professional. But from the day after Millie Fireflower's consignment to the Nothing, he'd returned as a feral animal in Preservation clothing, quick to rage and scanning for someone to blame in every corner. Everyone did their best to ride this strange tsunami without losing their jobs. Even Levit, Four Seven's capable assistant of the past seven years, was nervous. He was a young man who wasn't young anymore but couldn't lose the look of it for some reason. It happened sometimes in StoryEarth. He was on the phone with someone when Four Seven yelled from his office.

"What's happening with Cinderella?"

Levit put his hand over the receiver and poked his head in Four Seven's office. "Understudy had taken over, but..." Levit hesitated at the look on Four Seven's face.

"Spit it out. What?"

"Pauline Borb, the Player currently in the role of Hortensia, has applied for retirement."

"No! That's all. No."

"Can you hold just a moment, please?" he said into the receiver, then covered it again with his hand. "Yes, well, she said there's a stipulation in the Player contract that provides for this, should another cast member need replacing because of a breach. I checked. It does, and she's filled everything out correctly. She's calling to follow up."

Four Seven got up and came to Levit's desk, rubbing his thumb into the crook of his index finger, an old habit when anxiety threatened to upend him.

"What should I tell her?" Levit whispered to Four Seven, indicating the phone.

Four Seven had failed to notice that Levit was on the phone with Ms. Borb at that very moment. "Tell her I'll get back to her once I've reviewed the contract. What do we know about Agnes's whereabouts?"

Levit got Ms. Borb off the phone, then went with his boss into his office for some privacy. Levit told Four Seven what he'd heard from the agents. "It seems that Ms. Grath and Ms. Fireflower had somehow arranged to switch places."

An admin from the general pool knocked softly. "Agent Four Seven?"

"Black stars! What is it now?"

"You asked us to let you know when Mixko Stenfar had arrived at the interrogation wing. They just brought him in."

Four Seven threw on his coat and said, "Player Grath has been apprehended?"

"Yes, sir. She's currently being processed at the Correctional Facility."

Levit also confirmed that the Mama Bear understudy was ready to go.

"Both stories. Tell them to move ahead with the understudies," he said to Levit.

Levit never lost his cool. "Right away, sir," he said, already dialing numbers.

Four Seven barked at him, "And show me the Hortensia contract."

Levit handed him the contract, opened to the relevant page with a sticky note marking the passage in question. Four Seven scanned it and then muttered, "Set up an audition for Hortensia as soon as possible. Rat passings!" He slammed the contract down on the desk. "SBC is going to eat us alive."

Levit, juggling two calls simultaneously with his ear cocked into the receiver, called after him as he walked out of the office. "Agent Four Seven, you should know—Headquarters has sent down two additional special watchers to cover Stenfar's monitor room."

Four Seven looked at him for a moment, then turned to go. Levit opened his mouth for one more thing that he really didn't want to say. "Also, sir"—his hand still covering the mouthpiece of the phone—"President Woundliss asked for a personal report before you leave."

Agent Four Seven paused, came back in, then said, "I'll be in my office. See that no one disturbs me. And set up the Hortensia audition!"

"Yes, sir." Returning his attention to the phone, Levit said, "So, Ms. Fliggerby? Please post the following dates for the Hortensia audition on all media outlets."

Agent Four Seven closed the door behind him. He took a moment to calm himself, taking stock of everything he knew. Then he took a deep breath, faced the camera in his office, and pressed the record button on his HCb.

"Good afternoon, President Woundliss. It is with profound shock and disappointment that I must report to you the following unconscionable breach: The Players for Cinderella and Mama Bear somehow managed to switch places. This came to light yesterday, so there is no information yet about how this happened, but we do know the following:

"First, both stories—*Cinderella* and *Goldilocks and the Three Bears*—are up and running smoothly with their respective understudies fully integrated. The archival footage played until both stories were ready, so no gaps were experienced in the story continuum.

"Second, on our way to the Nothing, I questioned Millicent Fireflower, the unauthorized Cinderella Player, extensively, but she was utterly intractable, uncooperative in the extreme. She was officially decommissioned and sealed in the Nothing yesterday evening.

"Third, the unauthorized Player for Mama Bear, Agnes Grath, has been taken into custody and will be secured in the Preservation Precinct Correctional Facility for further questioning today. While she didn't alter the Goldilocks story, she does have crucial information regarding how this happened. We'll get it out of her one way or another, and then decide what should be done about determining her sentence.

"Which brings me to our most crucial concern: Whoever masterminded the technical aspect of this breach. I have a few suspects in mind, and they are in custody at present. Interrogations are underway today. I will keep you updated as we discover vital information."

He clapped his hands to send it, then left in a flash.

Part Three

The Nothing

Chapter 31

Zargamom

True to its name, the Nothing delivered. Millie waited. She waited so long that a stupor overcame her, so long that she forgot she was waiting. When her mother had told her about the Nothing, Millie didn't really believe "nothing" would happen. But nothing was happening.

She walked around, surveying the bleak landscape, already yearning for color, any color—the lush brown of Seth's furry face, or even the sweet, cozy softness of beige, a color she'd come to hate so much in the recent past. What she wouldn't give to see it again right now. She yearned for the soft blues and greens of their *Three Bears* set, of Sam's toys. She dared not even think of trees. She began to ache now physically.

"Get a grip. This is only the beginning," she told herself, suddenly aware of a nauseating fact. There was no beginning in the Nothing. There was no end, either. She looked around. There was nowhere even to stand or sit. The ground was both there and not there under her feet, not solid, not fluid, not even appreciable as somewhere to stand. She didn't even dare use her centering stone. There was truly nothing around for as far as the eye could see.

She was hungry. She wanted words. She wanted crisp, perfectly dressed words in tasty arrangements. She wanted all the delicious sentences she could have been eating right at this moment, had she not opened her mouth with the stupidest gaff known to Beings All.

When she thought she might go dark from starvation, she remembered what Frank had told her on the way there. Once every day, the Precinct sent just enough sustenance for the *deeks* (the abbreviation for "decommissioned Players") to stay alive. They were called 'un-meals.' The delivery system was intricate and very secret. The only beings trusted to deliver the food were known as Almosts. These were beings with fully formed human bodies, but only half-formed characters.

Some believed that there was a lingual deity running StoryEarth called Logos, and that sometimes Logos dismissed certain characters midway through the creation of a story. And the result was a sort of sub-race of humans called Almosts. (Few people actually believe this, both in the Precinct and the NetherJunctures, but it is a colorful explanation that everyone has agreed to keep alive. No one knows why.) What is indisputable is that Almosts have only ever been seen roaming at the edges between the Nothing and the bleak outer reaches of the NetherJunctures, usually Larkshen. Whatever their origin, the Preservation Precinct decided they were uniquely well-suited to deliver the meager sustenance meant for the deeks in the Nothing.

The un-meal was always a tasteless mush made up of either the words that the Player had uttered to get themselves into trouble (used for especially ungovernable Players to make them continually feel the pain of their transgressions) or an insufferably boring story, the same every single day. She hoped Frank would have mercy and give her the latter.

Millie sat down on the shifting, flickering ground, pondered for a moment, and then lay down on her back. This resulted in a feeling of falling—endless falling—but she had no more strength to resist. She gave herself to the free fall into nothing. Exhausted from the whole attempt—from a year of planning, a year of subterfuge, a year of desperate hopes, wild dreams, and giddy late-night hours with Agnes—she fell and fell and fell into a deep sleep, hoping with her last thought that this would all be just a very bad dream.

After some time—there was no time in the Nothing, but there were stubborn traces of it in a deek's mind—Millie, almost dark with boredom, opened her eyes. She lay still, wondering how long it had been. There was no way to tell because there were no shadows, there being no sun. All night? Seven minutes? Ten days? No, it can't have been more than a day because the Precinct hadn't been by yet with her un-meal. As she tried to sense how long it had been, the unthinkable happened—sound.

She bolted upright, listening with her whole body. This brought a new wave of nausea and disorientation. She heard mumbling and shuffling. She looked in the direction of the sound and eventually saw what she could only imagine was another decommissioned Player. This being was dressed in what must have been at one point an impressive, fantastical costume—but the colors were gone, and the graceful form of it drooped in a rotting curtsy of depression and grief.

Completely unaware of Millie, the apparition toddled generally forward with no particular direction, muttering, sometimes shrieking. Millie didn't know whether to approach her or hide. But there was nowhere to hide, so she just stood there with no footing on unreliable ground. The deek seemed to be trying to remember something.

"And then, what...it's...there's...um, oh! *Oh!* There were horses! Yes! *Clippety-clop, clip-clop, bippity-bop...*" She forgot again, lost her place, and then uttered gibberish peppered throughout her speaking. "Well, at least I...uh..." She saw Millie and froze in place.

Millie tried to be friendly. "Um, hi?" They stood watching each other, both immobilized by their own not knowing.

The deek bowed obsequiously, trembling, terrified, doing her best. "Don't remember anything!" she said quickly.

Millie tried to reassure her, saying, "Sorry? My name—"

Suddenly, the deek clutched Millie's arms with a strange mix of joy and desperation and whispered to her, "Name? Oh, name!" Her breath like the dust in a house left uninhabited for centuries, she whispered more gibberish into the world around her. "Knows! Name! Knows!"

Then she fixed her rheumy eyes on Millie and said, "Oooh, ooooh, tell! Say!"

Flustered and trying to free herself from the deek's grip, Millie responded, "Well, my name is Millie."

Working her mouth around it, the deek let go of Millie and turned in a circle, figuring out how to say it. "Mil-lie. Millie-Millie-Millie-Millie, Millie, Millie in the valley. Ha!" She found something in the fog of her past. "Millie in the valley! Flower? Yes! Name, flower! *Name! Flower! Remember!*"

"Actually, I think you mean lily of the valley."

The deek's face fell.

Millie reassured her, "But it does sound the same...I mean, you were very close...um, what's your name?"

The deek looked around, searching. "Gone...lost...not here. There." She pointed past the border. "You name here: Willie."

"Millie."

"Say. Again, again. Say. Keep."

"I will."

"Name?"

"Millie."

"Mm."

"I, uh...I was a Player, decommissioned."

The deek flinched. Pointing to herself, she commiserated, "Decommible."

"Really? You too? From what story? Mine was *Goldilocks and the Three Bears.*"

No reaction.

"I was Mama Bear, and then—well, it's complicated. Were you a Player?"

The deek nodded.

"What story?"

She tried to remember. As she spoke, she kept fading off and regrouping. "The horses! Heel! It was...there were big, *big...*

and they would, jogga-jogga *bla*therbit but no, not then, be-fore…yes, before, many souuuu-souuuu fa*na*gabi many big"—she mimed mean, selfish beings—"and…" She petered off into a busy, searching silence midsentence, from which she could not seem to recover.

Changing the subject, Millie asked, "Where do you live?"

The deek's whole body registered that there had been a ques-tion, and she tried to work out what it was while nervously twirling a flap of fabric that was once part of her skirt. It might have been blue silk long ago. She finally responded, "All. Any."

"I mean, when you go to sleep, where do you sleep?"

The deek's story had been going in circles, looking for itself during this conversation. Having almost found the thread, the deek jumped. "No! No! Something…else. It went there—no it was…oh, yes! Yes! That's it! Mice. Mice! And…birds! And…no. *Fffff*fff…Lairbey. Mairbey something. It…it was…it…was…" She was lost. She could not find it. She wandered off, muttering incoherently.

Millie called after her. "Wait! Wait. I have to know your— I have to, um, I'm very alone here. And I have no idea when I'll see you or anyone else again. I would like to call you something." She didn't want to set off another desperate outburst. But still, she went on, "Maybe we can make up a…a name? For you? So I know what to call you?"

But of course, a flurry of wild yearning and hopelessness ensued. "Name! *Name!* Willie in the Valley. Willie…Willi—"

"Actually, Millie."

"Millie."

"And I meant a name for you. What do you think?"

She was broken on this subject. "Gone. Not here."

"Not if we give you a new one. What do you think? A new name…for you."

This struck terror in the deek. She put her hand over Millie's mouth.

Millie took the hand gently into her own and said, "What can they do to us? I mean, we're already in the Nothing. We have 'nothing' to lose!" Pleased with her little pun, she smiled at the deek, who slowly warmed to the idea.

But then she said, "Name gone. You forget."

"Well, no, I don't think so because I'll be saying my own name over and over to remember, and I'll just say yours too. I'm fresh now, so I know to be careful, thanks to you. Will you help me? What name do you want to be called?"

The deek tried to think; it was painful to watch.

"How about I think one up? What about...Elizabeth?" This was comically inappropriate, and they both knew it. The deek gave Millie a small smile with an unsettling consciousness in her eyes. Millie tried with another. "Sierra?" Not at all. There was a long, awkward silence.

"How about Zargamom?"

"Like Zargamom. Zargamom. Zargamom."

"OK, Zargamom it is."

"OK! Bye, Nellie."

"Millie."

"Mellie. Ha! My name Nargazon! Ha ha! Not gone. Here. Nellie in the Valley. Zargabomb. Names. Know. Not there. *Here.*"

So Zargamom left, muttering and confused but much happier.

Chapter 32

The Stenfar Interrogation

Agent Four Seven sat across from Mixko Stenfar. He took his time. He sipped his confession coffee and offered some to Stenfar, who declined. Handcuffed and shackled for good measure, Mixko took his time too. He was no fool.

When enough time had passed, Four Seven said, "OK, Stenfar. What happened?"

"I don't know. The power went down and—"

"Don't insult me! There's nothing you don't know about these systems. You put them in place. What happened?"

"Look." Mix lowered his voice, looked the agent straight in the eye, and said, "You asked me to redesign the surveillance system, which I did. I focused on their visual reach, the sound sensors built into the lenses. I built up their energetics, made them more robust without sacrificing sensitivity. You made it clear that my career was on the line. I had to succeed at this, or else I'm cleaning toilets at the Seed Center Dock. Why in the name of All Things Told would I jeopardize the very power grid crucial to this impossible task—for some outrageous Player scheme?"

"I don't know. But we don't have anyone else on staff who could have pulled this off. So why did you do it? What happened?"

"I don't know! The only thing I can think of that might have caused this is—while I was working, I noticed that some of the circuits on the bigger sets looked a little, I don't know, frayed, and I made a note to tell you so we could address that next, but—"

"Frayed circuits? And you were going to tell me later?"

"They weren't connected to anything crucial. It didn't signal any imminent danger. It was a minor maintenance issue. And you were in a hurry to announce its the new—"

"Listen to me. A shutdown of this magnitude—one that happened so thoroughly that no one even knew it was happening *while it was happening*—A) doesn't boil down to a minor maintenance issue; and B) requires a level of genius that surpasses pretty much everyone we know of, except you.

"A great cost has already been paid in lives. I've just escorted Ms. Fireflower to the Nothing and sealed her off! You do realize that no one going back millions of years has ever returned from the Nothing. We've got Ms. Grath, too, and if you don't start talking, we'll get her to talk, by whatever means necessary."

Mixko locked his expression in place.

"I trusted you with this enormous job, and two days after you confirmed it was done, one of the biggest breaches in StoryEarth history went down. On the *Cinderella* set! I'm not done with you, Mixko." Four Seven started to get up.

"Sir—"

"What?"

"Agnes Grath is...she's—why would you punish her? She hasn't deviated from the script in her role."

"First of all, how do you know that? And you've skipped over the part where she isn't in 'her role'? Where she participated in one of the biggest Preservation subversions since the *Snow White* affair? In whose world is that *not* a high crime?"

"But, sir! All you really want is preservation of Story, right? That the story be whole. The *Goldilocks* story is still whole."

"It's still whole because we had archival footage and an understudy who's in place." Four Seven got up to leave but then stopped abruptly.

"*You,*" he said, turning toward Mix.

"Sir?"

"You said all *you* want. When did you stop including yourself in that principle? You, Mixko Stenfar from the long line of Preservation agents? When did *we* become *you* to you? I pity your parents." Then turning to the guards as he opened the door to leave, he said, "Lock him up."

"What for? I haven't done anything!"

"Yeah, well, we're going to give you a little time to think about it, just to make sure there isn't something you forgot to tell us."

They blindfolded Mix, handcuffed and shackled him, and escorted him downstairs to the Precinct cells under the building.

Chapter 33

The Scaredy-Pair

Millie tried to understand the boundary. It was invisible, but she knew where at least part of it was because she hadn't gone anywhere since arriving. It was just behind her, if she was still where she thought she was. She tried feeling her way toward StoryEarth and walked with her arms outstretched, palms forward. The boundary soon spoke with a mud-deep voice, the bottom-most notes of *no*. It was just a sound, but as soon as she heard it, her hands melted right off her wrists!

She screamed and pulled back in a panic. Her hands rematerialized, but the shock took her strength away, and she plopped down on the ground, now paralyzed with fear. She didn't want to move in any direction.

The memory of Zargamom haunted her. How would she keep herself from degenerating? She began cataloging everything she knew about anything—numbers, for instance. She counted until it got boring. Somewhere in the five hundreds, she remembered Zargamom again and doubled down on words, names, and stories.

My name is Millie. Millie is my name. I used to be part of the Goldilocks *story,* Goldilocks and the Three Bears. *Goldilocks sampled the porridge, tried all the chairs, and slept in the beds; then we bears discovered that our porridge, our chairs, and our beds had all been violated. We found Goldilocks, she screamed, and she left. The end. Porridge, chairs, beds, scream, the end. Porridge, chairs, beds...oh All Things Told, what am I doing? Do I really want to cement that stupid story into my brain?*

So she chose better stories. *Cinderella* was too painful, but she mined *Hansel and Gretel, Peter Pan,* and *Snow White,* challenging herself to recall every detail. She fell into this process so deeply that she failed to notice the two approaching figures—no doubt other deeks—who were holding on to each other for dear life, terrified but unable to squelch their curiosity.

They were faded like Zargamom but in much worse shape both physically and mentally. They were maybe male deeks, but their costuming had unraveled so badly that it was hard to tell. They could be Both-ers. They could be anything. She decided that, if they spoke, she would use the pronouns that she'd learned for Blaze. Hopefully, it would work.

She moved to get up, and they both screamed, which of course pulled an involuntary yelp out of Millie as well. She recovered and assured them gently, "I won't hurt you. I promise. Who are you?"

One of them ran away fast, muttering, "No, no, no, no, no," like a triple-time mantra, with the other in hot pursuit. The other caught up, and they did a coward's do-si-do, trying to hide behind each other, each pushing the other in front, neither one brave enough to just stand there. During this comic scaredy-dance, they took turns making guttural sounds that flourished into a back-and-forth duet.

"*Ghhbrhhhvrwwwwhaaaaa*fraidyscared!"

"*Ghhbrhhhvrwwwwhaaaaa*what is it?"

They frightened each other into a frenzy, until Millie yelled out, *"Stop!"*

They froze.

"I'm scared too, OK?" she said. "But I'm not gonna hurt you. I'm just a Player who's been decommissioned."

They flinched and trembled.

"What's your, uh—do you have a"—*careful here*—"name?"

They had long since lost the association of the word to its

meaning. One of them fished in their clothes for something that might be a "name" to hold out to her. The other examined their own body, thinking maybe it was a physical feature. Unable to arrive at the idea, they decided (looking at each other for confirmation) to move their arms in a faintly beseeching, inscrutable hand dance that might mean "name." They ended it in a still life that looked like they were both holding the same imaginary ball. They were shaking against the possibility of having gotten it wrong.

"Thank you, but no. I mean, but, um...let's do it this way. My name is Millie," she said, pointing to herself. "If you"—she pointed to one of them—"were far, far away, and you wanted to be with them"—she pointed to the other—"what would you do?"

They snuggled close, held hands, and smiled really big, certain for once of the right answer.

"Oh boy," she mumbled. "This is gonna be harder than I thought."

She approached one of them gently, separated them from the other, and walked as far away as possible. This was difficult for everyone. The other kept following as she tried to create distance. She kept replacing them back at the start. It went on for a while. All this time, they mumbled frightened gibberish. But eventually, she got them separated.

"Now"—she was speaking to the first one—"calm down. It's fine. Your friend is right over there, see? OK, so let's say you needed them to come over to you. What would you do?"

They screamed a bloodcurdling scream. The faraway one came running. It was mayhem. They comforted each other and hurled hostile gibberish at Millie. She apologized, rattled, and the whole thing escalated, until she blurted out, "OK, OK, *OK!* Who are you people? What in the mess of meanings happened to you? I just wanted to know your names. What's going to happen to me? I cannot end up like you!"

They were undone. They ran. They ran and ran into the gray nothing.

"My name is Millie!" she yelled into the emptiness. "*I have a name.* It's Millie, and I know it, and I'm not forgetting it, not now, not ever!" She yelled it in their direction like an assault. "My name is Millie!"

And then sorrow that had been running in her like a river for much longer than she knew began to flow. She thought of her mothers. She remembered Wrem and all the things he'd made for her with his own hands. She remembered the trees she'd known, which had loved and carried her through her childhood; her room; her Ddrymmian friends; the safety she'd always felt without ever knowing she was safe. She remembered her Mama Linn's tired face the last time she saw her and their embrace. She physically ached for home. Her heart was a boulder.

After nine or ten breaths, she called out, "Zargamom?" She waited for a response. She waited for a long nontime. Nothing happened.

It could have been twenty minutes. It could have been three lifetimes. By now, it didn't matter anymore. She fell asleep.

Chapter 34

The Grath Interrogation

Agnes had been sitting at the interrogation table for an hour. It was an impossibly small room with a round half-silvered mirror on the door. Two guards stood in front of it. She tried to recall what little she knew of the Players' Defense Manual, something she'd only skimmed, thinking she'd never need it. She was practically royalty in StoryEarth. What could they do to her without disrupting the natural order of things? The incident was day before yesterday. With both relief and dread, she knew her mother would be there any minute.

She heard confident footsteps echoing down the hallway, and royalty or not, her stomach clenched. Agent Four Seven was tall and energetic, his shoes shined, his clothes crisp and clean. Detective Storp looked like he had slept in his "suit." (The jacket almost matched the pants.) His shirt was haphazardly tucked in, and there were stains on his vest from one too many appetizers at the Pirate's Parrot. Four Seven had worked with him before and had requested his presence that day. Storp was a slob, but he was the best at getting at the truth.

The guards outside the door clicked their heels as the men approached. Four Seven looked through the window and saw Agnes seated at the table, looking down. His recent contact with Millie had unearthed his memories, and he was, for a split second, back in high school, sitting at the lunch table with Millie and Agnes, all of them in their oblivious teens, laughing into the abyss. And now this.

He nodded, and the guards stepped out of the way. Four Seven and Storp placed their palms on the energy sheet for access. The door opened, and Agnes sat up straight. Storp followed Four Seven in, closing the door behind him. They stood there for a moment. Four Seven shook his head at her after a long silence.

He spoke first. "Ms. Grath, this is Detective Storp, chief detective for the Preservation Precinct. Detective Storp, Agnes Grath."

Storp began, "Ms. Grath—"

"Where is my mother?" she asked. "She should be here by now."

The men gave a low chuckle. Four Seven nodded to Storp to deliver the news.

"Your mother isn't coming, Ms. Grath," he said with feigned sympathy. "In fact, we had to restrain her and help her back out of the building. 'I'm gonna darken her with my own hands!' she says. If you ask me, I wouldn't be in your shoes for nothin'. So you can check that particular ally off your list." They watched her take that in.

"I don't believe it. How do I know she wasn't coming to—"

"We have security footage if you'd like to review it." Four Seven figured the interview would be over very soon. Agnes would know no one was going to rescue her, and she'd spill the beans.

"No," she said glumly. "Never mind."

Four Seven proceeded in a calm, congenial tone. "We've been over your file, and from what we know so far, for the life of me," he began, "I cannot fathom why someone like you would throw away an entire family line, an ancestry, a past and a future, as well as a soft-cushioned present, for a supporting role in a minor story. You seem like one of the brighter members of your family. Can you help me understand this?"

A long moment passed while she tried to decide whether

to say anything at all or just wait for the Player rep. Storp was ahead of her. "If you're waiting for a Player rep, you should know there is no Player representation for what you've done. There's only prison or the Nothing."

She blanched.

"The question is which one. And if it's prison, for how long? Those are your options, missy," Storp said.

"I don't understand. I thought there was always a Player rep."

"Not in this case."

"Why not? What are the charges?"

Storp obliged. "Subversion, role abandonment, perjury, collusion, insubordination. And those are just the ER charges. There are more."

"What are ER charges?"

"Excludes Representation."

Agnes interrupted, "But...but wait. Subversion? Isn't subversion about trying to disrupt the existing order? I was actually trying to maintain it. All we wanted—"

"We? We who?" Four Seven asked as his eyes checked the corner cameras in the room for the red recording light.

"Millie and I."

"OK, go on. All you and Ms. Fireflower wanted was..."

"Was to embody different stories, to step into different roles."

Four Seven was shocked at this bald-faced candor.

"Ms. Grath! That is expressly against all Preservation principles. How could you even...*want* this?"

"How could I want this? Agent Four Seven, with all due respect, have you ever done the same thing over and over and over every single day without ever—" Then she remembered the obsessive skinny boy he was in high school.

"Of course," he replied before she could finish.

"Don't you get bored?"

"No, Ms. Grath, I do not get *bored*. It has always been an honor to hold to tradition. It's what keeps the fabric of StoryEarth together, the predictability, the inviolate security of knowing what comes next. That was in your earliest training manual.

What's the first thing you learned? 'Our whole existence hinges on the integrity of Story. Without it, we all go dark.'"

"I know, I know. But that's what I'm trying to tell you. We understood that Story integrity was important, so we studied each other's roles for a year."

Storp jumped on that. "A whole year? That's a very long time. So this wasn't an off-the-cuff thing? It was planned. Ms. Grath, forgive me, but even with the luxury of a year, neither you nor Ms. Fireflower had the training or education to disable the entire Preservation Precinct security system. Who were you working with?"

Her eyes went to her lap, and she wrapped into herself tight.

Four Seven held up his hand to redirect this line of questioning. "So," he said, turning to Agnes, "you studied each other's roles for a year, and..."

After a moment, Agnes went on, "We knew it would be crucial that every word, every gesture be exactly the same. What I'm trying to say is we worked very hard to keep everything Preservation compliant. And my embodiment as Mama Bear was flawless."

"For the seven minutes and thirteen seconds that you illegally embodied it."

"Well, I don't think I should be penalized just because Millie flubbed her lines."

Four Seven lost it here. "This is not about Ms. Fireflower 'flubbing her lines'! Or you saying the right ones! This is about planning for a year to subvert the express orders of the StoryEarth Preservation Precinct. We take casting very seriously, Ms. Grath. I'm not sure if you noticed. And there is a reason why you were cast as Cinderella, as 'boring' as you may have found it. There is a reason why Ms. Fireflower was cast as Mama Bear. And this whole situation proves our point. Everything was fine until you, in your infinite wisdom, decided to change things."

Agnes clammed up. Everything was not fine, but he would never understand it.

"Who helped you?" Four Seven asked.

"No one."

"We already know. You know that, right? We know who helped you. He's already confessed."

"Then you don't need me."

"Agnes," he said with genuine sympathy, "do you have any idea how much danger you're in?"

Nothing.

He went on, "If you come clean right now about your part in it, you can make most of this go away."

Nothing.

He looked at Storp, resigned. They would have to move to the next step. Without a word, they lifted her from her seat and led her out of the room. The guards cuffed her hands behind her back and blindfolded her as Four Seven gave the order.

"Solitary. And make sure Stenfar sees her on the way."

"No! *No!* Agent Four Seven, Detective Storp, please. Can't we work something out?"

"Ms. Grath, you had your chance. It's over now." He and Storp walked away, and without looking back, Four Seven said to the guards, "Go."

After they'd gone, he said to Storp, "We'll let her think about it for a while. See if she changes her mind after some time to sort things out."

Chapter 35

Millie's Un-Meals

Days passed, weeks, maybe a handful of seasons by the StoryEarth calendar. But in all stories, there was only ever the once, the once upon whatever time they were telling. Baby Bear never saw puberty. Snow White never went through menopause. Nor did Prince Charming ever rev his midlife stallion at the pretty maidens in the village square. But the stories' Players did age, just like Preservation agents and janitors and set dressers. They all eventually lost their vigor and faded to either white or black, depending on whether they retired or died.

In the Nothing, Millie had gone exploring, but there was no word for what that was like. She noticed some very modest nearby hills. She took ten or fifteen paces, arrived at the top of one hill, and then noticed she was somehow back exactly where she started. She was looking at a modest group of hills nearby with no trees, no vegetation to speak of, just gray, utilitarian sadgrass—never grew, never died.

She was starving for some proper food, the kind they used to serve at Great Vocabulary, a restaurant only the Players and higher-ups in the Precinct could afford—great, steaming turns of phrase, delicious sides of plot twist, meaty metaphors garnished with an artful smattering of crisp pronunciations. Oh, that blessed food!

She remembered that, at the end of a long day, she'd go to

the Player's Spa and stand in a comfort shower of her favorite colors and fragrances, then Shamsar would give her the healing massage, where she'd feel herself slip from her Mama Bear state and emerge again as Millie. Taking off the costume in the spa next to the changing rooms was the first step. This blessed massage was the second. She'd change back into her own clothes and meet up with other Players at the GV (as they'd come to call it), and they'd eat and trade jokes and stories about close calls. How she missed them all. Mimi, the Player for the *Hansel and Gretel* witch, was hilarious at these gatherings, and always had them holding their sides, gasping for air.

Just before she thought she'd actually expire, the shabby little wheels of the Continuity Cart would wobble up to deliver her meal. The delivery boy—an Almost who'd found his perfect calling—had a book of everyone's pictures, the deeks he was in charge of feeding. He would pull out the book, look through it till he found Millie's picture, then produce a beat-up cardboard box from a locked container marked "Decommissioned no. 2576.75rls5*(s)." The box had the words "My name is Millie" on it.

With a notable absence of decorum, he would open the box and pull out a bowl with an unappetizing glop of that one sentence, mashed. No descriptors, no adjectives or adverbs, no similes or metaphors. Nothing. Just the tasteless, viscous sentence:

"Someone was born, lived, and then they died."

That's all she'd get. It was always the same sentence. She'd tried to talk with him, but he was an Almost, so he had no capacity for engagement.

She ate her un-meal and watched him leave, pushing that crappy little cart to his next poor victim. She knew better than to try to follow. It would only make her sick to her stomach.

Chapter 36

Agent Four Seven's Hail Mary Pass

Agent Four Seven walked back to his office, somewhat shaken by Agnes's intransigence. His thumbs rubbed his index fingers. He tried to shore up the crumbling walls around his heart, a heart heaving with grief—grief for his career, for his reputation, for his childhood, for everything he thought he knew, everything he knew he couldn't control. Then there was grief, finally, for Millie. *What to do now?*

It had only taken three days for Woundliss to commandeer Four Seven's monitor rooms. Other agents had been given charge over the Grath and Stenfar interrogations. Over the successive weeks, he was being systematically edged out of everything. The breach had happened on his watch, and there were many questions with no answers.

He could tell that Levit was being needled for information, and he watched from inside himself as his assistant feigned compliance, even agreement with hostile Precinct agents, while still protecting Four Seven in whatever way he could. What a friend he'd been. Something was visible to him now that he'd never noticed before: Levit was his only real friend left.

Never one to give up, Agent Four Seven took stock of his situation. He'd lost influence with his superiors, and his credibility was decreasing by the minute with his staff. How could he pull

StoryEarth back from the abyss? What options were left? He hadn't gotten this far in the Preservation Precinct by being an automaton. He was resourceful. *Think.* What did he have?

He looked up from his desk. Through the window, he could see his whole staff answering no over and over again to Players wanting to switch or ditch their roles. One of the bee Players for *Winnie the Pooh* wanted to switch with *Itsy Bitsy Spider,* but the spider Player wanted Charlotte's role in *Charlotte's Web.* Charlotte didn't want to switch with anyone. It was a mess.

He got up, opened his door and addressed his staff. "Please issue a blanket statement throughout the Precinct, but especially in our division. Millicent Fireflower is already in the Nothing. Agnes Grath will very likely follow her there. Others will no doubt be going to prison for this catastrophe. Make it clear to everyone that they'll be in danger of losing their very positions *just for asking* for a role change. That should shut this nonsense down immediately.

"Oh! And bring in all the staff members of each of their High Homes. I want each one marked with the, the—"

"Tracker tattoos," Levit whispered.

"The tattoo trackers. Let's put special Watchers on them once that's done. I want a record of their every sleeping and waking moments. All of them. GO!"

The department jumped into action, some of them arranging for the tracking. Most of them answering call after call, issuing Agent Four Seven's warning to every Player wanting a different role. All the other calls ended with:

"No, Preservation has not changed policy."

"Yes, the investigation is underway, and—"

"No. No further information is available."

He put his mind back to the situation at hand, saving StoryEarth from cataclysmic change—preservation of the integrity of Story. He fiddled with a pencil, twiddling it between his fingers. And then he lit up.

This was a very long shot, but there was a ghost's granddaughter of a chance. The idea was bold but still rooted in regulations, even if they were as outdated as the laws allowing a Ddrymmian to attend a Precinct school. Turnabout is fair play.

He went to the reading nook in his office and found the book his mother had given him when he'd graduated from his Precinct permanency training, *The Glemsynne Memorial Encyclopedia,* compiled five hundred years ago by the famed brother-and-sister team Milova and Emigrier Glemsynne, renowned judge and StoryEarth historian respectively. Agent Four Seven had been so moved by this gift that he'd put it in a special glass case and never touched it. Now it was time to break it out and see if his idea could work.

He opened the case, carefully lifted the book out of its pristine home, and brought it over to the comfortable chair in his office. He settled in for a nice, long read. It took all night, but he found what he was looking for, in the section entitled "Rare Exceptions: Returning Errant Players After a Breach."

In one of the subsections, it stipulated that, at the discretion of the Precinct judge in charge, a Player who'd been sentenced to prison for breaching a story could be recalled into service. In this event, the Player would sleep in prison and take their morning and evening meals in prison but would serve their particular story during the day, having been escorted there morning and evening by prison escorts.

He checked that the regulation was still active. He wrote out all the pros and cons. He argued with himself aloud, taking strong opposition to his own idea. He thought it through until no argument against it would hold up. The night rolled by without him noticing.

Eventually, he saw the cleaning crew finishing up and the early bird agents coming in, hanging up their coats, making their morning cups of coherence, clearing their desks for action. Levit arrived shortly after them. "Sir! Good morning. Have you been here all night?"

"Yes, good morning, Levit. Can you get me Woundliss, please, right away?"

A hologram of Woundliss showed up soon after, in Four

Seven's office. He was a portly, irritated man with graying mutton-chop sideburns and a very long mustache. "What is it?" he asked in a hurry, crumbs of compliments biscuits still in his mustache.

"Sir, Players are beginning to call with requests for other roles, and—"

"Well, shut them down! That's no affair of mine. Do your job, dammit."

"Sir! The team is doing a very good job of clarif—"

"They're doing their jobs. Bully for them. What do you wan—"

"Sir, I have an idea that might be more effective than any damage control we could imagine. Please just hear me out. It won't take a minute."

"All right, make it fast."

"What if we put both the original Players—the ones who switched roles—back in their original roles?"

"Are you mad? You already sent one of them to the Nothing! The worst we can mete out. You're suggesting we undo that?"

"On the contrary, sir. I'm suggesting we mete out something worse. I'm suggesting the punishment be more *visible*. I'm suggesting they stay in prison for the rest of their lives while embodying the original roles they tried to escape."

"But—"

"Sir, the threat of the Nothing was obviously not frightening enough to keep them from trying it—and almost getting away with it. When a Player goes to the Nothing, they just drop out of view, and SBC moves on to its next news cycle. Don't you see? If Grath and Fireflower just disappear, the Players will eventually forget what happened, and we will continue to be vulnerable to breaches.

"But if the prisoners were visible every day, shackled, and being escorted by prison guards to and from work, it would send a message to everyone: 'Don't even try this, or you will be publicly shamed every morning and every evening for the rest of your life.'"

Woundliss turned this over for a moment.

"Sir, this breach happened on my watch. I must give my all to repair it in any way possible."

"How do you plan to 'retrieve' the Mama Bear Player? No full human has ever come back from the Nothing."

"I've sealed off a fair number of Players into the Nothing, so I'm quite familiar with the ritual. I've also done a great deal of research in creating and unraveling energetic boundaries. I've studied spells and glamors. I've interviewed many working witches and warlocks in StoryEarth—both as Players and as prisoners. All these things give me something of an edge. I think I can do it. If I don't make it back, then at least I'll know I did everything I could to repair the harm StoryEarth has sustained. I have to try, sir. I have to."

Woundliss shook his head as he thought it over. It would be a PR nightmare, and they didn't have time to mount the proper campaign, but he agreed—the visible suffering would be a much more effective deterrent. "Listen, I'm gonna send two agents with you to the boundary—agents I trust. If you actually pull this off and everything goes as you've laid out, then you can still have your job. If not, you'll have trouble getting a job cleaning the toilets at the Hammer & Nail."

"Thank you, sir."

"Okay, get on with it. Oh, Four Seven?"

"Yes, sir?"

"If the deeks are in prison already, they have nothing to lose. What's to keep them from making a mistake on purpose, just to get out of doing it?"

"If they mess up, then they are darkened by starvation. They don't even get their un-meals, nothing. It will be a slow and ex-cruciating dark. No Player would want to risk it."

Woundliss ran this possibility in his mind for a while. *Four Seven was naive. The dark might be attractive to someone with nothing to lose. Torture might be a better deterrent. Perhaps...*

Frank went on, "Each woman would live in solitary at the prison. During the day, Fireflower is back on the *Goldilocks* set, and Grath is back on the *Cinderella* set. Top security there and back. We put out a press release with the details of their sentence."

"I don't think it's legal," Woundliss replied.

"It's against Precinct convention, but not against the law. I've been reviewing the legal precedents. There is one case on the books that deals with this very situation. *StoryEarth Magistrates v. Klerry Beusom*, Player (Mouse), Aesop's Fables, 4.de. 3d Cir. 587BfrSplt. The Player for Mouse in *The Lion and the Mouse* wanted out of his contract and deliberately threw a wrong line. He was imprisoned by night and forced to continue playing his role by day under threat of darkening. He did so until he went dark by old age.

"The Preservation Precinct has since adopted other practices, mainly using the Nothing as unending torture. But the actual law was never repealed. I checked. I would prefer not to resort to such a primitive tactic, but I think in this case, it is necessary for the greater good of StoryEarth's Preservation."

"I'll send Ralph and Stillwell over immediately."

Four Seven was looking over some papers when the guards arrived. Like waking from a dream into a nightmare, he realized he'd just negotiated his way into an early dark to save the Preservation Precinct, his good name, and—he hadn't felt it until now—his friend Millie. Even the most legendary Preservation agents had never attempted going into the Nothing and coming back out. What in the scope of All Things Told had given him this suicidal confidence?

He remembered his mother, who was living in the Precinct Elders Hall. He had to make sure the paperwork was in order for her continued comfort should he not return. This triggered a flurry of opening drawers and rifling through filing cabinets. He noticed Levit hovering in the doorway and motioned him to come in.

Levit put a cup of steaming liquid on Four Seven's desk. "I thought you might enjoy some hot coherence this morning. Also, here is the Precinct Elders Hall file in case you need it."

Four Seven stopped and looked up. It was as though he were seeing Levit for the very first time—his posture, his face, his blue eyes, steady, open, sharp. In one moment, one connection through the eyes, he became aware of Levit's thousand kindnesses, the hundred thousand prescient acts of support. He had nowhere to put this gratitude. It had a quality of tenderness that was almost unprofessional. The best he could muster at the time was an awkward "thank you." He grabbed the file from Levit, opened it, and pretended to read the topmost document until Levit left.

Agent Four Seven was on the phone with the administrator at Precinct Elders Hall when he saw Ralph and Stillwell coming through the outer doors. They had on full protective gear, complete with helmets, stunners, and emergency dark guns. Oscar Woundliss had evidently designated Agent Four Seven as a possible flight risk.

Frank was beginning to seep up through the layers of Agent Four Seven, beginning to surface. Indignant and terrified at the same time, he sipped his coherence and shook his head. He could not believe it had come to this. But he thought, given all the unknowns, he might've done the same thing were he in Woundliss's place. As they approached his office, he asked them to wait for him outside the door while he finalized things with Levit. He tried to think of everything Levit might need to know for a transition to another manager, should that be necessary. But as usual, Levit was a step ahead.

"Sir, I'm sorry. I was wondering what would happen in the interim, after you leave but...before...if it should be necessary, before a new department head would be assigned to this office. I took the liberty of applying for an override for the palm ID sheet so that I can get into your office for any necessary documents—"

"Of course," Four Seven interrupted. And he paused for a moment before saying it. "I really don't know what I would have done without you, Levit. All these years..." The two men, unaccustomed to this break from professionalism, spoke in sentences that lost their way halfway through.

"Yes, it's— I have often..." Levit faltered.

Four Seven reached for a piece of paper across his desk, almost knocking the cup over, and Levit was right there with his hands—catching the cup before the spill. For a split second, their eyes met again. Levit's throat tightened with emotion. "Please, sir. Do you really have to do this? Is there no other—"

"Levit, you know as well I do that it's either this or I lose my position and any hope of a future."

His assistant gave him the pen. He waited while Four Seven checked through the override application, initialed where necessary, then signed it. A small group of loyal employees gathered to say goodbye, several of them with tears in their eyes. This confounded Four Seven. *What's that about?* he thought. He couldn't wait to leave. They watched as he made his way to the door, flanked by the heavily armed agents.

He turned one last time and looked at Levit, who stood motionless as Four Seven nodded, turned, and went out the door. Everyone slowly returned to their work.

Someone eventually had to gently tap Levit on the shoulder and say, "Thrish, the phone."

In something of a daze, he went back to his desk and said, "Agent Four Seven's office, Fairytale Division, Acting Manager Levit Thrish."

Part Four

Here

Chapter 37

The True Nothing

Millie, sitting nowhere in the Nothing, continued her mental exercises, repeating as many stories as she could in an effort to maintain her sanity; *Snow White,* for instance.

"Once upon a time," she said to herself, "in a kingdom far, far away, the royal king and queen had a baby daughter. She was beautiful and kind and growing into a lovely, young girl when her mother suddenly took ill and died.

"Before long, her father remarried, and her stepmother was fiercely jealous and insecure. Every day she would consult her magic mirror. 'Mirror, mirror on the wall, who's the fairest of them all?' And every day she would get her reassuring answer. 'Why, you, madam, are the fairest, most revered in all the land.'"

But this was the thousandth time Millie had been over the story, so when it came to the part where Snow White was the fairest and the queen ordered the huntsman to go kill her, she rolled her eyes and stopped mid-story. She sighed. "I don't want that to be how it goes."

She heard a cough somewhere or a gasp. But there was no one anywhere for long stretches of knowing or seeing. She dismissed this feeling as perhaps her mind coming slightly apart at the hinges, but at this point she didn't care anymore. She sat and thought for a moment. What did she want?

Well, for starters, it just didn't make sense how these stories went. For instance, where were all the *fathers*? Cinderella and Snow White both had terrible stepmothers; Hansel and Gretel had a terrible *mother*! So where were the fathers in all this? Why did they never intervene? Why were they so blind, powerless, and inept? She began to feel angry and heard herself finish the story another way aloud, "But the father overheard her plotting to kill Snow White and hatched a plan of his own."

No sooner had the words left her mouth than she remembered her training, and terror set in. She waited for the sirens and the earsplitting buzz. Her heart raced, her face flushed, she braced herself. But nothing happened.

She went on. "Yes, her father overheard, and...and was appalled, because he *loved* his daughter, and he wouldn't let any harm come to her no matter what." She cocked her ear. Nothing, again. "So he made a plan of his own, and he sent his horrible wife and her horrible daughters packing, and he saved his own precious daughter, and that happened because I said so. Me. Millie. My name," she said, as tears came up in her throat, "is Millie. My name is Millie!" Now she was yelling it into the air. "And I think it's stupid to make people suffer till they die, just for making mistakes. Or for changing."

Then just behind her, there was the sound—a sound like a thousand costumes gently falling off their hangers to the ground. Suddenly, she was everywhere. Suddenly, there was no cast, no costume, no set, no score, no script, no translation, just a gasp and then her breathing in and out. Eyes wide, her bones reached for meaning, for a way to hold this strangeness.

She reached out to hold onto something, anything, kicked around for a foothold, and when she realized that supports were not part of this experience, she dove backward into void. There was no scene, no music, no emotion, no language, no character, no story. But she was in touch with the roots of all those things, their essence, their presence.

There was no quality of embodiment and so on up to no quality of speaking and no quality of message. There were no villains and no shortage of villains. There were no heroes or heroines and no shortage of heroes or heroines. Everything was true all at once. And nothing was true as well.

She felt herself dissolve from the confines of "Millie" and coalesce into a profound union with every event, person, thought, and energy she'd ever known. A deep humming sound made its way into her consciousness. She began to feel a rhythm, like a sister to the sound, pulsating in her body. A gentle hand touched her shoulder.

She stirred, and an old woman with skin tanned by the heat of many fire seasons, said, "Lie still. Take your time. You've come a very long way."

Millie opened her eyes and saw a very large group of beings standing around her in a circle. She tried to sit up and immediately felt dizzy, lying back down. "What happened? Where am I?"

"Shhh," the old woman said. "Lie still. Let us bring you all the way here."

Millie saw hundreds of beings surrounding her in a large circle, and there was a tickling of faerie drums beating in the distance. The beings made a sound that originated from somewhere under their feet and traveled upward, vibrating through their skin. This sound reminded Millie of the Ddrymmian ceremonies of her young life. How the community became a conduit for vowel sounds and spiritwords.

Her hearing felt different. She heard not so much with her ears but with her heart, with her inmost longing. She sat up as the sounds around her died down, ending in a long, single note. "Mmmmmmmmmmmmm." It opened the gates within her, and what came rushing through was beyond her ability to hold.

Every moment of fatigue, boredom, rage, ambition, defeat, and remorse made its way into her sorrow. Everything she'd wrestled with and won and then lost, everything she couldn't possibly reconcile or understand, she felt it all. It flattened her. She keened and swayed, sobbing.

The elderly woman approached her. She was stooped and somber with long, soft-green braids that smelled of sage. Her feet were gnarled, bare, and broadened by much walking. She sat down behind Millie and put her arms around her from behind and held her steady, swaying with her as she rode her grief. After many breaths, Millie went mute, spent and still.

"Millicent Fireflower," she whispered into Millie's ear, "we have been waiting for you."

Millie, exhausted and hoarse, stammered, "How do you know my name?"

They just smiled at her.

Feeling the scope of her suffering for the first time, she said, "My friends are in prison because of me. All I've done is cause... irreparable harm—to my fellow Players, to my closest friends, and to my family, who will now suffer terribly—*again*—for my actions." And her weeping returned.

The old woman summoned a man who wore his years well. "River?"

He was a man with salt-and-pepper braids and a kind face. He'd already read the woman's thoughts and knelt down, holding a cup of warmed wonder to Millie's lips. "Drink," he said, and she did. Her first swallow rendered her limp with relief. It was so delicious.

While she continued to swallow the nectar—slowly to make it last longer—the old woman said to her, "My name is Alayzha Windwalker, and this"—she pointed to the one who had given her the cup of wonder—"is River. We are deepfriends."

Millie looked at the woman. "You're Sting?"

The woman smiled and nodded.

"But, where am I? And how did I get here? I don't–"

"You are Here, and you are safe. We will talk tomorrow. Right now, you've been through too much. We'll talk tomorrow, and someone will watch over you tonight."

When Millie finished drinking, Alayzha and a few of the closest beings approached her slowly, emanating their healing lights. Receiving this familiar greeting, she summoned her own light and sent it out in all directions to her new friends.

Her mind filled with all the new sensations and questions.

She wanted conversation and answers and connection with everyone, all at once. But Alayzha and River had helped her with a sleeping draft, and the warmed wonder did its work. There was time for all the talk tomorrow. Within minutes, a sweet, heavy nighttime release crept into her eyelids.

River escorted her to the place they'd prepared—a nook in the ground protected by a canopy of trees. Several of that inner circle stayed with her that first night. She lay down in a bed of soft mosses—mosses that sighed audibly with welcome as they received her weight. Someone brought a blanket made from all their tender moments and covered her with it. As she fell away into slumber, she didn't care about anything, only this moment and nothing else, a moment of sweetness—inviolate, palpable sweetness. She slept as she had never slept in her lifetime, all the way through to morning.

When Millie woke up, she stretched, and the ground she'd slept on stretched with her. She arched her back, and it swelled up against her spine, supporting the length of it, retreating to its original shape as soon as she did. She opened her eyes, expecting the gray sadgrasses of the Nothing, and instead, she saw the daybright green of a lush world pulsating at her with delight. She smelled something warm and sweet. Picking up her head, she saw someone she thought she knew from before, maybe.

This woman held a tray laden with morning sacred oaths, a hot cup of possibilities, and a clean set of clothes. She put the tray down and summoned a vibrant, rose-colored light up from her heart and into her palm. Millie smiled and, pushing back years of Precinct habit, summoned her own light and came toward the woman to complete the greeting. Their globes met, merged, then swam back home from where they came. It had been years since she had felt the velvet of someone else's light in her hand.

Millie looked at the woman and said, "You all know my name, but I don't know yours."

"All Things Told! So sorry. I am Jelleric, guardian of the

boundary between Here and the Nothing. I come with friendship and nourishment. Tend to your rituals. I will keep this warm."

Millie stumbled to a nearby tree to release the night's dreams through her feet into the base of its trunk. Then she relieved herself behind it, wiping herself with a fistful of grasses. Afterward, she started the Preservation Pledge out of habit, then caught herself, a little embarrassed. Suddenly, she didn't know what to do. She had no story to embody. She didn't know the protocol for a decommissioned Player. She'd released her dreams into the tree and now found herself just standing there, arms hanging with nothing to pledge to, looking at this "Jelleric, guardian of the boundary," trying to work something out. She looked so familiar.

"What is it?" the woman asked.

"I thought you were someone else. You look very much like—"

A knowing smile rose into the woman's face. "You're not wrong, Millie. We have met." With this, she placed her hand on her own heart and turned in a complete circle, summoning her disguise as a decaying deek. Suddenly, there was Zargamom in all her decrepit glory! Millie's jaw dropped.

The woman toyed with her for a bit. "Billie in the Valley? No! Nellie. Nillie..."

They laughed together.

"I don't understand. Zargamom? But—"

"I am Jelleric. We felt your presence as soon as you arrived in the Nothing. But to make it into Here, you had to go through two gates: one was unselfishness, and the other was surrender. I took the form of Zargamom to see what you'd do. You took pity on me, gave me a name, tried to help me."

"What was the surrender?" Millie said.

"The True Nothing."

"I don't understand."

"Before you saw us, you changed a story, yes? And you owned that change, you put your name on it, so to speak. And once you did that, you found yourself in a state beyond words, yes?"

"I really have no idea how to talk about it. It's..." Millie trailed off, not wanting to stain the experience with any attempt at description. "Yes."

"Well, that was the True Nothing. Most beings recoil from the implications of the True Nothing. They can't handle it, so they end up back in the Nothing. You surrendered. You gave yourself completely to it, experiencing the whole thing. That was the second gateway. Now come. Eat."

Jelleric served up the oaths, nice and hot, fresh from the pot they'd been stewing in, with a small pitcher of compliments to drizzle over it, if she wanted. Millie lifted the spoonful of oaths with compliments to her mouth, she closed her eyes and almost cried. This was nourishment that made High Home meals look pitiful. It was simpler but infinitely more complex and powerful. Millie felt the language taking root in her bones, feeding her strength.

They talked about their childhoods. Jelleric had grown up in Near Emmering. They realized they were almost kin. They shared favorite forest places, epic ritual events, and the like. Jelleric had even known of Balimaya but had never met her. Millie wanted to know how long they'd all been here. How had they gotten here? What did they do?

And at the same time, she felt the True Nothing radiating from somewhere inside her bones. Her consciousness squinted at the indecipherable map of it, trying to pick the lock, to crack the code.

She and Jelleric had fallen silent, sipping their possibilities, when a Hereian came running at full speed.

Chapter 38

The Deep

Laefle, what is it?" Jelleric asked as she jumped to her feet.

"Jelleric, quick! Take her deeper. He's coming for her. Windwalker saw it."

"What do you mean 'he's coming for her'?" Jelleric asked.

"She just sent me to tell you to get the Ddrymmian Player into the Deep. He's coming to take her back."

"Who? What's happening?" Millie found herself almost unable to remember what she'd left, what there was to go back to. She felt something dart behind her heart.

Jelleric simply said, "We must go. Come with me right now."

Picking up her bowl of sacred oaths and her cup, Millie struggled to catch what was happening. "Who's coming?"

"A Preservation agent from the Precinct." Seeing that Millie was concerned about taking her food with her, she reassured her, "Don't worry, we're not going away like that. Put them back down."

Millie complied. "Jelleric, please tell me who it is."

"We must get you to safety."

"But...but—"

"Millie!" A practiced tone in Jelleric's voice stopped all thought in Millie's mind. She went on, "No matter what, stay inside your feet, anchor your light, and don't look down, don't look away, don't let go of my gaze—right here, Millie—not for anything."

For a while, there was nothing but Jelleric's gaze. Then Millie's feet began to tingle, and she was tempted to look down but remembered the instruction. She planted her feet, strengthened the light in her breast, and held on to Jelleric's gaze for all she was worth. The world went black around her. And then it fell, spinning. She heard the sound that had first ushered her into Here— the thousand beings, the gentle "mmmmmmmmmmm"— until there was no more sound.

Jelleric said, "That should do it."

Millie looked around. Nothing was different. They were still right where they'd been. The half-eaten sacred oaths were still on plates next to half-empty cups of possibilities. "But how is this a hiding place?"

"You are in the Deep now. No one from outside Here can see you. Even if they manage to pierce through the two gates and make it Here, they might be able to see me but not you, not while you're in the Deep. From where you are now, only Hereians can see you."

Millie wasn't sure. She knew the range of Preservation's reach and couldn't be absolutely certain that they didn't have cameras everywhere, even in Here.

"Careful though," Jelleric warned. "Being in the Deep opens your Sight. I don't have time to protect you from it, so if you start to feel yourself drifting into visions, *and you probably will*— Millie? Listen to me. If you start drifting, return your attention to everything you're experiencing physically. Press your feet into the ground, look at colors, be aware of textures. Stay present. Talk with Laefle here. He's your guard."

Millie's mind had wandered.

"Millie!"

She jumped back into the present. "Yes."

"Did you hear what I just said? It's crucial that you don't fall into the Sight. It can be very problematic. It's a hard gift to close once opened. Repeat what I told you to do."

"Yes, the Sight. Stay present. Look at colors, textures. Feet into the ground. Know what I'm feeling physically."

"All right, and talk with Laefle."

"Talk with Laefle," Millie repeated.

"I must go now. Laefle, don't leave her for anything."

He nodded.

Millie took hold of the woman's sleeve as she turned to go. "Jelleric? How long do I have to stay in the Deep?"

"For as long as we need to keep you safe." Jelleric left in a flash once she knew Millie was secure.

Laefle, somewhat starstruck and awkward in Millie's presence, kept tripping over himself, trying to please her. "Honored One, how may I serve you? Have you had enough of—oh! The sacred oaths. I interrupted your breakfast. I can reheat them."

"No, it's OK. I'm not hungry right now. What is your name again?"

"Laefle. I'm a messenger for the Hereians. I can move very fast."

She smiled. He looked away, not knowing what to do about that. He seemed much more comfortable with movement than with stasis. She thought of something. "Laefle, can you tell me more about being in the Deep? What does it mean, really? Am I trapped here?"

"Oh no, Honored One. Noth—"

"Wait, wait, wait. Laefle, please. Look at me."

He obeyed.

"Please stop calling me Honored One. My name is Millie. Will you call me 'Millie,' please?"

"Yes, Honored One."

She raised an eyebrow.

He tried again. "Yes...ma'am. Uh, M-M-M-Millie." He looked around to see if anyone had caught him being so familiar with her.

"Thank you. Now go on. You say I'm not trapped here in the Deep."

"No, not at all. It is only for your safety that we have you in hiding. The Deep is simply a perceptual device. It is a manipulation of frequencies that makes you invisible to anyone not fully integrated into our location."

She thought about this for a moment. "But if I'm not trapped, then how do I get out? If I wanted to be visible—"

"Oh no, no, no! You mustn't...uh, er...visibility would be—well, um, there's a reason for Windwalker's decision to give you sanctuary in the Deep, and if she thought it was important, Jelleric probably made the spell carefully so it would be...*diffi-cult*...to take a different path."

Millie thought that over for a bit. "I think I'd like to sit for a while and just be quiet. Can you leave me alone for a minute?"

"No, ma'am. I am sworn to stay with you. However, I will step away for a bit. But I must be close enough to protect you in case of an attack."

"Who could attack me Here? The place is so filled with pres-ence and well-being. Anyone originally intending to attack, if they ever made it in, would surely lose their desire to harm."

"Yes, well, that is not always the case. Our beings have been Here for millennia, and it's...not always the case."

"All right, then, I need a little time to myself."

Laefle picked up the cue and walked a respectable distance away and looked in the other direction while keeping watch through his backsight.

Millie sat still. She tried to remember what Jelleric had said about the Sight, something about conversing with Laefle or sound and texture or something. She was disappointed that her lovely morning with her new friend had been inter-rupted. She struggled to piece it all together, something about Preservation looking for her. She couldn't even remember why or how she got Here. And the True Nothing, she was still trying to...

It was so wonderful in Here; why even bother about yester-day or before? But as she gave her thoughts free rein, she ended up at the moment on the *Cinderella* set, in a deep curtsy when he said, "Your name, Miss?" and she said: "My name is Millie."

But in the end, that had gone well enough, hadn't it? What

a holy place this was. She only wished she could share it with Agnes—and then like a bucket of ice water thrown against her chest and down her back all at once, she remembered everything else.

Chapter 39

What Millie Sees

What's happened to Agnes? The air warped around Millie a little with a wobbling sound, and then smack in front of her, there was Agnes! Agnes, in a dark, cold cell with nothing in it, no bed even, just a hole in the ground for going to the bathroom.

"Agnes." Millie called out with clarity.

Agnes turned her head toward Millie.

"Agnes! I—"

But she wasn't responding to Millie. She was looking toward the sound of heavy locks clunking around the tiny window of her cell door. Millie flinched as a bag came flying through it into the cell. She watched Agnes pick up the bag with effort, then sit back down, leaning her head against the wall behind her. After a while, she began to pick at the moldy recrimination crusts.

Millie couldn't stand this. She grew afraid of her own power to See. Her ears began to twitch. This was not at all like Ddrymmian Seeing. Ddrymmian Seeing came unbidden, but when it came, you only entered into another's feelings in your heart; you knew their pain or their joy. This was a complete Seeing of structures, events, people, weather, words; and if Jelleric hadn't been so pressed for time, she would have trained her to open and close it at will. But there hadn't been time.

Millie pressed her forehead against Agnes's, and watched in wonder as Agnes's body flickered with light. *There's hope!* she thought, but then Agnes bent over with pain, wailing, "Millie! What did you do? Where are you?" As Agnes swayed back and forth in her anguish, the light through her cell window caught her face, over and over. That's when Millie saw the bruises, the cut on her upper lip, and in horror she redoubled her efforts. She got as close as she could to her deepfriend, and tried one last time.

"Agnes, listen. It's me, Millie. If you get sealed off into the Nothing, it could be the best thing that ever happened to you." She stood behind her and aimed her voice into the back of her heart. "You have no idea! Agnes. It's beautiful in Here. Do something to provoke them! Make them send you Here!" She stood directly in front of her, screaming as loud as possible right into her friend's face. *"Agnes!"*

Laefle stiffened a bit where he was sitting and watched her carefully. She didn't seem to be moving.

"Miss Millie." Laefle put a hand on her shoulder.

She didn't feel it right away.

"Miss Millie." He shook a little harder.

Notice colors, textures. She forced her eyes somewhere besides Agnes's face. There were lilies of the valley nearby. She looked at them hard. She conjured how they would smell, then remembered she could move closer to them and smell them for real with her own nose. As soon as she did, the air wobbled around her again, and the lush forest reappeared around her. Laefle was at her side, steadying her arm under the elbow.

Millie got up and paced, walking around aimlessly. Laefle stepped back to give her room. Finally, she sat back down and nibbled one of the partially eaten oaths. It was so good. It made her think of her mother's baking, which she could smell now, the unmistakable aroma of hooray!cakes.

The air wobbled again, sending her into the NetherJunctures, into her childhood kitchen, only it was clean, unused, except for some crumbs left by the last person who had eaten there— probably Wrem. He never cleaned up after himself. Millie's heart raced and her breath shallowed as she moved through the hallway of her Ddrymmian home to where she heard her mothers murmuring in their bedroom. She peeked through the doorway.

Mama Linn! So frail. How did she get so frail? Mama Bette was fixing the bedding roughly and with an expertise that belied much experience. How long had Mama Linn been this sick?

"Ow." Linn grimaced.

"Well, I got to tuck it in, hon."

"Bette, please." She tried to clear her throat. "I mean it."

"All right." She stopped, softened, and stood there looking at her wife.

When Linn looked up and caught the tenderness in her face, she reached out. "Sit with me, will you?" Linn asked. Bette faltered, blew her nose, and tossed the handkerchief to the floor.

Millie squirmed and tried desperately to think of something or someone else to focus on. She wanted to find the lilies again. She even remembered her centering stone, but she couldn't tear her eyes off her mothers, one gray, haggard, and bony in the bed, the other still stout and overworked, exhausted and depressed. It seemed like they were only days, maybe hours, away from Mama Linn reaching the dark Door to Elsewhere.

"Come on, my lightbringer, we don't have to talk about anything. Just be with me."

Bette wrestled her fleeing impulse down, turned, and sat on the bed, kicking off her shoes. She opened the covers to climb in with Linn. Millie saw Mama Linn's fully ravaged body—marks of malnourishment, her legs' thinly veiled bones. As she reached up for Bette's embrace, Millie saw that the skin hung off her arm bones like an afterthought. Her hair had fallen out somewhat unevenly, whole patches of scalp showed through, and what was left was gray, not in color so much as in sorrow, in starvation of the soul. There were spots on her face that she'd never seen before. What in black stars had happened?

Millie tried to get herself out of there. Her ears had gone from intermittent twitching to a constant tremble as she looked for the hallway to walk out of the house and back to Here. It almost worked. She found herself sitting on the log where she'd started, but her mothers were still in their bed right next to her. She'd forgotten all about her centering stone.

Then Bette got up very gently out of the bed and told Linn, "Sweetlight, I'll be right back. I just have to pee."

When she got into the hallway, Wrem had just closed the front door behind him. He leaned heavily on a cane, and even in his late thirties, even with a pronounced limp, he still looked like the lumbering teenager she had loved, coming down the hall, trying to be quiet. Millie's heart broke at the sight of him. She forgot everything and fell hard into the Seeing.

"Where's Drauml? I thought she was helpin' you today," he asked.

"She'll be back soon. Had to go do some errands. Ah, my Wrem." Bette wrapped her arms around him and wept. He stood there long and held her.

"What did they say?" she asked him when she got her composure back.

"I give 'er the papers, the waitin' room lady, and she says is this a joke, and I says no. I tell her Mama's dyin', and she says—" He stopped and thought better of it. "Never mind. Anyway, papers are only good for kindlin' now."

"Well, Alphabet Delights is dark. What will we do?"

"Don't worry, Mama, we'll figure it out."

"Drauml couldn't get any orders, even from that *Rumpelstiltskin* character. No one will touch us."

"I know, I know."

"How are you doin'?"

"Grelle been workin' on me good. Won't be able to work the trees no more, though."

"Ah, my Wremmy. I don't know. People been bringin' us food all day, but..." And she wept again. "I can't lose her. I can't."

He held her for a moment, then said, "Lemme go see her. I'll sit with her, and you eat and rest a bit."

Bette went to the kitchen to heat up some water for Wrem and herself. On the countertop, there were two bowls someone had left for them. She lifted the towels to see and spooned some of the dense dictionary porridge into her mouth like she hadn't eaten in days. She stopped herself, to ration the food, then put her head down in her arms on the table, and fell into a deep sleep.

Millie dug her fingers into the soil by her right foot and tried hard to pull herself back into Here, but she couldn't take her eyes off her brother, who looked so much older than he was. Stooped over, his face sharpened into a map of suffering and forbearance. When he spoke, she noticed that some of his teeth were missing. And what had happened to his leg? Wrem not in the forest tending trees? He would go dark within a year.

Overcome, Millie wrapped her arms around her stomach and began to rock while a low, growing howl came up from her entrails. She tried to be quiet, forgetting that her family couldn't hear her. But finally, she cried out, "Mama Linn! I'm sorry. Mama Bette! Wrem! Where's Grelle? Find the healer! Somebody help Mama Linn!"

The storm boiling in her belly could no longer be contained. She felt sick and faint and managed to run behind a tree just in time to throw up. Laefle had been trying to get her attention. He'd seen it coming and was already there, holding her hair back, ready with a cool, lavendered cloth in his hands. He dipped it into psalms water and wrung it out, speaking a healing chant in Hereian. He gave it to Millie. She wiped her face with it and tossed it into the clean bucket he offered her. A good vomit can really clear the mind.

She leaned on his arm as he led her to another sitting place, a large stone this time, warmed by the sun. Her legs would barely carry her. He sat her down with skill and tenderness. He put his left palm on her back, just between her shoulder blades, and began to hum through his arm into his hand and into her back. She felt a warm sense of well-being seep in through the back door of her heart, the beginnings of peace. Gratitude welled up in her eyes.

"Thank you, L-Ler— I forgot your name."

"Laefle."

"Laefle. Thank you."

They sat in silence for a while.

"Please help me. I don't want the Sight. I...I'm so afraid to See anything else. I've...I'm—can you take this away from me somehow?"

"Shhhh. Quiet now." Gently, he tried to remind her of how to calm herself. "It's part of being in the Deep, so I can't take it away from you. But remember Jelleric's words. 'Stay present.' Notice textures, colors. This will keep you in Here and safe in the now, in the Deep—but only if you concentrate. It can't be intermittent. It's hard when you're just beginning. So let's practice. Look at this grass over here, right here." He pointed to it. "See it? See this little tuft of grass?"

"Yes."

"Notice how a couple of the blades are much higher than the rest. What else do you see?"

"I see...some tiny pebbles at the base, to the left of the tuft."

His palm was still at her back, but he was pulling it away very slowly so she wouldn't notice, encouraging her to stand in her own peace. "Yes, good. How many are there?"

She spent a moment counting them. "Seventeen tiny ones, eight larger ones."

"What else do you notice?"

"The lilies of the valley...next to it. I love lilies of the valley." Then she remembered. "Zargamom, she called me 'Nellie in the valley.'" And with that memory, the whole mess of what she'd wrought came back—the Nothing, the scaredy-pair.

Laefle was ahead of this. "Millie, listen to my voice. Stay in Here. Go closer so you can really smell them." He placed his hand gently on her back again, in the same place between her shoulder blades. Together, they walked closer to the flowers. She bent down and sniffed, feeling their sweetness, and leaned back into the deep peace offered by Laefle's support. She let herself be comforted and eventually grew oblivious to her surroundings in a dreamy deliciousness of quietude.

Despite her state, though, she was still aware. All around, she saw signs of intense watchfulness and activity. Someone trotted by with purpose, pausing to acknowledge her presence with a respectful nod. Someone else called out to Laefle from off in the distance. Laefle answered but did not move from where he was. He had sealed his presence in with Millie.

Then Alayzha Windwalker's voice came into the space through the trees, almost as if carried there on the air. "All beings, Preservation agents are nearing the boundary. Remember our Oneness—Oneness in everything, even with beings from other lands. We must strengthen our kindness, our senses—sight, our hearing—and we must call on a deeper Oneness. It's doubtful they will be able to see us, but if for any reason they do, remember, we must go about our normal business. They must not know the Ddrymmian Player is here. She is safe in the Deep now. If you meet a Preservation agent, greet with kindness and engage the heart. Perhaps they will open. If so, bring them to me. If not, distract. The Ddrymmian Player must be kept safe at all costs."

Millie's dreamy state started chafing against something else inside her. She smiled at Laefle with heavy-lidded confusion. *So much random stuff going on. What's the big deal? And anyway, what could they possibly want from me? I have nothing more to give and certainly nothing to lose. It doesn't matter. Nothing matters.*

Remember to focus. Stay present. Look at the lilies—lilies and their little white heads lined up and down the green stem, sweet lilies of the valley, lilies of the valley, Nellie in the valley, Billie in the willie. She laughed again at how Zargamom could never get it right. She thought of Zargamom and meeting her and naming her and all the panic and desperation she'd felt between the Nothing and Here and the Almost with his crappy little box of un-meals.

There was her mother's baking again. Then, the nauseating soup of her mothers and the bedroom and Agnes in her cell and all the meetings with Mix and the Precinct and her

High Home and—oh Beings All! Her High Home! That invisible thousand-year-old sanctuary. And with a start, she remembered Blaze. What had happened to her staff? What had they done to Shank? To Lydia? *My name is Millie.*

She tried to shake off the visions by focusing on the lilies and the grasses around her. But suddenly, she didn't want the dreamy lilies of the valley anymore. She didn't want to be hidden in the Deep. She wanted out. She wanted to go home. She wanted her family.

Chapter 40

The Decision to See

Millie knew nothing of this spell Jelleric had invoked. But she and Jelleric had Ddrym in common, so perhaps old trainings might work to free her from this "containment." Still, Millie was shrewd enough to know she needed more information before escaping. With shaking legs and a pounding heart, she decided to See who was coming for her from the Precinct and why. Then she could make a plan.

She was terrified, so to address this first, she grounded her feet, lengthened her spine, and remembered the centering stone. She didn't have hers anymore, so she checked her surroundings mindfully. She let her eyes touch all the stones on the earth around her, and then she saw it—a perfect, small, flat, oblong pebble with a thumb-rub hollow just right for her hand.

Laefle approached, saying, "Honored—Miss Millie, are you all right?"

She jumped and replied, "Oh! Yes, Laefle. I'm just remembering a technique I learned as a girl to help me stay calm."

Afraid he might distract her from Seeing again, she added, "I'll need to stand over here for a moment."

He gave her the distance, but locked his eyes on her.

She picked up the stone and stilled herself, sending all her anxieties and fears downward into the stone. She felt them travel through her arms and into her hands, and the stone received them and transmuted them. Then to keep Laefle quiet, she smiled and intentionally tried to say the word "Ddrym." Immediately, both she and he felt the seductive sweetness, and she went to work right away, weaving together Ddrymmian and Hereian Seeing.

All of Balimaya's teachings were coming back now. *Let the whole heart flow into every act. Release all desire for any given outcome. Just act with and for and inside Oneness.*

She asked the question silently, *Who is coming for me?*

The air warbled and shimmered around her. She saw Frank as a determined Agent Four Seven marching through Larkshen flanked by two heavily armed guards. She felt an overwhelming desperation in him, terror of what he was about to do, an almost certainty that he would go dark doing it. Several Larksheners along the path bowed to them when they passed, as was the custom.

Since it was Frank coming, she intensified her resolve to escape the Deep. She kept alive the Seeing, watching as they approached the graying landscape that had made her so physically ill on her way to the Nothing. As they progressed down the pathway, her Ddrymmian Seeing helped her feel him: he was reviewing the sequence in his mind, the sequence of spells needed to open the Nothing. She felt him working out how he might say them in reverse to get back out. She heard him practice the syllables silently in his heart. She felt him wondering if he should just leave the gateway open to the Nothing, thereby increasing their chances of getting back out. He wondered if the guards would allow it.

This confused her. If the guards would *allow* it? Frank was one of the highest agents in the Precinct. He would *tell* them to allow it, unless... What was going on here? Were they delivering *him* to the Nothing?

Everything came into stark focus. She would meet Frank head-on. She would negotiate with him. She had to get to her mothers. Nothing else mattered—not her career, not her happiness in Here, not her own life. And with a singularity of intent she'd never felt before, she willed herself to freedom, to visibility.

Laefle saw the energy shift all around her and watched in horror as she worked herself free of the Deep. No one had ever been capable of this, and he was afraid. There had been a meeting the night before while Millie slept. Alayzha Windwalker had reminded them of the foretelling. The Ddrymmian Player would initiate a return to Oneness throughout StoryEarth. There would be no more divisions. Hereians would roam freely, visible to all. New stories could have new breath and live anywhere and be told to and by anyone. The tyranny of Preservation would be lifted—but only if the Ddrymmian Player was kept safe until the way forward could be revealed.

Laefle used every piece of training he'd been taught. He opened his heart to her and shared with her the importance of her safety. He pleaded with her while trying to approach her with his left hand to induce the sleepy sense of well-being again. She never let him get that close.

"Millie, please. You don't understand."

"What is there to understand, Laefle? Why do you feel such a sense of threat in this place where Oneness prevails and all things are possible? I don't."

"The threat is the interruption of process. You are in Here! That, in itself, is a miracle. It is the fulfillment of the foretelling. We must keep you safe until we know the way forward, and that has not been told yet."

"How do you know this isn't the way forward? That what I'm doing isn't the very way forward you're all waiting for?"

Laefle paused to consider this, and in that instant, the truth in her questions filled Millie's body with the power of flight. She shot out of the Deep and into the present, and then up into the air, physically, with a loud rush of something like the sound of wind and water dancing hard against each other. She felt herself climbing, rising, her will, spirit, and muscles all firing to this end, up and up and up until she saw the forestry underneath her. She hovered over the tops of the tallest trees.

Alayzha Windwalker saw it and rushed up to meet her. The elder opened her own inmost self to Millie. She opened her soul to Millie, expanding in the sky, with wings of light keeping her aloft. Millie held fast, but faltered in the face of this extraordinary vision.

Alayzha's team surrounded the two, facing outward, ready for anything. Then she spoke to Millie, saying, "Millicent Fireflower, you must return to the Deep for all our sakes. We are oathbound to protect you from forces that threaten your well-being. And we have seen it coming. They mean to return you to a life of stasis and suffering. We cannot let that happen. You are safe in the Deep. But we cannot protect you outside of Here."

Millie—hovering, face-to-face with the fiercest, most beautiful creature she'd ever seen—still had Frank in her backsight. She saw the terror, the resolve, the integrity in his eyes. She didn't know what he was up to, but she felt her respect for his essence, and she felt her own mother's imminent passage as well. She would have to speak to Windwalker in a language that would reach her, something that addressed saving all StoryEarth.

"Honored Windwalker, I must ask the same question of you that I asked of Laefle only moments ago. How do you know this isn't part of the unfolding? Every great endeavor is fraught with risk. I see them coming too. And as luck would have it, I know one of them very well. To fulfill this mission, I must speak with him directly." Technically, she wasn't lying.

Windwalker spoke with a compelling voice. "This being you speak of whom you know well, Millicent, you do not know what they're capable of with us. We developed the skill to go Deep for a reason. There are things I cannot tell you. There's no time. Please, for your sake, for all our sakes, for the good of StoryEarth itself, listen to my voice." Something deep inside Millie was arrested by Windwalker's tone. "Listen to my voice,

Millicent. Come inside and feel the hearts that beat for you, hearts that have been waiting for you for thousands of years."

Millie looked around her. While they'd been talking, Windwalker had managed to bring her down to the ground, to the center of the field where she had landed the day before. All the Hereians were there, their attention focused on Millie's face and Windwalker's words.

"Beings have wasted in the Nothing, they have gone dark in Here, they have suffered throughout Ddrym. They've suffered in the Precinct, all waiting for the chance, working for the chance to experience Oneness. Thousands, hundreds of thousands, have given their whole lives to it. Please don't let hasty, fearful thoughts squander the one opportunity we have to see Oneness prevail once and for all."

Millie's head was bowed, and her eyes filled with tears. How much did her desire to be with her mothers weigh in relation to all that suffering? She hadn't asked for all this responsibility. They were foisting it onto her, just like the family business had been foisted onto her years ago, everyone painting all their hopes onto her body. It wouldn't work. She wasn't who they thought she was. She decided to speak the absolute truth, *her* absolute truth.

"Alayzha Windwalker, Honored One, all of you, there is nothing special about me. You renounce Oneness and increase the sense of separation by making me something special, something that you are not. My mothers need me. I never felt it before, but I know it now." Tears were catching at her throat. "I know it now!" she shouted it up into the sky as though maybe her mothers would be able to hear it.

"You clearly have the power to keep me in Here against my will, but if you do, you are no better than the Preservation agents coming for me. Let us each have our path. You must be in Here. I must be with my family. StoryEarth must be whatever it is without our intervention. All of it, *all of it,* is held in Oneness anyway, whether we see it or not."

Windwalker held Millie's gaze for several breaths. A circle of beings had formed around them. Several were moved to tears. Someone from the circle began to hum, and the tone was picked up by another and another until everyone had joined in the sound.

While they hummed, Millie walked around the circle, looking in their eyes as she continued, "All of you have experienced the True Nothing, or you wouldn't be in Here. So you know it exists, and you know it's everywhere, that its very nature lives inside, outside, with, without, and within Oneness. Nothing matters in the True Nothing." She planted her feet and opened the fullest extent of her will and her inmost self to them all. "And everything matters."

Then she engaged the engine of her intent, her love for her mothers. It roared, and in a split second, she was up again—up and up and up and up, until she took flight and propelled forward, outward, onward, and up, away from the lush beauty of Here. The moment happened so fast that no one, not even Alayzha Windwalker, registered that it had happened until Millie had disappeared from view.

Millie flew as if she'd done it all her life. She'd never been so terrified, so thrilled, or so certain. Her body found its shape in just the right ways to ride the shoulders of the air, until she finally arrived at her destination, the edge of the bleak, endless, colorless, featureless Nothing. For an instant, she invoked the memory of the True Nothing, and it gave her peace.

She landed roughly on the ground. It was the place with the nearby hills just off in the distance, where she had first met Jelleric, naming her Zargamom. Her body pulsated with life and power, and this power radiated outward into this place. It was the opposite of the shrinking diminishment she'd felt when she'd first arrived. The Nothing had no power over her now.

She wasn't sure where the boundary was, so she stood still and reached into her own heart for access to the love and concern she felt for her mothers. She stood for a long time, her legs almost faltering. She pressed her feet ever more firmly into ground that wasn't there. So she lengthening her spine instead, softening the backs of her lungs. She waited without "waiting," aware of what could almost be called joy, aware of the blood circulating in her veins, her breath moving in and out, fulfilling its transactions, keeping her alive.

Before long, she heard the warbling sound of the boundary behind her. She turned around and saw him through the transparent veil.

"Frank."

Chapter 41

A Surprise for
Agent Four Seven

With the boundary gap still shimmering behind him, Millie could see the two guards waiting.

"Millie." When Frank saw her face, relief flooded his body. He recovered his professional stance quickly, but—who knows why—he tried an uncharacteristically solicitous approach. Perhaps he felt his own vulnerability, not knowing whether he would get them back out of there alive. Perhaps it was seeing her again unharmed, unmolested by the Nothing. "Millie, I have come—"

They were interrupted by a gaggle of deeks making a ruckus. Dressed in what might once have been soldiers' uniforms, two of them were limping and shuffling next to a very tall, broad, extremely voluptuous woman, a former dancer (evidently the ballet diva from the beloved Big Girls Dance Troupe). Her leotard was ripped in the back, and her tutu had unraveled so badly that it threatened to trip her. Agent Four Seven looked on in horror.

One of the soldiers said to the diva, "*Always* guarding you. Won't do it anymore. *You* guard *us*. Do the story, do the story, do the story, do the story."

"Shut up, shut up, shut up," she muttered.

"Shut up, shut up, shut up," they mimicked.

"*Don't remember it!*" she finally shrieked, looking around frantically for hints.

"You can't remember it, you can't remember it," they chanted neener-neener style, dancing around, pointing at her, taunting, mean as fifth graders.

Then the diva gave a hearty raspberry in response, turned around, and aimed a loud, flabby fart at them. It was epic. She cackled with glee.

The soldiers screamed and ran away, nearly knocking over an old deek toddling his way toward them with two canes made from rude branches, on his way to nowhere. His suit had bleached out completely, if it had ever had any color in the first place. His pants were held up on his skeletal frame by sashes he'd no doubt stolen or bartered off more recent prisoners. He was pretty far gone.

"Stupid idiots, verbaidy bick flick phllllllh," he muttered, his head searching left and right, eyes gone a little blind with time. "No snow here. Ble ble hffffsgreh." He walked with a dogged unwillingness to submit to the pain. His breath reeked so bad that Millie and Frank could smell it from twenty feet away. He was unintentionally hiccupping toward the boundary, but not where they were standing.

Frank returned to the business at hand. "M-Millie. I'm here to...to...escort you back. StoryEarth is in chaos, and only one thing will set it straight. You...you...will be...Mama Bear, and, uh, the other one, the, uh...will return as Cinderella. Everything goes back to how it was."

"OK, Frank, but I need a fav—" This was going to be much easier than she thought.

"Only difference is you will live at the Preservation Precinct Forrectional Cafility. If more mistake, you—" He pointed to her, drew his index finger across his neck, and said, "Dark. Poof." He couldn't seem to get the words he wanted.

The mud-deep, bottommost *no* spoke itself into their conversation, and Millie knew the old deek had probably bumped into the boundary. He screeched with horror at losing his left arm and came hobbling/scuttling toward them, crying, "My arm!"

Millie tried to calm him. "Don't worry, sir, it's still there.

See?" She took his arm gently and showed him it was still there. "This happened to me once too. You just bumped into the boundary. It's very frightening, isn't it? But you're OK now."

He was clearly not. Trembling and weeping, he shoved her away. "Get away, you...you...witch!" The shove threw him off-balance, and she instinctively helped him recover it. "I said, get away!" he yelled, brandishing one of his canes.

Frank grabbed the old deek and pulled him away from Millie with one rough jerk. "Watch yourself, old man!"

Shocked by the intervention, the deek wheeled around to face his assailant, almost falling again. Their eyes met, and Frank's hair stood on end. The old man suddenly rose into his own eyes. With wonder and grief, he whispered, "Frank?"

Four Seven went down the list of people he'd consigned to the Nothing. Who would have known him by name? No one even remotely met this description. He pushed the man's hands onto his canes. "I am...Preservation agent...chief of...the kind of story where, um, you tell the story to somebo...to a young...a kid..." He grimaced and put his hand to his forehead.

"Fairy Tales," Millie offered. *Why is he disintegrating so fast?*

"Fairy Tales."

"I'm sorry, Frank," the old man said, choking the words out.

Four Seven, barely able to hold himself together as it was, said between his teeth, "Leave this place before you meet a worse end."

The old man, still inside his eyes, chuckled darkly. "A worse end? What might that be, Frank?"

"Not Frank. *Agent Four—*"

"You don't know your own father." Worlds hung in the air between them while Millie looked on. "There is no worse end." He said it like a man watching him from the other side of the darkness.

Frank stared at him. His hands started trembling, and he rubbed his right thumb against the crook of his index finger. His legs grew weak, his breathing shallow. "Dad?"

But the old man had fallen through a hole in the psychic netting, back into his gibberish. "It was fun the blickerbang. Blickerbang *bang*. Fffflitthskjsdfious. Backstack flickla shickledeedee."

"Dad! Pain. Mom gave up *everything*...still giving up. You... *belong*...in Nothing! *Bad dad*."

"Frank, look at me—" Millie tried to distract him.

"Don't. Not Frank." He had to think. "Agent." He stamped his feet, trying to find it. "I'm Agent Four S-s-s..."

"Seven, Frank. You're Agent Four Seven."

He had started sweating profusely.

"Frank? Look at me!"

"Is it hot? It's hot in here. Hot, hot, hot, hot, hot, hot." He was pulling at his collar, untying his tie.

"OK, good. Undo your tie," she said, trying to help him.

"Undo *tie*? No. We go. *Now!* No tie. We—you...go...you back to...back to..." He was looking for the exit. "Where is it?"

During this conversation, the old deek had made his arduous way back to where he came from, another nowhere neighborhood in the Nothing. They let him go.

"Which way? Where's the—I think it's—come." He took her arm and headed resolutely away from the boundary.

"Nope. It's over here," she said, deftly taking charge, walking beside him while she turned them back around. She hadn't ever seen him in this much disrepair, not even in high school during his father's betrayal.

Why didn't this ever happen to me? she thought.

And then she remembered. She had imagined a different outcome to the *Snow White* story. This was the very thing he could never do. All he had was a Preservation ethic so deeply entrenched that it had lost all its access to oxygen. It had become a kind of rigor mortis of the mind. He could not change anything, could not go outside the lines in any way. The Nothing would eat him alive within minutes. That's what it was, to him. So that's what would happen.

"Agent Four Seven, I'll go with you to the Precinct."

"Yes."

"Right now." She'd figure out how to get to her mothers later. For now, she had to get them both out of there.

"Right now," he repeated, not seeming to know what to do next.

Millie panicked. *"Frank! The boundary!"*

She saw it. They would have to run. When Agent Four Seven had opened it, he hadn't closed it behind him. But Millie noticed it was "healing" shut on its own. When Frank saw it, his muscle memory and survival instincts kicked in. He thrust his arms through it, holding the opening awake. He automatically spoke the words he'd practiced backward a thousand times on the way there, the entering spell spoken in reverse as an exit strategy. Thanks to Beings All, those words were still in the frontmost part of his mind. His mouth seemed to move of its own accord, and he got the opening just large enough for both of them to get through in one push. Once they were on the other side of it, Frank grabbed his throat, gasped for air, and collapsed.

Part Five

The Road Back

Chapter 42

Agent Four Seven Collapses

The guards jumped into action, one performing emergency protocols on his body while the heftier one sealed the gateway to the Nothing.

"Come on, Frank. You can do this," Millie said, moving toward him.

The one who'd sealed off the Nothing grabbed her hands and cuffed her, adding, "How dare you address a Preservation agent by his name!"

"I've known him since we were fifteen. He's going dark on your watch, if you don't set me free."

The brute wrote something on his little notepad. She didn't care. She watched as the other guard lifted Frank's eyelids, shined a flashlight in his eyes, and listened to his heart. He opened Four Seven's mouth and placed two tiny capsules, Revivatrols, in the back of his throat. Nothing happened. The guard tending to Frank tried one last thing: Using what little esoteric training he'd had, he tried awakening Frank's energetic core. (Learning this skill was optional in an agent's training. Almost no one was interested in it.) He spoke the words woodenly and ran his palm over the chakras. No response.

"Sirs, I have Ddrymmian training in healing. There are

things I can do to help," she said. "But I will need the use of my hands."

Four Seven seemed beyond help, but the one who'd been tending him uncuffed her anyway. The beefy guard was not pleased. "Stillwell, are you crazy? What are you doing?"

"Ralph, come on. I've done all the protocols. He's not responding to anything. She's Ddrymmian. She might be able to save him."

Ralph made a sound of disgust, watching for the slightest wrong move on her part.

She walked over to where Frank was lying and kneeled beside him. He was on his back, breathing but only barely, and his face was sheet white. She inspected his hands and told the guards to remove his shoes. She put her ear to his chest, listening for both the rhythm of his breathing and its connection to his heartbeat. She thought for a moment, then abruptly got up to look for a certain plant. The guards were startled into an aggressive stance.

"I have to find some gotsmer leaves. Can you help me?"

They had blank faces. "Ms. Fireflower, there's no vegetation here, not for miles."

"Right. Right. OK." *Think fast, Millie. Come on. Oh, Balimaya, what now? How do I save him?* She remembered being taught over and over that desperation clouded the mind. Ears twitching, she sat at Frank's feet, facing his body. Even though she could feel his life force slipping away. She took the little stone with the thumb hollow out of its special hiding place, and concentrated her own thoughts downward into her hands.

With every fiber of her being, she centered herself, opening her own channels so the energy would flow freely. She heard the guards step away, startled. Her concentration must have resulted in a burgeoning of light from within her. When she felt fully grounded, she put the stone back, then placed her palms on his feet, fingers pointing downward, the center of each palm in the arch of each foot.

His energy had been receding through the top of his head.

She called it back down toward her hands. She was patient. The pull was strong in the other direction. He had suffered two shocks: first the Nothing and its deep strangeness and then meeting his father. She summoned his life force back, feeling her own Ddrymmian pull toward light, and began to feel the reversal of direction. The energies swam back down through his throat, through the thoracic area of his spine, down his vertebrae, through his pelvis, and into his legs.

As soon as his life force made contact with her hands, she switched directions. Focusing her own channels, she let her force flow into his legs, up through his skeletal system, all the way through his skull. Simultaneously, she channeled a healing essence from the air around her and sent it swirling through his circulatory system, through his heart. Together, these efforts brought some color back into his face. The more sympathetic guard said, "Look! His eyes are fluttering."

She continued her ministrations, modulating the intensities based on the energetic information she received. She pulled something invisible out of his feet, then flicked it away with her fingers vigorously, off to the side. She did this several times. Eventually, she was quiet.

The beefy guard said, "What now?"

She was tired. "We wait. If it worked, I may have to modulate his system a bit to balance it. We'll see. Shouldn't be long."

About five minutes went by. Then his breathing deepened, his fingers twitched, and he opened his eyes. Millie stayed at his feet, ready to resume if necessary. Now his eyes were wide open, and he looked up at Ralph.

Ralph said roughly, "Agent Four Seven, we almost lost you."

"I don't know if I can move," he replied.

Ralph said, "Maybe you shouldn't try just yet. We don't know what all she did to you."

"Oh, Cuss Words Custard, Ralph! She saved his life," Stillwell said. They glared at each other.

Forgetting all protocol, Frank not only introduced her to his guards but also used their family names. "Millie, this is Ralph.

Ralph, Millie. That guy over there is Stillwell. I don't know what his first name is."

They were all embarrassed enough to pretend it was normal.

"Frank, can you push into my hand with this foot? Let me see. Push," Millie instructed.

He did.

"Good. Other foot?" Also good. "Now," she said, moving closer to his chest and taking hold of his hand, "can you squeeze my hand? Good. OK, give me your other hand." All the indications looked good. She very slowly helped him up to a sitting position and, after a fashion, got him standing. She had to support him by putting his left arm around her shoulders.

"There you go. See? All good." She made eye contact with the two guards. Ralph, still stinging from having his name tossed to a prisoner, looked away. Stillwell smiled.

Now it was time to start the journey back.

Chapter 43

A Compromise

Frank let himself be supported by her for the first few yards, with Ralph and Stillwell flanking them. When he felt secure enough, he thanked her and walked on his own, though it slowed them down a little.

Millie thought she saw something flicker at the edge of her vision, but when she turned her head, nothing was there. This part of the NetherJunctures was completely barren, with sadgrasses languishing on the borders of a gray path leading toward the luxurious greenery of Larkshen. She said, "Frank, I need to ask you a favor."

"Agent Four Seven," he replied curtly.

She looked at Ralph and Stillwell. "Yep, he's all better now." Stillwell acknowledged the humor. Ralph did not. "OK, Agent Four Seven, the Door to Elsewhere is right at the foot of my mother's bed, my mama Linn. Remember her? Is there any way we could go there together on our way to the set? I'm not asking for a reduction of sentence or anything, just the opportunity to see my mother before she goes dark."

He squirmed. She had saved his life. But his job was still on the line, and any concessions he made would surely feed Woundliss's paranoia—plus, because of her, they were already trying to dig the Precinct out of a disastrous PR hole. They walked in silence for a while. A faint green bled into blades of grass here and there. A tiny shock of gold showed up in the centers of little daisies. There was the flicker again, at the other edge of her vision this time. What was it?

She knew better than to push him. Everything depended on how well she could manage the tension between feeling her own overwhelming need and giving him space to make the decision she wanted. She began to feel ever stronger in response to the colors around her, which deepened as they made their way toward Larkshen. Frank also seemed to be getting stronger with every step. More and more color animated the grass and the trees along the way, which was comforting to them all.

Again, there was the flickering, but this time a little more was visible. It looked like—could it be?—Jelleric. She let the thought all the way in and then saw her walking right beside her! She calmed herself and opened to more of her own vision, and like a photograph developing in the darkroom, she began to see them all materializing around her. Plain as day, there they were—Jelleric, Laefle, and eight or ten of the Hereians, even Alayzha Windwalker, walking calmly beside and around them. Millie waved at them, then winked at Ralph and Stillwell in a conspiratorial way. "Don't worry," she said, "they're my friends from Here."

The two guards looked at each other, confused.

She whispered to Frank, "Agent Four Seven, don't worry, these are some of the friends I made from Here—a place I found after I'd been in the Nothing for a while."

Frank looked at Stillwell, then at Ralph. They shrugged back at him. He said to her, "Ms. Fireflower, let's sit down for a bit. You seem confused."

"Actually, I'd really rather keep going. I need to get to Mama Linn's."

"OK," he said. "But just for a moment, let's sit. I think perhaps the healing services you performed for me have taxed you overmuch. Here." He signaled to Ralph to give her his emergency flask. "Ralph will give you some liquid coherence. Drink."

"I feel great. I feel great, so much better now that Laefle is here." She went to hold Laefle's hand, but he shook his head and mouthed something she couldn't hear. She squinted at him to understand it better but really couldn't hear him.

"Laefle," she said, "this is my friend, Preservation Precinct Agent Four Seven." They continued walking. "Only, if you were in Here," she said to Four Seven, risking a foolhardy sense of intimacy, "your name would be Frank."

"Ms. Fireflower, I *am* here. To whom are you talking?"

"No, no," she said. "No, I mean if you were in Here, inside or beyond the Nothing or whatever." She gave a half-hearted laugh, realizing that he couldn't possibly understand.

"Yes, well, no matter. Drink up!" he said cheerily, tilting the flask into her mouth, hoping it would clarify her mind and they could put this moment behind them. It helped some. After a bit, they got up again and continued walking. Agent Four Seven, Ralph, Stillwell, Millie, and all her friends from Here made their way slowly toward Larkshen.

They had reached its outer edges, and the NetherJunctures around them had gradually become fresh and vibrant with color. Flowers stood in their places with shouting reds, shy reds, burnt oranges, singing yellows, lavenders, periwinkle, and turquoise blues. Leaves puffed out in their fullness now, plump and green.

As they progressed farther into Larkshen, the residents got wind of her presence and signed their respect for her secretly, with their hands, as she passed. The men walked a little taller for the adoring crowd. Millie took a chance at moving her fingers discreetly to say, *Thank you, May Oneness prevail.* Speaking their language reminded her of Shank. She searched for his craggy face among the beings—their green skin, such a comfort to see—who had come to pay their respects.

"Agent Four Seven, may I ask what has become of my staff?"

"Everyone working in the Fireflower High Home, and the Grath High Home actually, has been given tracers, pending the results of the investigation."

"But they had absolutely no knowledge of our plans. I swear it."

"Yes, well, we will be the ones to determine that. All in good time."

It was clear that she and he were resuming their adversarial roles.

Millie watched Jelleric out of the corner of her eye, understanding finally that Agent Four Seven and his boys couldn't see them. She wondered about her friends' safety outside of Here. Looking around for Jelleric, she noticed her friend had faded some. Jelleric was only half as visible now, Laefle as well. They were all still there, but had receded somewhat from the group. Ralph and Stillwell held her for security on either side.

"My mothers. If we go up that path, we'll get there sooner."

"Ms. Fireflower, surely you understand that we can't bring you to your mothers. It's very unfortunate, but..."

Millie stopped and looked at Four Seven. She dropped to her knees and cried as she begged him, "Please, Agent Four Seven. Mama Linn is dying. Please. You are a good man. I know this. You can somehow double my punishment afterward, but..."

Four Seven tried to lift her, clearly uncomfortable with this unchecked show of raw emotion, but she pulled away. He conferred with Ralph and Stillwell.

Millie dropped her head into her hands and wept. As she tried to let the river of her grief flow through her, she began to feel something tender. Peace melted in through her back like butter on pancakes. Unexpected relief! And then she was aware of what had to be Laefle's hand at her back, radiating the healing energy. She wanted to acknowledge him, but her bliss had replaced any sense of agency she might have had. She just wanted to lie down and feel it all day long.

Mama Linn! Millie stood up abruptly, a little too fast, and had to sit down again. Four Seven came over to her with an idea—a compromise.

"Officer Stillwell has brought to light that there is a provision in Precinct security procedures that sanctions special treatment to formerly convicted criminals who give substantial aid to the department. It only goes so far, though, so this is what we can offer: You will record a holographic greeting for your mothers on Officer Stillwell's HCb."

"But I don't think they can receive it. They've never been very good with technology. And even if they were, all their equipment would have been repossessed by now."

"Well, that's where Officer Stillwell comes in. He has said he'd be willing to deliver the hologram himself."

Millie looked up at Stillwell. She couldn't tell for sure, but it looked like he might have been suppressing a very faint greeting light. It wasn't clear.

He spoke. "Ms. Fireflower, my great-grandfather was from your family's neighborhood, Droaze; we don't talk about it, but some of my family's friends still live there. We have friends all over Ddrym, so I know some of the territory."

"But...I mean, thank you. Thank you, but is there no way I can go myself?"

"I'm afraid not," Four Seven intervened. "There's no time. StoryEarth is unraveling as we speak, and we need to get through Larkshen. It's crucial that we put you back in place as soon as possible. A car will be waiting for us at the Precinct, to expedite this plan."

Stillwell fished his HCb out of his pack and took a couple of test shots while Millie prepared herself. She tried to keep negotiating with Four Seven. She got him to make one more concession. Stillwell was confident now. "Ready?"

"Yes." Millie smoothed her hair a little and sat up straighter.

"OK, go ahead. Start speaking. Whenever you're ready."

She started, but Stillwell interrupted, saying, "Um, you need to look here." He pointed to a tiny light at the bottom right hand of the machine. "That's where its eyes are. It can't see you until you do."

"Oh. I remember. Thanks. OK." And then she began in earnest, "Mama Linn, Mama Bette, beloved Wrem, and Drauml...I..." She faltered. She thought for a moment. "Please forgive me for all the pain I've caused you and everyone else. I know you're very sick, Mama Linn, and I tried everything—everything"—she was now fighting the tears—"to get to you, but they will not let me come to you. I have to go back to the *Goldilocks* set." She let go a bitter chuckle. "The thing I most wanted years ago, the thing I thought was my dream, now my prison."

She collected her thoughts, and then went on, "The Preservation Precinct Correctional Facility will be my home now, which is as it should be, given all the terrible decisions I've made in my life. As I think about it, this is right where I belong.

"I want you to know one thing. I've negotiated with them so that you could see one of their doctors if you wish. I imagine Grelle is doing everything she can. But *please* let one of the Precinct doctors see you as soon as possible. I've been assured it will be free of charge.

"Mama Bette." And for a moment, she longed with everything in her body to hear her rougher mother admonish her about the faerie offerings, to hear her call her *squirt* just one more time. With a broken heart, she said, "I wish I had listened to you. I honor your wisdom, many years too late. Thank you for finding me, and bringing me home. And thank you for this," she said, fishing out the centering stone to show her. "And, Wrem...Wrem..."

Here, she put her face in her hands and wept for a moment. "My dearest, true brother, I will always hold you in my inmost heart. May the forest hold you forever in the heart of her leafy breast. May she feed your soul, and may you and Drauml and the children be blessed and happy all your lives.

"I wish I could come home. I wish..." She struggled for a moment to keep her energies within her, then finished with "The roads are so many. All begin and end in Oneness. May it prevail in everyone's story."

As she blew her nose into her handkerchief, Stillwell checked that the transmission had been lodged securely in his device. Agent Four Seven felt a lurching unease in his mind and looked away.

"The main road from Larkshen to Droaze?" she said to him. "There's a path that splits off from that road to the big meadow. Our house has the biggest garden on the path. You'll see it."

"I know where it is," he said softly. And that sentence, five words long, contained a whole book of words he would never say to her, things she would never know, could never know. He put the HCb in his pack and started off.

"Wait!" she called out.

He turned around. The last concession she'd wheedled out of Frank—that she could send a gift back as well. She looked frantically around for something to give her Mama Linn, something tangible. The only "thing" she had was her centering stone, and she knew she would need it to get through whatever lay ahead. She searched all her pockets. When she couldn't come up with anything, she stopped—for a long time.

Agent Four Seven was impatient. "Mil—Ms. Fireflower."

Then she took a deep breath and held out her left hand. Stillwell looked at her warily.

Four Seven noticed this, alarmed. "What's going on? Stillwell?"

Stillwell responded, "No, Agent Four Seven. She's just sending her greeting light. It's a skill all the children in the NetherJunctures are taught. It allows the bearer to receive, carry, and deliver someone's light to another being as a very special greeting. Under the circumstances, I think it's fine."

"Very well. But be quick about it."

Then Stillwell said to Millie, "Isn't this done with the right hand?"

"Yes, for the greeting light, but this is different. This is a way more important light. You do it exactly the same way, but you *have* to deliver it with your *left hand*."

"OK, I hope this works. I haven't done this since I was a sprout."

"Promise me."

"I promise."

"When you see Mama Bette—stout woman, very short hair—just make sure it goes this way: Greet with the right hand. Show them the hologram. Then give them the gift with the left hand."

He nodded. He held out his left hand, and they closed their

eyes. She summoned a small globe of brilliant white light from within her. It materialized in the center of her heart and swam up through her left arm and into her hand. There, it intensified and began pulsating. She gave his hand a squeeze and sent it up his arm and into his own heart.

He felt it land, let go, and jumped back a little. This one had power and intent. He'd never felt anything like it. "I'll do my best," he said, and took off running.

Chapter 44

Millie Struggles

Agent Four Seven turned to Millie and said, "OK, let's go now. There's no time to lose."

She stood up tall, centered herself, and said, "I'm ready." She scanned for her friends. They were fast losing substance. Jelleric approached her as they walked. Millie noticed Jelleric had a look of confusion and questioning on her face. She had taken hold of Millie's hand, but Millie could only see it now—not feel it. They walked this way for a bit. Millie saw Jelleric pushing her strength and support into her hand. Sometimes she was there, sometimes not.

The Precinct agent, the guard and their prisoner walked for a few hours. Hereians stayed with them for as long as possible, but eventually Jelleric had to let go. Millie looked at her. She'd stopped walking and was standing still, arms open wide, palms toward Millie—but her eyes had filled with tears. Millie received what she thought might be a blessing and returned it with her own form of blessing. She returned Jelleric's look of sorrow with an expression full of love, acceptance, and wisdom.

"Ms. Fireflower, what are you doing? There's no one back there. Please keep moving," Ralph said.

She looked back and saw the half-remembered dream of Jelleric, Zargamom, friend and protector, standing there amid a Larkshener crowd who seemed to know someone was there but couldn't see her. Her head was bowed, but then she looked up, joined her palms, and mouthed, *Oneness everywhere.*

"Ms. Fireflower, move along!" Ralph had had it with coddling this traitor, this prisoner.

Millie walked the Larkshener road with Four Seven on her left and Ralph on her right. Four Seven was in his full strength now, his strides nice and long, more confident with every step. The prospect of her hologram and her special light reaching her mothers buoyed Millie's spirits, but the trip from the Nothing seemed to have worn her down. The Larksheners who had been lining the path started dissipating. They always made themselves scarce near the Precinct boundary. Her walking was suddenly labored, as if she were walking through water.

As they rounded the corner and saw the Precinct cottages cozied together far off in the distance, Millie got nauseated, and her bones hurt. She knew that they'd be reaching the *Goldilocks* set fairly soon, but they still had to get through the Precinct border. Could she make it? She hoped Laefle was nearby somewhere, but she couldn't see any of her Hereian friends. They were gone. Cold—she was cold and sweating.

"Come on, Ms. Fireflower," Four Seven said, trying to encourage her. "We're almost to the border. You can do this. Think of it. You don't have to live out your life in the Nothing. You've made a terrible mistake, but this will help restore order and peace to all StoryEarth. It's the beginning of making everything right again."

She nodded. "I'm trying. Frank—Agent Four Seven, I..." She paused, panting. "I don't feel so good." With that, she promptly lurched to the edge of the path and threw up.

Ralph picked her up roughly and said, "Keep going."

She tried. It took both of them holding her up to achieve any forward movement. Ralph asked Four Seven as they dragged her along, "Not to put a damper on things, but, Agent Four Seven, how is she going to embody the role in this shape?"

In his single-mindedness, Four Seven had thought only about arriving, not about what shape she'd be in to perform her task once they got there. This was not like him. They stopped to let her rest. But immediately, she lay down, shaking all over. He felt her forehead. She was burning. She would not be able to even get there, much less embody, if they didn't do something fast. Four Seven asked Ralph how many Revivatrol capsules he had left in his pack. "I've got seven."

"Give her all of them."

Ralph raised an eyebrow but followed through, tipping her head, helping her drink the coherence from his flask. She choked on some of them, and he had to slow down. Four Seven looked at his pocket watch. They were losing momentum as it was. But they would have to wait for the capsules to take effect. "Come on, Millie, you can do this."

Hearing him speak her given name touched her. Together with the Revivatrol capsules, it filled her with a renewed sense of energy. Her color came back; her breathing slowed. She seemed in the best shape they'd seen since the beginning of this trek.

They gave her a moment to clean herself up a bit and dry off. She found a specific herb somewhere in the brush and rubbed it on the insides of her wrists, behind her knees, under her arms, and behind her ears. She couldn't wait to have a good, hot shower. Then she remembered it wouldn't be at her High Home. But still, she would be clean again at some point. *Anyway, onward,* she thought. *I can do this.*

Chapter 45

Stillwell Delivers

Stillwell covered ground. He was an effective Precinct guard, but he also had an innate sense of the NetherJunctures and knew which paths would get him to the Fireflower Farm the fastest.

He knew Millie from when she'd been chosen as the turner at the Turning ceremony. At the time, she was the youngest one ever chosen (she was only nine), and she'd done an amazing job of honoring the turning of all things during that ceremony. People talked about it for years. He'd had one of those young crushes at that time. That was before they told him Sting babies grew up to love in a completely different way, that their intimacy was shown through friendship and affection. But he never forgot her.

He was dressed as a Precinct security guard and knew this would be a bad way to come in, so he looked around for the appropriate herbs with which to make a bouquet to show his respect for their current moment of grief. He remembered the combination from when his mother had died. Hawthorn berries and a few wild roses were easy enough to find on his path. He wrapped the small bouquet with a wide blade of grass. It wasn't great, but it would have to do.

He followed the main road and turned off toward the farm. As he approached the front door, he realized with some misgivings what a potent task he'd been given. He knocked. A man lumbered unevenly toward it from within. He heard the locks jiggle and click, and the door opened on an imposing presence, despite leaning heavily on his cane.

"I'm so sorry to disturb you," Stillwell said, offering Wrem the bouquet he'd made. "But I come bearing a message and a gift for the elders of this house."

"Who from?" Wrem didn't take the bouquet, instead looking Stillwell up and down with contempt, resisting the urge to spit on his Precinct uniform.

"It's from Millie," he said with some tenderness.

"You work for the Precinct?"

"Yes, sir, but—"

"Take it away!" Wrem barked. "We don't need any more pain from her or from the likes of you. Enough." He started to close the door.

Stillwell blocked the door with his foot. He couldn't oppose him in his own house, yet he knew the importance of this delivery. Then he remembered his manners—his greeting light. He hoped he could summon it after so many years. It was uneven, but he did it, holding the globe of light in his outstretched right palm.

Wrem was taken aback seeing a Precinct employee offer a greeting light. He opened the door and returned the greeting, if reluctantly. Mama Linn had been so desperate to hear from Millie; this might help revive her a bit, or at least smooth her way through the Door. He took the bouquet and let the Precinct man in.

"Come with me," he said, and Stillwell followed, trying to keep his eyes down out of respect for the privacy of the crowd gathered there. Many were crying, comforting one another. The home was full of light from candles burning on tables and all along the shelves lining the hallway. Beings of all types and ages were sitting on the ground in the warmroom and along the windowsills. Faeries flickered here and there. A woman moved around in the kitchen, placing food on plates from the offerings others had brought, and distributed them to the group. All this was a Ddrymmian custom for someone near their Doorway to Elsewhere. Stillwell worried he'd gotten there too late.

Wrem led him down the hallway to his mothers' bedroom, where Bette sat by Linn's bedside. "Mama Bette, there's a man here from…over there…says he has a message and a gift. From Millie."

Bette barked, "Took him long enough to deliver it. She's been in the Nothing for a while now. A long while."

"Actually, ma'am, she's back out."

"What?" Wrem and Bette were now all ears. Linn was past hearing, lying in the bed, in another set of worlds.

"My name is Stillwell, ma'am, and I have family friends who live all over the NetherJunctures. I've been sent with a special message and a gift to deliver." And with that, he summoned his greeting light again (right hand) while they stared at him, confused.

Mama Bette recovered her manners and returned the greeting with her own.

Stillwell continued, "Agent Four Seven went into the Nothing to retrieve her and bring her back so she could reprise her role as Mama Bear in the *Goldilocks* story—"

"But so, what does that mean? Is everything back how it was?" Bette asked, glancing back at Linn to see if she could hear any of this.

"No," he replied, and as gently as possible, he delivered the rest of the news. "She'll be spending the rest of her days in custody at the Preservation Precinct Correctional Facility. Normally, a being in her position wouldn't be allowed to communicate with anyone, but she saved Agent Four Seven's life this morning, so she was given this one opportunity to send a hologram."

"We can't play it," Wrem said bitterly. "Your people took everything we had when…when…"

"Well, that's why I'm here. I've brought the recording, but I've also brought something I can play it on. Is there anything you'd like to do before I play this?"

"Just a moment," Bette said. She put her hand on Linn's shoulder. "Sweetlight." She put her face very near Linn's ear. "Hey, troublemaker, we have a message from Millie. There's a man here who says he can play it for us. Wanna see it?"

Linn took a very long time registering that anything had been said. She'd been on her side, turned away from them. She opened her eyes and moved herself onto her back. Wrem and Bette arranged some pillows to prop her up. She was extremely pale. "Who's that?" she asked.

"It's someone delivering a message from Millie." Bette tried to position her so the hologram would be in Linn's line of sight.

"But she's—"

"Linn, I'll explain it all later. Let's just see the message. All right?"

"OK," she said. "Where is it? Do we need plates?"

Everyone smiled.

"No, honey. It's not something to eat. It's something we're going to see. This nice man is going to play a hologram for us." And turning to him, she asked, "Where should we look?"

He indicated where, and all their eyes went to that space in the room. He pulled his HCb out of his pack, turned it on, found the file, aimed it, and pressed Play. Visual static showed up, and then like a tablecloth unfurling, there was Millie in forest pants and a simple green shirt with a kerchief around her hair. All three of them inhaled without exhaling.

"Mama Linn, Mama Bette, beloved Wrem, and Drauml...I— please forgive me for all the pain I've caused you and everyone else."

They listened, rapt, unmoving throughout the entire message. Linn wept right away at the sight of her. Bette fought her emotions hard but didn't win. Wrem left the room, listening from the hallway. They looked at Stillwell. Linn had lain back, unable to process any more. Bette leaned over her with concern, putting a cool cloth on her forehead, stroking her hand.

Stillwell approached Bette. "Ma'am?"

"What?"

"I must deliver the gift now."

"We got the bouquet. Wrem showed me."

"No. It's this." And he held out his left hand as his palm bloomed with a globe of bright white light.

She had to size him up all over again, having initially assumed he would know nothing of greeting lights, much less healing ones. She stood up slowly and approached him. "This is done with the right hand," she said evenly.

He replied, "Ms. Fireflower specifically instructed me to deliver it with my left."

Bette's eyes filled with tears, but she kept her face immobile. "Are you quite sure?" she whispered.

"Yes. She made me promise."

Bette clasped his left hand with hers. Nothing happened.

He stammered, "She, uh, she told me to do it with the same action as the greeting light, but it's not working."

"You forgot it's not you givin' it. Get yerself gone, and let the light come *through* you, instead of *from* you."

Internally, he stepped out of the way of the white light he carried in his heart. He just opened all the valves in his being, and the intensity swam out of his chest, down his arm, through his hand, and into her body. She took a sharp breath in and cried out, "Oh!" She covered her face and steadied herself on the bedpost. "Ah, Milliebug, what did you do?"

Stillwell panicked. "Did I do it wrong?"

"No, not you. I was— No. You did fine, sir. Thank you. Please leave us now."

He turned to leave, and she changed her mind.

"No! Stay. Just...I will need you to play the message again when it's time."

"Where would you like me to wait?"

"Please stay with Mama Linn, in case she wants to hear it again."

Then she turned to Linn. "Sweetlight, I have to be in the kitchen for a minute. Don't go anywhere." It was a feeble joke, but it made Linn smile a little.

Bette would have to prepare her for this. The light Millie had sent would be much too powerful to just transmit all in one shot. She went to find the right herbs and potions.

She passed Wrem in the hallway, who was still recovering from the hologram. "She sent her...light, Wremmy," she told him on her way to the kitchen. "Gonna have to strengthen your mama before I give it over."

Opening cupboard doors and drawers, she searched for all the right ingredients for a time-stretching, strengthening tea: logic, peace talk, reconciliation, calming buds, sermons, hymns, cloves of chant, prayer sprigs, perspective buds, and backtalk berries. She kept having to blow her nose as she chopped, ground, combined, separated, and sorted everything necessary to administer this medicine so that Linn would be strong enough to handle the light she was about to receive. Bette had never been the one most comfortable in the kitchen, but right then, you would have thought it was her who had done the cooking and the baking all along.

Finally, when everything was ready, she steeped the herbs in hot water, then brought it back to the bedroom. As Bette had predicted, Linn had asked Stillwell to play the message again, so Bette came in to hear the end of it one more time: "The roads are so many. All begin and end in Oneness. May it prevail in everyone's story."

Chapter 46

Millie Goes Back to Work

Miraculously, they arrived at the *Goldilocks* set intact. But still, Millie wondered. *What is Seth thinking? Where is Agnes right now? And did Mama Linn get her gift? Did it work?* She remembered that Agnes was probably on the *Cinderella* set, ready to embody the story she loathed.

A few moments before, when they were still a ways off from set, Four Seven stopped them for one last check-in before completing this mission. He went down the list with Ralph. They communicated with headquarters, making sure Agnes was at *Cinderella* and all the other pieces were in place for this event. They couldn't believe he'd pulled it off. It was a momentary distraction. But Agent Four Seven, never one for a fuss, kept things on track.

Tourists usually hung out by the stage door, but Precinct personnel had cordoned off the area, forbidding access. Unfortunately, they still had to deal with the press. "Agent Four Seven, what should I say to them?" Millie asked.

"Just go with 'no comment.' All I want is for them to see you returning to work. We'll supply Elizabeth with any quotes she needs for the story."

"OK." She suddenly felt very tired of it all.

"You ready?" He looked her over one last time for any signs

of deterioration. She seemed to have weathered the worst of it relatively unscathed.

Millie felt a twinge, followed by some cranking around and jerking up in her ears. She clutched her centering stone, closed her eyes, and put her training to work. She sent all the anxiety and despair down through her arms and into the stone. She pressed her feet into the ground and did her best to open her heart to the terrible moment at hand.

She looked at Frank and nodded. Four Seven and Ralph then clutched each of Millie's arms and walked her briskly toward the vultures waiting at the stage door.

With Mix in custody and many new Watchers at work, there was no more juice in the monitor rooms. Fobbler never said anything. Bink was glum and punctual. Jayth managed some politeness, but it wasn't his native language. No one made eye contact with anything but the screens. They would pick up the Working Draft coffee that Preservation provided them, press their palms into the scanners at the door, greet the outgoing Watchers with a word or two, and then sit down at their screens all day, making notations, reporting the infractions, then pressing their palms into the scanners again on the way out.

Today, though, things were different. The replacement watchers—Melva Charple for *Goldilocks* and Brambic Strup for *Cinderella*—took special pains to ensure their equipment was working. They fiddled with settings and checked and double-checked the transmission quality. There was just a little too much hypervigilance for this to be a normal shift. Something was up. Of course, nobody told the old crew anything, due to the ongoing investigation. They didn't fire them, because sometimes it serves to keep one's enemies close. But they didn't let them in on any crucial developments, either.

Meanwhile, wildfires of scuttlebutt blazed through the Precinct. Someone saw the news crews outside both the *Goldilocks* and *Cinderella* sets, and speculations took flight. There was no shortage of blowhards in the bars making predictions, claiming inside information. The gossip mill churned, snickering into its sleeve. The Pirate's Parrot, Rules & Regulations, Plot Pivot—basically all the gathering places—were filled to capacity. Everyone was glued to screens, and bartenders sneaked glances too between filling nonstop orders.

The top of the hour came, the tone sounded, and all eyes were on screens in homes, kitchens, offices, spas, bars, libraries, stores, and most important of all the monitor rooms. Everyone stopped what they were doing when the hour struck.

Millie approached the back door to the *Goldilocks* set while reporters shoved their microphones in her face. They all asked their questions at the same time. "Ms. Fireflower!"

"What was the Nothing like?"

"How does it feel to be back home?"

"Can you tell us anything at all about—"

"No comment," she said.

Four Seven spoke over his shoulder as he and Ralph pushed her through the crowd and into the building. "There's a press conference later this evening at the Precinct headquarters, and you can ask your questions at that time. Until then, our agents will escort you off this property. We need to focus."

With a big push, they got through the door, closed it behind them, and locked it. Millie looked around. Seth, Sam, and Tiffany were all suited up and ready to go, their shocked expressions at odds with the cozy tenderness of their costumes and the set. The understudy had taken off her bear suit, ready to hand it over to Millie. No one knew what to say.

Seth looked at Millie, his relief at seeing her eclipsing all the anger and hurt he'd felt in the past week. But none of his emotions could wrestle the others into submission. Sam had been warned repeatedly against saying anything at all, and you could tell. Tiffany's fury infiltrated her blank expression.

Four Seven took over. "As you all know, Ms. Fireflower will resume her role as Mama Bear. She will be escorted here each day from the Preservation Precinct Correctional Facility and back, where she will serve out a life sentence for her crimes. No one is to exchange any communication whatsoever with her, whether written or verbal or with any kind of eye contact or gesture, except what is scripted in the story. Is that understood?"

They nodded and mumbled their assent, except for Tiffany, who said in a clear voice, "Yes, sir."

He turned to Millie and said, "Please put on the costume and begin. Archival footage has been running to end right as you take your entrance." The understudy handed her the bear suit. The minute Millie held it in her arms, a shiver went through her body. She shook the feeling off and went into the changing room, accompanied by the female guard assigned to her for the purpose. Millie took the leg piece and stepped into it, remembering a warm familiarity with this act. She never thought this would be the one place of comfort in her life, but here she was, looking forward to it. *At least this sweetness, for now.*

The leg piece hugged her legs, and it hurt a little but not enough to mention. The guard helped her on with the top piece, the arms and the torso. She remembered her paws and the many classes she'd taken to learn how to hang up her coat, pick things up, put things down, and eat her soup—all with bear paws. The bear forearms took hold of her arms; the torso gripped itself around her. She gasped a little at how tight it felt, but relaxed into it as best as she could, knowing she had no other choice. Finally, she took the head and placed it over hers, brought her eyes into its eyes, and opened and closed her mouth to seal the embodiment.

She had lost everything dear to her in all three worlds— Ddrym, the Preservation Precinct, and Here—and now she faced a life of imprisonment in the one story she didn't want. She walked out onto the set, picked up her basket of berries, and took her place beside Seth. She joined hands with Sam, and it felt odd. For the first time ever, he didn't really want to hold her hand. But he did it anyway. And besides, it would soon be over. Everyone knew their part.

The story bell rang, and they went into action. Walking

toward their front door, Papa Bear opened it, and they filed in. Millie felt sick. She tried to keep going. They were at the coat-hanging part. She took off her coat with shaking paws and missed her hook. She tried again, and the room spun around. Millie couldn't breathe. She fell to her knees and ripped the bear head off. Sirens—the big, low buzzing—raged through her ears. But her brain had let go of her body. Right there on set, in a violent spasm, she vomited blood and went into a full seizure.

The watchers had been warned that anything could happen. Melva, a seasoned Precinct employee in her fifties, was an old hand, so she stayed calm and put the protocols in place. She got the archival footage going immediately, and hooked it up to the transmission. It ran on a loop while the live story was suspended till they could get things worked out. She checked in with Brambic and the others to make sure no other stories were affected. Everything was fine for now. Agnes Grath seemed to be following through per the plan.

Set medics rushed over to Millie while her castmates huddled together off to the side. Her body jerked, saliva dripped from the corners of her mouth, and her eyes rolled around while the medics tried to protect her from hurting herself. The head doctor barked, "Siren solution, please." Someone gave the doctor a syringe. "And I want a Revivatrol drip. Right now! Move! Jenny, put one of those coats under her head."

They worked as fast as they could. The doctor stuck a needle into her arm, and Millie's body went stiff as a board, her head thrown all the way back. He completed the injection, and her body went limp. The injection had stopped the seizure.

Four Seven looked on, numb, scrambling for solutions. Something strange was rumbling inside him, wanting out. *Maybe it won't be so bad*, he thought. *Grath is back in place. Fireflower is back in place. But she's ill, so we have an uncontroversial way of replacing her with the understudy. It's been done many times due to illness. This could work.* But the animal inside of him was snarling, lunging at his heart. His eyes went blurry. He watched the doctor's face as he checked her vitals.

In the monitor room, no one had ever seen this. Nor was it for the faint of heart. The camera lenses showed without mercy the whole event: her costume head flung off to the side, the blood, her messy seizure, the group of medics huddled over her body, the injection, the collapse. Melva zoomed the camera in so they could see. They did mouth-to-mouth resuscitation. They did chest compressions. They tried this twice more, until the head medic told them to stop.

Millie's face was gray and still. Sprays of blood were all over her costume and the floor. Her hair was glued to her head with sweat, her eyes still open. No one moved. The mic picked up the doctor's pronouncement. "She's dark."

"No," Four Seven said. The words escaped his mouth in a whisper. "No, that was *not* our agreement!"

Everyone was still for a moment. As the cast's mouths opened in shock, the crew made ready to wrap her body in a sheet to place it on a gurney. But there was some protocol that had to be followed—photographing the scene, documenting what happened, passing out waivers to be signed by the people present—so they asked the crew to wait a moment while that was done.

Frank had to act fast. He called Levit to notify Millie's family *before* sending a press release announcing Millie's darkening. He told him to clear the press release with Woundliss before sending it to Maggish. Then he told everyone that once the formalities were observed, they should go home for the day, and he left the set.

He made his way around the back of the set hangar, then walked a little farther into a small stand of trees, making sure he wasn't followed. Finally, he stopped, his heart hammering against his chest and tears climbing out of his eyes. He found himself saying, "No, no, no, no, no, Millie, *no*. I had the perfect answer. Everything was supposed to go back like it was."

He remembered meeting her that first time and his lame attempt to save her from the bullies. He remembered her brave friendship with him after his father's fall. Then he remembered something she'd told him when they were in school. They had argued about continuity and how things needed to remain exactly the same to remain whole. She'd replied, "If you can't change anything, you can't grow. You'll go dark."

"Wait, Millie! I know now," he said into the air. "Listen. Wherever you are, Millie, listen to me."

He planted his feet firmly, took a breath, and said, "'Two and two is...three.' No. 'Two and two is five!' See? I did it. I changed something." He watched the door of the hangar to see if it worked, half-expecting her to walk out of there and come find him. He shook his head and balled up his fists.

"No, that wasn't good enough. I can do better. Come on, Millie, how about this?" He shouted it up into the sky, "'Cinderella moves into the palace, and she and the prince bicker about everything. The divorce gets ugly, and evil spells are exchanged all around.'"

He kept going, laughing maniacally through his tears. "'Snow White is never awakened with a kiss. The prince finds her asleep in the forest and darkens her on the spot.' Was that different enough for you? Huh?! 'Tinkerbell is a trick! She's not real!' Millie, come back!" He was now sobbing against a tree trunk, forgetting to be quiet about it.

All the air had gone out of the monitor room. Melva was the senior watcher but new to the group, so she hadn't had time to establish her authority. She checked in on the other watchers anyway. "Jayth, who do you have? *Winnie the Pooh?*"

"Yeah, it's all good. He and Tigger are talking."

"Who else? Fobbler? Where are you at with the, uh, *Peter Pan* story?"

"Uh, yeah. Hook is doing his thing, terrorizing the children. Everything's on track."

"OK. How about you, Bink? You have, um"—she consulted her cheat sheet—"*Rumpelstiltskin.* What's the status there?"

"He's on the first go-around. She's in the tower, and he's spinning the gold for her. No abnormalities."

"All right." The whole conversation was conducted without

any of them, not even Melva, taking their eyes off the screen for the *Goldilocks* story. "Gentlemen, I know this will be a challenge," she said. "But please continue watching your given stories. There will be enough chaos to go around once this hits the press. Stay steady and shut everything else out. Earphones on."

"Yes, ma'am," they answered. All three men put on their earphones and returned to watching their stories.

Chapter 47

News Reaches Ddrym

Mama," Wrem said, "what's goin' on?" He'd never seen Mama Bette move with such determination in the kitchen.

She took his face in her hands and brought it down so she could kiss his forehead. "Go get some rest, my love. Come back by evening, OK? You won't be sorry."

"I ain't leavin' you."

"I said go," she said, pointing out the door.

He was tired of dashing her hopes about Mama Linn. He knew she was going dark, but Mama Bette didn't have to accept that until the very last moment. But Wrem did notice on his way out that their family friends had picked up on something—that the energy had definitely shifted. They were trying to listen for information that would fill in the blanks. But so far, nothing was clear except that the frequency had definitely gone *up* in this house.

Bette got everything ready on the tray: the tea, a lit candle, a clutch of hummingbird feathers they'd found years ago, and a small bowl of soil from the garden. She sweetened the tea with haiku. Blimmer held the door for her as Bette came through with the tray. She asked Blimmer to please thank everyone and tell them to go home. Blimmer hugged her friend and closed the bedroom door.

Bette set the tray down on the nightstand.

"Thank you, um, Mr..."

"Stillwell. I'll be going now. *All roads lead to Oneness.*" And as he left, Bette was left speechless with an unnameable, disoriented gratitude. Stillwell joined the large group of friends, all leaving at Bette's request.

"OK, my sweetlight, it's time."

Linn was unresponsive. Bette set the tray down on the bedside table. She moved Linn's tiny frame so she was sitting upright. She took the teacup in one hand and cradled Linn's head in the other. Carefully, she said, "All roads begin and end in Oneness, my love. Let's remember that. Now please take just one sip." She put the cup to Linn's lips. A tiny bit went in.

"Bette?" she asked, struggling for breath.

"What, my darling?"

"I don't want to keep going. I'm too tired. Let me go."

"All right," Bette answered, almost smiling. "I will let you go after you drink this one cup of tea and after I give you the gift Millie sent you. Those two things have to happen, and then I promise I'll let you go if you still want to go."

"OK," Linn said, and fell back to sleep.

Over the space of about an hour, Bette got Linn to drink the whole cup of tea. Linn even laughed at a joke during that time, clearly getting stronger. When the tea was done, Bette looked at Linn and said, "My love, you gotta be mad strong now. Our daughter has given you the most precious gift anyone can give, and you gotta be strong now. Are you ready?"

"I don't know. What is it? Why are you crying?"

Bette just let her tears roll without explanation. "Just lie back and rest. I'm going to give it to you now."

Linn lay back gratefully. She still felt spent from the effort of drinking the tea. Bette planted her feet and summoned the light Millie had sent. It materialized in her belly and then traveled up into her left shoulder and into her left hand. There it was, a brilliant, almost blinding white light that practically heated up the whole room.

With all the composure she could muster, she said, "Linn, give me your left hand."

Linn opened her eyes and frowned at Bette, questioning. She held out her left hand. Bette pressed the light into Linn's palm, and in an instant, Linn's entire body filled with light, and there was a sound, a chord vibrating in the air around her. Linn sat up slowly, filling with more power every second, smiling. Her eyes were wide with surprise and the deep sense of well-being. She looked at Bette, and they laughed, tears of joy washing both their faces.

Bette swooped down and embraced her wife. She whispered in Linn's ear, "Are you all right? Am I holding you too tight?"

"No, sweetheart. No. It's great. I feel *wonderful*. I feel...I feel..."

And then Linn felt it—a sharp blade in the heart of her bliss. Their daughter had given up her last remaining life light. Linn's phenomenal strength meant that Millie had gone dark. The last and only thing she had to give, she gave. And grief was the heart beating inside the body of joy that now lived in their house.

Linn began a slow wail. "Oh, Bette, why? Why? No. Let me go. Take it back. Bring it out of me and take it back to her." She pummeled Bette, who held her, trying to steady her through this storm.

She rocked her as they sobbed together. Bette finally said, "Linn, listen to me. Listen to me." She put a stray strand of hair behind Linn's ear. She kissed her forehead. "Millie is free now. She did what she needed to do, to show her love for us. It's too late now. What's done is done. But we can honor her and love her forever for it. You have her strength now! We will weep for a long time. But the day will come when we take up our lives and honor her sacrifice with every shred of our being."

They heard Wrem limping down the hallway as quickly as he could, calling out in alarm, "Mama Bette! Where is everybody? Why aren't they—" And then he saw Mama Linn sitting up, flushed, bright, strong, alive. Both his mothers wore expressions he couldn't fathom.

"Mama Linn?" he whispered.

Linn smiled and beckoned him to her. He folded her in his arms gently, the tiny bird that she was after so much time of not eating, and she began to sob.

"What happened?" he asked.

Neither of them could answer. Finally, Bette tried. "Millie... she...um...she sent—remember the Precinct soldier who came and delivered her message?"

"Yeah."

"She sent her life light. She's surely gone by now."

Wrem was struck dumb. He searched his mothers' eyes, both of them, for how to hold this. Neither one could help.

The little light-filled Sting baby that Mama Bette had brought home so long ago; the little girl who followed him everywhere, who could best anyone on a horse, who could honor Oneness without ever making you feel that you didn't; the one who'd sent him countless unanswered treespeaks, footcalls, and messages. And he had given her only his silence. He bowed his head, and his throat gave up its years of sorrow.

Chapter 48

Levit Finds Frank

Stillwell drove from his spot at the Precinct border to the *Goldilocks* set after delivering Millie's light, shocked at the amount of security. What did they think she was capable of? There were eight or nine security vehicles! There were two ambulances. What the hell was going on? He picked up his pace, trotting, then running toward the backstage door. When he got there, he couldn't believe his eyes.

A doctor was looking over Millie's body as though she had gone dark. And then he realized it was Flemming, the coroner.

"What happened?" Stillwell asked one of the guards who let him in.

"She was suited up and everything. Then right at the beginning of the scene, she just collapsed. Four Seven called his assistant, then let everybody go for the day. He should be around here somewhere."

"But...but...she's gone dark? Are you sure?"

"Look at her, man. She's all the way through the Door."

Stillwell wanted to get a closer look, but Seth was kneeling at her side, and so was Sam. They were speechless, crying. Seth was speaking to her body. "Millie, I missed you. Nobody was as good a Mama Bear as you. I was so happy you were coming back. And now..."

Sam was overcome. "Mama!" he cried, and laid his head down on her belly.

One of the coroner's crew gestured to Seth that they should clear the area around Millie, so he got up and gently pulled Sam away. That was when Stillwell got a chance to see her body. They'd cleaned off as much of the blood as they could. Evidently, during the resuscitation attempts, they had cut off the costume, so she had only her underthings on. She had been a lovely, strange being in the world. A woman's body like any other. You would never have known how much she'd been through, or how much she'd given.

Someone covered her with a sheet. Stillwell came in close and lifted it away just enough to whisper in Millie's ear, "I delivered the message and the gift. They loved it." He waited, half-expecting her to open her eyes and smile at him. Nothing.

The med tech nudged Stillwell aside so she could close Millie's mouth. Then she covered Millie's face again and said, "Bob, Willie, help me get her up on the gurney." Stillwell went home stupefied.

After the set had shut down and everyone had gone home, a little blue Shim, one of the old, boxy models, scratched and dented from years of use, arrived and parked in the empty lot. The security cameras would have recorded a man of slim build exiting his car, looking around, unsure of where to go. They would have seen him circling the building, trying the doors, then turning to get back into his car. They would also have seen him hesitating just before leaving, listening for something. And then they would have seen him walk toward the forest, out of range of the cameras.

Off in the distance, Agent Four Seven sat slumped against a tree trunk, disconsolate.

"Agent Four Seven."

Four Seven looked up, and there was Levit with a look of wonder on his face.

"Oh, Levit. How did you find me?" he asked.

"It's what I do," he said, not smiling, not knowing where to go from here. He pulled a flask of Things We Don't Want To Know from his inside pocket and offered it to his boss, who thanked him and took a swig.

After a moment had passed, Levit said, "I'm sorry about Ms. Fireflower."

Frank looked away, handing the flask back to Levit, who continued, hesitant, "But you're back...from the Nothing. No small feat, sir. Congratulations."

"I would never have made it without her," he said, his head bowed. "She saved my life."

Levit sat down next to him and listened. The flask went back and forth.

"She was my only friend in high school. Did I ever tell you that?" Frank took a drink. "I mean, I had other friends, but they all jumped ship when my father..." And then he went mute, remembering his father in all his raw decrepitude at the boundary of the Nothing, aching for all that was irretrievably lost.

"She never gave up on me. I shut her out, even when I didn't need to. We'd known each other before my permanency assignment. I could have been her friend all those years, but I...I just..."

"Well, actually, you *were* her friend," Levit reminded him. He'd read the files. He knew how influential Four Seven had been in her placement as Mama Bear. "You did so much for her in the background." Levit had also read all the memos defending her honor in the early days, during the controversy about whether a Ddrymmian was capable of holding such a position. He'd put his own career at considerable risk, something Millie probably never knew. "You made her dreams come true and never asked for a thing in return."

Frank looked at Levit until one of them should have looked away, but neither did. Levit finally looked down and bumped him on the shoulder with his own. "Sir, I'm so glad you're—I mean, I thought I'd—*we'd*—never see you again."

Chapter 49

Breaking News

It was a normal crowd for a Friday night at the beginning of Turning season. Ever since the Big Switch, beings throughout the Precinct were troubled by a strange excitement—some more happily than others. The customers at the Plot Pivot were jovial. The Rules & Regulations crowd was a little muted but not overly so. Everyone at the Pirate's Parrot was in rare form. The bartenders were busy, the blowhards were busy, the busboys were busy. Screens on, music on, dartboards up, pool tables clicking—the place was jumping.

At the height of the evening, someone whistled loudly over the crowd. A bunch of people yelled, *"Shut up!"* Everyone quieted to a murmur for a moment while the bartender turned up the volume on the screen. There was Elizabeth Maggish's somber face with a crawl at the bottom of the screen: BREAKING NEWS! DDRYMMIAN PLAYER GOES DARK ON SET! The place went still.

"From SBC with breaking news in the heart of the Preservation Precinct, on the set of *Goldilocks and the Three Bears*. Millicent Araklane Fireflower, much better known as Millie Fireflower, the Ddrymmian Player originally slated to reprise her role as Mama Bear, was pronounced dark today on set.

"In a plan to restore order to StoryEarth, a heroic feat was performed by renowned Preservation agent Four Seven and two top security guards. Agent Four Seven retrieved Ms. Fireflower from the Nothing and delivered her to an alternate sentence: life imprisonment and a return to the role she had tried to escape from in collusion with Agnes Grath and an as yet unknown accomplice.

"Ms. Fireflower was to have begun serving her sentence today, but the Ddrymmian Player suffered violent convulsions and went dark just as she was beginning her shift on set. Cause of dark is unknown at present.

"Ms. Grath began serving her sentence yesterday and is expected to continue into the foreseeable future.

"Agent Four Seven was not available for comment. He will certainly go down in StoryEarth history for his extreme bravery, venturing into the Nothing to retrieve Ms. Fireflower and bringing her out alive—a feat never before accomplished. The entire Preservation Precinct extends its heartfelt gratitude for a job well done."

She signed off, and the volume went down. There was a moment of recalibration where everyone tried to decide whether this was worth ruining the whole evening. They decided not. It just rerouted a lot of the conversations. Drinking resumed. Darts resumed. Pool playing resumed.

They wondered, though, if Preservation had darkened her with some mysterious pill. Or was the whole thing a hoax to scare Preservation Players back into submission? Maybe Millie Fireflower hadn't really gone through the Door. Plus, they hadn't shown any images of Agent Four Seven, so maybe that hadn't actually happened either.

Ever since the Big Switch, the Preservation Precinct had lost all credibility.

Chapter 50

A Hero's Welcome

Levit took Four Seven home. He was reluctant to leave him alone there, but professionalism still drove Four Seven. He thanked Levit sincerely and waved him away. As Levit left, he told Four Seven to please call him at any time of the day or night if necessary.

Frank poured himself a stiff cometojeezus and drank it as the room darkened into night. His mind was blank. He couldn't follow one thought all the way to its end before another would take him in the other direction. Finally, he got into bed and tried to sleep.

He wandered into a bear suit that was a little too small for him. It was all right though. Over to his left, there was a lot of hustle-bustle, with everyone preparing for some big event that had something to do with Preservation, and he was going to be a keynote speaker or something. Sparkles hung in the air around an enormous poster, but he couldn't tell what it said. Everyone seemed to be preparing for his entrance.

On the right, there was a slim man sitting in a meadow near a tree, facing away from him, with a bright yellow bird on his shoulder. He was curious about the man, but didn't want to let the people down. He started walking toward the celebration, and immediately, the suit constricted against his body, almost strangling him. As he struggled to free himself from it, light began to form inside his belly. Then he heard Millie's voice. "Frank."

He shot up and out of the bed, breathing hard. Everything came into focus. He stood there for a moment, realizing he'd actually been dreaming, even though he hadn't had a dream since he was a child.

When he opened the door to his office the next day, his staff gave him a standing ovation. Clearly uncomfortable, Four Seven smiled a little. "Good morning...please...please." He raised his hands, beseeching them to stop. They grew quiet.

"You should all know..." He paused, wondering how to say it. "I was only doing my job. And I had a lot of help." He remembered Millie saving his life, but looked around the office, realizing how everyone there, too, in some way, had helped him in his life. He made eye contact with everyone, one at a time, Levit last.

Four Seven went on, "I know today will be tough. Yesterday's tragedy has affected many beings in the Precinct, to say nothing of the Player's family. We must do our best to keep our heads about us. I would like to request complete privacy for this first hour, and then, Levit, you and I will meet. After that, I will come out, and we will meet as a group and begin the triage. Until then, take messages. You can tell everyone there will be another press conference at the end of the day."

Everyone returned to their desks and began answering phones, fielding requests for access.

Levit looked at him for a moment. Today of all days, Levit would have to double down on his own game. His phone never stopped. Calls, messages, and holograms were coming in from all sides for all reasons—supportive fans, aggressive reporters, detectives chasing down rumors of foul play, SBC angling for exclusives. It was absolute chaos.

The entire Precinct population was upside down with this double whammy—Frank's heroic journey into the Nothing, emerging triumphant with his intended prisoner, then her dramatic fall into darkness. It was just too much. Depending on whom you spoke to, Four Seven was either a hero who saved the Preservation Precinct or a villain who murdered a beloved Player.

Levit would do his best.

Once secured in his office, out of view, Four Seven sat motionless at his desk. Millie's ordeal had undone him. Levit's friendship haunted him. He wanted to stop everything. For just a moment, he wanted to know what he was feeling. He had never cared about that before. He felt terrible for wanting that. He had no idea how to conduct himself.

His phone rang. "Levit, please, I—"

"It's President Woundliss."

There was a quick pause. "OK, put him through."

"Agent Four Seven," Woundliss said. "Well done, my man. I didn't think it was possible, I have to admit. How are you doing?"

"I'm all right, sir." Woundliss had never asked him how he was doing.

Their conversation was cordial, almost friendly. They discussed how to spin the incident with the press. They obviously couldn't give her a full Player funeral. They weren't about to honor a criminal. But there was enormous goodwill toward her among most Precinct beings. And they didn't want to be seen as callous. It was a treacherous PR tightrope.

Toward the end of their discussion, Woundliss said as an aside, "Too bad that half-wit Ddrymmian bitch left you such a mess to deal with on her way out."

Too shocked to speak, Four Seven muttered, "Yes, well, I'll see to the funeral arrangements." And he hung up. In that moment, he felt himself make a quarter turn from his office to the memory of his dream—the commotion, the bear suit, and the slim man with the yellow bird on his shoulder. "Levit!"

His assistant was there in an instant.

"Shut the door."

Chapter 51

The Funeral

After much discussion, they decided on the following funeral plans. They would dispense with the official StoryEarth Player touches. They wouldn't use a hearse—that would give her too much status. They'd have to get the casket to the Ceremony Hall by horse and carriage. (Frank took secret satisfaction in how much Millie would have preferred that anyway.) There would be no drummers in front of the casket, no castmates allowed to walk beside it, and no posters of her in costume at the hall.

Then Four Seven told Levit, "Please hold my calls. There's something important I need to do. I'll be back as soon as possible." He left the office.

The prison guard at the PCF entrance came to attention. "Agent Four Seven, sir."

"Please show me to Agnes Grath's cell."

The guard hesitated. "We have strict orders from President Woundliss to keep her in complete solitary."

Frank whipped out his HCb, called Woundliss, and convinced him that he had one last strategy for getting a confession out of her. Woundliss didn't see what they had to lose.

The guard called for escorts, who led Agent Four Seven down several flights into the bowels of the building and through so many twists and turns that it would be impossible to remember his way back without help. When they arrived at the cell door, they went through protocol: One guard pressed his palm to the scanner, then a camera took the photo of each of their faces, after which Four Seven had to look into the lens to verify his iris pattern. When the green light signaled that the cell door was unlocked, Four Seven turned to the guards and said, "Please come back for me in thirty minutes. This shouldn't take much longer than that."

They clicked their heels and saluted. "Yes, sir."

He went into the cell, where he heard a small movement in the corner as they closed the door behind him and locked it. As their footsteps faded, his eyes adjusted to the dark. There was not much light to go by. He fumbled for a bench, but soon realized there was nothing. So he sat down on the ground.

"Ms. Grath?" There was no answer.

He waited a long time. "Agnes?"

After several breaths, she said, "Wow. You used my first name."

He was glad she couldn't see him blush.

She went on, "I don't think I've heard you do it since high school."

A moment went by while they both remembered lunches at the cafeteria, and times they would never share again.

"Hey listen," Agnes said suddenly, "On my way back from the set, there was crazy, weird energy. All the guards were whispering about something, but I couldn't tell what it was about. What's going on out there?"

"Agnes, I'm afraid I have some really bad news."

A bitter half laugh spilled out of her. "Bad news? You have bad news for me. That's hilarious. Hit me with it."

"Ms. Fireflower went dark."

Agnes whispered, "What?"

"It's...it's Millie." Frank's throat choked on the name, trying to keep it in. "I meant for everything to go back the way it was. You were in place at the *Cinderella* set, and we got Millie to the

Goldilocks set. I went and got her back from the Nothing. And as soon as she embodied the costume, she went into seizures, and...she's..."

"Agent Four Seven, I can't—"

"Please. Please call me Frank."

"I can't feel this again." It was like a thousand razors to the heart. "I cannot go through this again. I already lost her once." They sat in silence for a moment. "What caused the seizures?"

"I don't know," Frank said. "She started showing signs of illness after she sent a message to one of her mothers who was sick. Could her mothers have done it to her?"

"Words, Frank! Don't even think it. Tell me what happened."

And he relived the whole awful sequence of events for her.

Agnes, gutted, finally said, "Millie, the best friend anyone could dream of having."

In a voice she could barely hear, Frank said, "I know. She was your best friend. But she was my *only* friend. And I never told her that." He sat with her on the floor and grieved with her.

On the day of the funeral, try as they might to mute its effect with adamant directives, the Precinct was unable to keep things low-key. Thousands of people dressed in black lined the streets anyway, all along the route from the morgue to the Ceremony Hall. Peppered here and there were Larksheners holding their hands in the sign of love and connection: thumb and forefingers together, interlocked, held at the heart.

Seth and Sam flouted the directives, riding their bikes next to the casket anyway so that, technically, they weren't "walking" by it. Tiffany followed the rules to the letter, and didn't even show up. But Blaze, ashen with grief, walked as upright as they could manage, showing some of the dignity Millie had inspired in them, and far enough behind the coffin that they couldn't be arrested. Next to Blaze, Breller sobbed, receiving tissues every now and then that Blaze had thoughtfully prepared for him. To the left of Blaze, Shank pushed Lydia in a wheelchair. She had been too overwrought to walk. Shank held his own heartbreak with tenderness, knowing that Millie's life was still flowing somewhere, just out of their immediate reach for now.

"Elizabeth Maggish here from SBC, where we are covering the route being taken by the funereal horse and carriage bearing the body of Player Millicent Araklane Fireflower from the morgue to the Ceremony Hall. President Woundliss was adamant that there should be no poster of the late Player in her costume at the hall. Also forbidden was walking beside or behind the coffin on this route. And no flowers.

"The Precinct is trying to balance justice with decency. They don't want to celebrate a blatant criminal, yet they also want to show respect to her family and many fans.

"But there seems to be some pushback on this. You can clearly see two figures riding bicycles at either side of the coffin. They look to be castmates from the *Goldilocks* set. And it also looks like her High Home staff are walking behind the coffin, only far enough behind it for impunity. But the most staggering show of insubordination is the generous spray of flowers covering Ms. Fireflower's coffin. It is completely blanketed. Jack, can you zoom in to show this? Yes. Look at that! No one knows who ordered them, and—wait a moment." There seemed to be some confusion in the newsroom. "I'm...I'm being contacted by..."

She paused a minute, her index finger gently pressing in on her earpiece. "OK. OK, Jack, I've got it." She looked directly into the camera. "Ladies and gentlemen, we were mistaken. Those are not—repeat, not—flowers covering the casket. It seems that every single faerie from the whole Ddrymmian realm has come to pay their respects. They have shaped themselves so that their wings form the 'petals' of thousands of blooms. Quite a sight, I must say."

When they arrived at the hall, everyone maintained a respectful silence as they filled it to capacity. In the entryway, they saw a poster that said, "The roads are many. All begin and end in Oneness," made by a friend who'd taken pains to remain anonymous. And somehow, the assemblage formed itself into a circle. Not a Precinct tradition, but a decidedly Ddrymmian one.

At the funeral, Agent Four Seven sat at the back, his face an inscrutable collage of grief, disorientation, and something else—something with no name to it.

Chapter 52

The Unraveling

Millie's coffin had been loaded into the horse and carriage destined for the Ddrymmian boundary, where Wrem and his friends would be waiting, with Cliffer and Paulie hooked up to a decorated funereal cart to take her home. Everyone was exiting the Ceremonial Hall when Agent Four Seven's alarm rang in his pocket. It was Levit.

"Agent Four Seven, Stenfar and Grath have escaped."

"What?"

"From the looks of it, it was timed to happen during the funeral, and was done by very experienced professionals. Could it have been Another Way? They say the underground subversives are—"

"Well, well, well, they're still out there." His voice trailed off.

Levit was equal parts amused and baffled by the casual ambivalence in Four Seven's voice.

"What else do we know about this prison break?"

"Nothing yet. It only just happened about fifteen minutes ago."

"All right, I'm coming. Sit tight and try to keep a lid on it."

"Agent Four Seven, may I say, your sense of humor has gotten extremely dry since your return from the Nothing." And even Four Seven had to laugh with him.

All screens throughout the Precinct and Ddrym went a little

haywire and then recovered with this: "We interrupt your pro-gramming for breaking news. This is Elizabeth Maggish from SBC with an emergency transmission. There has been a prison break—I repeat, a prison break—from the Preservation Precinct Maximum Security Correctional Facility. The two prisoners are at large, and they may be armed and dangerous.

"At present, there is no information about who helped them escape, but unnamed sources have speculated that the sub-versive underground group Another Way may be involved. The escapees are Mixko Stenfar, a former watcher with the Preservation Precinct administration, and Player Agnes Grath, who had collaborated to switch roles with the late Player Millie Fireflower.

"The culprits no doubt planned it to coincide with Ms. Fireflower's funeral. This story is still unfolding, and we'll keep you updated as we get information."

And then the unending talking heads took over, with mug shots of Agnes and Mix appearing every few minutes.

Four Seven arrived at his office in a hurry. He dispatched sev-eral top aides to accompany Millie's casket to Ddrym, putting Stillwell in charge of them. "Wait for me," he told Stillwell. "I want to accompany her to the border."

When the aides had left the building, he asked for every-one's attention. There were nineteen employees working under him, twenty counting Levit. "Let the phones ring. I don't care. Everyone, mute all devices." And then he locked the door. "I don't know what to say. There is no protocol for what is happen-ing right now. I mean, of course, there's protocol. But I'm not sure it's relevant anymore."

They shifted uneasily.

"As of tonight, I am leaving my post here."

Even Levit's mouth opened. No one had seen this coming. "Why?" many of them asked.

"I'm not sure I'll be able to answer that to anyone's satisfac-tion, but I'll try. When I went to retrieve Mill—Ms. Fireflower—oh words, Millie, from the Nothing, I did manage to get in. But I never would have made it back out without her.

"I know how some of you feel about Ddrymmians, but it's time to reassess." He let it sink in for a moment, then continued, "Just after we got out of the Nothing, I collapsed. Stillwell told me I had no pulse. I wasn't breathing. But Millie is a Ddrymmian. She knows energy, and she'd been *a friend* to me since we were in school. She brought me back to life. She quite literally saved my life.

"During our trek back to the *Goldilocks* set, she tried so hard to follow orders, even though it literally dragged her through the Door to Elsewhere to do it. She was trying to make up for the damage she'd inflicted." His words caught in his throat. He stopped for a moment.

"What damage?" he asked them. There was a long pause while he composed himself. "All she wanted to do was play a different role. She didn't even want to change a story, but embody a different role. That's not a sin. It's natural! I'm told people get bored doing the same thing over and over again, unless you're like me."

Some of them smiled. Levit noticed the blinking lights of the many people he'd put on hold on his phones.

"Only I have no idea who I am right now. I just know I can't do this anymore."

Someone asked, "Agent Four Seven, what will you do?"

"I have no idea. This is all I've ever known. I really don't know."

There was an awkward moment when no one knew what to do or say.

"So for now, the priorities are to send out an APB asking for any information regarding Stenfar's and Grath's whereabouts. Lilly, make flyers. And, Sally, you go with Dave and Phillip to distribute them throughout the Precinct. Joe, take care of getting this in all the libraries, grocery stores, bars, and Player spas, and make sure there's a constant crawl at the bottom of every screen in StoryEarth."

"Sir?" It was Joe.

"Yes?"

"Who will take your place here?"

"Woundliss will have to appoint someone. Levit? Come with me for a moment. We have some things to go over before I leave." To the rest, he said, "Stay off the phones. I mean it. Stay off the phones until you receive word from me."

Levit and Four Seven went into his office. Four Seven sat at his desk and said, "Close the door." He motioned for Levit to sit.

He asked Levit, "Do you want this job?"

"Not in the least," Levit said, nervous and alive.

"Not in the least? Don't be a fool. You excel at everything. They'd be so lucky to have you."

He looked at Four Seven. "Yeah. Well, they don't have that kind of luck."

"I thought you'd—maybe, that—"

"You thought I'd want this job?"

"Well, I...I—it just seemed logical. I mean, you're the most qualif—"

"Sir, I am the most qualified person in all of StoryEarth to work with *you*. I know your files backward and forward. I can feel when you're ready for another cup of coherence and when it should wait. I know you turn your plate a quarter turn before eating. I know you despise fried admonition sticks. I know you love statutes soup, but only if there are slices of toasted debate to go with it.

"I've never known another human being with as much generosity or integrity as you have. I can recite every single instance in the past eight years when you've foregone advancement at Preservation because it would have been at the expense of a fellow agent who needed it more, when you've let someone else take the credit for a win that was yours because it wasn't important enough to make a fuss over it."

"Levit, listen to me."

"No, Frank, you listen to me." The use of his first name

brought Four Seven to his feet. Levit stood up now too. "I can call you that now because you're leaving anyway. I've got nothing to lose."

"I guess that's true," Frank said, incredulous.

Levit went on, "When you left for the Nothing, I knew I'd never see you again. I couldn't put two sentences together in a row that whole day. I promised myself that if I ever saw you again, if you came back alive, I would tell you how I felt, Preservation Precinct be damned.

"Frank Horace Grambling, you are a boneheaded, neurotic, obsessive-compulsive control freak. But you are *my* boneheaded, neurotic, obsessive-compulsive control freak. If you're done here, I'm done here. We'll go together. You can't survive without me anyway."

Frank laughed, the first true, big smile he might have ever felt in his face. Levit laughed back into Frank's eyes, and neither one knew what to do. Frank, nearly sick to his stomach with nervousness, finally walked around his desk to embrace Levit. Levit gathered him up in his arms, and Frank was overcome with emotion.

Standing in that embrace, in that silence, each man felt that he'd finally made it home after lifetimes at sea. They stood there for a moment, breathing, holding their breath, not believing, knowing the truth of it, neither one wanting to let go.

Finally, Frank held Levit at arm's length and looked at him. "What?" Levit said.

"It doesn't matter. I have the rest of my life to tell you," he said as he pulled away to look for something on his desk. "And it will probably take that long."

Levit laughed.

Frank's eyes held Levit's for a second, then Frank blushed and wrestled himself back into his professionalism. "Get your things. Let's go."

They wasted no time. Levit popped back into Frank's office and said, "I—are we going to be back? I mean, should I leave the—I should leave the log, right?"

Frank said, "Leave them as much information as you can. Just make sure you have your ID and whatever cash you've got on you."

The office staff watched with their mouths agape as Frank and Levit walked through the main office to the door. "Sir, what's going on?" Joe asked.

Frank turned to Sarah and said, "Sarah, I need you to take over until Woundliss makes his permanent assignment. And David, help her out. Levit has left everything there for you—the log, the calls list, everything. It's on his desk to refer to. You can contact him if you get stuck. Joe, cover all the watchers. And… thank you, guys! For everything." There was a ghost of giddiness in his voice.

Chapter 53

Insubordination

As Frank put on his coat, they heard Lilly say, her voice trembling, "What if we want to go with you?" Lilly was just a low-level copier who had been there for decades. She rarely spoke. Everyone's jaw dropped.

Frank's face softened, and he said, "That's not prudent, uh, uh..."

"Lilly," Levit whispered.

"Lilly. I don't think it's a good idea. I don't even know where I'm going," Frank responded.

"What if maybe that doesn't matter?" she stammered.

Joe walked over to her, saying, "Lilly, don't be ridiculous. How will you pay your bills?"

She said, "How's he gonna pay *his* bills? He doesn't know, and he's still going. I don't wanna do this anymore, Joe. Do you?"

The office heaved with unrest.

Frank broke the moment. "Listen, we have to go *now*. I will stay in contact with Joe. That will be safer for you, Sarah," he said, adding under his breath, "in case I engage in some kind of noncompliant behavior."

"That's it. I'm in," Stope said, shoving piles of papers into his desk and getting his jacket on. He'd gone to school with Frank and never thought he'd see the day that Frank would break a rule, but here it was. The staff was looking from Stope to Lilly to Sarah to Frank to Levit to one another.

The door at the entrance of their building opened and slammed shut, and they all jumped. Then, louder and louder, heavy boots pummeled toward them. Frank had the presence of mind to unlock the doors and open them, a gesture that placed him firmly in alignment with the coming aggressors. He was there to greet them, three enforcement goons headed up by a fourth whom he recognized from his legendary trip to the Nothing.

Ralph barreled in. *"Everybody, freeze!* Precinct Enforcement!" It was comical, because they were already frozen, trying to process what they'd just been talking about. Still, nobody moved.

Frank was steady. "Hello, Ralph. What's the problem?"

"You know very well what the problem is, Agent Four Seven," he said, sneering the name. "Two prisoners have escaped from the correctional facility, and *nine more stories* have suffered major breaches, all at the same time."

A gasp gripped the room. Everyone knew about the prisoners. No one had heard about the breaches. This explained why the silenced phones were continually lit up like fireworks at the StoryEarth Good Will Ball. Frank's single-mindedness, plus his gift for compartmentalizing, kicked in. "Look, Ralph, I've got a funeral to oversee. We have to follow protocol. Step aside."

"I don't think so," Ralph said, blocking Frank's way. "We have orders from the top to lock this place down."

Frank said evenly. "Step aside, Officer."

Ralph pulled his gun. Everyone held their breath.

Then, one of Ralph's own men yelled, "Drop it!" and suddenly the cold barrel of another gun was at the back of Ralph's head.

Stunned, Ralph didn't drop anything. He said, "Flaerity, don't be an idiot."

"Sir, I can't let you do this."

Ralph said, "Bobby! Lims! What are you waiting for?"

The other two enforcers were caught off guard. Lims responded first. Brand-new to the agency, he fumbled with the safety latch on his gun. Bobby, who'd never drawn his weapon at anyone, said to Lims, "Are you really gonna let this happen? You want your name to go down like *this*?"

"Well...yeah," Lims said, backing up toward Ralph with his gun in both hands aimed at the other two.

"Lims! This is *Agent Four Seven* we're talking about here," Bobby said. "It would be like ending Superman."

"Look, you guys," Lims said, his hands shaking, his fingers uncomfortably snug on the trigger, "I'm not willing to be court-martialed and sent to the Nothing for some Precinct agent with a good story to tell. We have orders to follow."

"Good boy, Lims," Ralph whispered.

But nobody expected what came next. Lims swiveled left and deftly shot the gun right out of Ralph's hand.

Bobby and Flaerity tackled Ralph, eventually cuffing his hands behind his back, while Lims covered them, waving everyone out. He yelled, "OK, *go!* Everybody, go, go, go, go!"

Some fumbled for their things, some ran for the door, but everyone understood that the moment had arrived. They left to the sound of Ralph shouting expletives from his chair. "You're all going on the list! We're gonna round up each and every one of you scumbags and dump you off in the Nothing where you belong."

Frank said to Flaerity, Bobby and Lims, who'd waited till everyone was out safely, "I have no idea who you guys are or how to thank you."

They told him, "Don't worry about it. Maybe you buy us a drink sometime."

"Count on it," Frank said, giving the office one last long look before telling Levit, "I think we're done here."

Chapter 54

Uninvited Guests

Tragic as it was, Millie's funeral gave the members of Another Way exactly what they needed for their long-term plan to come to fruition—a massive, Precinct-wide distraction. They'd been waiting for an opportunity like this for years. When she died, Millie struck a match that lit up the revolution. That day came to be called Opening Day.

While Millie's mourners remembered her at the service, Mix and Agnes were freed, smuggled into Ddrym, and given refuge at the Fireflower farm. The coordinated story breaches took place just as they were making their way through the border. Preservation couldn't possibly arrest, much less process, everyone involved; and the secret operatives for Another Way used the ensuing chaos (along with crucial assistance from the faerie world) to implement their campaign for reformation and renewal of the Preservation Precinct.

The time had come. Too many Players and Agents had chafed under the now obsolete rules. Their world had long outgrown these antiquated ways of being. Communications began to improve among opposing forces. It wasn't by far a happily ever after outcome, but it wasn't a blood bath either, as so many of the Precinct/Ddrym wars had been. Conversations were facilitated—mostly by Sting operatives, whose unfailing friendship and empathy blew gently on the little coals of trust still alive in everyone.

Little by little, the Precinct began seeing the upside of renewal and change. They softened toward Ddrym. Orders for Linn's incomparable dishes started coming in, and Alphabet Delights swirled back to life. The kitchen was rolling again. Agnes taught Drauml how to drive. Drauml taught Agnes Mama Linn's famous grumble recipe. Mama Linn taught Mix how to work with light. Mix taught Wrem the joys of prank. And Wrem taught everyone how to properly listen to a tree.

All StoryEarth now celebrated Opening Day every year, which came on the first day of Turning season. It was honored with spontaneous improv skits, fairy tales embodied by gender-bending casts, and modern interpretations of old chestnuts like *Cinderella,* sometimes even with a choose-your-own-ending option.

The problems with the Precinct still existed, of course. Friction between the traditionalists and the creatives would no doubt never disappear altogether. But at least now it wasn't illegal to have the conversation. And this was a big step forward.

Two years after the original Opening Day, Mix and Agnes were joined. It seemed so fitting, especially since Millie's mothers had offered their home for the reception.

When the day came, the kitchen was alive with Mama Linn's brisk movements—carrying platters loaded with giggles and murmurs to helpers for circulation, making extra frosting, checking the oven so the chocolate Pop the Questions didn't burn. The cinnamon I Dos were already in the fridge.

Bette directed traffic outside, barked at the children not to wander off, and made sure people had water for their horses and room for their cars. (She'd softened in her old age about this.) She was coming back into the house when she bumped into Agnes coming out, resplendent in her pale-green silk gown dotted with tiny live roses. Agnes greeted her Precinct friends who'd just arrived. She had taught them how to offer their greeting light. They giggled as they tried, some succeeding to squeals of delight. Bette looked on in wonder, never dreaming she'd see this in her lifetime.

Drauml and her friends set up the feast and gathered flowers from the garden for the table. Wrem and his friends made sure there were enough tables and chairs (borrowing from neighbors where necessary) and sang all the plants and trees into their maximum loveliness. Wrem and Drauml's two children ran around with reckless abandon, making their parents cross.

As to the setting, Pim Pfahler had donated his services as his joining gift. He created magical depths of sweetness in lavender tones all throughout the house. At the tables, the chair backs wore lavender chiffon shawls around their shoulders, with bouquets of lily of the valley peeking out from the folds. Down the length of each table, Pim had placed a shimmering soft gold runner with living leaves at its edges. An egg cup holding a small globe of light sat at each setting.

This gave Flurjahm a last-minute idea for his own gift to the couple. The faerie world had developed quite a strong link with Mix. It was probably a kind of "honor among thieves" nod to him in appreciation of his pranksmanship. Whatever the reason, Flurjahm honored the link by rallying the bravest of his friends, persuading them to bestow the highest honor a faerie can bestow—the willingness to be seen. During the dessert course, they materialized, one at each place setting, inside Pim's globes of light—ready, willing, and able to grant one modest wish.

Of course, Frank and Levit were in attendance, both so handsome. It seemed that Frank had lost ten years in his face. He had worried so about what to give the couple. Frank ended up giving Agnes a lovely locket that he'd received from his mother's estate. Inscribed on the back was, "Your friends in Oneness, Frank and Levit."

Frank circulated with all the adults while Levit played with the kids. One of Wrem's boys ran by him, and Levit tickled him fast as he passed. The delighted boy squealed, and Levit went after him like a monster, stumbling; a giant, roaring; lashing out with his arms, and missing. All the children joined in. Frank caught sight of this while talking with one of Mix's friends. He cocked his head and smiled at the fun they were having, his face full of tenderness.

The sun blinked through the trees in the late afternoon. When dinner was ready, Mama Linn rang the bell. All fell silent as they found their seats. They'd set an extra place of honor for Millie's memory between Mama Linn and Mama Bette. Drauml sat at Agnes's left, beaming at the woman who'd become her best friend. Wrem took his place at Mix's right, giving him his true face as he said, "Welcome, brother." Mix nodded.

By the time the loving felicitations cake was served and the wishes had been granted, the party was deep into the slurred-words wine. There was music and singing and dancing and more wine while more people showed up to the party. Friends from the community came in with other friends. Nobody seemed to notice.

"Do you think they know we're here?" one of them asked the older man standing with her.

"Oh, I doubt it. They're way too far gone. And anyway, you've gone through the Door to Elsewhere, so they won't see you till they go through it too. I'm still in Here, but someday we'll be visible to everyone living. I feel sure of it."

She turned and looked in her friend's eyes. "I think so too. It's coming. How is this for you, seeing him there so happy? Your son has come such a very long way."

"Yes, he has. And you were no small part of that, Millie."

"Well, he was a great Preservation agent too." She thought for a bit. "It almost darkened him to see you there in the Nothing."

"I know. But I couldn't let him go without telling him how sorry I was. I had to disguise myself for the same reason Jelleric disguised herself to you. It's the only way we can tell if someone can stand being in Here, and I knew he was on the edge."

"Yeah, he wasn't ready yet. But on our way back from there, you know he let me send my light to my mother. It was a big risk for him, but he let me do it. And look at her. She's so happy."

"Yes, she is. And look at him now, a Preservation Precinct

consultant secretly running Another Way. Would you ever have guessed it?"

"Not in a million years."

They stood off to the side, taking in the scene, enjoying the joy. "I like his husband too. He chose well," Millie said.

"Yes, he did."

After a while, they agreed it was time to go. "I'm glad we got to see this," she said. "Goodbye, my friend. I must go now."

There was a little commotion over by the garden. A humming-bird with a shimmering blue-green body had lit on Bette's shoulder. Linn's eyes grew wide, and she whispered, "Bette, don't move."

But Bette turned her head and said, "What? *Oh!*"

The startled hummingbird took flight again, but returned in front of Bette and bowed in the air. Then it whizzed up and over, returning, alighting on Mama Linn's shoulder before tak-ing flight again and bowing in front of her. Linn stilled herself, cherishing this magical presence, letting reverence prevail over excitement at this intentional act.

Then the bird rose straight in the air, chirping a few times before swooping down on Agnes's shoulder, almost nuzzling her neck, then jumping off and bowing in front of her. The blue-green brilliance then hovered for a while in front of Wrem, be-fore landing on his head, and plucking out a few hairs. This drew a laughing yelp out of his throat and tears of a finally ripened forgiveness from his heart.

"Millie," he whispered.

"Millie," everyone murmured, their heads bowed.

Then she did aerobatics over the whole wedding table, giving aerial bows of respect to Mix, to Drauml, and to Frank. She hov-ered high, dive-bombing, chirping, spinning, interacting with all the other guests in various ways. When she felt complete, she simply disappeared in a blink.

Millie felt herself dissolve. Each quark, every impulse, every thought she'd ever had, all memory, the totality of every story she'd ever heard, told, believed, or embodied—all of it was soft-ening, thawing, liquefying.

Her essence dissolved like salt in water, without plot, point, story arc, or message. Her life force was everywhere now, and nowhere, air in spaciousness, too rich for words or message. Her body no longer an entity, it exhaled into the True Nothing, joyful and at peace.

The End

Acknowledgments

In 2006, I wrote the book for a twenty-minute musical (an assignment for my MFA at Tisch School of the Arts). Composer Kevin Cummines and lyricist Tony Asaro traveled with me to StoryEarth. Thank you, Kevin and Tony, for finding and feeding the first seedling of these StoryEarth chronicles with me.

Years later, the musical grew roots and blossomed into a novel. Thank you, Shaunta Grimes, for your unstinting encouragement, and to the Ninja Writers community for helping keep my feet to the fire.

Thank you, NaNoWriMo friends, for helping me get all the way to "The End" of my first draft.

Thank you, Arlaina Tibensky, book doctor at Gotham Writers, for being a trusted and extremely helpful guide as I took my first real steps into crafting a novel from a first draft.

Love to my beta readers Emilia Negri, Jill Yancey, Louise Foerster, Krista Buccellato, and Heather Principe for reading the manuscript in its infancy and for your intelligent, invaluable feedback.

Thank you to author, editor, proofreader and friend Sean Patrick Brennan for keeping me from overworking the story, for helping me clarify myself, and for authentically feeding the fire of this story's worth.

Unending gratitude to Susan Miller and Lisa Ries for their listening, their questions, and their insightful feedback that enriched and deepened the narrative.

Thank you, Marc Spencer, for your advanced novel-writing course, and thank you, Jacob Spencer, for your insightful proofreading.

Thank you, Liz Carbonell, for having the best, last eyes on this work as an editor, before I let it go out into the world.

Thank you to my deepest friend, Courtney Campbell. Your creative spirit, your music, your humor, your compassion, your big ears, and your presence and our parallel paths make me grateful every day that you were born.

Thank you to my friends at Archway Publishing for all the support, guidance, and encouragement.

But most of all, a grateful embrace to my wife, Elena Terrone, whose belief in me blesses me every day. With her indefatigable heart, her no-bullshit Brooklyn common sense, and her magical skills in the kitchen, she has given my soul a sanctuary that surpasses the beauty of Millie's High Home.

About the Author

Tina Lear is an award-winning singer/songwriter and published composer/lyricist for musical theatre. Her songs have received nationwide acclaim. She is also a novelist, poet, and blogger. She taught yoga to inmates at Rikers Island and drove cattle in Wyoming. She met Queen Elizabeth and is fluent in Italian. The accomplishment she is most proud of is birthing three interesting, truly good people—and earning her beloved wife's respect.

Made in United States
Troutdale, OR
09/05/2023

12653531R00219